# THE
# BRANGUS
## REBELLION

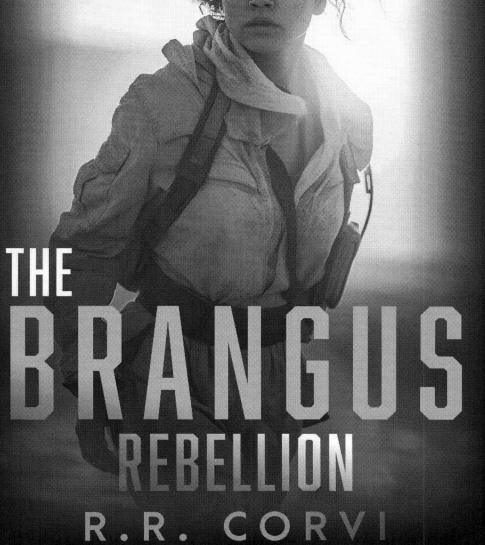

THE UNION TOWNSHIP SERIES: VOL. 1

THE STUNNING DEBUT NOVEL
A CLIMATE FICTION THRILLER

# THE
# BRANGUS
## REBELLION

### R.R. CORVI

Published by R. R. Corvi

ISBN: 979-8-9875611-0-2

Cover design & interior formatting:
Mark Thomas / Coverness.com

*To my dazzling wife Rosie, who was always there*
*with love and encouragement,*
*and often with a thoughtful, detailed critique.*

# FROM COLLAPSE TO UNION

*We brought it on ourselves.*

> *True, humankind survived. This time. But have we learned anything?*

*The origins of Earth's global Collapse in the late twenty-first century can be traced to more than a hundred years earlier, notably to the remarkable successes of capitalism, consumerism, and mass-marketing techniques that flowered after World War II. These forces, based as they were on notions of perpetual exponential growth, took only a generation to drive human society into an era of shortages: shortage of air to dilute combustion products, shortage of fuel, of fresh water, of arable land, of genetic diversity, of peace and privacy. Attempts to reconcile these shortages with prevailing ideologies led, in turn, to the period we now call the Crazy Years, when public debate was increasingly consumed by the efforts of various power groups to ignore, deny, and distract from the plain truth: untrammeled consumerism applied on a finite planet must, in a brief time, lead to tragedy.*

*The latent tragedies showed themselves in the decades of*

*the Civil Wars, spanning roughly the last half of the twenty-first century. Systemic governance failures, aggravated by worsening climate change, spawned a worldwide turn to violent and demagogic politics. Old grudges resurfaced, scapegoats were sought and found. Arms for local rebellions became more readily available. Three centuries later, it is pointless to detail who rebelled against whom in those years or with what outcomes. What is clear is that, during that time, almost everywhere on Earth, people warred perpetually with their kin and neighbors. Civil wars tend to be more brutal and destructive than those with strangers; these wars fit that pattern. By 2100, the human population had shrunk by about half from its all-time high in the 2050s. The damage to non-human life on Earth was even worse, with uncounted species driven to extinction.*

*During the wars, climate warming went from bad to worse. Along with the combat, these changes drove massive refugee movements, mostly away from the equatorial regions. Millions perished in these migrations, but millions more survived, remaking the ethnic mix in the Northern Hemisphere.*

*Early in the 2100s, as global warfare sputtered out, the climate delivered a deadly surprise. Human forcing had pushed the Earth's systems of oceanic and atmospheric circulation too far. In a mere decade, these flipped away from the stable, "cool" state that they had occupied for millions of years. Flow patterns broke up and reformed in new configurations, leading to a sudden shift to a hotter stable state. Global land temperatures rose by 5°C virtually overnight. Life on Earth baked. Crop failure, thirst, and starvation became the norm. Social organization foundered, making the terrible conditions worse. Over the next few decades (now called the Bad Days), more than nine-tenths of the Civil Wars' survivors died, and humankind's vaunted civilization collapsed into scattered communities of subsistence farmers, each waging a drawn-out but usually losing battle with the elements.*

*It was in this unpromising soil that the North American Union was planted and grew. In this, it was served by three advantages. By global standards, the climate of North America's eastern seaboard was benign, being survivable by humans from roughly the Chesapeake Bay northward into what once was Canada. By pure chance, the region surrounding Trenton had suffered little during the Civil Wars. And through foresight and planning, massive digital archives were stored at the University there, along with machinery and materials for many kinds of manufacturing. The staff of the University shrank but survived, propagating a core of essential skills but also a worldview—one scarred by disaster and entirely different from that of the pre-Collapse days. From this little core of practical imagination came Eapy Fox, the "Mother of the Union," and her egalitarian, collectivist, ecology-attuned system of government. It was Fox who worked out the rules for small interlocking townships (twps), with specialized functions, as the fundamental administrative units in Union governance. Within two decades, by judiciously exploiting their ability to re-create selected technology from the pre-Collapse, the "toop soup" that makes up the North American Union evolved from a clutch of like-minded farmers surrounding the University into a durable nation-state. At the time, it was, and so far as we know, it remains, the only such state in the world.*

*A century and a half after Eapy Fox, the Union provides security and health, if not wealth or luxury, to its twenty million citizens. Geographically, it has spread up the east coast of North America and far into the old Canada, reaching away from the ocean almost to the boundaries of the Western Waste. But around its edges, both physical and metaphorical, there remain those who do not accept its dominion or its philosophy.*

*Patri twp UniHist Gibbs, from twp UniHist Ph.D. qualifying exam, July 2335.*

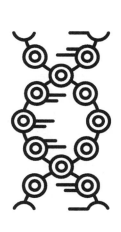

# THE MAYOR

Lani hunched in the main refectory of Township EEE and muttered a curse. Lately, her attention acted like a scared rabbit, dashing from one bad refuge to another. With a sigh, she surveyed the room, then dragged her eyes back to the screen of her computer deck, jammed now with notes for her course at the Uni. It was near the end of serving hours for the refectory's second seating, and latecomers hurried in to catch a meal before the kitchen closed. Already a group was rearranging seats down near the stage for a meeting, and card games had started in another corner. Poirot, the township's bloodhound mascot, slouched around the food pickup line, hoping for a handout, or at least for dropped crumbs.

The room had terraces and a stage so that it could be used for performances. Displayed above stage center was the township's full name, in relief, in large golden letters:

*"Equality Environment Evidence."*

The sign reminded anyone who needed reminding that the function of the township (whose name was usually abbreviated "twp EEE," and pronounced "toop Triple-E") was to protect and defend these fundamental pillars of the

Union: Eapy Fox's "three E's." A dozen years earlier, when she was adopted into the twp, Lani had found the words inspiring. Lately, they only made her feel weary and depressed. Fine, the twp had special status as a kind of highbrow national police force. But at bottom, it was just a bunch of cops.

On the rare occasions when the mayor called for a meeting of the whole twp, the entire six-hundred-plus membership—all of its twple— would crowd into this space. Indeed, while Lani watched from her seat in the back corner, the mayor herself bustled in with a couple of aides, probably on a break from some long-running meeting.

Half a dozen kids, freshly released from the discipline of table manners, played a furiously fast game of tag up and down the aisles. This griped Lani for reasons she couldn't have explained, so she buried herself further behind the screen of her deck and tried to concentrate on schoolwork. She had picked an empty corner of the refectory for her hangout. For classwork, the lack of near neighbors suited her, and it saved other twple the trouble of actively avoiding her.

It was a surprise, then, when the mayor slid her tray onto the table next to Lani, sat down, and gave her a cheery smile. "Hello, Lani. How've you been?"

Lani looked at her with suspicion, concealed as best she could. She had no recent reason to dislike the mayor, but they had not spoken since Lani's hearing a year and a half ago. For her to turn up out of the blue had a sour smell to it.

"Can't complain, luv. Super, really," she replied with her own perkiest smile. She had to wince at herself. She was overdoing the bonhomie, she knew, looking like a marketer and a fool.

"Good, good." The mayor subsided and let the silence linger. She poked at her bowl, which was full of one of the twp kitchen's signature dishes—big chunks of various root vegetables swimming in a spicy fish broth. "Twp soup," she said.

Lani cringed. If the mayor was forced to haul out rhyming puns for three-year-olds right at the start, this conversation could turn very bad indeed.

After a moment, the mayor tried again. "Classwork?" she offered, craning to get a look at Lani's screen. "Math? How's it going?"

"Hmph. Tolerable, I guess." Actually, Lani was having quite a good time with second-year calculus. She had always liked math, though she was not unusually good at it. It was reassuringly definite, with right and wrong answers and a feeling of stability that came from deep foundations. More than that, going to class meant getting out of the twp campus, which was fine with her. That made math class the high point of many days. But she was not dim enough to say such a thing to the mayor.

The mayor wasn't saying much either. She just sat there looking matronly and worrying a tough crust of bread, but her eyes were on Lani with an attention that never let up. The story was that she had been a tough cop in her day. Maybe every conversation was an interrogation to her. But then she surprised Lani with a quick girlish grin.

"How is it, being a movie star?" she asked.

Lani snorted. "Luv," she said, "if you mean *The Hendrikson Raid*, you're confused. I hear there's a kid in it who plays a character with my name and does some things that I did back then. And also lots of things I didn't. That makes *her* the movie star, not me. Potwee Evans, her name is. From twp Inuit-ion."

"You hear?" the mayor asked. "It's been featured on the Daily Drop for weeks, and everybody's talking about it. But you haven't even watched it?"

"Nope, and not going to. I didn't like that story when it was happening. I don't like dwelling on it now. Not my idea of a good time."

The mayor sat and considered this as if trying to decide if her wrist had been slapped. For her part, Lani assumed the mayor was working around to something, and she was pretty sure that it wouldn't be pleasant. In principle, Lani could stall and wait her out; there must be someplace else the mayor needed to be. But Lani had never been good at the waiting game.

"Something on your mind, luv?" she asked at last.

"Well, yes, dear, actually there is. How much longer does your probation have to run?"

Lani had been suspicious. Now she was angry. "Six months. Which you know perfectly well. You recommended the sentence."

3

"Yes. Too bad how all of that worked out. Everybody knows it wasn't entirely your fault, dear. Bad luck, really. But you know…"

"Of course. The Council can't let twps slide when one of their own kills some outsider for no good reason. Especially not Triple-E. Undermines the twp's reputation and all. Somebody's got to pay." She slapped her deck shut in hopes of making a quick escape. But the mayor wasn't done.

"Dear, I don't think you quite understand how seriously that business was taken," she said. "At the highest levels, too. We did the best we could for you. You're lucky you didn't get cashiered. But we had a good advocate."

"So here I am for two years, sitting at a desk counting duck feathers."

"Yes, Lani. Here you are. I know it's the shits, and I don't mind that you're resentful. But remember that at the end of your probation, you come up for review. The panel won't necessarily let you back on the streets just because you've done your time. You're a smart kid, Lani. Smart and tough, and you can handle yourself. We need you. But I'm worried. I don't like the stories I've been hearing."

"What stories?"

The mayor managed to look unhappy. "You know. Burning the candle at both ends—and the middle as well. Spending all your free time partying. And outside the twp to boot. Drinking too much. Never a good sign, that."

"People are mad because I like to party?"

"Of course not, dear. But people say you're sleeping around. Easier to count the folks you haven't boffed than the ones you have."

"'People' say, huh? Who are these 'people'? Anyway, I'm twenty-four years old. I can manage my own *fucking* love life, thank you."

"The point, Lani, is that such behavior means you don't respect yourself. And if you don't respect yourself, nobody else will. Certainly not the panel who will hear your case in six months' time."

"Thanks, luv. Wizard advice. Anything else? Ways I can improve? Live up to expectations?"

"I hear you've been missing therapy sessions. You could start again."

"That bitch!" Lani snarled. "I knew that sanctimonious turd was ratting me out all this time!"

4

The mayor seemed genuinely shocked. "He would *never!* That's really not done. Honestly, Lani. I'm the head of a twp full of the best cops in the world. You think I don't have other sources of information? You get serious about things. Straighten up. Keep your nose clean. For six lousy months. Then you can carouse all you want. In the meantime, don't do anything stupid."

She drilled Lani with a stare from under her eyebrows. "I think we're done here."

"Damn straight," Lani said, snatched up her deck, and stalked out.

# DAY OF THE DUDE

Like many urban twps, EEE spread its people across a number of rented apartment buildings and other residences, loosely concentrated in the neighborhood of the refectories and the other main twp facilities. Some of these buildings were shared with other twps, and some were not, but the EEE twple tried to keep themselves segregated by floors at least. Because of its uncommon emphasis on physical conditioning, twp EEE had chosen a location some distance from the center of Trenton to give it ready access to parkland and athletic facilities. These were nominally shared with other citizens, but in practice, the semi-military nature and the grim fixity of the EEE twple's training tended to intimidate and discourage other users. The twp leadership made a public display of downplaying this kind of distance between themselves and regular folks, but in truth, they cultivated it.

Lani's room was a couple of blocks from the refectory, up four flights of stairs. A good location: she stayed in shape, and the less fit riff-raff stayed away. She walked in, tossed her deck on the bed, picked her small deck off the desk and stuck it in her pocket, and walked out. After a quick stop in the washroom down the hall to sluice water on her face, she was off.

Three minutes later, she pounded on her friend Evar's door, a few buildings away. "Open up, Eve!" she shouted. "I need you!"

Presently the door opened. Lani took one look, shrieked, and jumped backward with arms flung wide. "Crap!" she gulped gleefully. "What have you done?"

"Come on in," Evar whispered, pantomiming a survey of the dorm hallway. "Nobody else knows."

She closed the door behind Lani and did a slow pirouette, her hands over her head. "It's a costume," she said.

"No lie," Lani agreed. It was a scarlet sheath with swirls of orange, topped with a headpiece that had cheekbones like a centurion's helmet and puffy feathers—red, yellow, and orange—on top. The thing was cut away in back, nearly to the place where a long, furry tail, reaching almost to the floor, sprang from the base of Evar's spine.

"Need to let out the seams a little. The dancer who wore this was a stick. Also paint on the face, hands, and shoes. I think a yellow background, with black swoops back from the eyes and blood-red lipstick. Will it work?"

"Great God, it's shocking. Of course it'll work. Nobody will wear Union issue ever again."

Lani herself was in Union issue, as almost everybody was, almost all the time. Provided for free, everywhere, the Union white cotton shirt and street-dirt-gray pants had no aesthetic appeal, but their tent-like fit was practical in the hot climate, and their interchangeable absence of style was a point of pride among the militantly possession-averse Unionites. When luvs wanted to dress up, they would dye their hair or wear a fancy belt or a colored scarf. By this standard, Evar's dress hailed from many light-years away.

"Where'd you get it?" Lani asked.

"That dance studio on Leghorn. Cast off. Something to do with the new artistic director."

"What? Is the dancer's twp reorganizing again?"

"Wouldn't know. I only root in their trash."

"Great. So what's it for?"

Evar twisted around and posed, then posed again, stretching to gauge the effect as best she could in her little doorway mirror. She didn't like the picture, so she spun over to her desk and set her server deck's camera and the big monitor to self-view.

Evar was the deputy chief communications guru for twp EEE. Three years back, she had authored a popular text on communications. This got her noticed and, ultimately, recruited from her twp at a Canadian university to join the EEE cops. It had worked out well for everybody but her, as she fought through endless battles with her much older, underqualified boss. Her oversized place was crammed with routers and other hardware, including a giant screen that would have been declared unnecessary and excessive if she had any other job. The bright, high-res view of her own flouncing pleased her.

"Halween," she said at last. "I'm going to a Halween party." She struck another pose. "Say, the beau's gonna like this."

Evar's partner, whom nobody at EEE had ever seen, lived someplace far to the north. Their joint life was conducted through the mail, and in person during week-long vacations, three or four times a year. Presumably, this lifestyle had influenced the choice of topic for her current book, which had the working title, *Action at a Distance: Modern Love by Rail and Post*.

Lani asked, "What's Halween?"

"Old pagan holiday. Honors the dead or something. Got appropriated by the Christians and then by the corporate consumptionists years before the Collapse. People spent fortunes on costumes."

"Hmph. We don't have fortunes these days. Good thing we have friends. Speaking of which, I could use one." Lani's tone was pleading.

Evar stopped her preening to pay attention. "Something wrong, kid?" she asked.

"Nothing much. Just got reamed by the mayor herself, is all."

"Oof. She can peel your paint for you. I know. I've spent too much time in her office explaining myself. What did you do to rile Her Honor?"

"Never mind. Point is, I gotta get out of here, right now. Going downtown, place I've heard of. Can you come with me? Back me up? Drag me out if I need dragging?"

Evar hesitated for a long time. "Aw, shit, Lani, I can't," she said at last. "Got work to do. And seams to rip. Any other night. Except tomorrow; that's the party. Hell, I'm so, so sorry. Forgive me?"

Lani stood up straighter and gave herself a little shake. "Sure, Eve. I'll manage. It'd be better with you, is all."

"Okay, Lani. Drink before you go?"

"Oh, yeah."

Evar produced two glasses and a bottle of vodka. Put a gurgle worth in each glass. Lani raised hers in Evar's direction, drained it, put it down. "Thanks," she said, reaching for the door. "Gotta go."

"Okay. Have fun. Don't do anything stupid."

"Why," asked Lani, "do people keep telling me that?"

# BACK CANAL

The Back Canal, run by twp BarNGrill, sat in the old part of town near the University. It attracted the student crowd with cheap watery beer, low lights, and a dance floor that was partly partitioned off from the main room, letting drinkers actually sit and talk if they wanted to. Among EEE twple, it had a poor reputation because the students were deemed over-educated (even by Union standards), self-absorbed, and snooty. Now that Lani had spent some time sitting with them in her calculus class, her judgment was not so harsh. On this night in particular, with the mayor's scorn still burning her ears, the last thing she wanted was to sit around the twp, drinking with cops. Old cops, especially, with their interminable stories. With their memories.

She didn't much like weak beer, though. Once in the door, she settled onto a barstool, told the bartender, "Whiskey, neat," and sat back to survey the scene. Four large tables with backless benches dominated the room, lined up with Cartesian precision in a two-by-two grid parallel to the bar, while a half-dozen tables for two hugged the walls. There seemed to be an age gradient in effect, with undergraduates near the door and Uni staff and grad students toward the back. On the opposite wall from the bar, a large opening gave access to the dance room, which was better-lit and seemed to be the place's only source of music. The tune playing at the moment was a scratchy polka. Nobody was dancing.

To Lani, the bar's playlist resembled that at any other place she knew: a grab bag of tunes from an era several centuries gone. When explained in those terms, this sounded odd. But it was also inevitable. Little popular culture of any kind survived from the time of the Civil Wars; people then had no time for frivolities. Even more so during the Bad Days, and indeed for the first century of the Union and more, when all of people's efforts went to surviving the next day or burying those who didn't. It was only when Lani's parents were young that the notion of "leisure time" was no longer an obvious fallacy. By then, nobody remembered how to make music or art. To fill the gap, people turned to the archives, where quantities of high-quality work was free for the taking. In this way, a long-lived, multi-generational fad grew up, in which social status depended on immersion in pre-Collapse movies and music. Tunes in bars propagated the trend, and though Lani and her age group were getting a little bored by the musical chaos, there were no alternatives on offer. Many of her peers ended up as self-styled experts and often culture snobs. Lani was not that extreme. As long as she wasn't dancing, she was prepared to tolerate polka. But not to defend it.

Pretty quickly, somebody at the far back table stood up and waved to Lani. She looked familiar, and as Lani moved over, glass in hand, she recognized Mizi, a grad student in her math class. Mizi specialized in journalism or some damn thing, and like Lani, she was learning more math than she needed, just for the fun of it. The table was full, and to make room Lani had to squash in next to a couple who were deep in conversation.

Mizi gestured grandly. "Everybody, Lani," she announced. "Lani, everybody." This introduction got all the attention it deserved—which is to say, none.

"Sorry!" Mizi laughed. "Mostly here, people talk shop. From what I've seen, you're not all that work-obsessed. But that's okay. Jump in."

Lani snuggled into the too-small space and tried to tap into the flow of conversation. The pair next to her seemed to be discussing sex techniques, though at a shockingly elementary level.

"...so be careful when it slides in," he warned. "Wrinkles are bad."

"And how about size?"

"Most important thing. Bigger is better, but not too tight. Too loose is really bad. You want to try it out for a long time before you commit."

"And salt water? I've heard that…"

"Old wives' tale. Don't waste your time. I tried all that stuff. All that works for me is two pair of socks. Thin synthetic under heavy wool, and my boots have never given me another blister."

Well. Not sex at all. A pitcher of beer sat in the middle of the table, with a bunch of upside-down mugs around it. Lani finished her whiskey and reached for a mug.

# NEMATODES

It turned out that the folks at Lani's table were mostly genetic biologists and ecological engineers. This wasn't surprising. The Union couldn't afford large research infrastructure—no particle accelerators or giant telescope arrays. Instead, they excelled at desktop and lab-scale subjects: math and computer science, nanotech and genetics. Especially genetics. There was a whole school of people at the Uni who did such stuff, and to all appearances, half of them were here at the Canal, having a beer. For the most part, they were acting as Mizi said, huddled in twos and threes and going on at length about technical details of nutrient cycles, dependency networks, activation thresholds, and so on. Finally, she got the guy next to her, the one with the double socks, to open up a little and tell her about it.

"Mostly," he said, "we're trying to unfuck ecosystems that have been screwed up by climate change."

Lani waited for amplification. But the wait got too long for her. "That's just too wonderfully peachy for words," she finally pronounced. "Don't suppose you want to tell me what that means? Or how you do it? Hmm?"

He stared at his beer for a while, then looked at her sideways. "Nobody ever wants to listen to that part. Are you sure you do?"

She gave him her best wide-eyed enchanted look (he was at least medium-cute) and nodded.

"Okay." He stared at his beer again and sighed. "Ecologies are like webs, okay? Everything connects to everything else. So when the climate went seriously to hell, say two hundred years ago, it blew holes in all those webs. Which then started to unravel around the hole edges, and that caused more unraveling, and so on. Runaway de-speciation, we call it, when we talk to the Council's staff. Go all in for polysyllables, they do."

"Yeah, okay. And so?"

"And so, we're left with whole wide chunks of land where nothing much grows. Bad, bad dirt. The cycles that should be moving water and minerals around, changing critters into crap into fertilizer into plants into critters, they're all broken. There's zillions of species missing now, from bacteria on up, and all of 'em used to do something useful."

He paused to pull on his beer and waited morosely for Lani to refill hers.

"Not to complain," Lani said. "Just saying, you're not lifting my mood."

"I told you nobody wants to listen. It's not surprising. It's just important. And depressing."

"So, what do you *do* about it?"

"We try to build local systems that work in the current conditions. We can't hope to put in all the species that ought to be there; instead, we aim for a toy version of the whole ecosystem, ideally the minimal one that works. Then let nature fill in the gaps, which it will do, eventually. But even getting that far means tons of computer modeling. That's where most of my time goes."

"And then you transplant the rabbits and mosquitos and grass and mule deer and whatever else you need into your plot, and bingo! A little slice of Eden?"

"Well, yeah, but we never aim that high. People always want tigers and grizzly bears and apex predators, don't they? And, you know, milk cows. Llamas. Crap like that. But we can't do that. Sure, even though lots of those species are gone, we have full DNA sequences in our databases. And our exotic-husbandry techniques are getting pretty good. Means we can make 'em in labs.

But for them to thrive, first we need what they eat. And their breakfast needs whatever *it* eats. And so on. We start at the bottom and work up to something that's still in our range. If we're feeling frisky, at the top end, we might breed something brand new, with genes tailored to fit exactly into a slot we can't fill any other way. But that's tricky, and we need a ton of modeling. And Council approval every time."

"Well, that's news to me. Brand new species, huh? How far up the ladder do you go? What do your miracle beasts look like?"

"Nematodes, usually. When we're playing God, as a rule we tailor nematodes."

"What's a nematode?"

"Little roundworm. Hundreds of thousands of species. Do awful good stuff in the soil."

"You mean, like earthworms?"

"Naw. Different thing entirely; much smaller. Earthworms eat nematodes. Nematodes are parasites on earthworms. It's complicated."

"Great." Lani drained her mug. "I've had it, though. Wanna dance?"

# RESOLUTION

It was almost 04:00 when Lani pushed open the door to her room. She shucked out of her clothes, lifted a light robe out of the closet, gathered the clothes under one arm, and set off down the hall to shower. The robe was optional. EEE twple spent enough time training their own bodies and dealing with other people's in odd circumstances, that few of them found casual nudity shocking or even rude. But Lani was in a foul mood, and she felt better wrapped up.

She padded down the empty hall, dumped her dirty clothes in the laundry chute, and picked up replacements from the supply closet. Turning into the women's loo, she stacked her stuff in a cubby, pulled her toothbrush from the wall rack containing it and a dozen others, and examined herself disapprovingly while she brushed her teeth.

"Moron," she muttered through the toothpaste.

A shower helped, but not much. The water was tepid because the water heaters didn't power up until 05:00. And besides, her dissatisfaction was way above shower grade. And above bender grade (she was, in fact, still drunk and not yet hungover). It was even above intercourse grade. Actually, intercourse was more part of the problem than the solution.

The dancing had started well, then went south in a hurry. The first tune was something unidentifiable but Latin, and she'd coached Luv Nematode through

16

it with some success. "Just walk," she'd told him. "Left, right, left, right. Forward and back. Good. Listen to the drums for the rhythm. Now put some hips in it. More. More. Latin dancing is all about the hips. Now we can do this apart, like we've been doing, or together…like this. You're doing fine. Don't look down, look at me. You're supposed to be smitten. Good. Now we go back and forth, keep the beat, and when we want to, we can do things." She took his hands and did something, with the effect that they were no longer facing each other but dancing side by side, with one of his arms around her waist. "Or this…" and she did something more complicated, ending with him seeming to have spun her a couple of times, when, in fact, he had just stood there with his hand up.

The tune ended. As often happened, the playlist then jumped back half a century to something jazzy with a swing beat, and Lani made her first and most damaging mistake. "Hey, perfect!" she said. "We can do the Lindy! It's easy. You'll love it!"

It wasn't easy, and he didn't love it. She tried to coach him through the six basic steps, but it was too fast, he didn't get the feel, and he ended up pivoting slowly and miserably in one humiliating spot while she literally danced circles around him. She tried to recover, but the music wasn't any help (one fast dance after another, some of them mid- to late twenty-first-century stuff that put a premium on gymnastic feats such as standing on one leg for thirty seconds at a time while waggling all of one's other limbs). Soon he was sweating and angry. He finally stalked off the floor and escaped to the men's room to regain his composure.

Nothing went right after that. She had started the night intending to get good and drunk, but she overdid it even by those standards. In the end, she went home with a guy from another table, a whiney astronomer who couldn't talk about anything except how, sure, you could still learn things from the old data banks, but it was impossible to get new observations to help answer the inevitable follow-up questions. He struck Lani as inflexible in mind and body. Stiff, in fact, in every way except the one that mattered. They had finally gotten the deed done, but it wasn't pretty, and it wasn't fun. As soon as he was snoring, she abandoned him and came straight home. Not a night to remember. All things considered, a lukewarm shower was probably better than she deserved.

She dressed in running gear and did mindless cleanup chores in her room until the dorm came alive at about 05:00. Then she went out with the rest and started her daily physical training. Normally she enjoyed this part of the day: warm-up calisthenics, a few quick kilometers around the park in the cooler air before sunup, then back to the gym for weights, stretches, floor work, and five hundred meters in the pool. But on this day, it felt as if her limbs were made of bread dough and her lungs were on vacation. Her brain throbbed, and when her head went below her heart, the pain became piercing. The coach for the day kept looking at her, checking his timer, and shaking his head.

Breakfast was a trial, too, because her stomach felt no better than her head. She was determined to stick to schedule, though, even to the extent of taking food she had no intention of eating. In the Union, this was a social crime, on a par with kicking dogs or smoking tobacco, but she figured she could get away with it once. Then back to her dorm for another shower (this one hot), and off to her cubicle in the twp EEE main offices, where she spent four hours doing the mindless collation of operational statistics that was the best they would allow her to work on while her probation lasted. It would have been practical to do this in her room, where she could dog it for a bit and not be noticed, except that the reports on which she based her stats were confidential and could be accessed only from a deck operating inside the main office building.

Another downside to being in the offices was increased exposure to verbal darts from her colleagues. Today it was Gido Watanabe, an otherwise likable kid barely out of his teens, who wandered by her spot while explaining to somebody that this was the local headquarters of the Coco guild. Possibly, with typical youthful self-regard, he thought he was the only one who knew that Coco was a mythical child-eater. Well, Lani did know. But it didn't matter. Both of them knew it was a silly accusation. She didn't eat children; she just… never mind.

After her stint at work, she began to feel a little better, so she dared to follow her usual routine and skip lunch in favor of sparring with a pick-up group in the well-watered, grassy courtyard next to the refectory. The late-October weather was overcast, humid, and blistering hot. They were scheduled for kendo, and if she had faced real swords, she would have died many times over. As it was, she only felt she wanted to.

Then back to the basement of the gym for the welcome anonymity of weapons training, on this occasion mostly short-range firearms. Next, her dance/martial arts class. (Twp EEE instructors drew no distinction between dancing and fighting with people; both were simply special cases of movement in space.) There, Madame asked her twice where her head was, and could she please the hell bring it back? She then changed back into her Union standards and hustled across town to the Uni for her three-times-weekly math meet-up. She often ran this route, but this time she used a city scooter because she felt she was verging on breakdown. The lecture was wasted; she didn't hear a thing or think for a minute about Euler's equation. Then back to the twp for a late supper in the smaller refectory where she could sit at a table by herself and largely escape observation by seniors, and a brief trudge back to her room. Once inside, she dumped her deck, decided to blow off her homework, stripped to underwear, and fell into bed.

And couldn't sleep.

For the next hour or maybe two, she lay in a disembodied state brought on by exhaustion, reflecting with what felt like great clarity on her situation and recent behavior. By precept, example, and experience, she had learned that she supported her family and her twp, and the twp supported the Union. The Union then reflected and returned support back down to the twps and thence to the individual citizens. And more, that every person owed this web of obligations all that they had in the way of love, loyalty, energy, flexibility, and intelligence. Because the survival of humanity hung in the balance. If Lani and her fellows failed in their duties, the Bad Days might well come again, and a second such catastrophe would likely end with everybody dead. Everybody.

Lani knew all this and believed it. She also knew that she herself was falling short. What she couldn't believe was that her failure was her own fault.

Her panel meeting was scheduled for the day after her probation expired, one hundred eighty-two days hence. (Not that she would admit to anyone that she was counting.) The mayor was right, she supposed, in that something had to change to prevent the panel from posting her to indefinite kitchen duty, or making her into a tax auditor, or possibly even kicking her out of the twp. But though the mayor's conclusion had merit, her reasoning was all wrong. No, the problem was not that Lani was acting out and overindulging. And there was nothing wrong with her self-respect, thank you kindly. The problem was that nobody could look like anything but a toad, doing the work she was assigned to do. Rather than flying under the radar as the mayor wanted, she was going to have to rise above feather counting and get herself noticed. But in a good way; she was going to have to do some real police work. So, she swore, that's what she would do. Obstacles be damned.

# DATA HEIST

Lani perched on the edge of the chair in her office cubicle, contemplating her next move. She felt compelled to prove herself, and she fully intended to. She had been in full-on mental revolt against her own twp for—she consulted the clock on her screen—ten hours and forty minutes. This fact alone made her profoundly uneasy. The tight relation between twps and their twple pervaded the Union system: twps had rights guaranteed by the Union; individuals didn't. You counted on your twp to take care of your welfare and on the Union to take care of your twp. From this perspective, revolting against your twp was not merely injudicious; it was more like self-mutilation. An act that damaged society but that also carried its own punishment. So there was reason for Lani to feel nervous.

So far, however, she showed no outward signs of distress. She had slept, exercised, eaten, dressed, checked in on time. All completely according to routine. She then blazed through four hours' worth of tedious work in half that time. Now she had nearly two hours all to herself, with access to most of twp EEE's operational data, and it was time to do something overt. Something that she would surely have to explain later. Something that only a huge success could excuse.

Her aim was to take down a by-God bad guy. All on her own. Never mind that she had no authority to do any such thing and would not have even if she were not on probation. Forget that. She reckoned she was born to operate in the thick of it, out on the streets, and if she couldn't do that, then she didn't care what she did.

The problem was, to bust a bad guy, he had to have committed a crime. And for her purpose, not just any crime—it should be something flashy, attention-getting, and wholly, unarguably perverse. But in the Union, this kind of thing was hard to find.

Among EEE's twple, cop-years of spare time was spent watching pre-Collapse videos centered on big-city police work. These had certain points of contact with daily life in the twp, but the differences were obvious, jarring, and a source of endless amusement. This was because most of the crimes being investigated in the videos simply did not exist in the Union or were vanishingly rare. In the Union, nobody (almost exactly nobody) had significant amounts of money. Or needed it. Or could do anything much with it if they had it. It was not just that most people were, by pre-Collapse standards, dirt poor. Nor that they understood conspicuous consumption as a pernicious form of mental illness and treated it as such. Nor that drug dealing and addiction were not even illegal. Rather, it was simply that expensive luxuries scarcely existed in a society that had emerged from starvation rations only a generation or two earlier, and also that enterprises of any size were collectively owned with their profits distributed among all their twple. Moreover, the central government taxed really successful enterprises back to a notional ten-sigma outlier level so that other twps could share in the good fortune. As a result of all this, the soul and subject matter of old cop shows (bank robberies, jewel heists, car thefts, art fraud, insurance fraud, kidnapping, inheritance fights, drug deals gone bad, mugging, burglary, prostitution, gang violence, confidence games, gun running, and so on) had simply vanished. There remained a certain level of petty theft, murder, and rape, and some described shoplifting as the national sport. But most of these crimes involved perpetrators and victims in the same twp and were almost always handled by the twp's own bailiff, according to the twp's own rules. As the closest approximation there was to a Union national police agency, EEE involved itself only in actions that crossed twp boundaries, or that threatened the stability of the Union itself.

Of course, there were still financial incentives for businesses to under-report earnings and exaggerate expenses, and as long as their twp got its cut, everyone at the local level was happy; but all the other twps suffered. These were, therefore, crimes against Equality. The dishonesties involved (at the expense of others) were, in themselves, offenses against Evidence. In short, tax fraud was a serious crime, and the Union took it seriously. The result was that a large majority of twp EEE's effort and resources went to investigating tax evasion. About two-thirds of the twp's operatives were accountants, people who spent their days in front of computer screens, chasing credit around. Only a few special teams engaged in the kind of derring-do that Lani had been up to when things went bad for her, causing her probation. Lani's deep-seated fear was that she would never have such freedom again. That she would be stuck indefinitely at a desk, mumbling the computer accountant's mantra: "One plus one is zero. Carry the one."

Lani's probationary job was, basically, data entry. This was even worse than accounting. It involved reading the daily reports submitted by cops on the beat, some of them EEE field agents, but mostly from other, lower-level law enforcement twps. The idea was to tag each report with the metadata that you might want in searching for a particular incident, and then load reports and metadata into the twp's "events" database. An automated system pre-filled the metadata slots, but many of the search fields wanted information that was subjective, and pretty often, the AI made choices that humans found unnatural. To catch these, Lani vetted the machine's classifications and fixed stuff that looked wrong. On a good day, she might read two dozen reports and catch one or two bugs. The metadata work was a soul-destroying bore, but the original incident reports could sometimes be fun. Without having to sweat on the street, she was getting a pretty good overview of stupidity, negligence, and crime in the Trenton area.

On this day, however, Lani didn't care about stuffing information into the database; she wanted to get some out. Doing this would attract attention because she was only authorized to make queries on behalf of other, higher-ranking staff. She had the permissions and certs needed, but each request she submitted would generate a report sent to the putative requestor, with her name on the distribution. Twp EEE officers were suspicious by nature; if they started getting reports they had not asked for, sooner or later, they would want to know why. Her solution to this quandary had the simplicity of most successful larceny. On the twp roster were a number of long-retired relics who nevertheless maintained active data access privileges. These twple probably looked at their secure screens no more than annually, when they checked, before sending a gift, to see if their favorite grandson had recently besmirched the family name. In fact, she knew one such old guy moderately well, named Moran. She held her breath, crossed her toes, and typed in her first query using his work ID.

# TRUTHS AND LIES

Lani's search request returned incidents that occurred fairly nearby, fairly recently, that involved a modestly large (by Union standards) amount of money, that required from the perpetrator some face-to-face initiative (no computer crime) but not violence, and that had not been followed up by either local or Union law enforcement. This last was very important. She was trying to impress people, but she would make no friends by poaching on their turf.

She found a major annoyance in the non-crime of the month, in which a handful of police officers had disappeared in the span of a dozen weeks or so without explanation. The smart money held that there was no criminal activity involved. Union customs were such that it was fairly easy for a citizen to walk away without notice, change twps and names, and seem to vanish. Combine this facility with a growing population, the high stress of police work, and small-number statistics, and you had your explanation. But not everyone bought into his argument. So, for now, there was quite a lot of chatter in the "events" stream about interviews, forensics, and other doings of the Missing Officers Investigation (which already had built up enough momentum to get its own acronym: MOI). Lani wanted none of these nonsense affairs, but their variety made it difficult to weed them out of her search results. Eventually, however, she succeeded, at least well enough.

When she collated her results, she was appalled by the number of documented events that met all her restrictive criteria. For a generally peaceful citizenry who talked endlessly of brotherhood, the six hundred thousand Union citizens in her greater Trenton search space, spread over about a thousand twps, seemed to cause an awful lot of trouble. Or maybe she just had no proper intuition for how large even a fractional million was. In the end, she set thresholds so the search yielded about thirty candidates, broke the rules by copying the results to her small personal deck, and quit for the day.

She didn't yet want to risk attention by dropping her usual afternoon schedule, so she had no time to prune her hit list until the evening. After supper, she settled into her room with a bottle of not-bad whiskey, normally reserved for guests, and patiently sipped her way through the possibilities.

By a little after midnight, she had rejected all but four items. The rest were clearly unsuitable, most often because, though possibly criminal events, they were banal and boring. All of the four survivors needed more research, but one of them stood out. The crime itself presented as simple fraud—a straightforward and minor offense against Evidence. But as her teachers had been at pains to explain, even though Evidence crimes came last in the traditional litany of deadly sins, it didn't follow that they were the least important. Quite the contrary. The world is internally consistent, after all. Therefore any lie is a malicious act that splits a fantasy world off from the real one. And even a tiny split can grow and ramify until it threatens everyone. Indeed, until the very notion of truth is in danger.

A lie, they said, is like a piece of masonry poking above the sand of the Western desert. It could mean anything or nothing, depending on how deep it goes. And because a lie lives in an inconsistent world, there is no way to judge its importance from what shows on the surface. To distinguish a minor fib from deeply damaging duplicity, you just have to dig. The circumstances of Lani's chosen incident had, she thought, a whiff of the bizarre. It was this smell that made her think that simple fraud might turn out to be something bigger. Something worse. She couldn't fully explain it, but her impulse was to dig.

She read through the incident report again. It had been submitted by a detective in twp MetPD3, a force that operated south of the river, in M-Town. The detective, Kalkin by name, had been undercover, looking into something else entirely, when she met a woman with a strange story. Details were scanty. To be sure of anything, Lani needed to talk to the detective. Unfortunately, twp MetPD3's headquarters were in a different comms region than twp EEE. Audio and video connections could be arranged, but only from her own HQ building, and such calls would surely be logged, AI-monitored, and recorded. Lani didn't want any of that. Instead, she would mail a stamp asking for a face-to-face.

From her desk, she pulled a stamp, noting absently that her supply was getting low; she should buy another pack the next time she passed the PO. A "stamp" in postal parlance was a compact, robust memory device (her favored size was the cheapest available, 100 GB) designed to be handled by the postal system's mailboxes and physical sorters. She plugged the stamp into her small deck and loaded it with a twenty-second video clip of herself asking Detective Kalkin for a meeting at some convenient place to discuss case such-and-such, which had become of interest to twp EEE. This last part was a stretch. Almost for sure, nobody at EEE other than Lani knew or cared about it. But then, so what?

It was a little after 01:00. Lani trotted downstairs and dropped her stamp in the building mailbox, where the next day's early-morning pickup would happen in four hours. For a metro area delivery, there was a good chance that the detective would get her stamp by mid-afternoon. With any luck, Lani could be talking to Kalkin in a couple of days.

This sluggish mode of communication between twps arose from policy that was as old as the Union. Its purpose was precisely to slow long-distance conversations and re-postings. Inside twps (more precisely, inside geographical domains called "wicks" that were sized to contain, at most, a handful of twps), painless high-bandwidth communication was the rule. Lani could connect with her adoptive family a half-kilometer away at any time, audio or video, for as long as she liked and at no cost. Or with anybody else in her wick. After all, the whole point of recognizing diminutive social groups was connectivity.

But to go outside the wick, there were just a few low-bandwidth voice-only channels available, and most of these were allocated full-time to emergency services. The Union's makers had seen the consequences of viral spread of anonymous lies and rumors, and they wanted none of it. Instead, they arranged to stretch the doubling time for malicious chatter from minutes to days. If that slowed the transmission of news and added friction to the nation's economic activities, so be it. That was an acceptable price to pay. In real emergencies, special channels could be opened. But if you wanted to deliver an image of your newborn to Uncle Gubi, three hundred kilometers away, then tomorrow or the next day would do fine. Send him a damn stamp.

Lani went back upstairs, brushed her teeth, and went to bed. And couldn't sleep. After pretending to doze for an hour, she turned on the light and read until it was nearly time for morning PT. She went downstairs ten minutes early to stand in the lobby and watch the mail pickup.

"Me, obsessive?" she murmured as she jogged to the park. "Why would you say that?"

# THE SNAP

As often happened with her morning workouts, Lani didn't encounter anyone interested in running at her speed, so she set off solo along the well-known park paths. Ten minutes in, she had crossed the park from south to north and came out on a paved road with apartment blocks on the other side. She turned left and edged over for a pair of runners, male and female, going the other way. As they trotted by, their steady breathing, the rhythmic scuff of their boots, and the dark street combined with Lani's rebellious mood to launch a sudden flock of memories that threatened to mug her mind. She stopped dead in the street, desperately fighting them off. *Didn't need such nonsense; had things to do, places to go.* They were crafty, though. They double- and triple-teamed her. She struggled fiercely and was actually getting the upper hand until she turned and saw the moon setting bright through a gap in the clouds. Only a couple of days past full, hugely gibbous, barely asymmetric. Paralyzed by recall, she stopped short. She'd seen that before.

Assaulted from both sides, her defenses collapsed. Her vision swirled until, with a snap that hurt her eye teeth, her mind skipped backward a year and a half. Once again, she waited at the Ohio frontier, with the raw odor of the unnamed village in her nose and McRae looming bulky beside her.

"Chief," she grumbled, "these guys are small-time…"

# REBEL VILLAGE

"Losers. If all the Union's enemies look like this, we're overtrained."

McRae grunted back at her. "Enough of that," he said. "Bravado doesn't impress me. I know you're scared. Who wouldn't be? There's two of us and a bunch of them. But we don't have to take them all on, and we won't. Just do your job. Our business with Chaupi comes first. Intelligence, as we can grab it, is second. Full stop. Don't pick any fights. Don't hurt anybody unless you must."

He stood and glowered. "And put a boot in that smart mouth of yours, especially with people around. Leave the talking to me, you hear?"

"But…Bernardo Chaupi," Lani said, with an exaggerated trilling of the 'r's. "Who names their kids 'Bernardo' anymore?"

McRae ran a hand through his hair and tried to stare her down. Failed. "He's an immigrant. From whatever they call that feudal federation in the old Argentina, this year. Way down south. Patagon? Doesn't matter. Now quit asking fool questions and pay attention. We have work to do."

"Yes, Chief. Got it. Time to go?"

"Not yet."

The two stood immobile on what was probably a defunct highway embankment, adjacent to the main road, while the sun sank behind the town's huddled buildings, and horse carts trundled below. It was all Union traffic headed east to be well out of town before dark. The day breeze off the Lake, only a few klicks to the north, was fading. What replaced it was a waft of agro-industrial stink from the village. There was no place around higher than their mound, but still, they weren't high enough for the shape of the place to reveal itself. All Lani could make out was the bulk of the distillery—the village's excuse for being—and a straggle of mismatched dwelling units nearer at hand, on both sides of the road. Lots of them had improvised chimneys, with smoke coming out. Inadequate electricity, evidently. Very primitive and enviro-offensive.

McRae was tall, with a neat beard barely showing gray, and blue Irish eyes that were an oddity in that time of well-mixed races. Lani was shorter and much younger, in appearance more typical of the Union: dark of skin, eyes, and hair, with an ambiguous ethnic provenance. They both wore shabby standard-issue Union work clothes and little waist packs. Both displayed a certain blocky solidity that, in most times and places, evoked the word "cop."

At last, the final fleck of sun edged out of sight. The sky was uncommonly clear, and a sharply defined fat moon, a couple of days from full, rose behind them.

"Okay, now."

They turned and scooped up the long Union Railroad coats they had shed earlier. These were excessive for Ohio's tropical weather but provided a practical way to hide a smallsword. McRae's coat concealed such a weapon. In the Union, it was a policeman's badge of authority, which in this place, he didn't want to show unless he had to. Lani's coat did not hide a sword. She had something better.

They stumped down the steep slope to the road and crossed it. The village's main gate was nearby to the west, but they wanted nothing to do with it. Instead, they headed north among the dwellings, mixing with villagers going home from their shifts at the distillery. They turned west toward the center of town only when they were well-screened from the gate.

The village was too small to have outskirts, but it had them. A similar-size Union twp tended to be organized like a fruitcake: a sharply bounded homogeneous matrix of dormitories, kitchens, refectories, and businesses, sprinkled with random larger nuggets of industry and administration. At the twp boundaries, this conglomeration just stopped, surrounded by local agriculture and civic services that need space: water treatment, solar panel arrays, and such.

The village they entered didn't look like that. From their moving vantage, they could see that the town center contained a clutch of large, imposing buildings in addition to the sprawling distillery. Outside this central zone was a ring of about a dozen shops, none of them new construction, showing various levels of enthusiasm for upkeep and appearance. Closer to Lani and McRae, there was a relatively classy residential district with a group of impressive structures (could they really be private homes?) clustered together. The rest was a ramshackle collection of single- and multi-person dwelling units. These seemed built of various salvaged materials and lay scattered any which way for hundreds of meters from the center, separated by irregular spaces filled with piles of rotting garbage and all manner of junk.

Picking her way alongside McRae among the outlying buildings, Lani shrank into her greatcoat and wrinkled her nose. Between the wood smoke and house-size mounds of used-up sour mash, the smell was enough to water the eyes and fog the brain.

"God, Chief," she whispered. "It's medieval. Why do we want them back?"

Between them, "Chief" served more as nickname than title. Technically, he was her uncle; in the Union culture, this superseded their positions in the twp hierarchy, but only by a little. This made it feel weird for her to call him Captain. Still, when they were on duty, they needed a term more formal than Unc, and they had long ago settled on Chief.

McRae didn't answer. Lani knew the answer to her own question; she'd read all the briefing docs and discussed them ad nauseam back at the home twp. Her queasiness came from seeing, for the first time, a place where the Union's fundamental principles—respect for Environment, Evidence, and Equality—were being violated, out in the open and all at once.

When McRae spoke, it was to change the subject. "Looks like our population guess was short by a thousand or two," he said out of the corner of his mouth. "I wouldn't call conditions medieval, though. More like something out of Dickens."

# BAD MONEY

The village had no common refectory, unlike virtually all Union twps. It did have something that had once been one, six years back when it still claimed membership in the Union. The building wasn't hard to find—it was the newest and largest of those in the border strip of shops surrounding the distillery, and it had the distinctive flat archway entrance and high-ceilinged interior that usually identified Union refectories. But the double entrance doors were locked, with boards over the tall windows. A peek through the cracks showed what appeared to be a warehouse for sacks of grain and large pieces of mechanical equipment.

"No dinner, huh?" McRae said, unsurprised. "Well, they must sell food somewhere."

There were few people on the streets, but by noting those who carried parcels and following them back to their source, they found the town general store pretty quickly. It sold not only food (all boxed or canned; no produce) but also work clothes, boots, eyeglasses, and other sundries.

"Something edible—precooked, not fancy, okay?" McRae murmured to Lani. "Take your time looking, and check prices."

Lani sniffed. This was all according to plan; for McRae to remind her was a minor insult. Either that, or he was as tense as she was. That could be true. As he drifted away toward the clothing section, she noticed his left hand cradling the scabbard of his sword for a quick draw, bunching the fabric of his coat. This made the coat's qualities as concealment, marginal to begin with, nearly nonexistent. She shrugged and went to look at canned goods.

She returned sooner than intended because she didn't like the way other customers looked at her. Drab as they were, her clothes were enough to set her apart. McRae was waiting empty-handed. "Let's go," he said.

Lani put her goods—three vacuum-sealed cubes of potted chicken—on the counter, along with two silver coins that should have been more than enough. The gnome-like guardian of the cash register ignored all these things, gave her and McRae a rude stare, and twisted to look over his shoulder and signal to the manager sitting behind him in a glassed-in office. In no time, the manager came out, and half a minute later, a guard appeared as well, with his own sword and a swagger. In the Union, a sword signified authority, showing that someone important had your back. It wasn't clear whether that rule applied here. The manager's suit was dapper, even by Union standards. The guard, shirtless in a form-fitting double-breasted vest and turban, belonged in a stage play.

"Terribly sorry, Miss," said the manager, with no sliver of contrition. "Your money is no good here."

"But it's silver," she said. "Not Union bills. It's good anywhere."

"The gentleman told you that your silver is not welcome here," the guard interrupted with a sneer, loosening his sword in its scabbard. "In truth, your persons are unwelcome also. Unwelcome in this establishment, unwelcome in this city. Be gone. Now. Take your money with you."

This scene had not taken long, but already it had drawn a clump of spectators. No place for a fight. Lani bit back what she judged a withering riposte, scooped her coins off the counter, and followed McRae to the exit.

Outside, a scrawny boy, maybe eight years old, waited for them. He had a sword, too, made of wood. It was a nice piece of work, in the style of the Knights of the Round Table, straight, sanded to a double edge, with a long grip, cross guard, and pommel. He waved it at McRae and Lani and bragged,

"That's my dad in there! He's the best. You mess with him, he'll cut you up for fish bait!"

McRae studied the kid seriously. "Don't worry, son," he said gently, setting off down the street. "We've got no quarrel with your dad."

"Not worried!" the kid yelled. "Fish bait!"

"Nice blade," said Lani, over her shoulder.

# ON THE STREET

"Our *persons*!" Lani fumed, stretching her gait to match McRae's. "Where did he learn to talk like that?"

"Movies, most likely," McRae replied absently. "Something from the 1930s, with a butler. That goon wants to be an aristocrat but can't aim higher than Jeeves. Needs a lesson in ambition."

He strode on for a block in the gathering dark. The streetlights in the center of town were paltry and rare, but they were on. Outside the central core, it looked like there were none.

Lani changed the subject. "Prices were out of sight," she said tonelessly. "Three times what you'd pay back home. Lousy goods, too. Half the bread was moldy."

"Same for the dry goods," McRae agreed. "Mostly castoffs. All part of the pattern. Pay the workers next to nothing, then steal it all back." He turned a corner and stopped. "But here's the stable," he said. "Check it out. Two minutes."

Lani nodded and walked through the wide-open doors without slowing down. To go with healed fractures and other fruits of a years-long childhood equine obsession, she had a sure knowledge of horseflesh. There were four mounts tied to a hitching rail along one wall of the stable, available for immediate rental. More were in stalls at the back and probably more yet in a nearby field. But in two minutes, she would never get a look at those. The rent-a-nags up front would have to do.

There was no attendant in sight. She moved into the center of the line, calming the nervous animals with gentle noises and a touch of her hand. She looked at the eyes and teeth of the two nearest her, stroked their legs and sides, and lifted a forehoof on each. Nearby there was a little cart loaded with the day's manure, ready to be taken wherever shit went in this town.

"Hey, boy!" a voice shouted at her from the back. Somebody had finally noticed her.

"Who you calling boy, dickhead?" she shouted back, turned on her heel, and marched out.

"From the size of the manure pile, something like forty head in all," she reported back to McRae. "The ones for rent are broken down. Old, overworked, underfed. Okay for getting around town, but not much more. But there are likely some good ones out back, being boarded. Not all that poop started as bad hay. And there's some pretty nice tack hung up on the walls."

"How many good ones, do you think?"

"Hard to say, Chief. Ten?"

"Crap. Well, let's not get ourselves chased. Nice job. Now let's move along. Time to do what we came for."

# CHAUPI'S DIGS

The building they wanted was on the boundary between the city core and the scattered residential zone, near a little creek that straggled through the town. Apart from its complete anonymity (it didn't even have an external street address), it was not noteworthy in any way, just an average office building in a worse-than-average town. Apart from the distillery, it was the only building in town whose purpose their scanty intelligence identified with any certainty.

Lani and McRae climbed steps to find an unadorned porch with nothing resembling a doorbell. McRae tugged at the doorknobs, but both were solidly locked.

"Anybody watching us?" he asked. He waited while Lani did a slow scan of the neighborhood.

"Nope, nobody in sight."

He fished a little box out of his coat pocket, flipped it open, and carefully chose one of the plastic bottles it contained. He checked the label twice and grinned at Lani. "Don't get this stuff on you. It's supposed to eat metal, not bio, but why take chances?"

He turned back to the door, stuck the bottle's snout into the lock mechanism, and squeezed. In seconds the lock bulged and began to squirm. So did the strike plate on the other door and even the big brass doorknobs. As Lani watched, the

39

whole assembly took on the consistency of warm pudding and slopped down the front of the door to make a puddle on the porch, where it solidified.

"…twenty-nine, thirty," said McRae. "They claim that's the lifetime of those little bots. I always give them some extra, though."

He didn't wait long, however, before he bounced the door ajar with a shove, grabbed the exposed edge with his fingernails, pulled it open, and slid inside. Lani came right behind him, alert, checking the spaces. There was a stairway to their left, and to the right, a long hallway, surfaced with what looked like honest-to-God polished marble and hung with antique framed paintings. Nobody was in sight, but music wafted from a wide portico, halfway down the hall. They followed the sound. Turning left through the portal, they found a pleasant anteroom, a spotless desk guarding a closed door, and an irate middle-aged woman sitting at the desk, eyeing them with scorn and disbelief.

"How did you get in here? What do you want? You have no idea what you're…who *are* you?" she gobbled without stopping for breath.

McRae waved her to silence. "No worries, luv," he said. "We just stopped by to talk with Mr. Chaupi."

At that, she rose halfway out of her chair and bared her teeth. "Don't you give me any of your Union 'luv,' you monster!" she hissed. "*Nobody* sees him unless I say so, and I say you *can't!* Now get lost! Mannerless commies…"

"Ah. Well," McRae said, walking around the desk and waving for Lani to follow. "I say we can, and we will, and right now, too. Our discussion with Mr. Chaupi will take some time, so please see that we aren't disturbed." To Lani he added, "She's probably not armed. But if she does anything you don't like, kill her."

He paused at the threshold. "And luv, if you open that door after we're inside, neither of us will like it at all."

He tried the door to Chaupi's sanctum, found it unlocked, and breezed in.

# EDGY NANOTECH

Chaupi's office hit Lani like a fist in the face. It was, by a wide margin, the most opulent room she had ever seen. Mr. Bernardo Chaupi himself stood near its middle, on an expanse of shiny hardwood floor, playing what she took to be a violin or possibly a viola; she had never before seen either one up close.

He stopped playing when she and McRae appeared, looking briefly surprised but not concerned. Certainly not frightened. The music went on from speakers at the back of the room. It was missing something, though. Lani realized that it was a student's recording mixed with one of the instruments left out. Chaupi was filling in the absent part. McRae started to say something, but Chaupi shot him a look and waved his bow hand, silencing him exactly as McRae had silenced the assistant outside.

"Not now," he said pleasantly. "Please take a seat. Almost done." He nodded for a time, mentally found his place in the streaming music, and joined back in. Lani didn't have enough experience to be sure, but she thought he was pretty good.

McRae took a chair in front of Chaupi's desk. Lani remained standing, picking a place between McRae and the door. While Chaupi wound up to the piece's finale, she studied him and the room. He looked to be in his forties,

41

with a high forehead, a close-trimmed beard, and long black hair tied in a queue. Inside snug tailored clothes, he had an athlete's physique but more that of a distance runner than a fighter. An attractive guy, she thought. The room was expansive and high-ceilinged, its substantial wall space densely packed with eye-catching stuff: paintings and photographs, hanging sculptures, minerals, gems and jewelry, technical artifacts from prehistoric spear points to computer hardware made soon before the Collapse. There were perhaps a dozen musical instruments, mostly stringed but also some horns and woodwinds. A grand piano sat in one corner, and what might have been Persian rugs covered half the floor. Several mobiles hung from the ceiling. In fact, it was a remarkable museum of art, music, science, and technology, all in one room, all well-tended and carefully lighted. The net effect was to blow the breakers in several of Lani's "miserable excess" categories and leave her feeling dazed and light-headed. Fucking saints, what had it *cost*? Maybe McRae was feeling the same way; how else to explain him sitting there complacently while Madam Dracula outside was doubtless calling for help?

Presently Chaupi finished his part, and the speakers went quiet. He loosened the tension on his bow, hung the instrument in one of the scattered empty spaces on a side wall, and calmly sat down behind his desk.

"Now, how may I help you?" he asked.

"I am Captain Ryg McRae, and this is my assistant, Investigator Lani Maxwell," McRae explained in a formal sing-song. "As you doubtless surmise, we represent the NAU. We are from twp Triple-E."

That got a raised eyebrow. "Triple-E, huh? That's something. But you're out of your jurisdiction, Captain."

"Jurisdiction, schmurisdiction," McRae said with a comfortable smile. "You know why we're here. You are making problems for your Union neighbors. You run a company town that is an object lesson in wage slavery. You use monopolistic advantage to stifle competition from inside the Union. You use your wealth to suborn the leaders of Union twps. Your town stands in the way of developing Union farming, irrigated from the Lake. In short, to the Union, you have become an intolerable nuisance. All this has to stop."

"A large order. But why come to me? You should be talking to the mayor or..."

McRae dismissed this objection with a wave and a chuckle. "Be serious, please, Mr. Chaupi. It's clear who's in charge here."

Chaupi opened his mouth to say something but shut it as the door banged wide and two armed goons rushed in. They wore the same turban-and-vest getup as the guard in the general store. It was a uniform, not a fashion choice, Lani realized. Somehow this made her feel better. They carried mismatched swords, one almost a rapier, the other more like a machete. But matched or not, they were long and pointy, and the guards looked like they meant business.

"Lani," said the Chief.

Lani had been standing demurely a little to one side, more or less in a dancer's fourth position. At the sound of her name, she flowed forward, interposed herself between McRae and the guards, and dropped into a fighting stance. Attached to the left side of her belt was a little device that looked like a tape measure. She took this with her right hand and, with a swooping motion, whipped out something long and skinny, like a length of wire or a stiff willow switch.

Her two adversaries stopped short and shot each other a puzzled look. But before they could get their focus back where it belonged, Lani hopped forward, hopped sideways, and fell back *en garde*. With each hop, she flicked her wrist, and with each flick there came a musical *ting*, and a length of steel blade clattered to the floor. The goons were left dumbfounded, staring at the stumps of their swords, each sheared off cleanly a few centimeters above the hilt. Lani's willow switch waved gently in their faces.

"Nanotech," observed McRae from his chair. "It's *really* sharp." He examined the two for a moment. "Lani, do you have any advice for these gentlemen?"

Lani thought about it. "Run," she suggested.

They ran. They got in a mess getting through the door but quickly sorted it out and soon could be heard pounding down the corridor.

Chaupi had been sitting quietly, but now he edged closer to his desk.

"Nuh-uh," McRae chided. "Put your hands up and keep 'em up unless you want them cut off."

McRae rose and went to Chaupi's side of the desk, careful not to get between him and Lani. He opened all the drawers and, from one, pulled a heavy revolver, ancient but clean and polished, like so many things in the room. He sighed heavily.

"Somebody always has a gun," he complained. "Lani, take this."

She did something on the hilt of her weapon that made it curl up from the tip backward, very fast. She clipped the resulting disk back onto her belt and took the pistol.

The Chief's complaint notwithstanding, she knew he had his unsanctioned tiny automatic concealed somewhere. She hadn't seen it on this trip and didn't expect to unless it was really needed. But it was good to know it was there.

McRae sat down on the desk and looked hard at Chaupi. "So here's the thing," he said. "Your life is gonna change, starting now. At this moment, I have a good deal of discretion about the terms of that change. But if you and I can't agree, then real soon you'll wake up and find a detachment of Union Marines in charge of this place. And that day will end with your neck stretching a rope. So you and I, we need to negotiate a deal that you can and will live with. Is that clear?"

Chaupi rolled his eyes, perhaps at the lack of subtlety, but he nodded.

"I can't hear you."

"Yes," said Chaupi. "Let's talk."

"Good. Lani, take that cannon and stand guard outside. Don't shoot anybody if you can help it. Mr. Chaupi and I are going to dicker."

# STANDOFF

Lani took up a position right outside the grouchy lady's anteroom, now vacant, where she could keep an eye on the whole corridor but had a bolt-hole if she needed it. She broke open the pistol, dumped the cartridges into her hand, and examined them with a skeptical eye. None of them met her standards, but she took the two best-looking rounds and stuck them back into the cylinder, followed by two that might possibly fire. The last two she put in her pocket. She wanted an empty under the hammer, so the damn museum piece wouldn't go off on its own, and another empty after that, in case she needed to scare somebody by being willing to pull the trigger. All this took a minute or so, and there was still nobody in sight. She thought about dragging the desk into the hall for cover but rejected the idea as ineffective, time-consuming, and bad psychology. Instead, she let the gun hang in the open, pointed at the floor, took a deep breath, and relaxed, waiting for something to happen.

After a little while, something did. She heard a soft rustling from the stairwell. Then a silence. Then a bald head popped partway into the hallway and popped out of sight again. Another pause, this time for a longish mumbled conference. At last, two empty hands came into sight, followed by the same head as before and, finally, a body. The guy stepped into the middle of the hall with his hands up. He wore the same outfit as the others, minus the turban, and with his sword sheathed. He reminded Lani of Yul Brynner in *The King and I*, possibly her favorite movie when she was eight. Cute, she thought, but she ignored him and shifted her focus back to the stairwell, where real danger might emerge at any time.

"You there. What's going on?" Baldy asked, nervous, a little too loud.

"Got nothing to say to you," she replied. "Send your honcho out."

"What?"

She sighed elaborately, a mannerism she had learned from the Chief. "Red Rover, Red Rover, let your god-damned honcho come over."

That brought a laugh from the end of the hall, and another guard sauntered into the open. He was older than the first one, tall and lanky, and evidently comfortable with the idea of getting shot at or possibly sliced and diced by semi-magical nanotech.

"So what *is* going on?" he asked.

She shrugged at him. "Nothing dangerous. My boss is talking with your boss."

"Is he, now? And what do you think that means we should do?"

"I think we should let them talk. Most likely, they're becoming best buds. There's plenty of time for us to kill each other if they come out fighting."

"I expect you're right," he said. "Truce, then, at least for now. But don't go anywhere."

"Wouldn't dream," she replied and slid back to put herself mostly in the cover of the anteroom. She was by no means sure that she and the Chief had the only guns in the building.

# TORN CURTAIN

"Nothing much," McRae replied to Lani. This was unhelpful. He and Lani were back on the street, in the clear, a third of a klick from the scene of their recent excitement. But he volunteered nothing. They were headed roughly toward the main East Road, skirting the boundary between occasional streetlights and none, expecting to spend another night camped out near the road. Lani badly wanted to know what had happened back there and whether they had won or lost, but the Chief was in a thoughtful, silent mood. Finally, she broke with protocol and just asked him.

"Not good enough," she persisted as they strode along. "What happens to Chaupi?"

Chaupi and McRae had emerged from the office after half an hour, both pretending to modest satisfaction. Lani knew the Chief well enough to see that under his bland demeanor, there was a glint of victory, along with something sneaky and furtive that she couldn't place. Chaupi, however, was only putting the best face on a bad situation. Lani guessed he had made a deal that he didn't like but hadn't yet figured out how to get out of. At least he had instructed the palace guards to give McRae and Lani free passage out of town and to pass that order to the outlying stations. Especially the one blocking the East Road. They had been given leave to go, and they were going. But McRae still wasn't talking.

"Huh?" Lani said. "Huh? C'mon, Chief, out with it. You know I'll get it out of you. So tell me now. What's the story?"

"Well, first," McRae explained at last, "the Marines will sure-nuff be here. Soon as we make our report. Few days, less than a week. By that time, Mr. Chaupi and his lieutenants will be gone—scattered who knows where. We take over the town, establish a new twp to run the distillery, start making the place fit to live in. We'll reel in the lieutenants in time, mostly. Any we catch will find themselves drafted for five years reforesting Pennsylvania or some such."

"But what about Chaupi?"

"Ah. Special case, that one. He'll disappear, likely with Union help. We confiscate all his stuff, of course, and put it in museums or whatnot. But long as we know where to reach him, he's free as a bug."

"Why, for shit's sake? He's the boss. This,"—with a gesture—"this mess is all his fault."

"Yep, true fact. But he's got real horsepower, he does, and someday we might need that."

McRae had been facing straight ahead while he talked. Now he turned for a long serious look at Lani. "You don't suppose that the Union has the world licked, do you? We squeaked through a mighty narrow place just a lifetime ago. It could happen again. To see it doesn't, or to deal if it does, we'll need people like him. So he gets a pass. At least this time."

"Well, crap, Chief. Is that justice? It doesn't sound like it."

"You want to be careful about dispensing justice. We don't do that much. The judges even *say* they don't do that. Best of bad alternatives. That's our stock in…"

"Ambush!" Lani grunted and surged ahead faster than thought. They had rounded the corner of an unlighted single housing unit in the part of town where hung blankets stood in for doors. The only streetlight was a hundred meters away, but in its pale light, she could see part of a foot poking from under a door curtain and the tip of an upthrust sword at head height. In an instant, she could visualize the whole setup: there would be a squad inside, waiting for the fellow at the door to sweep the curtain aside and thrust as he crossed the threshold. Her only chance was to drop him in the doorway, where his mates would get tangled up with him as they tried to charge.

She yanked out the willow wand as she lunged, uncurling it to full length quick as a finger snap. It sliced the heavy blanket like a whip through soap suds, and she could barely feel the tug as it went through flesh and bone beyond. She withdrew fast, holding her wand high. From behind the blanket, there came a gasp and a shriek as a tiny body tumbled out into the street and dropped a sword with a dull, non-metallic clunk. The sword was made of wood. The body was the kid from earlier, the one who had called them fish bait. His left leg was gone, about mid-thigh.

# RUN

Lani stood paralyzed, gaping at the thing she'd done. The leg wasn't completely severed; the lower part held on by a thin cord of tissue, making it slide back and forth as the kid sat bolt upright and tried to grab it. His blood was everywhere, black in the dim light and terrifying in its quantity. The boy stared at her with his mouth working, eyes like dry wells begging her to help him, breathing in fast gulping sobs.

"Lani, wake up," McRae said sharply. He jerked his belt off in a motion so smooth that it had to have been rehearsed. Made sense, really; lots of nasty things you can do to an opponent with a belt. Lani remained frozen, wanting to comfort the kid, knowing it was useless.

"Break the handle off that sword. Do it now. *Move!*"

She remembered to let her wand wrap itself up so it would do no more damage. Stiffly, she bent over and lifted the sword out of the pool of blood where it lay. McRae was looping his belt around the kid's thigh for a tourniquet. Lani finally saw what he was about. With a convulsive jerk, she broke the sword blade over her knee and gave him the short end. He stuck it through the loop of his belt and twisted it until it squeezed off the pulsing blood flow. The kid tried to scream again, but nothing much came out. McRae slid him over against the door jamb, took his hands, and placed them on the tourniquet.

"Hold this," he told the boy. "Hold it hard. Don't let go, or you'll die. Do you understand?"

Maybe the boy nodded. His eyes were still enormous; he was still sobbing.

McCrae shook Lani by the shoulder. "We've gotta go."

She stammered something.

"Shut up," he told her. "He'll be found soon, and when he is, they aren't gonna like it a bit. All our deals will be busted. That's it. We need to blow."

"What do we do?" she said, barely audible.

"It's our turn," he said. "Like those other guys. We run. Follow me."

And he was off. He dashed along the front of the house in the direction they had been going, turned hard around its far corner, and disappeared. Lani dithered for a couple of seconds, then did her best to run after him.

It was awful. She lurched and spasmed on legs that had turned to water. She made the mistake of trying to peek over her shoulder for one last view of the kid and nearly fell. Twisting violently, she barely made the turn and lumbered after McRae like a pregnant nanny goat. He was far down what seemed to be a scruffy alleyway, rapidly opening his lead.

Lani mumbled curses to herself, trying to get her body to behave. It was a stupid situation. She knew she could outrun McRae any day, on any surface, at any distance. Hell, he was twice her age. Almost three times. But there he was, gaining ground. In desperation, she dropped back to a jog and tried to pick up speed slowly. This worked better. She started to lengthen her stride, stay on the balls of her feet, use her arms as she had been taught. She had run a couple of hundred meters before she realized that the sobbing she heard was not the kid's but her own. That wouldn't do. If she wasn't careful, she would run up an oxygen debt and keel over. Gradually her breathing smoothed out, and her legs regained their snap. That was good news because, after the first little bit, the ground was more like an obstacle course than a street. McRae had been making erratic turns. She didn't know why, but soon they were holding a fairly constant course toward the southwest, almost directly away from the East Road. By this time, they were well away from the lighted part of town, amid fields, trash dumps, and wasteland, running by the light of the waxing moon, nearly full. The moon phase had been a factor in planning this affair; she had pooh-poohed this idea at the time, but now she was glad. No dogs barked as they powered out of the village's built-up area. She recalled the reason from the Union intelligence assessment: all the dogs had been eaten by the local workers.

She was still carrying Chaupi's gun, stuck in her belt in the back. But it bothered her, messing with her stride and always threatening to fall out. She was hoping to persuade McRae that she could get rid of it. For more emotional reasons, she would also have liked to lose the nanotech willow wand, but there was no hope for permission to do that. The head of the Triple-E nanotech division herself had checked it out to her, making clear that there were only four like it in the world. She didn't care if Lani came back, so long as the weapon did.

About the time the gun really started to annoy her, McRae stopped and waited for her to catch up. They looked at each other. They both were sweating and breathing hard, but neither was anywhere near exhaustion. For the moment, they were on familiar ground, with thousands of days' PT experience to fall back on.

"You okay?" he asked.

She nodded. "Yes, Chief."

"Need anything?"

"This gun. It's a problem. We got to have it?"

He considered briefly. "Your call."

"I think," she said, "it's more dangerous to us than it is to them."

"Okay. Ditch it. Somewhere it won't be found right away. Also, we're gonna drop our coats a little way ahead. Make sure you empty the pockets, save what you need. Water bags and iodine."

"Right."

He stood for a moment, carefully not looking at her.

"Don't worry about the boy," he said at last. "I'm sure they found him in time."

She glared at him. "*Goddammit, Chief,*" she breathed. "Don't jolly me, okay?

I'm not an idiot. I cut his leg off, right? Above the fucking *knee!* He was going into shock before we turned the corner. If he lived long enough to see a doctor, it would be a damn miracle. So don't tell me that stuff. It's insulting."

She stared into the distance for a while, then back at his face. "Can we run some more, please, Unc? It's better when we run."

"Okay, Lani. Here we go."

# MOONSET

The little wash where Lani lay shivering was filled and fringed with stunted thorny shrubs. They were thick enough to shield her from observation but not enough to protect her from the daytime sun. Come noon, it would be hellishly hot. For now, it was still chilly after the night's storm. The thorns were long and sharp, and it had taken her forever to find a spot where she could lie on her back and not be punctured. She and the Chief had been on the run for a day and two nights. It had been chancy, but now she was pretty sure they had honestly gotten away. They would find real beds soon if they didn't die of exhaustion first. She was as tired as she could ever remember. And she couldn't sleep.

That first night, the Chief had led them in a widening spiral away from the village and around it. They had waded the sluggish little stream that flowed out of the village, waist-deep and smelling of sewage, yeast, and chemicals. After that, they headed nearly straight west for a while, running easily on ground that was mostly pretty good. It had once been semi-rural suburbs, with little residential clusters separated by bands of trees and fields. They would come on the remains of the neighborhoods suddenly. Chimneys, near-buried foundations, and piles of corroded rubble would appear from the night as if condensing from the sultry air. The former trees were reduced to low waves of springy mulch, except for rare linear piles where the trunk of some suburban giant had not yet completely rotted away. Vegetation was sparse and shrubby. One day the ecology would find its way to something like a short-grass prairie, but that day was far off.

After several kilometers, they turned south and then a little east. The aim was to avoid roads while getting as far as was practical from the village, in what they hoped was an unexpected direction. After they gained some distance, they would turn east, eventually coming back into Union territory south of the dead city of Cleveland.

There were certain problems with this plan. They had no food to speak of, and water was hard to find in a landscape that now consisted of thin or absent layers of indifferent soil atop deep glacial till. And the topography was bare and gently rolling. There were hardly any places to hide, and traveling by day would expose them to view from far away. Last, the country was crisscrossed with decayed roads, little used but still passable to horse traffic. That meant riders could show up pretty much anywhere. The game, then, was to lie up during the daylight hours, travel at night, and leave as few tracks as possible.

Toward the end of the first night, they found a negligible dry wash eroded in the bottom of a barely noticeable valley, where they holed up for the day. The Chief and Lani traded two-hour watches. By early afternoon, they had seen dozens of tiny lizards and one small rodent; the Chief claimed to have seen a skeletal coyote round about sunrise, but Lani thought he was making it up. They also saw three riders at various times, going who knew where, but none came closer than a kilometer to their roost.

During Lani's first afternoon watch, piled-up cumulus clouds appeared over the northwest horizon and, with surprising speed, resolved into a massive squall line, roaring down on them from the Canadian plains. The weather had been uncommonly settled for several days, but plainly, she joked feebly to herself, that was coming to an end. By the time the Chief took the watch, the nearest thunderheads towered almost straight above them, with blinding white crowns bashing into the stratosphere, bases that were lost in sullen cloud-wrack, and everything in between visibly churning. "Get ready to move," he had said, craning his neck at the oncoming storm. "This is our chance."

When the weather arrived, it was all at once, like an avalanche. The wind kicked up with swirling gusts that could knock you over, the temperature dropped ten degrees, lightning was everywhere, and the rain was day twenty of Noah's flood. Most importantly, to their thinking, the visibility shrank to tens of meters. Nobody would be following or sniping at them from a klick away. And the rain would obliterate their tracks.

The lightning terrified Lani. Much too often, as the leading edge of the storm rolled past, bang followed flash with no perceptible pause. But on that terrain, there was nothing you could do that would help. It was like descriptions she had read of shelling in combat. You went about your job, and what happened, happened. The rain was not a serious problem, except that every wash became a stream. These were seldom too deep to wade easily, but the footing in the stream beds was bad, and there were a lot of them. They crossed many of these side by side, with elbows locked for mutual support. Even so, several times, they toppled into frothing torrents.

After half an hour, the rain slackened a bit, but then it resumed, worse than ever, with hail. It wasn't bad hail, just pellets the size of cherries, but it was cold, and it hurt. The rain stopped about sunset, and briefly, they could see under the cloud base all the way to a clear horizon. Far to the north, a tornado tracked along slowly as if it belonged there.

After dark, they continued slogging eastward. The temporary streams mostly subsided, but sometime after midnight, they ran afoul of a fairly large one that was still running. The Chief stepped in a hole and fell, dragging them both into the water and spraining his ankle. Wet and annoyed, he insisted that they press on, so for the last several hours, Lani was his crutch, holding him up on her shoulder as they stumbled across the endless slippery glacial rubble. A couple of hours before dawn, they had given up, exhausted, and found this low thorny place to hide.

The sky had cleared; with the moon down, it was very dark except for rippling lightning still visible on the eastern horizon. The summer Milky

Way ran overhead, its majestic sweep confused by the Low Earth Orbit dawn swarm: thousands of colliding relics of the fabled space age that variously slid or tumbled or twinkled through near space, above the spoiled atmosphere. She hugged herself to stop shivering, cried quietly for a time, and, at last, dozed.

# SWEEPER

Lani opened her eyes and shook her head. She was back in her own time, in Trenton, near the territory of the EEE twp. How long had she been out? The moon had moved, but not very much. About fifteen minutes, then. Still a long time for this sort of thing.

"Are you all right, luv? Do you need help?" The voice was masculine, non-threatening, subtly artificial. It came from a street sweeper, squatting on its wheels a meter in front of her.

Swell, she thought. Now, when she could most use a bit of human touch, the only one to come to her aid was a garbage machine. "I'm fine," she told it. "I don't need help."

"Glad to hear it," it said. "In that case, can you please move? You are obstructing the completion of my rounds."

Lani looked around. She was squatting on the sidewalk curb with her feet in the gutter. Her left boot rested halfway into a medium-sized pile of horse manure—always first priority for the city's automated sweepers. She stood up, still shaky and disoriented, and managed to stand back from the street far enough for the machine to roll up and ingest the horse patty with a mechanical *gulp*. "Good evening, luv," it said and rolled on about its business.

Lani wiped tears from her face and considered her situation. The park was at her back. Twp EEE, and her life's center, lay a kilometer that way, on the park's other side. A modestly large distance, but it could be much farther, and she would still feel the twp's pull. The EEE acronym was supposed to be a reminder of the virtues that the twp championed. But cops being cops, Triple-E twple usually presented the name in terms of failures. These were precisely Eapy Fox's list of fatal pre-Collapse mistakes: crimes against Equality, against the Environment, against Evidence-based mental habits. That was fine, she thought. Always good to know what evils you opposed. But that advice was so negative. It didn't tell you where you *should* go, or how to get there. She loved her twp, but by now, she felt sure that it was not going to mend her guilt and depression. To free herself from that, she was, this very minute, as her stamp worked its way through the postal system, engaged in open rebellion against EEE. That made the twp the center of her life again, just in a different way. She felt no urge to abandon her play for the twp's validation. But she needed more. At the very least, she thought, she needed a wider circle of friends. Ones who weren't cops.

She shook herself and looked around. She wasn't going to find better chums here, except maybe for the street sweeper.

She now felt stable enough to run to someplace more promising. She took some deep breaths, bounced twice on her toes, and set off.

# REMATCH

Four days later, Lani still had nothing back from Kalkin. *Niente.* Zero. Way less than epsilon squared. This worried her. A lot. She worried that Kalkin herself had become a missing officer. She worried that Kalkin had blown the whistle on her nascent investigation, killing it (and Lani's chance of redemption) before it even got out the door. She worried that she was worrying too much.

Somehow, she made it through her day. She threw consistency to the wind, battering her sparring partners until they were thoroughly scared of her and shredding targets at the shooting range with ferocious concentration, but then submitting to dangerous lifts in dance class, executed by guys she didn't trust, with blithe disregard of possible consequences. For supper, she went to the early serving at the big refectory and went out of her way to hobnob with officers above her rank and people on her dorm floor whom she never saw, simply to prove she could. She focused on charming twple who had been silently shunning her for months, people who hoped she would just vanish from the twp without making a fuss. By the time the second seating started, she had made up her mind about the evening.

It was apple season, so she swooped down to the serving level and grabbed a couple, fresh from the Maritimes. Then back to her room to drop off her laptop deck and return to the street. The air was like a steam bath, but for a change, the sky was clear. The big square of Pegasus floated overhead. She read this as celestial affirmation of her next stop— the local stable. The hands there all knew her; nobody said boo when she strode back to the stalls to give her first apple to her favorite mount, a compact roan stallion named Rocky. She spent ten minutes fawning over him and making up for having been gone so long. The apologies had little effect, but the apple did. Then she was off again and headed toward the Uni, munching her other apple. She didn't relish the memory of her last encounter with academics at the Back Canal, so she had decided to give it another try. Get back in the saddle.

Things were not yet rolling at the Canal; it was still pretty early. She nevertheless managed to attach herself to a group of three guys at one of the back tables, who promptly offered up their names: Gennu, Spol, and Patri. The attachment process had been dead easy. She had walked over with a pitcher of beer and said, "Hiya, luvs. I'm Lani. Mind if I join you?" And that was that.

The General Assembly was in session, meaning the talk was mostly politics—not Lani's strong suit. Gennu went on about how the "Assy," as he called it, was considering loosening restrictions on advertising, especially ads about food and restaurants.

"This same argument has come up about once a decade for the last sixty years," he lectured. "Greens are for, Birds are against, Birds always win. But this time the Chips are likely to vote in favor, so who knows what will happen."

"Food ads? Why food ads?" Lani asked, mostly to stake out a little conversational space.

Spol smoothly picked up the loose ball. "Images, really," he said. "Photos or video. Policy forbids them in ads about restaurants or anything to do with food. The gripe is that they're always staged. Misleading at best; lies at worst. Have you ever seen a picture of crispy veggies in a restaurant window that looks anything like what you get on your plate? So that's it. A basic offense against Evidence." He smirked over Lani's right shoulder and leaned back from the table, looking smug.

"They argue about that? For sixty years? Are they nuts?" Lani wondered out loud. "Don't they have real problems?" She aimed a finger at the third guy, who hadn't yet said anything. "You. Patri? Yeah, Patri. You want to weigh in on this?"

Patri looked her over for a moment, then unfolded a genial smile. Quite a nice smile, really. "Well, yes. I do. It's one of my pet topics, which is your bad luck. I learned most of what I know about it from my friend Vaun, who can lecture about it for hours. But she's not here, so to shorten a long, old story: Most everything distinctive in Union culture is a reaction against the Bad Days and everything that led up to them. Think about religion. Before the Collapse, religious doctrine was pervasive in most cultures. But we Unionites never do *anything* for religious reasons, and most religious vocabulary has vanished from the language, except for use as curses. Or take our given names. Patri, Lani, Gennu, Spol. Not a William, or Caroline, or Sebastian, or Anastasia in the bunch. We don't give kids names like that. We like names short, and if not actually unique, then very uncommon. And for sure, nothing intentionally biblical or attached to some long-dead white monarch. That's a social habit. It started even before the Union was formed—think of Eapy Fox, Mother of the Country, for God's sake—and it stuck. Or gender roles. All the old societies were patriarchal. We go with matriarchy by default. Eighty percent of twp mayors and Union reps are women; same for Council members. A man has to be better, work harder, if he wants to get elected to anything. That used to be true of women, so we hate it. Anything that smacks of the bad old days has become anathema."

"Yeah, but advertising?" Lani interrupted.

"Same deal with advertising. Advertising, propaganda, marketing, the makers figured that beyond the minimal level of informing about price, function, and availability—let's call it advertising for engineers—all that stuff amounts to sneaky ways to fly under your mental radar and make you want to do something that's bad for you. It's an assault on Evidence, almost always. So they banned it. Like most good ideas, that one can be overdone, and likely has been. But there are pros and cons, and times change, which makes the question keep coming back. And here we are. Is that an answer?"

"Wow, yes," Lani grinned. "Do you teach classes? Can I sit in?"

This prompted a period of embarrassed murmuring and shifty glances.

"No," Patri said at last. "I'm just a student. And I talk too much. What about you? Tell us about yourself. You're not that Lani from the Hendrikson Mine film, are you?"

"Nope," she said carelessly. "That was some different kid." She paused and took a deep breath, thinking about what came next. She wasn't about to tell these guys she was a cop. Fortunately, she had a plan.

"Not much to tell, really," she said, with demure and downcast eyes. "I'm visiting from the University of Saratoga. It's a little school, not many options. So I'm here, looking around, see what's a fit. Maybe demographics."

The others didn't exactly hoot, but there was derision in the air. "Demography? Really?" Gennu chuckled. "Do you know who goes into demographics?"

"Uh, well…No."

"People who are good with numbers but don't have enough personality to be accountants."

"Great. Thanks for that."

"No, seriously," said Patri. "You're a demographer, fine. Me, I breed marsupials at the zoo. No kangaroos, mostly quokkas and long-nosed bandicoots. The odd opossum. You know."

"You're making fun of me."

"Yep, 'fraid so." He stood up. "Let me make it up to you. Care to dance?"

Lani opened her mouth and closed it again. She finally got her tongue working. "You dance?"

"Hell yes. Before grad school, I spent some time in the Navy." He raised his eyebrows at the other two, who nodded their agreement. Yes, it was true.

"The thing is, all us sailors know how to dance. You know, hornpipes and shit. So are you coming or not?"

# CONFIDENCES

At the usual time, Lani woke up and found that she was not, in fact, freezing in a pre-dawn whiteout. It was pre-dawn, right enough, but Trenton was near the southern limit of year-round habitability. Even in mid-November, with the windows open, the feeling was more like a sauna than a snowstorm.

She made the first move toward sneaking out without waking Patri, but it was wasted effort. Faint lights from outside showed him sitting up in bed, wide awake, staring at her. As best she could make out in the semi-dark, he was worried.

"You okay?" he asked, with a hand on her bare shoulder. "That seemed like a bad one."

"No," she said. "No, I've had worse." She curled up in a ball beside his legs. "Not sleepy now. How about if I just, you know, go?"

"Seems like a waste. I'm wide awake too. How about if you just, you know, stay? We don't have to get all physical again. Some of the best conversations happen at three in the morning."

"Hmph. What about?"

"How about us? That's me and you. I'll start. I'm Patri twp UniHist Gibbs. Born and raised in eastern Ontario, twp Chard. Small place, only three twps make the town. We raised grapes. I joined the Navy at twenty, got out at twenty-five, now I'm working on a Ph.D. in North American history here at the Uni. Oh, yeah. And I think you're pretty super. Enough of me. Your turn."

"You get shot at, in the Navy?"

"Not to speak of. But it's your turn. None of that answer-a-question-with-a-question crap, please. I know that trick."

"You always talk in complete sentences? Makes you sound like a professor."

"I plan to be a professor one day. Still your turn. What's your name?"

"Lani. You know that."

"I mean your whole name."

Lani paused (stalled, actually), sorry that it was too dark to make her bat-the-eyes thing work. "Lani twp ModDance Harris," she said at last.

"Great. Now your real name, okay?"

"What makes you think that's not it?"

"You've got a tell, Lani. Don't ask me what it is; I won't say. But I know every time. Half the stuff that comes out of your mouth is lies."

"You bastard!"

"I don't mean to upset you. I like it. It's one of the things that makes you interesting. But I do want to know who I'm falling for. C'mon. What's your name?"

"No. You'll hate it. You'll hate me."

"I won't. Tell me, please. Give."

Lani tried to control her breathing and sat stiffly for a minute.

"Okay, dammit," she said at last. "I'm Lani twp Triple-E Maxwell. Happy?"

He leaned over and hugged her firmly. "I'm ecstatic. That's wonderful. Triple-E, huh? Damn. I never slept with an elite cop before. And Maxwell. So that *was* you in the Hendrikson flick."

"Yeah," she sighed. "I was there. Only it was nothing like in the movie. I didn't do a thing, really."

"Well. Anyway. But Maxwell. That's interesting, too. Pretty flashy, in fact. Think of it. We're Maxwell and Gibbs. You know. We practically invented statistical mechanics, the two of us."

"What?" she said, suddenly boiling mad, surprising even herself. "Are you crazy? We happen to share names with two long-beard physics nerds, and you think that's funny? You think that'll make me feel like we're connected? Like we're a couple? Don't you know *anything* about women?"

"I guess not. Nor ever will, most likely." She could hear his smile. "...But actually, I did learn one thing in the service. It goes like this."

He turned her around, so she lay face down, and began kissing behind her knees, slowly working up the insides of her thighs. After a while, she sighed and began to hum. "Now," she said, "we're getting somewhere."

# WALTHER LUNCH

Roughly once a quarter, McRae would take Lani out to lunch. The ostensible reason was to catch up, let hair down, talk over, act out, and otherwise prepositionally discuss their respective lives in reasonable privacy and away from the twp. Lani suspected that her uncle's real motive was to get two breakfasts in a day, which could be done at their habitual venue Comfood, but which the twp cooks at Triple-E would not countenance. In any case, there they were.

Comfood had a nice terrace overlooking the river. In a few months, the view would be mostly sandbars, but now, toward the end of hurricane season, the river was high and scenic. The weather was hot but not excessively so. Both Lani and McRae were working on large orders of scrambled eggs, pancakes, grapefruit juice, and bacon (a rarity but miraculously available if ordered early in the day). Everything should have been perfect. But nevertheless, the Chief's nose was out of joint.

"Those worthless buffoons," he grunted.

"Which ones, Unc?" It was a social occasion, so "Unc" was preferred.

"Politicians. Members of the goddamn governing Council."

"What is it now?"

"Firearms, kid. They've voted down a proposal to update the weapons list for law enforcement. Again. Comes up every five or ten years, and every time the Birds say 'Nope. We don't need that.' Who the hell are 'we' is what I want to know."

"Is this about the Walther again?"

"You got it. The Walther." He looked up from his food, trying to appear conciliating. "Not that it's a bad gun. It's okay for what it is. But that design is four hundred years old. Can you believe it? Four centuries! Hitler shot himself with one of those, you know."

Lani knew. She had heard all this before. It seemed to her that her uncle had changed—around about the time of their failure in Ohio. He had become somehow less patient. Less open. More resentful about little things. Well, the experience had certainly changed her; why not him?

"Least they could do," the Chief went on, "is let us use a 9mm. That little round the Walther fires won't stop a charging jackrabbit."

"Unc, there's not a 9mm cartridge on the planet. Or if there is, it's also hundreds of years old. And we know how those work."

McRae flashed her an anxious look. This was as close as Lani would ever come to talking about the Hendrikson Mine fiasco. But neither of them wanted to get into that.

"So," Lani went on, "the Council would have to start up a whole new production line, only to keep the police forces in training ammo. It's a budget decision; it's not personal. If it's stopping power you want, why do you carry that little popgun? If you're gonna keep a clandestine sidearm, why don't you ask your friend the gunsmith to make you something with more punch? Or just carry the Colt?"

"Concealability," McRae shrugged with a wan smile. "Why be obvious about packing? If it's a display of authority you want, we've got swords. And that little gun amuses me. I like the tip-up barrel. But you're right; ammo is always a problem."

The Chief was regaining some of his usual affability, but he wasn't quite done with politics. "While we're at it, you know what else those Birds have done? They turned down, *again*, Triple-E's proposal for public surveillance cameras. That would be easy and cheap, and give us a real tool to crack down on street crime. Why…"

"Of which there's almost none," Lani interrupted. "Unc, I've been reading the reports. I know. And besides, Union folks don't like people looking over their shoulders. They're too fond of shoplifting. Enough police crap. No, let's don't speculate about missing cops. Let's talk about something else."

McRae added syrup to his pancakes and considered. "Well, all right then. I hear you had a tussle with the mayor. How was that?"

Lani flushed. "Not great. Not fun at all. But I'm okay."

"She's another Bird, you know. Hidebound conservative. Not to say a prig."

For a moment, McRae fiddled with his eggs while he stared absently across the river. "There was a time," he said at last, "when I trusted her. Not so much anymore."

"When was that? What happened?"

McRae shook his head and refocused on Lani. "Long time ago. We were a lot younger then. You would have been in diapers. Never mind. Here and now, the Birds still run things."

"So you're Chip-ish, then?"

"Don't spread it around. I don't like people to know my politics. But I guess you should know, I never agreed with the sentence our mayor handed you. That may have been by the book, but I say she doesn't stand up for her twple."

"Well, even I would say that's not quite fair."

"Fair? I'll give you fair. Who in the twp is in better physical condition than you?"

"Huh? Well, I don't…"

"I do. I talk to the coaches. Nobody, that's who. Some of the guys are almost as good. Who can beat you with a blade, at least when you're not hung over?"

"Yeah, okay. Nobody."

"Damn right. Nobody. Who has your eye for horses or your memory for faces?"

"Stop it, Unc."

"Who knows the rules better than you? Who gets stuff done with a computer better than you?"

"Stop it. Lots of people. What's the point?"

"Wrong. A few people, most of 'em flabby and no good with a handgun. Point is, among three or four hundred top-drawer cops, you stand out. You're not the best in the twp, but that's mostly inexperience. You could be, given time. So what the bloody hell is the mayor doing putting you on the shelf for two years? For a mistake that any of us could have made?"

"But Unc, I killed a kid. Unarmed. Remember?"

"He wasn't even a Union kid!" McRae closed his mouth and huffed through his nose, then shut his eyes and visibly forced himself to relax. Remarkably soon, he was back, the picture of genial rationality.

"Sorry," he said. "I get carried away sometimes. But it does gripe me that we at Triple-E do dangerous, dirty, highly skilled work. And some of us are pretty good at it. But do we get rewarded? We do not. Every month your take-home pay, and mine, is only a trifle more than what they pay that witless greengrocer's apprentice down on Delaware Street. I know, equality, equality. The reward for good work is the work itself, and not material at all. But there's something cockeyed when we risk our lives every day, aren't given the tools we need to do the job, and then our equals in society don't even show some tangible respect when we get things right."

"Well, *I* respect you, Unc," Lani said. "There's nobody I respect more."

There was an embarrassed silence. Lani finally broke it. "So who *is* the best cop in the twp?"

McRae's smile came back, and then he laughed. "I suppose," he chuckled, "that would have to be me."

# KALKIN

It took three more days for Detective Kalkin to get back to Lani. She was duly apologetic and had a good excuse: she had been traveling on business and had not been getting her mail. The meeting was arranged for a south-side coffee shop, not far from the MetPD3 station, in the afternoon. This cost Lani a dance/martial arts/fencing sequence and even a special segment on rock climbing, which she enjoyed. But she didn't mind all that. The Uni was on her way to the meeting anyway, so she picked up a city scooter after her math class and hummed south for ten minutes, across the bridge, and into M-town.

The coffee shop was known to her, as was Detective Kalkin's face, from the mailed video she had received. Lani arrived a little early, but Kalkin was already there, on the patio at a shaded table for two. She came across as experienced and self-assured, mid-thirties, wiry, with long bleached hair. She stood up and stuck out her hand.

"Hi," she said. "Rakka twp MetPD3 Kalkin. Thanks for coming over."

"Lani twp Triple-E Maxwell. Glad to meet you."

Since they were meeting for the first time, on confidential business, they took the precaution of exchanging ID sticks. Each of them licked a stick and poked their sample of the other's saliva into the gene sequencer in their own deck. They small-talked for a minute while the sequencers did their magic and then got down to substance when the machines agreed that they were who they claimed to be.

"So, luv. Can you run me through this thing with the handbag?"

"Yeah. It was three weeks ago. I got dolled up to spend the evening at this club across the river, Trenton-side, in the warehouse district. The Open Horse. On another case."

"Can you tell me what that was? It might matter."

Kalkin grinned. "Sure. I was looking for leads into a stolen pet ring."

"Come on. Really? Sounds decadent."

"No joke. Dogs aren't common in Trenton, but even so, some dudes wear them like accessories. Other things, too. Ferrets are good. But the supply of, you know, Afghan hounds and such is pretty limited, hmmm? So *if* you happen to have purchased one of your own, and *if* you don't take unbrotherly precautions, like locking your doors, then you may come home one day and say, 'whoops, where's Rover?' Well, Rover is on somebody else's leash, strutting the streets of Rochester, or Bangor, or wherever. And somebody else has paid quite a lot to a procurer for the privilege. Twisted, hmmm?"

Lani shook her head. "Well, that sounds wrong in all sorts of ways. But it's basically dude bastards preying on other dudes, isn't it? I mean, except for the procurer, who could be anybody."

"Yup. Which is why I was at the Horse. You find a wealthy crowd there. Clueless, too. Club's only reason to exist is to give narcissistic over-earners a place to admire their own charms in the company of like-minded moneybags. To compete, even. Nothing like admiring yourself in the eyes of others."

"If you say so. Not my usual thing. Or crowd. Do you suppose some of those earnings are under-reported?"

"Seems likely. The Horse does things to discourage people like us from learning much about their customers. Like, first names only—a house rule. If they're invented, so much the better. You don't get in unless you're wearing a fortune in threads. And the bouncers will toss you out again if you do anything stupid, like taking notes or pictures. If you try to pin the owners down, they say they're 'providing a venue for successful citizens to enjoy creative fashion.' The dude patrons gotta know it's risky, and they pay triple prices for drinks and all. But maybe risk is the point, hmmm? If you're rich and bored, I mean."

"Guess so. Sounds like a great fishing hole for some people I work with. But that's not my line. What about the handbag?"

"Ah. Yes. The handbag. Pure tangent, that was. I was up at the bar, picking up drinks for me and the guy I was trying to wheedle."

"You paid for the drinks?"

"Yup. I was playing the rich bitch that night. Funded by the Department."

"Nice work if you can get it."

"Yeah, well. But just down the bar from me is this babe. Early twenties, tall, about 175 in flats, long, light-brown hair. A real looker, in about three months' salary worth of yellow silk. I'd noticed her earlier, playing the crowd, thought there was something funny about how she moved, but couldn't place it. There at the bar, I pinned it down. It was the bag. Nice enough item: shoulder strap, light brown leather, like her hair. But she was carrying it like it was full of pure palladium. Kept one hand on it all the time. I mean, *all* the time. Couldn't keep her eyes off it, either."

"So what did you do?"

"Hell, what could I do? Scooted down two seats on the bar and asked her about it."

"Pigshit. You didn't."

"Sure did. Leaned over and said, 'Nice bag. Can I see it?'"

"Then what?"

"She showed it to me. Damn me if she didn't. It was like she'd been busting herself all night, tryin' to find somebody to brag to. And here I come up and just ask her. So she let it all pour out. Her boyfriend bought it for her, she said, to soften her up before he told her he was going out of town for a couple of months. And now she's got this treasure but nobody to flaunt it to."

"Treasure?"

"That's what I asked. She said it was pure-bred cowhide, from before the Collapse. Three hundred years old. More. Last of a cache of leather goods that somehow stayed pickled in liquid air, all this time. Thawed out and fresh as a daisy."

"Did it look like cowhide?"

"How would I know? Nice enough leather, but far as I could tell, it coulda been anything. Horse, rabbit, you name it."

"Hmph." Lani sat and thought about it. This was the kicker, the thing that caught her attention in the first place. And that had caused Kalkin to put in a report about it. Because everybody knew that cows were extinct. Had been since the mid-2000s. They were victims of an astonishingly successful germ warfare attack by persons unknown. Its aim, people guessed, was to panic the British cattle industry. But the bug worked much better than expected. It was asymptomatic in humans but could be passed from them to cows. So it transmitted like crazy, catching the world as it did at a time of political confusion and lax travel control. In two years, every bovine on the planet was dead, and cowhide (to say nothing of steak and hamburger) became among the rarest of commodities. Two hundred years later, such things were the stuff of legends.

"So, luv. This female thought it was real?"

"I'd bet on it. But not on her. Kind of a twit, really."

"The cryo-preservation thing. Nonsense, you think?"

"Sounds like a scam to me."

"So, at a minimum, it's fraud. Misrepresentation. Whoever bought it is the victim, unless your babe tries to resell it."

"Uh-huh."

"Unless it really is cowhide, somehow."

"In which case, it's a shitstorm. How much of a one, depends."

"Yeah." Lani nodded. "This woman? She have a name?"

"Adri, she said. But I wouldn't bank on it." She looked at Lani narrowly. "You going to follow this up?"

"Yeah, I think so."

That earned an even more penetrating look. "This isn't official yet, is it? Are you freelancing?"

Lani considered a fib, but this cop was too smart. Lani was getting a bit alarmed at how easily the lies were coming to her these days, and her only a week into her revolt.

"Yeah," she said. "I am."

"Hmmm. You be careful, youngster. These people are rich. That makes 'em crazy, by definition, but not all of them are dumb. You got somebody to back you up, one of your own people? You know, if things get dicey?"

Lani thought about it. "Sure. My uncle's EEE, and he's good. He'll rally round if I need him."

"Great. Need anything else?"

"The name of this bar is bugging me. Does it mean anything?"

"Oh, that." Kalkin chuckled. "Underworld stuff—opposites slang. Open Horse, Closed Horse, Clothes Horse. Easy."

# COURTING EVAR

Evar opened up right away when Lani knocked. All the fabric and the sewing kit had disappeared, replaced with many small, round, fired clay pots that Eve was decorating, all different. Eve's work brought her in contact with everybody in the twp, so she had acquaintances beyond counting. And she liked to keep busy, though not much in a big-group social way. By choice, she was nocturnal as a raccoon and almost as solitary as Lani herself. But when she wasn't working or researching her next book, she was, singlehandedly, the twp gift factory. She sat down and went back to work with a little paintbrush.

"Wassup?" Evar asked. "And what are you drinking?"

"Whatever you're having."

"Good. Fish cooler. Rum, grapefruit juice, ice. Look in the fridge."

Evar's place was large enough to have a fridge. It was a small one, and packed with batteries and the glues that she used for connectors and minor dropped-deck repairs, but it also held a heavy pitcher that looked and smelled right. There were two ice cubes left in the freezer. Lani took them, refilled the tray from Eve's desk canister, and poured herself a cooler. She had been out in the sun all day, and she could feel the first sip lower her temperature and loosen her joints.

"So. How the fuck are you?"

"Good. Real busy. Look, Eve, I need a favor."

Eve eyed Lani skeptically.

"Nope. No you don't. Not yet. What kind of friend are you? Only come around when you need something. I'm gonna get you socialized yet. Small talk first. Gossip. Five minutes' worth." She waved at the wall clock. "I'm timing. Then *maybe*, if I don't feel disrespected, you get to ask me a favor. How's your mom? I never see her."

Lani sighed and submitted. It took more like twenty minutes than five, but finally, Eve was satisfied that she knew the score on all of Lani's adoptive family: how she videoed her mom for at least a couple of minutes every day, how her dad had a new hair color, how one of her brothers lost a tooth playing lacrosse, how her uncle stopped by her cubicle once a week just to buck up her spirits, how she never saw them at meals because of different schedules, and so on. Torture, really. But she could take it.

"Okay, kid, you done good. Refill? Now, what's that favor?"

"Um. Your dress. The Halween costume. By the way, it's 'Halloween'. I looked it up."

"Right. I don't care. What about the dress?"

"Can I borrow it? I need to look classy for a night."

"Sure, I guess. But why?"

So Lani told her a little bit of why, but that sounded thin, so she added detail and then explained *that*, and soon Evar knew pretty much everything, right down to the phony cowhide bag. But what good are friends, Lani wondered, if you can't trust them?

"So that's it," she finished. "Only you've gotta keep this to yourself, okay? I'm breaking rules here, and the only excuse is if I make it come out okay. If her honor the mayor gets onto me before I'm done, that's it. I'm finished. Clear?"

"What? Oh yeah, sure. Secret. No problem. But I'm thinking. It'll take a few days to make the alterations. And lose the tail, of course. Stand up against the wall over there. I'll get my tape measure."

# OPEN HORSE

Getting into the Open Horse was not nearly as hard as Lani had feared. She hated to go into situations unprepared, but she had found the Horse impossible to scout. The entrance was a nondescript door at one corner of a block of warehouses; behind the door lay a long windowless hallway with the major-domo or head bouncer or whatever he was at the end. That was all.

At the risk of being pegged as a cop, or worse, as a rube, Lani spent a while one weeknight lurking behind packing cases in a nearby alley, spying on people going in. *Almost* all of them wrapped up in railroad coats or equally drab outerwear, but sometimes a flash of color showed around the women's hemlines or collars. The men displayed a noteworthy excess of bowties, often with walking sticks or ceremonial swords. They had a bimodal age distribution; the men were of similar age to the club-goers in Lani's experience, but the women were older.

On Saturday, she was back, not too early, wearing The Dress under a battered waterproof cape. She had dispensed with the plumed headgear, which (like the tail) had seemed too much even for this scene. The dress alone would attract plenty of attention, she thought.

It did. Whipping off her cape and doing a pirouette was all it took to get her past the bouncer. "Clothes Horse," she said to herself. "Easy."

Once in, with the cape checked, she made a slow tour to get the feel of the place. It was spacious and high-ceilinged, with a central dance floor surrounded by lots of little tables. The immediate impression of obscene wealth resembled what she had felt in Chaupi's office, but the more she looked, the more she felt that Chaupi had done a better job. His collection was authentic and had a point of some sort. Here, the directing principle seemed to be merely a ragtag and inaccurate imitation of 1930s high-society movie sets. *Top Hat*, perhaps, or *The Lady Eve*. The owners probably wanted customers to feel that they might bump into Fred and Ginger at any moment, or at least William and Myrna, but after five minutes, Lani was pretty sure that none of that bunch would ever have set foot in the place.

The clothes looked pricey but kind of monotonous. Menswear came in two flavors: tuxedos (sometimes in colors) and pseudo-military from many centuries, with medals, sashes, high collars, epaulets, and the whole deal. Women showed more variety but tended toward what she tentatively identified as ballroom gowns, with lots of poof below the waist and nothing interesting above. She saw one outfit with a train longer than the 09:30 express to Saratoga; how it got in under a railroad coat was more than she could fathom.

Not for the first time, Lani struggled with the conflict between her nostalgic, movie-based dream world and the stern demands (Equality! Evidence!) that daily life enforced—and that every part of the Open Horse defied. But for all its boundary-breaking, the Horse's mood wasn't joyous or exhilarating. It had something fevered and hollow at its core. For years she had spent endless time watching old movies with friends, sometimes three a night, filling her head with great moments and reveling in the whole experience. Since her awful Ohio adventure, she'd watched all of two films total, and she couldn't recall either one. Something had melted out of her life, and she missed it. Whatever it was, she wasn't going to find it here. In this overdressed zoo, the best she could hope for was a lead. Some days, you have to take what you can get.

A small minority of the dresses seemed built for real dancing, while her own certainly was. And it was drawing unconcealed stares, even without the footwork. Enough mooning, she thought. Back to work.

Everything was on track until she heard a familiar voice and turned to look. There, not two meters away, was Bokun Yardley. He, too, belonged to twp EEE, and she knew him pretty well. He sometimes joined her noontime hand-to-hand combat group; she had sparred with him many times. Though she winced at the thought, she had slept with him twice, not too many months ago. She was pretty sure that he wanted more, while she definitely didn't. She couldn't spend the night fending him off. How, she fretted, could she get the freedom of action that she needed with him around?

Driven mostly by the urge to sort this mess out, *now*, Lani stepped straight into his line of sight and waved coyly. "Hullo, glamorous," she murmured.

He did a double take, blushed, and stuttered, "La-La-Lani!" before remembering that in this place, names were precious and not to be used lightly. He was dressed in something that might have looked good in Napoleon's court, but the expression on his face didn't belong on a dance floor in any century.

"What the hell…What are you *doing* here?" he demanded, *sotto voce*.

In a choice guided by strategy, not tact, she refrained from pointing out that she could ask him the same question. Instead, she raised her hands in a dancing posture, pouted, and shuffled her feet a bit. "The foxtrot?"

"Knock it off!" he shouted in his stage whisper. "I'm working here! Under*cover!* You'll scare off the big game. Stay away from me. Get lost! Now!"

"Okay, okay," she replied, with her most winning smile. "Give my love to the duchess." And she turned and flounced away. Her flounce even had a little more snap than usual—she had just spotted her evening's elegant prey, complete with the handbag.

With her target in view, now what Lani needed was a man. In the circumstances, this was not a problem. There were a fair number of couples dancing. The prevailing view in the Union was that sexual preferences were probabilistic, time-varying, and situational. The couples were mostly women with men, but pretty often otherwise. As usual, there were many people standing on the sideline. She picked a nearby tuxedo, a kid even younger than herself, who had been eyeing her for a minute or two already. Where, she wondered, did such pups get the money to dress like that? But even a glance around showed the answer to that question: they got it from older women. Suppressing a roll of her eyes, Lani marched up to him, took his hands, and said, "Let's dance." So far, so good. How could he possibly refuse?

The music was unfortunate—1980s whiney country western crossed with drugged-out rock 'n' roll, but that didn't matter. In fact, she decided, it was good. Her objective at this point was to get everybody looking at her without herself casting even a glance at the handbagger. Since partners were superfluous when dancing to this kind of schlock, she could stretch herself a bit and leave the tuxedo to do what he wanted. To her, this meant lots of energy: arms-up hip and upper body motion, with pirouettes and bent-knee stomping, and once she had cleared a space for herself, near what felt like the end of the song, an unmotivated split. She squeezed back up without even putting a hand on the floor and danced once around her nominal partner before the music stopped. Sure enough, the whole room was goggling at her. Good deal.

She presented her hand to be kissed by partner number one and moved on to a guy in pale pink pants and a khaki Eisenhower jacket. Next tune up: a lugubrious waltz. She spent most of it glued to the guy's coat, leading unobtrusively and staring blankly over his left shoulder, the picture of boredom. It was only toward the end of the dance that she steered by the bar and, with a startled flash of brows, locked eyes for a beat with her quarry. She then urged her partner into double time, staring longingly at the woman at the bar whenever she got a chance and leaving her World War II general dizzy and confused.

For her finale, she took four slow steps straight away from her target, then looked slyly but briefly back over her shoulder (with her eyes and the down-to-there cutaway back of The Dress giving the lady a double-barreled load of sex appeal). Then she stopped, visibly changed her mind, turned fast on her heel, and strode back to perch on the adjacent barstool and confront her intended. "Can I..." she said, and froze. "Can I...I...oh, *merde*," she finished in a small, miserable voice.

The handbagger was baffled. "What? What is it?"

"I don't know what happened," Lani said, staring down at her feet. "I was dancing with that…that dub over there, and then I saw you sitting here, and you smiled, and it was like all the air went out of me. I just had to impress you. To get to know you. But all that brassy…vamp…it's no way to behave. I'm sorry. Forgive me? Please?"

"But, yeah, sure, hon," the woman said in confusion. She didn't know whether to be put off or intimidated or flattered or attracted.

Lani gave her no time to figure it out. "Look," she said, "I'm a dancer. It's what I do. Sitting here, like this, I'm all in a bunch. Do you dance? Will you dance with me? We can chat while we dance, and maybe I'll make some kind of sense."

"Um…I do, a little. Nothing like you, though."

"Don't worry. It'll be fine."

"Okay, just a minute." She tossed off the last of her drink and slung her bag over her head and one shoulder. Then she attached it around her waist with a thin silvery chain and a tiny padlock.

"Wow," said Lani. "What's in there?"

"I'll tell you later—if you're nice. My name's Muam, by the way."

"So wonderful to meet you, Muam," Lani said, obviously losing herself in the other's eyes. "You can call me Dobs. Let's do it."

# BAKING MUFFINS

For the second time in a week, Lani woke up well after sunrise and missed PT. Her feeling of guilt about this astonished her. It exceeded by a wide margin her guilt over exploiting Muam by seducing her and then prying her for information, and that was by itself no small thing. She rolled over on her side and, for a minute or so, just watched Muam sleep. It must have been near thirty degrees in the apartment. The sheets were tangled around their feet, and the bed had the slightly damp, sticky feel that went with a night of heavy exertion. She decided she didn't really need the PT.

She slid out of bed and staggered the length of the apartment to the toilet in the far corner. On the way, she marveled at the icons of wealth and status that she had, so far, only seen in centuries-old videos. The Open Horse had tried to achieve this effect in a bumbling way, but here was the real thing. A private toilet (with shower!) An open closet showing at least two dozen different outfits, none of them Union standard wear, and ten (she counted) pairs of shoes. She reached in and stroked a pair of sky-blue pants, simply to feel them. What were they made of, and how would it feel to wear them? The thought was appealing and disgusting at the same time. And that was only Muam's part of the closet; the bulk of it was full of men's clothes. The place had its own kitchen. She stood in its center while it crowded around her with wonders, things that she didn't even know were made in the current century: a special sink to wash dishes in, a stovetop with three separate electric burners, a refrigerator as tall as she was, an honest-to-God oven, big enough to bake two loaves of bread at once. She had gathered that Muam was a baker by profession, but it was still unimaginable that she would bring such a power-hungry device into her own home. The style and aura of entitled convenience dazzled while the inefficiency revolted her, and the probable criminality involved in amassing all this stuff laid a heavy pall over everything. Muam had said she had a boyfriend, out of town at present. Lani reckoned this absent dude must be badly lacking in social conscience. Most likely, he and Muam were riding for a fall.

More, if Lani were half the citizen/cop she thought she was, she would have just reported the both of them and been done. Every day, they had to be committing serious offenses against Equality, and likely against the Environment too. And to convince themselves that their life choices were morally acceptable, they must draw on stores of self-delusion on a scale that mocked any supposed belief in Evidence.

But she needed answers, and for now, she needed to cover her tracks. Besides, oddly enough, she genuinely liked Muam. She might be reckless and shallow, but nothing about her was malignant, and she was generous and sensitive in and out of bed. An outstanding lay, in fact. And gorgeous.

Lani shook her head violently and took three deep, measured breaths to help center herself. This line of thought was getting her worse than nowhere. The boyfriend (Muam had told her his name was Jayro) and Muam would likely run afoul of twp EEE soon enough, without Lani doing the first thing to or for them. She had to stay on target. Where in all hell did that handbag come from?

Quite some time later, Muam made flopping noises from the bed, forced herself erect, and slid into a light cotton nightie. On her way through the kitchen, she put an arm around Lani's waist, bumped her with a hip, and kissed her on the cheek. "Damn shame Jayro's coming back soon," she said and continued on to the toilet. Lani turned away and sighed. Nothing like mornings to put things in perspective.

Soon Muam returned and started shuffling things in the kitchen. "Muffins okay?" she asked.

"Sure. Anything I can do?"

"Here. Slice me half a cup of strawberries."

Lani chopped in silence for a minute, then decided the time had come.

"Muam?" she said, as offhandedly as she could manage, "I've for sure gotta have something like that bag of yours. Where do I get one?"

Muam stopped whisking batter and looked over her shoulder at Lani. "Don't you dare get a copy of that bag. That's my trademark."

"Course not. I can't afford anything that nice anyway. But, you know, a little change purse. Or a pair of sandals. It would just be so cool to carry around part of a real cow, from all those ages ago."

"Yeah, it's wild. Like you're traveling back in time. Back when things were better. Let me get these in the oven. Then I'll tell you all about it." She went back to her strawberry muffins. Then, as a nervous afterthought, "Just don't let on that you heard it from me. If he finds out I told you anything, Jayro will snatch me bald-headed."

True to her word, Muam soon closed the oven door, opened her deck, and showed Lani where to go and what to do. It was pretty interesting.

# DEAD DROP

Lani made it back to twp EEE a little after noon. She had missed not only PT but lots of other scheduled events, including her lunchtime sparring meet-up. That wasn't good—people would be wondering about her—but it would all be worse if she didn't show up for her afternoon schedule on time.

She was wearing Union work togs taken from Muam's place and carrying The Dress in a paper bag. The attention it was designed to attract was the last thing she wanted, the morning after. She dropped the bag in her room, scooped up her regular deck, and headed over to the gym.

Sure enough, in her first hour moving around the HQ complex, four different people stopped her to make sure she was okay. One of them was the Chief. She always grinned when she saw his face; his relaxed good nature was contagious. But this was off his normal rotation. He had taken her to lunch only a few days before. She had to wonder what he had heard to make him come looking for her again so soon. In fact, what he had heard, and from whom. To all and sundry she excused her morning absence as a short-lived bout of stomach problems, flu maybe, or food poisoning. She smiled again at the implied insult to Muam's strawberry muffins, which had been fabulous.

Finally, after supper, math homework done, she decided she had time for more serious business. She bought a gift bottle of vodka at the refectory bar, popped it into the sack with the dress, and made her way to Evar's door.

Eve was miffed by the crushed and sweat-soaked state of The Dress, but mollified by the alcoholic peace offering.

"What do you want from me?" Lani said, in her own defense. "This thing was made to be danced in, and I danced in it."

"Yeah, but with hyenas? Unwashed ones?"

"Oh, pooh. Everybody knows hyenas are extinct. The dress did its job, though."

Evar perked up at that. "You catch a fish?"

"A little one, maybe."

"Tell Auntie Eve. Sit. Let's have the whole story."

So Lani related how she had found the owner of the handbag and how that particular accessory had been bought for cash (no specific amount here, but definitely a lot of money) from a little unnamed hole in the wall near the river, close to the docks. The shop, she had been told, was tiny and unmarked and only opened for a few hours every month or so, just long enough to sell off the latest shipment of super-special leather goods.

"You've checked this place out? In person?" Evar asked.

"No time today. I'll try to get down there tomorrow."

"The opening hours are irregular, you say? Not the third Thursday of the month, or some shit? So how do the customers know when to shop?"

Lani shook her head admiringly. "Ah, Eve. Count on you to get right to the core. I'll show you. Let's use your machine. You'll like this."

It took some time to sit down in front of Evar's giant screen; Eve insisted on mixing martinis in celebration of Lani's catch (whatever it was). These were not Lani's favorite, but she had been dry all day and was not going to object.

"Okay," said Lani, "Open up the Drop and go to the Quebec City Questioner. Look at the masthead."

The Daily Drop was a compendium of conceivably interesting updates for Union citizens. It included recordings of every theater and cinema performance in the Union in the last twenty-four hours, playlists of music in many different categories, made up by people whose job it was to do such things, photo essays by anybody who wanted to post them, updated catalogs pointing to many kinds of data in the central archives, and numerous other things, notably the full content of every newspaper published in the country. The thing typically ran to a petabyte or so each day. The Union didn't lack for communication resources, but it was very scrupulous about how it employed them.

Shortly Evar's screen showed the usual dull newspaper page of names and jobs, with photos of the managing editor and of the front of the Questioner's building, with a Union flag flapping merrily in its yard.

"Zoom on the ball on top of the flagpole. Now zoom in on the sun glint at the top of the ball. See that little dark speck off center at 2 o'clock? Zoom in on that."

Evar did. What opened up looked like a piece of half-size notepaper with a few lines of print:

> Mati's Antique Doll Clothes
> Have the chic-est Pre-C dolls in yr Twp!
> Low prices! 16.10 to 35.99
> Hand-tailored for best brands
> Brbie, ShrlyTmpl,AmerGrl,GermPorcHd,CbgPtch,ManyMore
> Finest wool/cotton mat'ls, NO plastic
> NOW OUT OF STOCK

"Well, well," Evar said with a tight smile. "A broadcast dead drop. And that,"—pointing at a notification now blinking in a corner of her screen— "is telling me that this image is encoded as a high-depth pyramid, which is what allows the kind of major zooming we just did."

"When I do this, my deck doesn't show me any notification."

"You, my dear, are not a big-shot systems honcho. I run a bunch of snooping code all the time. Stuff most people don't bother with. Hacking isn't quite dead yet; people try crafty stuff every now and then, and at EEE, we have secrets worth stealing."

"Okay. What's a deep pyramid?"

"High-depth pyramid. Oxymoronic, huh? An old standard for encoding images. It lets you do precisely this sort of thing—embed very high-rez sub-images inside a grainier one without wasted bytes. People used it a lot back about the time the Union was formed. Now there are handier ways to do the same thing. I guess it was common enough it got built into the standard OS way back when. Since then, it's fallen out of use but still survives in the later releases."

Evar stared at the document for half a minute. "Those prices—they've gotta be bogus. Looks like a date, don't you think?"

"Oh, yeah," Lani agreed. "I was gonna say. There's nothing doing at the shop right now. When there is, my source says the 'OUT OF STOCK' line goes away, and the open dates and times appear as the new prices, coded in some obvious way."

"Cute. Medium-clever bastards. Who, I guess, have something to hide. Wait'll I tell the boss. She'll be so confused. It'll stick in her craw, for sure. She'll never manage to swallow it or spit it out."

"Nope," said Lani. "No boss-telling. This stuff is embargoed, remember? If your boss learns about it, I'm in deep doo."

"Hmm. Sorry. Forgot for a minute." Evar sat for a while, drumming her fingers on her desk. After a while, she stopped thumping and turned to Lani.

"Two questions. First, why put so much algorithmic horsepower into a dead drop? There must be easier ways. Even I know three or four, right off the bat. And second, what's your next move?"

# OLD FARTS

Every ten days or so, like everybody, Lani drew duty looking after the twp's old or disabled population. An important feature of twp life was that everybody knew, if you became unable to contribute to the normal business of the twp, you would be taken care of. This was a point of honor. Twps that handled this obligation badly would soon become pariahs; their business suffered, they could no longer count on favors from their neighbors, and their population dropped as their twple quit and moved elsewhere. On the other hand, doing this chore well called for a lot of labor, both skilled and not. Lani was in the not-skilled category, but she didn't hate the duty. The work was seldom difficult, and compared to her probationary job, it conveyed a refreshing feeling that she was doing something useful.

To encourage inter-generational rapport and suchlike, she was usually paired up with the same two patients, for two hours each, on two consecutive shifts. She particularly liked her first charge, one-time Deputy Mayor Hapu Moran. He was the same old geezer whose credentials she had used to do her DB search the week before. Hap was old as the sea, had been everywhere and done everything, had used and abused every cliché. Nowadays, he was wheelchair-bound and suffered from a brain malady that affected his speech, both in recalling words and in producing intelligible sounds. After helping Hap for more than a year, Lani had become fairly good at interpreting his slurred talk, but some days were better than others. As soon as Lani walked through his door, she realized that he was in the best form she had ever seen.

"Lena, durr!" he mouthed, around a largely reconstructed toothy grin. "Gra' t'see yer."

"It's Lani, sir," she replied with a smile of her own.

"L'ni, shurr! Ri' yarr. Yrna's L'ni; nukne yusit! Swye lyk'u—yn'err take no shi' f'n n'buddy." ("*Lani, sure! Right you are. Your name's Lani; make me use it! That's why I like you—you never take no shit from nobody.*")

This was the longest speech Hap had ever uttered in her presence. She was impressed and excited. Maybe she could get a real story out of him. She took him by his shoulders and kissed his cheek.

"Only from you, Hap. And then not always. What'll we do today? Inside or out?"

(*"Outside!"*)

"Super. It's still not too hot out there. Off we go, then."

She folded up the deck that Hap had been reading and stuck it in the chair's side pocket. Then she grabbed his wide-brimmed hat from the hook, swung around to the back of the chair, nudged off the brakes, and rolled Hap smartly out into the hall. Hap liked speed and hated to be kept waiting.

"Roof or park?" she asked.

(*"Park."*)

Hap's room was on the second floor of the twp's hospital/rehab building. Because of his disability, it would have made sense to put him at ground level, but there was much competition from other EEE vets who were in wheelchairs or worse. Hap had vehemently refused to take a room from any of those, seniority be damned, so he and Lani habitually used the zig-zag ramp running along the building's front to get down to the entrance level. There was also a freight elevator, but Union pride being what it was, nobody who was not moving heavy furniture would dream of using it.

"What were you reading?" Lani asked as she steered the chair down-ramp at slightly subsonic speed.

(*"Politics. Depressing. Damn Chips. Ignorant, upstart kids."*)

This was enough chatter to get them down to ground level and out the front door. She popped the hat onto Hap's head and, at an easy jog, propelled the chair across the street and in among the palms and drought-stressed orange trees of the neighboring park, where they might find some shade.

Politics at the Union level didn't much interest Lani. Nobody talked about it except when the General Council was meeting, which it happened to be—just starting the winter session, she recalled. But Council proceedings were, at best, episodically interesting, and even when something was happening, decisions got made by way of inscrutable maneuvering among existing power blocs. She knew that the Chips were one of these, the newest and smallest of the three important claques, and the one most likely to advocate for re-introducing practices or technology that had gone into eclipse during the Bad Days. She was also aware that the Chips held power out of proportion to their votes because the two older claques (the Greens, who were more conservative than the Chips, and the Birds, who were even more so) were *almost* evenly matched. That gave the Chips power as self-interested tiebreakers. None of this sounded like promising material for a conversation with Hap. Well, perhaps if she approached it sideways...

"So, Hap, what would you say to the Chips, if they had to listen?"

She stopped the chair in a quiet spot next to a medium-sized fish pond and waited for Hap to get his thoughts together. She felt an attack of sadness, watching him struggle against his failing body. She would sometimes slop through this pond to cool off on her way back from her pre-dawn runs. She wished Hap had been young enough to run there with her, just one of those mornings.

(*"Remember, damn you!"*) he said at last. (*"You don't remember. How bad it was. Today you have five you love. Next month, one. Or none."*)

"But Hap, that was a long time ago. It's better now."

(*"Not so long. Eapy Fox knew those times. My grandma, nine years old. Saw Eapy Fox in person. Herself. Heard her talk. Like yesterday."*)

Lani stood and listened.

(*"How it was. Fat ones got skinny. Skinny ones died. It happened. Could happen again."*)

Suddenly Lani could hear the Chief telling her the same thing on that night in Ohio. The memory grabbed her and shook her, like a dog with a rat.

(*"Wanted too much. More than Earth can give. Greedy. Selfish."*)

She had been standing behind the chair, with both hands on its back. Abruptly she let go with one and pivoted about the other as her knees buckled, leaving her squatting against the chair's left wheel, face buried in her free hand, heaving with silent, racking sobs. Hap watched in silence for a moment, then reached over and stroked her hair.

Presently Lani was able to collect herself, get up, wash her face in the pond. Watch while a fat koi drifted by, fins barely moving. At last, she stood and rejoined Hap.

"I'm sorry, Hap," she said. "You didn't need this."

(*"It happens."*)

"Not to you."

That earned her another smile and a shrug.

(*"Every few days."*)

They sat there until it was time to go back, watching the grass and the trees and the sun on the water. On their return, Hap asked her to leave him in the downstairs lounge, where he could sit and listen to the other old farts talk. Then he looked up at her, embarrassed.

(*"One thing."*)

"Yes?"

(*"My name. Don't just use it. Right? Ask first."*)

Lani stood there, thunderstruck. Crap. He knew. He had known all along. And not ratted to anybody. What a man.

She leaned over and hugged him, and he whispered in her ear.

(*"I'm old. Not so dumb."*)

"Not at all," she said. "You're the best."

# THE BLIND

The warehouse district consisted of four blocks on two adjacent streets, running parallel to the gently curving river and not far from the docks. The streets were wide and paved to accommodate heavy wagon traffic; through the middle of each block ran a broad alley for accessing loading docks that didn't face the street. The buildings themselves were old, of heavy concrete construction to survive hurricanes, with wide blow-out panels below their roof lines to equalize pressures in case of a tornado. By the looks of them, they had weathered at least one and possibly both kinds of disaster since their last paint job.

The one Lani finally identified as her objective had four entrances spaced along the street front, with two big sliding doors in its middle, and two hole-in-the-wall offices at its ends. The right-hand office had the address that Muam had given her, scrawled on sun-bleached paper taped to the front door. There was no other identifying sign, the door was locked, and there was no window to peek into. Frustrated in front, she walked around to the back, but learned only that the little office had its own rear exit, also securely locked.

She wandered down the alley to get a look at her building from a little distance, dodging wagons and folks plying loaded hand trucks, and finally got lucky. Three adjacent buildings, including her object of interest, looked like they had been built at the same time, to the same plan. Each of them had a little crane mounted on top, positioned to lift stuff from the alleyway. That suggested a hatch in the roof to put the lifted goods into. She could see a ladder giving access to the roof of a warehouse across the alley; from that point, she could probably get a view of the one she cared about. But it was working hours, with too many people bustling up and down the alley; there didn't seem to be a way to get up there without calling attention to herself. She decided to take tomorrow's crack-of-dawn run through this alley and see what she could learn before daybreak when things were quieter.

Her outstanding bit of luck came quickly, two buildings farther along the line. The place seemed unusually run down, with a back door of lightweight, interior-grade foam board. It wasn't even locked, just secured with a hasp and a twist of wire. Beside the door was an official-looking yellow poster. It announced the place was condemned due to storm damage and would be demolished to make room for new construction before a date now six months past. Lani snorted. Typical Union bureaucracy. But in this case, handy. Could be very handy.

Without even looking around (always better if you appeared to be on normal business), Lani untwisted and pocketed the wire, and went in. While she waited for her eyes to dark-adapt, she fished gloves and a mask from her pockets, and put them on. There was a light switch by the door, but it didn't work; presumably, power was off to the whole building. Light was getting in, however. She could see that she was in a low empty space, overhung by some kind of loft, accessed by a stairway to her right. The light was sunlight coming from upstairs, diffusing down the stairwell and also shining out into the larger warehouse space at the front of the structure. She stood still and listened for a moment but heard nothing except outside noises.

"Anybody home?" she shouted, but got no reply.

"Okay, then," she said to herself and trotted up the stairs. The loft was bare, though the floor was littered with glass, broken from picture window frames that looked down on the warehouse's main floor. The light came from three of the blow-out panels that had warped partially out of their mountings but failed to blow out completely. The floor near them was soggy and stank of mildew but showed no signs of collapsing.

The leftmost damaged blow-out panel immediately drew her attention. Its lower left corner was folded out toward the alley, with a gap a full thirty centimeters wide at its bottom. Placing her head against that corner, she could see up the alley to her left. Because of the street's curve, she had an unobstructed view of her target office's back door and another ten meters into the alley. She would have preferred the front door, but this might be good enough. She could set up a stakeout here. She would.

For a moment, a contrary thought wormed into her mind. Making camp here would involve a ton of work, long, long hours, and a real chance of getting caught. All this for a lousy handbag? Was she going overboard?

But that worry didn't last. She was already getting a feel for the opposition. Eve was right. Planting their ad by jiggering the Daily Drop was itself serious work, and subverting such a core Union comms channel was an inescapably criminal deal. Whatever these snakes were doing, there was more to it than fraudulent leather. They merited some watching. And now she had just the place. Also, she thought, as conspirators, this gang seemed self-satisfied and not very subtle. When they wanted to do something secret, they might even be silly enough to try it through the back door in the dead of night.

# STAKEOUT BLUES

December, and getting dark early in Trenton. One hundred forty-seven days left in her probation. The weather's only concessions to the season were for the wind to blow and for the night air blast that tangled Lani's hair to be balmy, not baking. It hadn't snowed in Trenton for more than two hundred fifty years, and she was missing the days in Colorado when she was very young, when fat flakes spattered in her face, and her parents made her hot goat's milk when she got home.

Walking against the wind was a trudge, and she was tired of it. In fact, she was just tired. She studied the message on the dead drop every morning, and every morning it kept on saying "OUT OF STOCK." Work was a bore. Evar had been gone for days on one of her "visiting the beau" vacations. There was no relief to be had from that quarter. A few people at EEE, including the Chief, were working frantically on the Missing Officers Investigation, which looked like it might be a crime after all. But there was no chance of her getting close to a case like that. In fact, the only exciting hours were those she could tear away from the normal day's schedule to stock her observation blind with necessities: a camp stool, a thermos jug that she would fill with coffee each night at the refectory, a nice camera with a long lens and tripod she had borrowed from her long-suffering, blue-haired, bird-watching adoptive dad.

The only piece of good news was that she could get into the leather shop if she really wanted to. Her early-morning scouting had been productive in the sense that she learned that her target warehouse also had a ladder to its roof, on the far side from her blind. About halfway up, this was blocked by a locked mesh door, but at this point, the shop warehouse and its neighbor were close enough together that she could chimney around the blockage. This wasn't easy (the separation was a trifle too wide for comfort, and both building walls were on the slippery side), but she knew she could do it, because she had. On top, she indeed found a hatch, secured on the outside with an indifferent-quality padlock. One more little obstacle averted, she thought, with a sigh.

She was returning from stashing a city scooter on the blind's ground floor, so she could give chase quickly and silently if anything worth chasing ever presented itself. This appropriation of public property was, alone, a selfish and marginally criminal act. It would have gnawed at her conscience in any case, but was especially galling because she still had no practical way to watch both the front and back doors of the alleged cowhide shop. She was losing sleep and moral certitude, watching a blank door that might never open.

It didn't help that she was spending more and more time at the twp bar after dinners. Just hanging around, drinking with the other EEE cops was the last way she should be using her time. But the alternative seemed to be smuggling a bottle into her headquarters cubicle during work hours—a quick way to get suspended or dismissed from the twp. More and more, the sustained sneaking dishonesty of what she was doing was wearing on her, compounded by its likely ineffectiveness and her own apparent inability to discipline herself. Hence, to carry out this stupid, lonely half-assed investigation in a way that might lead somewhere.

"Sometimes, Lani, I don't understand you at all," she sighed as she turned the last corner to the refectory.

And there, sitting on the steps, was Patri Gibbs. Apparently waiting for her.

She pulled up a few meters away. "Shit!" she shouted over the wind.

"And good evening to you, too."

"What the hell brings you here?"

He shrugged, and there was that smile again. "I kept waiting for you to come back to the Canal, but you never did. So I came to find you."

"Shit!" she said again. "Go away. I'm beat. I've got no time for this. You want to go inside and bang me on a dining table? Or what?"

"Yeah," he said. "Oh, hell yeah. But not tonight. Tomorrow. Come with me tomorrow night. Dinner and a play. We can use one of your tables afterward."

"A date? You're asking me on a date?"

"Yup, I think that's what this is called."

"Why should I do that?"

"Well, we might get to know each other a little. Vaun tells me it improves the sex. With research to prove it, of course. A lot of people find the building anticipation...agreeable."

She shook her head in disbelief. "Really now? You should know something about me. I got no talent for delayed gratification. Stink at it, in fact."

"I see," he nodded. "That's tough. I guess we'll just have to cope."

# STRANGERS MEAT

Patri's plate featured farm-fed gopher snake and didn't bear too much thinking about, even though the little deep-fried nuggets looked appetizing enough. Patri swore that they tasted fine. Not unlike chicken, he insisted. Lani's grasshopper stew had a similar marketing problem; hers, too, tasted okay, but the texture took some getting used to.

The food supply had always been an issue in the Union. What with droughts, floods, hail, wildfires, windstorms, and pollination failures, most forms of agriculture were chancy and had been for more than two hundred years. Even feeding a population shrunk far below that found in the Pre-Collapse, the Union diet of necessity was largely vegetarian; it seldom made sense to raise crops to feed to livestock instead of humans. But as usual in the Union, there were exceptions. Twp refectories served fish pretty often, but chicken, goat, and horse only rarely, on holidays and other special occasions. In times of moderate plenty, one could find restaurants selling meat daily at exorbitant prices. But for most people who wanted a protein jolt or a change from refectory fare, or just a change of scene, the solution was one of the many mom-and-pop cafes such as the *Strangers Meat,* where Patri and Lani had indeed met for the evening meal. Like most such places, its dishes were nutritious but unusual, sometimes bizarre, and as a business concern, its life expectancy resembled that of a butterfly. But it was small, quiet, and private, and it served wine. And there they were.

"Okay, Patri, tell me about the Navy," Lani demanded as they got down to serious eating.

"You can call me Tree if you want. Everybody else does."

"Tree? Seriously?"

"Yup. Started with my parents. I've never answered to anything else, really."

"Okay, then. Tree, tell me about the Navy."

"Not much to tell. I was in it for five years."

"Were you an officer?"

"Not at all. Started as a plain old gob. Wound up as a sort of senior non-com."

Lani sipped her wine and squinted at him. "How 'bout if you're a little more forthcoming, huh? It'll smooth the conversation. You know what gets a woman's attention. Play to it, why don't you? Why'd you join up? Did you go to sea? If so, where did you go? Ever been ashore outside the Union? Did you have a partner in every port? Did you ever get shot at? I asked you that last one before, but you brushed me off. Maybe you remember."

"Okay, okay. I joined the Navy because I was sick of growing grapes. I wanted to see what's left of the world. I spent about half my time on the water, the rest in port, mostly in Nova Scotia, helping refit my ship before her next cruise. When we were at sea and under sail, which was most of the time, I usually worked with the team that took care of the rigging. Lots of fiddling on deck, running the winches that kept the sails trimmed. Patching sails, patching lines, patching sensors and cables, doing other repairs, sometimes aloft, on the mastheads."

"Did you like it?"

"That part was kind of fun, at least in good weather. Which we hardly ever saw, seemed like. Spent all of one hurricane season, eight months long, wallowing around the mid-Atlantic, where they breed and grow. We'd send back weather data until the old tub was too beat up to continue, then limp back to port, refit, and do it again."

"Yow. Somebody thought you were expendable."

"Exactly so. There've been some ships like that one get expended, too. It happens now and then."

"Goddamn." Lani chewed in silence for a while. She had heard lots of EEE war stories, but this business of drowning whole crews so folks on land could get better weather reports rattled her. It was so painfully large-scale, cruelly impersonal.

"Well, how about you?" Patri asked. "Done anything interesting since that Hendrikson affair?"

"Oh, no you don't. We're not going there. And you still haven't told me about getting shot at, but not to speak of. Can I try a piece of your snake?"

"Hmph. That. And sure, help yourself." He held his plate still while she forked a mini snake chop and continued to hold it while he collected his thoughts.

"It was off the coast of Central America, I think about where Belize used to be. I was on a different ship by then, an escort. We were riding shotgun for a freighter carrying manufactured goods and a little tanker loading cargo to take back to the Union."

"What kind of cargo?"

"Don't know in any detail. Some kind of petroleum product. The Union still needs oil derivatives in small doses, you know, and we don't produce much of our own. They still have working oil wells near where we were, and this little pocket refinery on an inlet, right near the water."

"You mean people *live* there? But that's way south. It's crazy hot, no? For that matter, how did *you* live there?"

"Well, you know. It's not unlivably hot and humid all the time, just part of it. Also, of course, it's better near the ocean. You work outdoors when it's cool enough, and when it isn't, you hide inside with air conditioning. That's what the freighter was carrying: HVAC parts, batteries, solar cells, whatever. A barter deal, really."

"And so?"

"And so there we were, close inshore, running on screws under battery power, all sails furled, and all of us at battle stations in water-cooled suits."

"Water-cooled suits?"

"Yeah. What a pain in the ass. Always too hot or too cold, or both at once. And the umbilical. Hell, talk about being on a short leash."

"Anyway…"

"Right. Anyway. We get the freighter unloaded and the tanker hooked up, when some poor idiots on the other side of the cove open up on us. Small arms only. One heavy machine gun, I think a twin fifty.

"I'm sure the skipper was expecting this kind of thing because about five seconds after the shooting starts, our marine squad gives them the same back again, and both our 20s let loose, and then our deck gun finishes the whole deal with five rounds of anti-personnel airburst at point-blank range. Then the skipper points the big gun at the refinery and tells whoever they're dealing with onshore that if there's any more nonsense, he'll use incendiaries and slag the whole place down."

"Goddamn. What then?"

"If you believe the rumors, the boss guy onshore didn't even apologize. He said, 'You know I had to try,' or some shit, then carried on with the deal as if nothing had happened. I guess his people were expendable, too."

"Casualties on your side?"

"Nothing serious. A few rounds came aboard; didn't hurt anything much. One officer on the bridge got cut by flying glass. She didn't get much sympathy; nobody liked her anyway."

"And where were you during all this?"

"Oh, me? I was at my station, supposedly loading drums of ammo into the forward 20mm. As it worked out, we'd emptied one, and I was lifting the second one in when we got the cease-fire."

Lani had stopped bullying and was watching him with a different expression. He picked up his wine glass, put it down, picked it up again, and took a long drink.

"It seems," she said, "that you guys knew what you were doing."

"Yeah, maybe so. Felt like murder to me. Anyway, that's the day I decided not to re-enlist."

*

"And now," she said, a good deal later, "you're a graduate student. In history."

It was, in fact, about three in the morning. A time when the world slept, but when the two of them, like magic, simultaneously sat up wakeful and curious. As a pleasant background change, on this night, her awful dreams were in abeyance.

"Yup," he said. "It seemed like a good idea."

"But now you don't think so?"

"No, it's not that. I think it's only mid-thesis doldrums. Vaun tells me it's normal, and so does my advisor. But I've been at it for months, doing the same things, and I still can't see the end. Life feels so static."

"Yeah, wait a minute. Who's this Vaun person?"

"A friend. Another history student. She's a damn genius. Likes the student life, I guess. She's been around the department forever."

"Should I worry? Is she competition?"

Patri chuckled. "For you, you mean? No. When you meet her, you'll understand."

"Okay. Very mysterious. How do you spend your days, then? Writing a thesis, I mean."

"Oh, it's history, you know. A lot of reading, a little thinking, a little writing."

"No wonder, then. You need more exercise."

"Oh, I work out."

She stroked his hard midriff. "I know you do. What's it about? Can you tell me?"

He had a ready answer. "Human folly."

"But that's everything," she snapped back.

He chuckled. "You're too wise. But yes. To be more specific, the Collapse. What the hell were people thinking in the hundred years before the world went to shit?"

"You mean, why didn't they stop it?"

"Precisely. No, don't stop that."

She resumed stroking. "And do you have the answer?"

"Of course not. But could be a new viewpoint. A different channel into their zeitgeist that nobody's looked at before. Not so much what people were thinking, as what they thought they were thinking."

"Sounds too meta for me. Too big." She let her stroking wander. "Not like *this*. This is just about right."

"I was hoping you'd think so," he said, and rolled toward her.

# STERN CHASE

It began to rain as Lani arrived at her blind and found a one-horse cart parked behind the supposed leather shop next to the loading dock. Her pulse suddenly racing, struggling to appear nonchalant, she strolled over to have a closer look.

The cart was a rental. Signs on the sides identified it as belonging to twp Loadit, which was mostly longshoremen who moved freight around the docks and the rail yard. They also ran a little stable that let out carts like this one for short-haul deliveries around town. Their culture was a little out of the norm, in that their refectory served fish but never meat; also that they went in for arranged marriages, and these nearly always inside the twp. But she had never heard anything to suggest that they weren't honest.

The cart had a canvas roof and sides, open in the back. The bed contained one wooden crate, about half a meter square and half that high, stenciled

*FRESH CATCH*
*twp AU-SOME*
*Ausable Forks*

Lani suppressed the urge to try the leather shop's back door for fear of leaving wet footprints on the protected loading dock. Instead, she continued to the far end of the warehouse block and circled around it, yanking the front door of the shop (still locked) as she went by. Then back to her blind, where she dashed upstairs and set up her camera, hoping to get a good shot of whoever was doing whatever inside, when they came out the back door.

As it turned out, she had half an hour to wait, and then her photo shoot was a bust. By the time the driver emerged, the rain had become steady—not a downpour, but enough for him to pull up a hood before he stepped into her clear field of view. Combined with the poor streetlight illumination and interference from the rain itself, and even though he pulled away driving the rig straight at her, she was pretty sure that, from the pictures, all she would ever identify with certainty was the horse.

That left pursuit. She was downstairs before the cart clop-clopped under her window and away; it took only another minute to extract her scooter from its hiding place and be out on the alleyway. When she emerged, still stripping off her mask and gloves, her chase was at the end of the block and turning right toward the river.

Tailing him was childishly easy. Her little scooter was much faster than any horse-cart and perfect for lurking at intersections, almost out of sight. Its only defect was that it lacked any kind of protection from the soaking rainstorm. But the rain was warm, and after a couple of minutes, she couldn't get any wetter. She happily ghosted along in the sparse evening traffic, mostly keeping a block away from her quarry to his left or behind. She toyed with the idea of tailing him from ahead, something she had read about and always wanted to try, but she reluctantly played the responsible cop and stuck with the sure thing.

Before long, he returned to the twp Loadit stable, as Lani had expected, and drove the cart in out of the rain. The stable had exits on two sides, one facing the river and the other the railway station. Lani positioned herself so that she could see the paths from both exits. This put her too far away to get any sort of description when he left, minutes later, surprisingly headed toward the river. Male, short-ish, maybe fat-ish. That was the best she could do. He was not carrying anything visible, certainly not the big crate that had been in the cart.

There were dormitories near the docks; Lani guessed that he would check into one of these and call it a night. Wrong again. The guy walked right by them and on toward the small-craft basin. The basin was laid out with four floating docks sticking straight out from the riverbank, numbered one to four from the upstream end. These were protected from the river current by long moles, one upstream and one down. The downstream one was shaped like an "L," with a long leg parallel to shore, leaving a narrow gap to the river proper near the end of dock number one. Lani's mark went directly down the main pier parallel to the shore, and turned off at dock number two. Halfway down, he stepped neatly onto a boat moored stern-in on the right-hand side. As best Lani could tell from two hundred meters away, he was methodically checking out his boat and unmooring it.

This made a problem for Lani. It certainly looked as if her chase was departing by water and not wasting any time doing it. In that case, Lani badly wanted to know the name of his boat. But to find that out without a telescope, in bad weather, she would have to get close to his stern. And the geometry of the harbor meant that she couldn't do that without getting close enough to her bad guy for *him* to describe *her*. Given her soaked Union work shirt, she thought, he would be able to do that right down to her bra size and color. Not good, if her description got back to twp EEE. If she weren't on probation, she would just wave her ID at the harbor master and ask. But that was no good either; she had no ID that she dared to wave. Nope, she admitted to herself, she was stuck. She would have to swim.

She got back on her scooter and purred over to the downstream entrance to the main dock. She put her scooter on the public rack, left her boots beside it, and with a feigned casual saunter, headed barefoot onto the main pier, down the staircase, and up the floating ramp to dock number four. This put her a good hundred and fifty meters from her target, with three rows of boats between them. It was raining harder.

She padded to the end of the dock, looking for evidence of people in the crowded boats tied up there. A few lights showed, but not many. Out near the end of the dock, she found a deserted grouping of pleasure vessels, water taxis, and small cargo lighters. She sat on the dock between two of these, facing her target. It still hadn't moved. Once it did, she wouldn't have much time. She didn't want to be seen in the water, so she reckoned brown skin was better than white cotton. She took off her shirt and pants and stuffed them under a coil of rope. With a last look around to be sure nobody was taking note of her yet, she grabbed a bumper on the dock's side and lowered herself noiselessly into the rain-splashed basin.

Her course took her away from shore to the tip of dock number three. She did it in three underwater pulls, coming up oftener than she really needed, to check her position. She worried because it was awfully hard to see anything from water level, with all the rain splashing. From there, it was a straight shot of perhaps sixty meters to the tip of dock two, visible to her target all the way. She tried to do it underwater in one go and nearly made it. At least she managed to surface and breathe without making much noise. From the stern of the last boat on dock two, she could see that the one she wanted was already edging out of its slip. She had to keep moving.

She headed for the middle of the channel that led to open water. For a little while, she would be around the end of the dock and invisible from the moving boat, so she indulged in a smooth breaststroke, for speed without splashing and to keep oxygenated. No telling when she might have to duck for a while. When she got to her chosen spot, she settled into a float, facing back toward where she expected the competition to appear and showing no more of her head than she had to. Very quickly, she got her first good look at the guy's boat as it slid out from behind the dock. About ten meters long, sloop rigged, perhaps unusually wide in the beam, now running on battery with no sails set. The guy, damn him, was scanning the water ahead of the bow with a searchlight to avoid floating obstacles. As he turned into the channel, Lani grabbed a breath and dove for the bottom.

She heard the swish of his screw as she swam deeper. When her hands hit mud, she turned and looked up, sculling to keep herself from floating. After what seemed a long time, she saw his searchlight flitting over the water above her, and then she could make out the dark ellipse of his hull, blocking the diffuse glow from other lights on the surface. He was passing directly over her. She kicked gently toward shore and let herself rise, popping up with a suppressed gasp less than five meters behind his spinning screw.

"Eapy Fux, Plattsb," she read, through the surface spray. "What the hell does that mean?"

# LOCK CAMS

Lani would not ordinarily have knocked on anybody's door at 01:45. But Evar, back from her travels and being who she was, was a special case. She would barely be getting started for the night. That didn't mean she would welcome an interruption.

"Who the fuck?" she shouted through the door. "Go away! I'm working!"

"Eve! It's Lani! I gotta talk to you!"

Eventually, she opened the door. "Lani," she said. "You look like a drowned... oh, fuck me." She screwed up her nose. "What's that smell? Where the hell have you been? Are you drunk?"

"Swimming. In the small-craft basin," Lani apologized. "I guess not all the boats are real careful with their, you know, facilities. And heading back for my clothes, I swam through a bunch of..."

"No, don't tell me. Damn. You're not coming in *my* apartment in *those* clothes. Here's a towel. Go trade those rags for clean ones and take a shower. With soap, goddammit. Then come back and be polite, and maybe I'm willing to talk to you. And do *not* forget your hair."

Sometime later, Lani sat nursing a beer, having told Evar all about the stakeout and tail job.

"That's all?" Evar complained. "Eapy Fux? Sure was a lot of trouble

111

for Eapy Fux. What *do* you think it means?"

"Well," Lani mused, "it's just a boat name. Could be nothing. Then again, pretty often they're private jokes."

"You think it's a dig at Eapy Fox, then? Maybe, by extension, the whole Union?"

"Well, for sure the Eapy Fox connection. And now you mention it, it's got a flavor to it, doesn't it? There are secessionists, you know, mostly up around the Great Lakes. We watch their chatter, a bit. Seems to me their humor comes across like this. Adolescent, snarky, potty-sexual stuff. But always deniable."

"You'd know that better than me. I only talk to machines."

"Lucky you. Anyhow, can we learn anything about this tub? Better yet, can we track her? Without getting caught doing it, of course?"

"Shouldn't be hard to find the basics in the Ship Registry." Evar turned to her deck and typed, looked, typed some more.

"Piece of cake," she said after a minute. "Eapy Fux, 20 tonnes, 11.5 meters, sail and electric, commissioned 2324, out of Plattsburgh. Rated for frozen freight. Owned by twp Au-some." She searched some more. "Au-some is a twp of fishermen operating in Lake Champlain. Smallish twp, but seems solid enough."

"Makes sense. After I got out of the basin, I went back to the stable where our guy rented his cart. Turns out he paid for the cart with a case of frozen fish. The night manager's a cheerful sort—he gave me a couple of filets to encourage me to go away."

"Imagine that. So the cart rental was a barter deal? That's illegal, no?"

"Sure. It's a way to avoid stating income. But enforcement at that level is lax; everybody does it. What about tracking?"

Evar smiled broadly. "Your old granny Evar has just the thing," she said. "You know about lock-cams?"

"Nope."

"Well, around here, you want to go anywhere with a boat that size, you use the canal system. Means you're always going through locks. This guy you were following, his first stop tonight was probably the entrance to the New Raritan

Canal, six or eight klicks downstream, where there's a nice lock to get you off the estuary and into the canal. More'n a hundred and fifty years ago, the Union put in a computerized monitoring system. Every time a lock cycles, they take images of all the boats. Matter of fact, that's how they bill the traffic for use of the canals. So there's a complete record of where your friend has been. Trouble is, these are privileged data, supposedly available only to the Canal Authority. And," she smiled warmly, again, "to a very few law enforcement organizations. Including EEE."

"Great. What are you waiting for?"

"Ah," said Evar, "Youth. Youth and impatience. But let's see."

She worked for a bit. "Hmph," she said. "It's blocked. That's odd." She sat thinking for a while. "This is going to take some time," she said at last. "Check back tomorrow. Or the day after."

"Take your time," Lani said, finishing her beer. "It's still pouring outside. Now I'm dry, can I borrow an umbrella to get home?"

"Sure. But one more thing. Be careful, Lani. This is getting scary. You're in the badass middle here. Smugglers and fraudsters on one side, EEE on the other. That's a lot to take on. You really don't want to do this alone. Don't you need a friend here? Somebody to help you? Somebody you can trust?"

Lani hugged her, hard. "But I've got a friend, Eve. And Triple-E, to boot. You're it."

Eve's eyebrows went up. "Not sure I signed up for all that."

She took a step away, looked Lani over, then stepped forward and hugged Lani back.

"Okay," she said. "Sounds interesting. But not too exciting, please. I like my action at the other end of a digital link."

Lani got her umbrella, but she didn't go home. Instead, she strolled through the warm rain to the Uni and let herself into Patri's dorm room. The lights were off. She shed her clothes on the floor and slid into bed, spooning against his smooth back.

"You'd better be Lani," he mumbled.

"Right first time," she whispered, and closed her eyes.

# WINDOW SHOPPING

Next morning, the "OUT OF STOCK" line in the dead drop had been replaced by "SALE TIMES" and some dates. The shop would be open for two days, starting in two days' time.

Lani skipped math class to go to her blind and start the camera running in automatic mode, one image every five seconds. If there were comings and goings at the shop's back door, even before the sale, she wanted to know about them. At that rate, the camera battery would run down in a fraction of a day, but she had anticipated that problem. She had a scooter battery as backup, charging the camera, a setup she figured would run for a month or more. If she didn't get busted for disassembling a city scooter, she'd be fine.

On the first day of the sale, she was up even earlier than usual. The shop doors wouldn't open until noon, so she was able to go through her normal routine with the smooth efficiency of a rusty push mower. She made excuses to her sparring buddies, called in sick to her data entry job for the day, and spent the afternoon and early evening watching for anybody to go in or out of the shop front door. It was a frustrating occupation, and it drove her crazy. On that street, there was no place for an extended stakeout; no matter where she squatted, she would soon become conspicuous. The best she could do was to wander by a couple of times an hour, varying speed, direction, and side of the street. Whatever she could see in this succession of two-minute visual snapshots, that's what she was going to get.

She learned, first, that no winter-solstice-gift mob scene was going on. She had hoped for a crowd out the door, but no luck. In total, all day long, she saw the door open only three times. Once for a male luv who went in but didn't come out—at least not when she was watching. Times two and three were the entrance and exit of a different guy. She caught him leaving when, on a hunch, she did a repeat pass only ten minutes after he went in. He entered empty-handed and came out carrying something in a bag. This helped to confirm that somebody was selling something in there, but this was hardly useful news. Neither man was distinctive in appearance, and both were dressed, as she was, in Union daily garb. She felt, though, that they didn't wear their clothes the way she did hers. Maybe she just imagined it, but they had some sense of righteousness, some subtle strut, that said they were better than she was. Better, in fact, than anyone she knew.

The shop was supposed to shut down at 20:00. Maybe it did; she couldn't tell. No mysterious proprietor came out. Her back-door camera showed action all day long. But there was enough normal traffic through that alley that deciding who was or was not tugging at the shop's door would take more study than she could afford that day. And she had missed lunch—and supper. All told, there was nothing to show, and she wanted a drink. Wanted it pretty bad.

# RAWHIDE RETAIL

On day two, Lani again skipped her work shift, this time to go shopping for real. She was as prepared as she could be to play the social elite: squeaky clean, clothes ironed, nice understated necklace of Evar's around her neck. And every cent she could scrape together in her fanny pack.

She was used to unlocked doors, but somehow, she expected the shop's front door to resist. It didn't. She stepped out of the morning heat into a poorly lit, undersized space with a counter facing the door and walls filled with shelves that held mostly second-hand footwear. Behind the counter was a closed door and a tall clerk, very erect and elegantly thin, wearing a vest that would have paid for the shop's contents four times over. When she came in, he looked up from his deck.

"Let me know if I can help you find anything, luv," he said. Nice voice. Pleasant, not pushy.

"Thanks. Thanks...." She turned slowly to scan the goods on display. Sandals made from scooter tires, aged athletic trainers, high-topped dancing shoes with the soles peeling off, torn treated-canvas rain gear. Junk, in short. All private-made, none of it official Union manufacture. The good stuff had to be behind that door.

"I'm looking for slippers," she said at last. "Men's. About twenty-four centimeters?"

"I doubt we can accommodate, luv. Our slippers are down there, near the floor behind you. But I fear they're all women's."

Lani had already spotted them but looked again. Three pairs of tatty things sporting fake fur and bunny ears.

"Hmm." She fixed the clerk with a soulful gaze. "I was hoping for something a little sleeker. And a lot…older. Does that help?"

"Ah. Well, luv, I think we might manage sleek and old. But not slippers. We are out of slippers at present. May I interest you in something else?"

"Well…Sure. Why not? May I see your stock?"

"Ah, no, luv. I'm sure you understand, we must adhere to a strict protocol. It works like this: You tell me what sort of item you desire; I search the inventory and show you a list of products with photos and prices. You make your selection, and pay me."

"Sight unseen?"

"Yes, luv. These are unique and desirable pieces, you see. It would astound you, luv, how often the unscrupulous will seek to view and even handle merchandise when they have no intention of purchasing. No ability, even. But to continue. Once you have purchased an item, I retrieve it for you, and if it does not meet with your approval, of course I will refund your payment. I should say, the quality of our products is such that this happens very rarely. Once you carry it out of the shop, the sale is final."

"Well. I see." She shrugged and dithered. She was working hard to keep in character. Trying to recall anything that she "owned" in this sense—bought, paid for, kept forever—and she was coming up empty. Her running shoes? She supposed so. They were Union manufacture, even though she had paid a little something to get ones that fit.

But the clerk was waiting. She had to say something to him. If anyone in the world was a living, breathing offense against both Equality and Evidence, it was this carefully supercilious clerk. Probably best, then, for her to tacitly admit that she was only a working girl, out of her league.

"I really don't have a backup plan here," she said. "I guess I'm looking for something special, to impress Bi...to impress the gentleman with my feelings for him. Some little accessory? Small, but nice?"

The skinny guy's expression was no longer blandly cheerful. In fact, it was shading into a sneer. But he played along.

"Of course, luv." He tapped on his deck and turned it to show her the screen. "This is our most, ah, economical item. A wide, tooled-leather wristband, suitable for mounting a large piece of jewelry. Or, if you have a taste for antiquities, a wristwatch."

If the place hadn't been so dark to start with, the price at the bottom of the image would have dilated Lani's pupils to the size of teacups. She did a quick calculation. If she gave up alcohol and eating out and lived entirely inside the twp, she might save that much cash in half a year. No wonder Muam kept her handbag chained to her body.

"I see," she said. "Mostly, I see that I came unprepared. I apologize for the misunderstanding."

"Yes, luv. It's a common mistake."

"Thank you for your time. Perhaps I'll return another time."

"And sooner than you think," she muttered once she was out the door.

# BREAKING AND ENTERING

Chimneying around the blocked ladder to the warehouse roof was still uncomfortable, but Lani managed. The unanswerable question had been when to make her move. The sale hours nominally ended at 20:00; she definitely wanted to wait until then, but if she delayed too long, the operators might have cleaned the whole place out before she got there. It didn't help that she had no idea how many people she was dealing with, nor whether they slept (if they slept at all) inside the building. In the end, she bundled all her uncertainties into one ball and then ignored them. Since it was near the longest night of the year, she picked 04:35 for her jump-off time. That gave her a couple of hours of darkness for cover, but also some concealing background noise from the awakening city. Her main worry (irrational, she knew) was how angry the Chief would be if she got caught after ignoring all of his precepts about covert ops. Starting with never, ever, get into anything serious without backup.

Once on the roof, she took off her boots and cat-footed across to the wide trap door. It was all as she remembered, still secured by the same crumby padlock. Twp EEE had access to some very high-tech ways to open locks, like the nanobots that the Chief had used on Chaupi's front door in Ohio. But if she tried anything like that, she might as well leave a sign in big block letters saying, "EEE was here." Instead, she waited until a trash collection cart rattling down the street made an adequate racket and then whacked the lock with the heel of her boot. It popped right open, exactly as similar locks on school lockers had always done when she was twelve years old and feeling nosey. Pretty much identical circumstances, she thought, as she swung the hatch open.

She switched on her headlamp and peered inside. She had a small selection of climbing gear, just in case, but was relieved to see that she wouldn't need it. As she had hoped, a ladder, attached to the inner wall of the building, led from the hatch down into the darkness. She put her boots back on, checked her gloves, and climbed down and in.

She found herself in a big dusty room, mostly empty. She held her breath and listened hard but could hear nothing but the trip-hammer beating of her heart. On one side of the room was the roll-up exit to the loading dock; on the other, a large swinging door with a grimy window leading toward the front of the warehouse and, presumably, the little shop she had seen. Next to that door, she found a workbench with hand tools and a clutter of wooden crates and loose packing materials. She counted six crates, all the same size, and all from twp Au-some.

Five on the floor were empty; one, up on the workbench, made her freeze. It contained a pair of high, dressy women's boots, the same coffee color as Muam's bag, with seven-centimeter heels and dangling leather fringe on top.

This was crazy. She knew what a watch band cost, and to all appearances, Muam's handbag had been a financial stretch for an unusually wealthy couple of dudes. At that rate, these things would bring a king's ransom. What were they doing in an empty workshop? Why hadn't they been sold?

But as she studied the boots, the mystery unraveled, and her face stretched in a wide, happy smile. "Oh, my," she whispered. "Someone's going to hear about *this*."

The goods were damaged. Seriously. Chewed by rats, if she was any judge. The top one in the box looked almost okay, but the one underneath was a real mess. She sniffed it. "Clawed, gnawed, with rat piss to boot," she giggled. Sometimes she cracked herself up.

But to business. This was better than the best she had hoped to find. She took the boots out of their box, opened her jackknife, and carefully sliced off a dangling fringe strand from each one. She pocketed the leather strings, replaced the boots in the box, packed in the same positions as before, and clicked off her light. She briefly considered going up front to see what she could learn in the shop but gave up the idea as too risky. Chances were good that the skinny clerk was asleep somewhere. Time to get out. She climbed the ladder carefully and quietly, closed the hatch, and replaced the padlock so it looked like it was doing something. Then off to her room for PT and breakfast.

# BINGE WATCHING

Lani let her camera run for another day to round up possible stragglers. Then she took the memory card back to her room and spent two long nights hunched over her deck, viewing the images. Her aim was to isolate people who showed an interest in the shop's back door from the crowd of citizens who were merely on their way to other business.

Right away, she concluded that if she ever did that again, she would make the time between frames two seconds, not five. With five-second separation, there was time for an active person to bounce out of the crowd, try the locked door, and bounce back to the alley. Not that people normally behave that way, just that interpolating people's movements from sparsely sampled photos was a problem and, at best, a learned skill.

When someone did seem to want to go into the shop, she copied all the images showing the new person of interest into a separate time-tagged file that she might show to a judge later. Of course, about half the time, the party would be moving away from the camera, and she got a good view only of the back of their head. But she took what she could get.

What she got was mostly diddly. There were mildly interesting cases, people she thought she had seen at the *Open Horse*, but she had no names to go with any of them. Only right at the end, in the hour before dawn, as she browsed among the stragglers, did she find two positive IDs. Both were quite alarming.

In a picture taken a little before noon on the day after her break-in, something about a woman walking toward the camera triggered Lani's tired synapses. "I know this bitch," she muttered, and zoomed in on her. It took a surprisingly long time for her to make the connection. Like a skunk on her desk, the woman was so out of place that Lani's mind at first refused to grasp what she was seeing.

"Hell damn fuck shit!" she whispered. "Venna, what are you *doing* here?" Because the woman was, beyond doubt, Venna twp EEE Keithley, age fifty-three, the hardest-assed lieutenant in the entire twp. And also the Chief's second in command and enforcer among his picked team of operatives. Lani had known her for years but never liked her much. Partly this was that Venna didn't give a damn if she was liked. Partly it was simple jealousy; Lani got the Chief's attention sometimes, but Venna always did. Mostly, though, it was Venna's unfailing, humorless, scrupulous rectitude, which always impressed Lani as disapproval of the world in general and of her, Lani, in particular.

There was one other oddity, something that had contributed to Lani's initial confusion. Venna always, always wore her sword, displaying her authority to the world. She carried it with her to the toilet. Rumor had it that she was born wearing that sword. But Lani's image was quite clear: no sword belt, no blade.

Subsequent images showed her up on the loading dock, trying the locked door, then moving around toward the front of the building and out of view, like the twenty-odd other presumed customers captured by Lani's camera. But the sale was over. Did she get in the front door? There was no way to know.

Venna's presence at that time and place raised such a lot of questions that Lani felt unable to deal with them on her second consecutive night of no sleep. So she put these worries on the shelf and plowed into the rest of the photos. Only a little later, she found herself looking at the skinny store clerk, coming out the back door of the shop and disappearing, headed away from the camera. Sixty images later, he was back and letting himself in, again through the back door. What had he been doing for those five minutes? She sat and mulled it over. He wasn't getting a doughnut, or going across the street for a change of scene, or to take a piss; if it were something like that, he would be doing it several times per day, but she had never before seen him poke his nose outside. No, it had to be something to do with closing down after the sale.

After a while, she shifted her attention to the top of the image. The camera's field of view was large enough (barely) to show the target warehouse's crane sticking out above the roofline. And on one image, taken near the middle of Skinny's five-minute absence, she could see a little rounded blob projected against the sky, close to the crane. On careful inspection, she decided it could be the top of someone's head. She looked some more, got the same result. Definitely a head. Skinny was a methodical bastard. He had been on the roof, checking the trapdoor lock.

When this idea struck her, Lani collected her school backpack and was out the door without conscious thought. It wasn't until she reached the street that she worked out in words why she was so spooked. Item: Skinny had now known for days that his store was breached, but nothing had been stolen. Therefore, somebody was snooping on his business. Item: Most of the explanations for Venna's showing up implied that some EEE twple had an interest. If they found out that the leather shop was under surveillance, they would want to know by whom, and they would want to know right away. When that happened, Lani didn't want a room full of her gear sitting in an open building only a hundred meters from the nominal crime scene.

# CONFESSIONS

The day had been long, what with Lani's sleep deficit and several high-stress visits to the blind to get her stuff out and, subsequently, to erase her tracks and to obscure the reason she had been there. She elected to spend the night with Patri, hoping to get a rare full night's rest. But of course, it didn't work.

It was three in the morning, their usual hour for deep conversations, when Lani chose to confess some of her secrets. It seemed like Patri had been waiting for them.

"So, first off, you've been thinking of me as a working copper. I am and I'm not." She was sitting upright on his bed, curled up, holding her knees, with her back to the wall.

"That's not very clear," he said.

"Yeah, yeah. Give me time, okay? Problem is, I'm on probation. Have been. For almost two years. Never mind what I did to get that, but it was bad. Somebody died. A kid, in fact. A kid, maybe eight…" she stopped and squeezed her eyes shut. "Never mind. A kid. You could call it an accident, but somebody had to pay for it, and I'm paying."

He slid over and put an arm around her shoulders, but she shrugged him off. "Stop it. I need to tell you this."

"Okay."

"Probation. It's like having leprosy or something. I have one good friend, and my family—adopted family—and my ex-boss, who is also my uncle, and you, and that's it. Everybody else treats me like earwax." She paused for a long time, her face a mask. When Patri tried to say something, she waved him to silence.

"Pretty soon my probation is up, and a committee is gonna decide if I'm rehabilitated. I don't think it matters. I think if they say nay, then I'm kicked out of the twp; if they say yea, I'm just sidelined for life. I think my only hope is to go at it another way. I've gotta do something good. On my own. I've gotta get everybody's attention, make them take me seriously."

"Are you…"

"Let me finish. So I'm doing it. Been doing it since right before we met. Got a fraud case that nobody else picked up, and lately, it's getting hot. Taking up a lot of time. Gonna take more." She shot him a thin smile. "Me sneaking around, making trouble. You can't help but notice. Probably already have. I just wanted you to know what's going on. What your crazy girlfriend is into."

"Can I talk now?"

"Be my guest." She wiped her nose on his sheet.

"Two questions. Any chance I can wheedle you out of this? Because you're nuts. I don't know the details, but I don't have to. It'll never work. If you pull it off, they'll hate you forever, and if you don't, they'll crucify you."

She looked at him sadly. "It's too late, Tree. I'm in too deep. Not just twp policies; I've broken serious rules. If I don't shut down a real damn criminal conspiracy, I'll spend years on a work crew for misuse of city property, breaking and entering, malicious surveillance, and who knows what else. Might have to do that anyway."

Patri stared into the distance for a while and sighed. "I was afraid of that. Okay, I'm not gonna run away because you're out of your damn mind. I guess I knew that already. So tell me if I can help. If you're gonna waste your life breaking rocks, I might as well do the same."

"Pigshit. You will not. But thanks for the reflex."

"It's my training. Second question: About your probation. For whatever it was you did, do you think your punishment was too harsh?"

It was Lani's turn to stare and sigh.

"Yes. No. I don't know. It was almost an accident, just really bad luck. Could've happened to anybody. I had a half second to make a decision, and I did, and I was wrong. Cops do worse all the time and don't get their chops busted. But that's the thing. Any civilian does what I did, she'd be in real trouble. The judge would be saying words like 'negligence' and 'manslaughter,' and she'd be up for years of hard labor. It hurts my heart. What did they say to the kid's parents? 'Oh, yeah. The rookie who chopped your son's leg off? We made her go sit in a corner for a while.' Doesn't seem like enough, does it?"

Tears were streaming down Lani's cheeks. She finally allowed Patri to comfort her, and they huddled together for a long time until her shakes subsided and she could control her grief. She turned and kissed his cheek.

"So here we are. Upright Gibbs and multiple offender Maxwell. I don't think I'll need your help, but if I do, I will surely ask. You want me to fill you in on the details?"

"Sure. It's only 3:20. We have lots of time."

# TREE

"Tree. I need to go back to the *Canal*," Lani told Patri the next evening after supper. They had eaten at his twp refectory, which was convenient for lots of reasons. For one thing, it was easy. The academic twps were used to having visitors, and they saw no purpose in checking them in and out like children. So she walked right in with Patri and got in line, and that was that. By EEE standards, the food was uninteresting, apart from using a great plenty of hot sauce. Part of the academic culture, Patri told her. He seemed to find more subtlety than she did in the various kinds of pepper.

"Easy enough; it's only around the corner," said Patri. "How come? Not the quality of the beer. Washing down the chili?"

"No, I need to find a guy."

"You've got a guy. Don't tell me you need more. I'm hurt."

She made the obligatory noises and fisted him lightly in the ribs, but she was tempted to hit him harder. This was serious, and she wanted him to pay attention.

"No. I'm looking for this genetics guy I was talking to a few nights before we met. I think he might be able to tell me where to send the leather sample."

"Must be a dozen people at the Uni who can tell you that. Why not wait 'til tomorrow? We've got better things to do."

"Tree." She turned to face him, straightened his shoulders, and patted him on the cheek. "I love making love with you, and we'll get around to it later, I promise. But stop talking about it all the time. It's boring."

"Is this the same cop who can't defer gratification?"

"*Ja*, by damn, it is. But there's work to do. And tomorrow is twelve hours down the road. This thing is starting to move, and if I don't move myself, I'll get run over. Also, I don't want to traipse all across campus explaining my situation to department secretaries. That sort of thing will get back to Triple-E. And so, if that other guy is at the *Canal*, I need to talk with him. Coming?"

He jogged to catch up with her, and they walked in thoughtful silence to the bar. Lani broke with habit by starting with a pitcher of the *Canal's* least-maligned beer. Her first scan of the room failed to turn up Luv Nematode, who, on this night, was the desired object of her attention.

"I've been thinking about last night—your whole story," Patri said while they waited.

"Really? What do you think?"

"Well, I'm wondering. What's your end game, Lani? When you've gone as far as you can by yourself, then what? And what has to happen to make you decide it's time?"

"Getting nervous?"

"Well, sure. And that will get worse before it gets better. But I'd like to know that you're not just winging it, one play at a time."

"Good question, really. I think that quitting time is pretty soon now. With Muam's story (which is hearsay) and her bag (which I handled but can't document), and the price tag on that watch band that I didn't see, and the circumstantial evidence that the stock they sell is getting smuggled in to avoid having to declare its inflated value, I don't have enough to make any judge charge anybody with anything. But I think there's enough that if I go meekly into the Chief's office and tearfully admit I've been a bad girl, and then roll out all that almost-evidence, and throw in the photos I got of people at the shop's back door, he's likely to think that there *is* enough to start a real investigation. I mean, at the very least, there's gotta be a person of interest or two among those customers, and the amount of money involved in one of those two-day sales makes it a medium-big deal. So next, he probably arranges to raid their sale next time they're in town. Then he can surely get some of the clientele to talk to him, so they themselves don't get charged with tax evasion, and also bust that guy behind the counter for straight-up fraud. Then if he rats out his bosses, well, that's when the fun really begins."

"Oh. Great. So you *have* thought about it."

"I haven't. All that is just me winging it. But there is one thing I want before I fess up to the Chief. I want some qualified, disinterested specialist to stand up and say no, those boots aren't three-hundred-year-old cowhide, they're last week's pigskin. Or whatever."

"And even if you get left out of the follow-up, you'll come out of it okay?"

"Yeah, I think so. Word will get around."

"And you're getting a line on this expert here, tonight?"

"Let's hope." She smiled warmly and squeezed his hand. "Now don't bug me while I'm working. You were right that first night. You talk too much."

"I love you, too."

"Cheers."

*

They sat in the *Canal* for a long time. People came, people went. Occasionally somebody would sit and start a conversation, but it was always about English lit or meteorology or physical therapy or, in the worst case, politics. Never genetic engineering. Tree got bored, and they danced for a while, but their hearts weren't in it. Sometime after 01:00, they realized that they were putting the first serious strain on their brand-new relationship. They were about to leave, cleaning up the evening's scattered litter, when doctoral candidate Nematode himself walked in, looking droopy.

He spotted Lani right away and nearly turned around and walked out. But Lani stood up and waved him over, somberly, not with smiles and good cheer. He hesitated, eyeing Tree, but finally came to stand by their table.

"Hi," said Lani. "You remember me; this is Tree. I owe you a proper apology.

Join us for a minute, if you will. I'll buy you a drink and say my piece, and then you can do what you want. Okay?"

Luv Nematode nodded and sat. Lani waved the waiter over and ordered drinks all around.

"Here's the thing," Lani said when they were settled. "I came here tonight looking for you because I wanted to ask you a question. But sitting here, it came to me that I don't have the right to ask you for anything. Last time we were here, I led you on and made fun of you and made you feel small in front of your friends. And the crappy part is that I wasn't really even being mean to you or trying to hurt you. The truth is, I was all wrapped up in me. Where you were concerned, I just didn't care. I didn't care. And that's no way to feel about another citizen. I'm really sorry. I promise not to do it again, if I can help it. That's it. I won't bother you anymore."

Luv N. considered this. "Okay," he said. Presently he sipped his drink and said, "So now you want me to answer your question?"

"Nope. This isn't a tit-for-tat. We're done. Unless you want something more from me, feel free to go hang out with a better kind of people."

He nodded and took another sip. Cautiously, he stood up and extended his hand. "Dance with me?" he said.

Lani cocked her head and laughed out loud. "You've got nerve," she said. "I like it. Sure, I'll dance with you."

She got up and let him lead her to the dance floor. Fortune smiled and, for the next tune, delivered a slow number, something he could keep up with. Nat King Cole, she thought. She snuggled up to him and did her formidable best to make him look good.

After a minute or so, he murmured in her ear, "Rumor says you have something to ask me."

"Yes. But it'll wait for a bit."

# ON THE FARM

The Uni's experimental farm was about fifteen klicks north of Trenton— far enough, and on bad enough roads, to make a commute by scooter impractical. So Lani took the train, which made the trip a short hop at small expense. The track ran straight for the first ten kilometers or so, then detoured to the north to start a clockwise circle around the dead city of Princeton. There were lots of such detours shown on the Union railway map. They bypassed places where, during the Civil Wars, one side or another besieged and exterminated the local population, leaving only rubble and unburied corpses. Princeton, as far as anybody knew, got the business for the crime of being populated by intellectuals. The main threats to safety in dead cities (collapsing buildings, vermin, disease) had, of course, expired long ago, but still hardly anybody went into them. This avoidance came at a huge price, especially for once-central transportation hubs such as New York. Nevertheless, Unionites let these places be and tip-toed around them. The Council wanted everybody to remember why the Union was formed to begin with.

Lani got off the train at the Rosedale stop and waited briefly for one of the farm's staff to pick her up, driving a well-worn surrey pulled by an excellent matched pair of chestnut mares. It turned out that the answer to Lani's question from the Back Canal was Professor Teti twp UniBio Yang. She was a biologist and geneticist, highly thought of in her department, but for the next month or two, she was spending all her time at the experimental farm, working on "something to do with Asian ungulates." Nematode had been sure that she could identify Lani's leather sample, could explain the results to laymen, and that she could and would otherwise keep her mouth shut. A few mail exchanges later, here Lani was.

The driver waited for Lani to board, and then, with a click, set the horses into a comfortable walk. "Reep," he said, sticking out his hand.

"Lani," she answered, giving him a firm shake in return.

"Don't think I've seen you before," Reep continued. "You one of the Yangsters?"

"Yangsters?"

"Oh. I guess not. What we call Teti's army of students and postdocs. Er, Prof Yang's, that is. Must be a dozen of 'em."

"And they come out here a lot?"

"From time to time, you know. Long's she's living here. When they need to talk face to face."

"And you live at the farm, too?"

"Oh, no, luv. Me and the other groundsman, we live in Rosedale. She's got the place to her lonesome, most nights. Reminds me, luv, we gotta get you back to the station by 16:30, so Briy and me can get ourselves home on time."

"No problem. I shouldn't take anywhere near that long."

Her copper's curiosity satisfied for the moment, Lani relaxed into her seat and enjoyed the ride. It was a hot and sunny day, for January. The road was good gravel and made a satisfying crunch under the wheels. The scenery consisted of gently rolling hills covered with typical Jersey scrub: short tufty grass, cactus, various shrubs about waist high, and the occasional mesquite tree. The farm, when it came into view, was something different. It was a good-size spread, maybe a hundred hectares, fenced off all around with high cyclone wire, presumably to keep animals out. It was much greener than the surroundings. Lesser fences subdivided it into many oddly-shaped plots, each one hung with labels, charts, images, and notations. Lani imagined, with a smile, that at least the key parts of all this paperwork would be in Latin. In the middle of the compound, reached by a long gravel drive, stood an antique house and a cluster of barns and outbuildings. The house had a roofed and screened veranda with a scrap of lawn in front, and it looked old enough that George Washington might have slept there. As Reep and Lani drove up, Professor Yang stood by the front-door steps, waiting for them.

"Lani, luv, welcome," she said in a soft voice. "You can call me Teti. Come have some lemonade."

Teti Yang set them up on the shady side of the veranda, on comfortable chairs and across the top of a wooden coffee table made from a giant stump, also very old. Teti herself was perhaps in her mid-fifties, medium height and a bit round, and endowed with an assertive calmness. She was dressed in many-times-washed Union issue, with a bright yellow scarf draped over her shoulders and across her back. After their mutual identification ritual, she stretched out on her chair, clasped one knee to her chest, and fixed Lani with a steady gaze.

"Let's talk about your business first, luv, if that suits you. Then if you like, I'd be happy to show you around and explain minutia to your heart's content. This is a bit of an occasion for me, you know. I get strangers visiting out here sometimes, but not very often."

Lani sipped her lemonade and nodded.

"So then. Police business, eh? Triple-E business, no less."

Lani nodded again and hoped she wasn't blushing.

"You have a sample that you would like me to sequence, then. May I see it? Can you tell me in some more detail this sample's circumstances and why you need my help? Without betraying any confidences, of course."

"Sure." Lani pulled one of the leather strings out of her pocket and handed it to Teti. She had retrieved it from its hiding place in the Trenton city park earlier that morning. Well before sunrise, in fact.

"This came from a boot," she said, "alleged to be made of three-hundred-year-old cowhide, cryo-frozen for almost all that time. To make a fraud case, we need to show that isn't true. So what I want to know is what animal this strip came from. Horse, pig, shark, bat, cow, whatever. Sorry it's tanned. Oh, yeah, and it may be contaminated with rat piss. Can you do that? If you can do it, will you tell your results to a judge?"

Yang rolled the strip between her fingers, sniffed it, and smiled. "I don't mind the rat piss. The tanning, that's a little challenge. But we can do it. We just have to work harder. And I won't say anything to you that I won't tell a judge."

She sat silent for a time, thinking. "Also, please understand that I don't do the sequencing myself. That's handled by one of the postdocs at my lab. He'll also run the pipeline to do the first round of data analysis. But I will be the one to look at his outputs and do the interpretation. This may not be the level of security that you want, but I don't know how else to make it happen."

"How long to get the answer?"

"A week. Could be more. Right now, we're pretty backed up."

"And you trust this postdoc?"

"Yes. Implicitly."

Lani thought about it. She felt a jarring urgency, but in truth, the case was unlikely to make any real progress until the time of the next sale, which was probably most of a month away. She didn't like expanding the circle of people who knew anything of what she was doing, but even if she looked for a brand-new expert, she would be doing that. She didn't seem to have a choice.

"Okay," she said. "Go to it."

# BLACKBUCKS

Teti Yang spent a minute packaging Lani's leather sample in a vial, in an envelope, in a plastic bag, and then writing a note to her postdoc telling him what she wanted him to do. She dropped the envelope into a mail pouch outside the front door.

"So much for that," she told Lani with a smile. "May I show you something, if you have half an hour?"

"Of course, Professor Yang. I'm at your disposal."

"No need for formality, Lani. This is supposed to be fun. Come with me."

She put on a straw hat that hung by the door and strode a hundred meters to the farthest of the outbuildings. On the outside, it looked like a large, low-roofed chicken coop, but inside, it was spotless gleaming wood floors and galvanized steel partitions, forming a dozen good-sized stalls. There were windows and an open barn door in the back, giving views onto a wide scrubby pasture. The building smelled like a barn, but only faintly.

Teti went to a refrigerator on the wall and pulled out a large milk bottle, complete with a nipple. She then opened one of the stalls and invited Lani in. "Meet Okki," she said.

Huddled in a corner at the back of the stall was a young animal. It was a dark fawn color, stood about thirty centimeters tall, and seemed to be all skinny legs and long neck.

"Okki is a female blackbuck, five weeks old," she said, going down on her knees to present Okki with the bottle. It was enthusiastically accepted. Teti went on talking while the fawn nursed. "She's one of six we have on the farm now, aiming for a breeding herd of thirty in a year or so. The interesting thing is, blackbucks have been extinct for about two hundred years."

Lani opened her mouth, but all she could think of to say was, "Can I do that?"

"You bet," Teti said with a broad smile, and gave her the bottle. "Keep it tipped up, so she doesn't swallow too much air."

Lani squatted in front of Okki and presented the nipple. Okki shied and dithered for a few seconds, then committed and grabbed on. After that, it was easy.

Lani was remembering the things that Luv Nematode had told her. "You used recorded DNA sequences to bring them back."

"That we did, child. It wasn't easy, but we did. Lots of steps to master. Learned to use goats as surrogate mothers."

"Why blackbucks?"

"Ah. Well, for one thing, they're genetically interesting. In most mammals, like you and me, the sex chromosomes account for about five percent of the genetic material. In blackbucks, the percentage is more like twenty. Very curious."

She paused, looking closely at Lani, as if testing her. Finally, she took a deep breath and continued.

"But that's not the reason. For you to understand what it is, I need to tell you a story. It's not a pretty story, I'm afraid. It doesn't reflect well on humankind. Not well at all. Are you sure you want to hear it, dear?"

This was sounding more and more like Luv Nematode. What *was* it about geneticists, anyway?

"I've seen some things," Lani replied. "You won't wreck my illusions."

"Well, then, blackbucks," Teti said. "They're antelope native to the Thar desert in northwest India. The mature animals are gorgeous. Black bodies with

137

white underneath, big white circles around the eyes, and improbable long spiral horns. In the early part of the twentieth century, they were hunted practically to extinction in their homeland before they got government protection. Then somebody had the bright idea of introducing them into Texas, where they did well. The Texans kept managed herds on huge plots of land and sold hunting rights to trophy collectors. Seems there's a certain kind of person who can't get enough of tracking down the world's prettiest animals and killing them. But I digress."

Okki had had her fill, it seemed. She wandered away from Lani, briefly rubbed against Teti's shins, and then lay down on the pile of straw in her corner. Teti took the bottle back to the refrigerator and kept talking.

"So there were two populations, one small and scattered in India, and the other bigger and concentrated in a handful of counties in Texas. Then, some decades later, came the Civil Wars. The herds in Texas got whittled down by various hungry militias wandering through, looking for meat. Then when the climate really turned hot, the habitat dried up and blew away, and the Texas blackbucks died out entirely.

"The story in India was different, and worse. We talk about the Civil Wars, plural, as if they were only a North American aberration. Not so. Climate pressures led to similar violence most places in the world. The fighting in Central and South Asia was as bad as ours and as senseless. One day some nihilist madman—I suppose it was a man—set off an enormous dirty bomb near the summit of Mt. Kailash. It's in southern Tibet, possibly the most sacred mountain in the pre-Collapse world. Four of the largest rivers in South Asia have their headwaters on its slopes. In one stroke, this madman managed to poison the water supply for most of the northern part of the subcontinent.

"And that did for the blackbucks, dear. And many other species. Also, by the way, for about a hundred million humans, who died horribly in the first month from prompt effects of radiation exposure, and several times that many who succumbed in the next little while, as people trying to run away found they had nowhere to go. It holds some kind of record for single-shot casualties. Impressive, eh? To this day, even on this side of the world, we suffer from elevated rates of cancer, miscarriage, and birth defects, and many of them arise from this one event. Both my daughters have serious health problems of those sorts."

Lani reached out and held Teti's hand in both of hers. There was no point in saying "I'm so sorry" to such a bald recitation of facts. No point at all.

"Best not to think about all this too much," Teti said. "It tends to darken one's day."

"And you decided to work on blackbucks...?"

"To try to reclaim something from that wreckage, you know. Can't do much about the humans. But blackbucks are within our grasp, and they fit into the local ecology, so we got the Council to agree. Been working on it for years, and now it's starting to pan out."

Teti Yang had been staring at nothing. Now she revived and turned her attention back to Lani.

"But I'm boring you. I'll be in touch," she said. "By the way, we have lots more lemonade. Would you like to take some with you to speed your journey?"

"Oh, hell yes. It's wonderful."

"It should be. We grow our own lemons here. Sugar cane, too, for that matter."

And she was off, leading Lani back to the house and to Reep.

# LIMBO

Days passed with nothing doing. Days left before the panel meeting, counting down through the one hundred twenties.

On the level of personal maintenance, Lani's sleep deprivation retreated from its acute spike around the time of the leather shop sale to its normal chronic level. She was able to get back onto her regular activity schedule with something like the dependability she had displayed in the old days, before her revolt began. This, she hoped, would repair some of the damage that her reputation probably suffered during her extended stakeout. She spent more or less every other night with Tree. He was proving himself a thoughtful, patient, entertaining, and enthusiastic lover, something she had never before experienced and didn't know what to do with. Too good to last, she feared. The MOI had gone into high gear. Rumor had it that bodies had been found. Overheard conversations in the refectory seemed to deal with nothing else, and the same for gossip in her martial arts classes. But these sources spread mostly elaborate speculation—no convincing or even agreed-to facts. From the higher echelons of twp EEE came a steady diet of nothing, nothing, nothing.

The great cowhide mystery was similarly stalled. Evar confirmed that the *Eapy Fux* had returned to Lake Champlain by the shortest route. Once there, she dropped out of sight because there were no locks to traverse. Evar had code running to keep an eye on all the water routes connecting to the lake, but none of these alarms had been tripped. There was no word from Teti Yang, nor any expected for a while. And Venna Keithley navigated the halls of twp EEE with her usual cold and punctilious demeanor, wearing her sword, and displaying no new leather goods.

Lani enjoyed the lowered stress level for a day or two; then the lack of stimulation became an obscure itch that she couldn't scratch, and at last, it began to drive her crazy.

One night during her customary sleepless wee hours, she went looking for inspiration in old images stored on her deck, in her personal files. One that caught her attention was a family relic from long ago, given to her, with written commentary, by her mother when she was perhaps seven years old. It showed her mom's great-grandmother as a young girl, early in the Bad Days, surrounded by her own family—her parents and six siblings. The picture came from California, late in the short, ill-starred history of the Russian River Republic, before the family fled north and east. The parents looked thin and worn out, the kids bright and happy, but skinny. Great-great-grandfather Ricardo was possibly a mestizo, his wife, Priyam, clearly South Asian. Lani's mom had drilled her on the kids' names, all of them aggressively mixing-pot American, names that were already going out of style: Paul, William, Isabelle, Lawrence, Patricia, Grace, and Merry. Merry was Lani's ancestor, middling in age, special as all children are. And the only one of the bunch, adult or child, to survive the next four years. The rest got picked off in various ways, by ones and twos. No single family disaster, just grinding, relentless attrition. "Remember them," Lani's mother had told her. "The ones who fell along the way. Never forget them. Never let such things happen again."

That was motivation, Union style. Everybody she knew had similar stories.

In the same folder was an image of Lani and her parents. Her younger brother, too, and a handful of friends from twp Moly. Taken on a picnic excursion in the hills above the mine. It was a good picture, she recalled. But she didn't look at it. It was too much.

# PARADISE

Lani couldn't reconstruct how it was done, but Tree had managed to get her talking about her childhood. They were lounging in her room in a pleasant post-coital glow, with windows open and lights off, sipping iced wine (which Tree assured her was not offensive to him or his wine-making forebears).

"The mine had been there forever, "she said, "like tin mines in Cornwall. But it hadn't been worked for maybe a hundred and fifty years. Then about a century ago, the Union railroad made it out to central Colorado. Our teachers said that was specifically to reopen some of the old mines, including the Hendrikson, because the Union needed minerals they couldn't get any place else."

"Not my specialty," said Tree, "but it sounds right. Fits with what I know."

"So anyhow, twp Moly was formed back then to clean out and operate the mine and send the molybdenum back east."

"So what's moly…molyb…molybdenum good for, anyway?"

"To make steel alloys, mostly. Hard, tough ones. Used a lot to make machine tools and such. Also weapons. Swords. Gun barrels."

"Okay. Go on."

"It was always a fairly small twp. Only about twenty actual miners; they ran multi-ton remote-control machines that did all the work below ground.

There was a solar/ethanol power station to make watts for the machines and the refinery, and the rest was support: refectory, houses, the school, infirmary. There was a little ag sector that worked greenhouses for vegetables. All pretty standard for a free-standing twp, just more isolated than most and more dependent on food shipments from the outside. Three or four times a year, we ran wagon trains over the pass to the railhead at Tabernash. Metal went out, food and supplies came in. Barrels of nano-goo for the refinery. Sacks of flour, pecans, whatever."

"Yeah. But to be a kid there...?"

"Was heaven. What a fucking glorious place. I mean, there were *trees* there. Down at mine level, they were pretty sparse, but up a bit higher, it was a regular forest almost up to the tops, any place the soil allowed. Pine trees half a meter thick growing out of cracks in the cliff no wider than your hand. Up high, in old fire scars, meadows where the grass and wildflowers would knock your eyes out. And horses. The twp had so many horses. I swear we learned to ride before we could walk. I don't know how many months, all told, my brother and I spent chasing each other around those mountains. A lot. Sometimes on foot but mostly mounted. We climbed every mountain for twenty kilometers in all directions, knew all the good streams and watering holes, knew how to make fires and put 'em out. The works."

"And what about your parents?"

"Mom taught school. Dad worked in the greenhouses and sometimes in the refinery. Mom was a fixer, too. She could repair pretty much anything mechanical, kitchen mixers, rock crushers. Most everybody at the twp was multi-skilled. Not enough people to do all the jobs, otherwise. The folks would go camping with us sometimes. Sometimes we organized several families for week-long horseback expeditions to some of the famous old places."

"So that's what people mean by the 'high islands'?"

"Yeah. Above three thousand meters, you can get spots that look like the old climate." She chuckled a little grimly. "Surrounded by desert, of course."

Tree sat silent for a long time, with Lani's head in his lap. Maybe gathering his nerve. Finally, he stirred.

"I know you don't want to. But can you tell me about the raid?"

As expected, Lani went stiff. "Why," she complained, "did I not see that coming?"

"I'm sorry, Lani. But I've got to know. How did all that go down? What was your part?"

"I told you. I went out the back door as they came in the front. Took a walk in the park over to the railhead and made a radio call. Nothing to it."

"Lani, please quit it. I can read a map. That ridge you walked is a couple of kilometers long and four thousand meters high."

Lani sniffed. "Thirty-eight hundred. Tops."

"And you up there in a winter storm. At night. Walk in the park, hell. Talk. I want to hear about it."

# HENDRIKSON

"It was about this time of year," Lani said, dully, after a short but stinging argument. Her delivery was sullen and grudging to begin with, but as she continued, it became dreamlike, fluent but abstracted. "Middle of January. The weather that time of year was mostly pretty nice, but sometimes a major storm would come through. The wind would kick up, the temperature would drop, and we could get snow sometimes all the way down below two thousand meters. One of those was just starting when they showed up. The raiders, on the main road outside the twp.

"Your people"—by which she meant historians— "say they were met by Ceri Gomez, one of the security detail, on the road a couple of hundred meters outside the main gate. Sure, I knew her. I knew everybody. It was getting dark, and she was looking for a wandering horse. They suppose the raider troop wanted in, she objected, and they gunned her down right there. Per regs, she was packing a Walther, but she never got a shot off.

"The shooting alerted the other two security twple, who had their two Walthers and a hunting rifle between them. Shooting from cover, they managed to hold off the raiders for a little while. But it was nothing like an even fight. There were something like twenty mounted raiders, and they had gotten into a cache of pre-Collapse military weapons. So as soon as the bad guys figured out

145

what they were up against, they just rode in and overran the guards.

"But you can read about all that. I bet you have. I didn't see any of it. Our 8-plex was at the other end of the mine compound, near the stable, five hundred meters away. All I know is I heard shooting, and then a couple of minutes later, Dad ran in, wet and scared. We spent so much time in the hills that we kept daypacks packed and ready to go, always. He stuffed a hunk of bread into his, threw my winter outdoor gear at me, shoved the pack onto my back, and told me to run for it. Get to the stable, grab a horse, and go, he said. Take the Wall trail up, he said, then north by the back way to Tabernash, where I could use the shortwave to yell for help. Then he pretty much threw me out the door and ran off to find Mom and my brother, Goss.

"Last time I saw him. Or any of them.

"So I dashed to the stable and found nobody human around. Bart, my favorite gelding, was handy. I saddled and watered him, slung a feed bag on one side and Dad's daypack on the other, and trotted out into the snow. It was coming down pretty hard already. I could hear noise and confusion off toward the main gate, but I couldn't see a thing.

"About the geography. You've looked at the map, you say. The mine is at the head of a big cirque that opens to the east. That's how the raiders came in. Dad figured, I guess, that I would never make it out that way. To the west is a near-vertical cliff face most of a thousand meters high, with no practical way up. To the north, there is a long steep-sided ridge that looks awful, but there's a trail that runs up it, off to the northwest. It goes diagonally up the south-facing wall of the ridge, starting at about the east end of the compound. We couldn't get there either, but I guessed I could lead Bart straight up the south side of that ridge for a couple of hundred meters until we hit the trail. Shit. Steep, loose, snow-slippery, us more than half blind. Shouting and screaming and shooting behind us. As a climb, that was the worst part of the whole thing. Bart was an everlasting hero to make it up there. At least nobody came after us. Nobody knew we were there.

"I mounted up, and we spent the next couple of hours on that uphill trail. Mostly I could ride because Bart and I had done this trail several times before, and he knew it. But near the top, it steepened, and more and more, I was leading him. Then things started to level out, and we got into the wind and new snow drifts, and I lost the trail. We struggled along for a while, ended up on a shallow talus slope. You know talus? Freeze-thaw cycle busted rocks, right? All sizes, from grapefruits to pianos, all shapes, tangled up, all covered with shin-deep new snow.

"So Bart stepped on one of these flat rocks about the size of a coffee table, and it tipped, and his left rear leg slid off it into a hole, and he broke it. He *screamed*, Tree. I never knew a horse could make a noise like that. I sat in the snow for a while with his head in my lap. I comforted him the best I could. And then I got my jackknife out of my belly pouch, and we said goodbye, and I cut his throat.

"After that, it was just a long nightmare. The route goes up over the top of one mountain, then kind of rolls up and down along that ridge of yours, mostly being more talus with occasional stone outcrops but sometimes trickier footing. Then it goes over the top of *another* mountain, and finally it starts down. But it was all straight into the wind, and it was blowing a gale, and it was snowing and cold as hell. I had a headlamp, a compass, an altimeter, and a map. But using any of that stuff was murder because with gloves off, my hands kept freezing up. It got to the point it was nearly impossible even to hold the compass. I had bad shivering spells. But the only thing to do was line the compass needle on north and keep going. Try not to fall off either edge of the ridge. Sometime before dawn, I crested that second mountain, and things began to look up.

"By sunup, the snow had pretty well stopped, though the wind was still bad. I was supposedly following a trail from here on in, but I couldn't find it in the snow. But with map and compass, I could tell pretty well where it had to be. I trudged on down until, eventually, warming air and lowering elevation got me below snow line and I found it, only fifty meters off my track. From there, it was twelve klicks following the crest of my ridge line to a trail junction, counting on my high route to preserve me from having to cross flooded streams. And after that to an old bridge that had still been standing two years ago, the only other time I had been there, and then another ten klicks following the rail line to Tabernash.

"Only twenty-few klicks, mostly downhill, but I didn't make it before dark. I found a hollow protected from the wind, used stuff from Dad's pack to make a fire, and got warm for the first time that I could remember. I slept bad, got up early, and made it to the unmanned Tabernash railhead, weather station, and emergency shelter at dawn on the second day. The place was armored like a vault. But Dad had long ago made us memorize the door combo, so I got right in, turned on the lights and heat, drank a liter of water and started another one heating, and fired up the shortwave. The folks at the other end were shocked to hear that anything bad at all was happening at the Hendrikson mine."

# ALPINE RESCUE

Patri forced Lani to take a break by leaving the room. The wine was gone, so he walked down to the loo for glasses of water. When he returned, she looked at the stuff doubtfully.

"Vodka?" she asked. He shook his head. She sighed, took a gulp of water, and started right in again.

"I sat there in the shelter for three days, eating up the emergency supplies and sleeping. The weather was cold for the first day, then warmed up a lot. I could see that the snow was melting off the higher elevations. Once a day, I would get an update on the shortwave, so I wasn't surprised when a train rolled up late on the third day. It was a good-size expeditionary force: a platoon of Marines, lots of horses and tons of supplies, and three officers from twp EEE, as advisors and observers. One of that group was this lieutenant, Ryg McRae."

"Your uncle. The Chief."

"That was later, after his brother adopted me. But yeah." She had a sudden attack of the shakes, weathered it, started once more.

"The plan was simple. The Marines detached a sergeant and his squad to take the wagon road over the pass and down to the mine on the other side. Meantime the main force would retrace my route up to the head of the cirque. The two groups would communicate by radio. When both were in position, the squad would make a demonstration at the mine entrance, distracting the raiders while the main group came down that exposed trail and in the back door. They gave me a horse and took me along as a guide. Reluctantly. I mean, they were reluctant, not me. Everybody I knew in the world was over there at the mine.

"Of course, it didn't work. It was a major fuck-up, from the beginning. The Marines were fit and game, but they weren't acclimated. They felt fine at the start, but by the time we were climbing through three thousand meters, lots of 'em were in sorry shape. Also, the horses were suffering. You have to be careful with horses, going uphill at altitude. They'll go too fast, overheat, dehydrate, and then they're good for nothing. These Marines didn't know squat about that. Didn't help that the route was chosen to avoid running water. You ever try watering eighty horses in puddles of snowmelt? Don't.

"We bivouacked that night high on the mountain. That didn't go well either. It was cold and windy, there was no flat ground anywhere. The horses hated it. Nobody slept.

"Next morning, we got into the talus for sure. The kind of ground that killed my horse, Bart. Well, these ones didn't like it any better than Bart did. Before the morning was well started, the Marine lieutenant decided he had to detail some guys to lead the stock back to the railhead, and his Marines would have to hump the supplies (mostly ammo) themselves. This was slow and painful. By the time we got in position at the top of the cirque, just out of sight of the mine, there were two broken tibias, one smashed elbow, and lots of sprained ankles. And we were shy a bunch of ammo boxes that had gotten left along the route.

"The squad on the other side of the mine had it worse. The raiders were too smart. They put out pickets along the wagon road, way farther from the mine than expected. And when that squad of Marines showed up, the raiders let them in a ways and then ambushed them, cut them up bad. Worse, they figured immediately that this tiny attack had to be a feint. By then, they had found the trail up toward the cirque, so they had lots of time and motivation to get themselves dug in down at the bottom, where they could enfilade the last few hundred meters of trail.

"The only reason we didn't get wiped out coming down was that the other side's guns were centuries old, and so was their ammunition. Automatic weapons lose their charm when every clip contains four or five jams. In the end, it all came down to ammo. We didn't have enough, and theirs wouldn't shoot. The Marines got the job done, but the last part was ugly. Hand-to-hand. In the end, Marine casualties were more than fifty percent. The Marine lieutenant and the senior EEE guy both were killed, and the Chief was injured.

"All that led to the final act. There was a monster unused bunker at the east end of the compound, dating back to the Civil Wars. Before our attack, the raiders jammed all of the Moly twple in there with a big fucking load of explosives. Then the last surviving raiders locked themselves in, and tried to negotiate their escape, shouting through the door. Nobody knows what happened next, but for sure, the Marines were in no mood to negotiate. Maybe they tried shooting through the door, or maybe the raiders decided to blow themselves up out of simple spite. Either way, the charges went up, and the bunker roof fell in, and everybody inside died. Some on the outside, too."

Lani paused for a long time. She had told her story carefully and clearly, but now her voice broke up, and she stuttered and staggered to the end.

"I don't think the falling concrete hurt anybody; they were already dead from the overpressure. It would've been quick. And I'm still here, so the politicians can still brag that no twp has ever been wiped out, to the last man, by anything. When the shooting started, they stashed me behind an outcrop up the trail, looked after by a corporal with a busted ankle. He had orders to hogtie me if I tried to get away from him, and I did, and he did. So I didn't see much of anything. I heard and felt this deep CRUMP, and a few rocks shook loose and rattled downhill. And then nothing—just the wind in the crags."

# BAG OF SYMPTOMS

Patri and Lani sat for a long time, holding each other close while they both shuddered and wept and tried to absorb or evade Lani's story. Finally, they got out of bed and shuffled down the hall to wash up.

Back in Lani's room, Patri held her again and kissed the top of her head.

"I thought I knew you were super, but I really had no idea."

She shrugged away irritably. "It's something that happened to me. I had good clothes and a good horse, I could follow a compass. I didn't quit. And I was lucky. I don't walk on water, and I don't wear a cape. Don't make a hero of me. I'll disappoint you."

"Can't I approve of you?"

"It's not like that. You put me on a pedestal, I'll fall off it. I guarantee."

"Well, thanks for telling me about it, anyway. I know it was hard for you. I feel like…"

Lani was looking out the window, where the first gray hint of dawn was beginning to show, scowling. "'Thanks for sharing!'" she mimicked. "'I know it was hard!' Lay off, will you? Right now, I don't much care how you feel."

"I don't get it! I want to help. I know I can help. I mean, just your nightmares…"

"Oh, fuck!" Lani snapped. "Here we go. Back in therapy! First, it's the nightmares. Then the flashbacks. Then you'll want to help with my alcoholic self-medication. Then you'll start to worry about my 'inability to maintain long-term relationships', and you'll think I'm too high-maintenance, and you'll be out the door! You think you're so smart. I can read, you know. I know what's wrong with me, and why. Do you think that helps?"

"Lani, calm down."

"Nope. Nope. Not gonna." She grabbed Patri's clothes, folded with Navy neatness, from her desk and flung them at him. "I'm not gonna do this. Get dressed and get out. I'm not gonna be your bag of symptoms. We're done."

"Lani, please."

"No. Get lost. Go dress in the hall. You screw around for about ten more seconds and I'll lose my temper and start breaking your bones. Beat it!"

And that, she thought, was that.

# BARFLIES

Evar had finally accepted an invitation from Lani to go drinking somewhere out of the twp, where they could avoid interruptions. They picked *the Frost*, a pub that Eve liked for reasons Lani couldn't appreciate and Eve couldn't explain. The best that Lani could say for it was that it was quiet and uncrowded. These features largely followed from its others (no music, no dancing, dwarf menu of drinks that Lani suspected were watered) in a logical, almost mathematical way that Lani found appropriate but not endearing. It was run by a retired professor of literature, and its shingle carried the improbable tagline "Stopping by the Woods on a Snowy Evening."

Lani had a different view. *The Frost*, she thought, was the place where, when you had to go there, they had to take you in. Anyway, there they were, and they had things to talk about.

"You dumped Patri?" Eve started. "The hell were you thinking? From all I've heard, he's Mister Perfect."

This was the last place Lani wanted to go, but indeed, what the hell? She waded right in.

"Don't stand there waiting to be hit, I say. He was getting ready to drop me. I could feel it. Why should I go through that?"

"Drop you because he thinks you drink too much? Is he crazy?"

"No, no. That's only a symptom. Drop me because he thinks I'll get all needy on him. Because he thinks I've got trauma syndrome."

"Well, don't you?"

"Sure, of course. More. Survivor's guilt, big time. At least the shrink said so, and that far, I believe him. But so what? So does a third of the population."

"I didn't know the numbers were that high."

"Okay, I made that one up. But it's a lot. Old Hap, the Triple-E Tiger? He told me he still gets flashbacks. Been retired for twenty years."

"Okay, okay. Point is, romance isn't a fight. You adore this guy. Then feel it. Let yourself go a little. He wants to dump you because you're a lush, you can't stop him. But make it his move, not yours. Have some faith. Drink up. Cheers."

"Thanks, Auntie Eve. Just what I need. But I'm not taking him back."

"Okay. Your funeral. What's next? You said something about loose ends."

"No, really, Eve. Patri and I are finished."

"Fine. Loose ends? I'm on a schedule here. Let's hear about the girl detective."

Lani sighed, finished her drink, waved for another. One thing about the *Frost*; with no customers around, service was quick.

"I'm still waiting to hear back from Doc Yang. Meantime, there are unanswered questions; I'd like to work on some of those. Trouble is, most of them aren't actionable. By me, at this time, anyway."

"Enough preamble. Tell me your list."

"All right. First, there's Venna. What was she doing there, at the shop, out of uniform? And after closing time?"

Evar pursed her lips. "What's the state set? One: it's a coincidence. Two: she's a customer. Three: she's one of them. Four: she's undercover, pretending to be either two or three. I think that's it. Exhaustive and mutually exclusive. What's your problem?"

"I can't distinguish among them without tailing her."

"Probably not a good idea, huh?"

"No. She's smart and no-nonsense and cop-paranoid. She'd catch me at it and cut me off at the knees. Maybe literally. Unless you can help. You know, track where her decks go."

"Bah. Without her knowing? Forget it. People used to do that, some centuries ago, when they didn't have our safeguards and they did have positioning satellites. No more. What else you got?"

"Okay. First time you went looking for lock cam data, you were blocked. What was that about?"

"Oh, yeah. I forgot about that. Somebody had changed the permissions so only the Canal Authority could access it. I couldn't figure out who or when. I talked to the CA systems chief, and she fixed it, no sweat."

"Somebody from EEE involved, you think?"

"There's no way to know. But with all the other weird shit going on, I'd say yeah, probably. May mean somebody's hiding a bunch of smuggling. And no, I don't feel good about that. And I don't feel good about not feeling good. What have you gotten me into?"

"Never mind. And what about the boat itself? The *Eapy Fux*? Looks like they're using a boat with a ten-tonne capacity to move what? Fifty kilos of leather? That makes me wonder if they use all that tonnage for something more. Any ideas?"

"Nope. Don't see that I have any angles on that one."

"Me neither. I think the place to start with them is accounting. Not my line, but other folks in Triple-E may think it's fascinating. So let's put that one in the 'ancillary investigations' box and come back to it after we break the news about the cowhide."

"Huh," Evar grunted. "Getting to be an awful lot of 'we's and 'us's in these plans. The way I see it, this is mostly a 'you' thing."

Lani reached across the little bar table and tugged on Evar's cheek. "Silly old lady," she said. "We use the royal 'we.'"

"What else?"

"I have photos of about twenty likely customers. It would be good to ID them. Then we can ask them if they'd like to talk with us about what they know about the operation, and who got them interested, or would they rather have their taxes checked? I'd like to rope you in on that one, but I'm afraid it's mine from the get-go. For now, it goes in the 'ancillary investigations' pile as well."

"Is two a pile?

"Shut up. The next one is really, really mine. Fucking Bokun Yardley."

"Didn't you already..."

"I said, shut up. He claimed he was doing something undercover that night at the *Horse*. Was he? If so, what? Maybe I can find out. Maybe it's related."

"This is getting old. Are we almost done? I hear my mommy calling."

"Don't worry. I saved the best for last. And it's all yours."

"You gonna share? Or do I have to guess?"

"About the dead drop. To set that up, they must have a person in Quebec City. Or at least working for the newspaper. Those little pyramids of theirs must get dumped into the photos by somebody with access to the raw files, the ones that get uploaded to the Daily Drop. Who is this person, then? Can't be too many possibilities. And I bet he/she has friends. Who are *they*? And you, your very own self, you said that it was odd to use all that algorithmic setup for something as simple as a dead drop. Is Luv Dead Drop in Quebec City playing this game with other pictures too? Or is it only the one flagpole-sitter pointing to our leather shop?"

"Oh. Hmm. Hate to say it, but that does kind of sound like it's up my alley. Might even be fun. Okay, I'll look into it for you."

"For an antique, you're just the sweetest thing. Let me know if you get something."

"You say 'if' not 'when.' Humph. I'll show you. Now I really gotta go."

She stood up. "Hey, Wam! Check, please."

# BLUNT SABERS

Lunchtime, and members of the little sparring crowd were in the courtyard, putting on their gear—padded long-sleeved jackets, screened masks, and gloves. Today they were working with sabers, and supposedly with tournament rules. This bunch was too aggressive to be strongly bound by rules, however. The weather was cool, so the group was a little larger than usual. Among them, Lani noted with interest, was Bokun Yardley. No time like the present, she thought.

"Hey, Boke!" she shouted. "Let's fight!"

This put Bokun in a spot. He knew she outclassed him with a blade. But handed a public challenge, how could he refuse? He put a good face on it, though.

"You're on!" he shouted back. "Get ready to bleed!"

"Three hits," Lani said ritually; they would continue until one of them had scored three legal touches. 'Legal' in tournament saber meant contact with the blunt point or front edge of the sword or partway down the back, but only above the opponent's waist. Lani reflected with satisfaction that there was no referee to ding her for unsportsmanlike behavior, and no need for the contest ever to end, if the only hits were illegal ones. She could clobber Boke as long as she wanted to until she got answers.

They faced off and came *en garde,* but then, when they would normally have taken a short step back before beginning in earnest, she lunged forward and jabbed Bokun hard in the upper arm. "Hey!" he yelled in protest, retreating for three quick shuffling steps.

"One, nothing," Lani laughed as she closed the gap between them. "Legal. Just not…sporty." There was a line she liked from one of Patrick O'Brian's books about how the Spaniards were not actually shy (meaning cowardly), but they were never *ready.* That described Bokun all too well.

"Hey, Boke! You look good in braid and epaulets. Let's see more of that."

"You bitch!" he snarled, and went for her.

They executed three quick phrases, feint, riposte, beat and attack, with no bodily contact made. But if Bokun had been paying attention, he would know that, with real weapons, if Lani had wanted, he would now be missing an ear, a kidney, and the tendons inside his right wrist.

"No joke," she said. "Must have been a shapely filly for you to spend money like that." She got inside his guard and caught him with an illegal fist swipe that knocked his mask awry. He jerked it back in place with his free hand.

"You keep quiet about that," he hissed.

Lani fell back and switched to pure defense, making sure he didn't get past her guard but not attacking. "What's that?" she shouted. "Can't hear you through the mask!"

"You keep quiet…Hey!" he started, but before he finished, she had rushed him, gone to full extension as he retreated, and whacked him across the shin.

"Illegal! Nothing done," she sang as she resumed her defensive fencing. "No, I want to talk about it. That whole night was an offense against Equality. And women. What's your excuse?"

"I told you! I was working!"

"A lie." She parried his head-cut in fifth, followed his blade down toward the ground, and then diverted to poke him in the kneecap, which must have hurt like hell. "You were out on your own, and now you're fibbing about it. Nothing done."

"Why, you…" She followed up one of his ill-advised lunges with a bruising slice that in a real fight would have taken off half his right buttock.

"Nothing done. That's crimes against Equality and Evidence, both." She reached in and stuck him again in the same kneecap. "Nothing done. You know what I think?"

"I don't care what you think, you crazy…Yow!" She had faked him with an apparent opening, got close enough to bind him up. Then in separating, she hit him on top of his mask with the middle of her blade, hard enough that the point flexed around and stung him on the back.

"Two, zero! I think it's camouflage. I think you and some rich dudes…" She baffled him with a high-line feint and then spanked him across the thigh. "…are working a scam on the Environment."

"Lani, I'm warning…"

"Let's even this up, huh?" She backed quickly and shifted her blade to her left hand. When he closed to take advantage, she ticked his blade aside and smacked him across the chest, backhand but hard, with the flat of her own.

"Nothing done! You want to…" She did it to him again. It was sort of sad to see how she could fool him all day long.

"…use your position in Triple-E…" And she did it again.

"…to deflect suspicion while you corner the market in genetically modified…" and suddenly, his defense dissolved, and he dropped his guard completely. She made a long lunge that took him in the middle of the chest, bending her blade in a huge arc and almost knocking him over. If it had been a real sword, it would have gone right through him.

"…goat bladders! Or some shit," she said. "That's three."

They stood for a moment, glaring at each other through their masks. Then Bokun took a roundhouse swing at her. Even with a blunt, lightweight tournament saber, it might have taken her head off, except that he had telegraphed the move far in advance. Almost absent-mindedly, she ducked and deflected his blow so it went over her head, and turned to other business.

# ON THE CARPET

Lani had barely reached her desk the next day when she got a ping from Venna Keithley. No video, no voice, just a summons. "Pls meet me my office asap." She reflected that, as messages went, it was not as rude as possible. After all, Venna didn't have to say "please," and she was kind enough to include the trailing full stop; that conveyed completeness. She toyed with the idea of delaying, since she didn't work for Venna, but could see no advantage. So she went.

Keithley's office was bigger than a coat closet, but not much. She waved Lani into the only other chair, closed the door with a flip of her foot, then made Lani wait for five minutes while she signed off on a stack of expense claims. When she was done, she didn't even look up before asking, "What are you up to, Lani?"

"Just the usual, luv."

"No. No, I don't think so. You're playing some game. What is it?"

"Nothing, luv. What's bothering you?"

"You, Lani. You're bothering me. You've been absent. Dragging around like a sick cat. Starting fights in that noontime tea party of yours."

"It's a sparring group, luv. Starting fights is the point."

"Did you just talk back to me?" Keithley was leaning forward with both fists on her desk.

This was starting to get serious. "No, luv," Lani said.

"Bokun Yardley says you assaulted him yesterday. Showed me bruises. What do you say about that?"

"We were sparring with sabers, luv. Sometimes you get in odd positions, and your blade doesn't go quite where you intended."

"Pigshit, Maxwell. You haven't missed with a sword since you had your first period. You hurt him on purpose. Assaulting a superior is a serious breach. Why'd you do it?"

Lani briefly considered telling some version of the truth, but it wasn't safe. Deny, deny, she decided. "No, luv," she said. "It wasn't intentional. I'm sorry if Boke is sore."

Keithley snorted. "If I decide you're shucking me, you could be looking for another twp tomorrow. Or something worse could happen."

"Yes, luv."

"Luv Yardley also says you insulted him. Said he was trying to start a monopoly in…" she consulted a form of some sort, "…genetically modified goat bladders. What was that about?" She put down the paper and slowly pulled back into her chair. Lani thought she looked like a moray eel shrinking into its crack in the rock. Not less threatening. Just less visible.

"Standard dueling doctrine, luv. Anger and distract the other fellow. Interfere with his judgment."

"Yes, but 'genetically modified goat bladders'? That's weirdly specific, Maxwell. What made you say that?"

"First disgusting thing that came to mind, luv."

"Thinking about goats lately, luv?" Keithley asked, peering intently at Lani.

"No, luv," said Lani. She was concentrating on her morning's breakfast, trying not to think about Teti Yang and her blackbucks born of goat surrogate mothers. It had been oatmeal. With…oops…goat's milk.

"You think there's something funny here, Maxwell?"

Lani snapped back to the moment. "No, luv."

"I hope not." Keithley shuffled papers for a moment. "I heard you were seen dancing at the *Open Horse* bar a few weeks ago. Is that true?"

"Yes, luv."

"That place is a disgrace. You have to be a compulsive propertarian even to get in the door. It says here you were wearing a revealing red dress that night. Very expensive. We in the Union don't get paid that well. We in EEE certainly don't. Where did you get the dress, Maxwell?"

Lani didn't have to think twice about not dragging Evar into this mess. "Theater company downtown, luv," she said. "Cast-off. Pulled out of a trash bin."

"Hmph. All right. But I don't want to hear about you gallivanting around that place again. Right, Maxwell? Right."

She leaned back in her chair and considered Lani with a hostile stare. "When does the panel meet to consider restoring your full status, Maxwell?"

Lani suppressed the urge to tell her, "one hundred thirteen days!" Instead, managed a respectful "About three months, luv."

"Well, if they met today, you would be in a great deal of trouble. Henceforth, Maxwell, I expect your behavior to be impeccable. You understand me? No beating up fellow twple. No late-night drunken forays to the University. No salacious dancing at establishments whose very existence is a crime against Equality. You get my meaning?"

"Yes, luv."

"Good. Then get out."

# POLONIUS

The Chief walked into a passion-fruit-scented birthday party early in Lani's work session the next day. But then, the EEE offices always smelled like passion fruit. Union gardeners had an informal rule, "don't plant anything you can't eat," so decades earlier, the twp groundskeepers had started passion fruit all around the building, and the vines had owned the exterior ever since. On this day, the office where Lani sat was celebrating Gido Watanabe's twentieth by easing through the open windows to harvest ripe fruit by way of various athletic stunts, some involving technical climbing gear.

The Chief took all this in good humor. He congratulated Gido and accepted a spoon and a fruit, and ate it, seeds and all, in the approved fashion. Then, in his genial way, he suggested to Lani that they take a walk. She suppressed a grimace and agreed. She feared another reprimand and would much rather have stayed at the party.

"What's up?" she asked as soon as they reached the street.

"Patience," the Chief said. "Let's walk a bit."

So walk they did, around the corner and down the street for three whole blocks, before the Chief finally pulled up at an unoccupied pocket park and chose a bench. Lani sat beside him. They admired the dry streamed that seemed to be the park's only reason for existence, and Lani visibly exercised patience.

"Well," the Chief said after a time. "How would you like to go back to work?"

"Huh?" said Lani. "What the hell?"

"Problem?"

"I mean, do you and your deputy ever talk? She grilled me just yesterday. *Hard.* Made it clear that if she had her way, she'd hang me from the yardarm."

"Oh, Venna's a little upset. She'll get over it. Bokun is sort of her protege, and she doesn't like seeing him humiliated. Good experience for him, I say, and overdue. The kid's a little full of himself. Next time, though, check with me before you beat up one of my guys. Could be I can suggest a better way. Okay?"

"Uh, sure. Okay. But about…"

"Going back to work. Yeah, I meant that. We're overstretched with this missing cops thing. That one's a stinker. Keep this to yourself, but we've got bodies now. Two, anyway. Both from around here. Both execution-style. Thing is, when somebody starts killing cops, not in the heat of action, the victims are nearly always dirty. They deserve it. These missing folks, there's a handful of them. Mostly from the Trenton vicinity, but some from far away. Means I don't know who I can trust anymore. And that's why I need you.

"I think I can persuade the mayor to let me put you back on light duty, under close supervision. She'll see it as in the twp's interest. Sort of ease you back into working status until your probation is up. You'd have to work for me, though. As part of my team. That includes Venna and Bokun. And you have to keep your nose clean. Are you up to that?"

Lani thought about it. "Yeah. I guess so. If Venna and Bokun do their bit."

"I can promise that. But I need better than an 'I guess so' from you. If we're going to do this, I need a commitment. Are you in or not?"

Lani started to answer, but the Chief talked over her. "Not yet," he said. "I need you to understand some things. I need to lecture a little. Can you hold still for that?"

Lani nodded.

"Okay. Here's the thing. It's all about loyalty. Way back through history, successful societies have depended on loyalty to hold together and get things done. Ours is no different. But loyalty to what, exactly? You can be loyal to yourself, your family, your twp, your nation, your principles. You're lucky, Lani. You're young, and though you've seen a lot, you have never really had to make an important choice between conflicting loyalties. So far, the right thing for you and your twp and your country have always been aligned, so you've jumped in and done what was necessary, even if it was hard. Right?"

Lani nodded again.

"Well, it's not always that way. Pretty soon, you'll find yourself in situations where it's not so simple. And when that happens, you want to know who's got the first call on your loyalty. When you're working in a small team, like my gang, then your team members need to know that, too. There will be times when they are laying their careers and even their lives on the line, with the outcome depending on what you choose to do. They need to be confident that you'll do the right thing. I've had people let me down that way. Once or twice, not very often. I believed in them completely, was sure that I had their personal loyalty, right down the line. And then they turned on me. When that happens, you can be sure, even if it doesn't kill you, it leaves a scar. One you'll remember. You understand?"

"Yes, Chief. I think so."

But maybe she didn't. She could not imagine being on the wrong side of her uncle. But Bokun and Venna? Yes, that could happen. Could she back the Chief but not his team? Was that choice open? Who had ever dumped the Chief for some other cause, and when, and why?

"But Chief…" she said, "Do you mind if I ask you about your own loyalties? How *you* order them?"

The Chief nodded slowly and rubbed his beard. "Good question. Me, I start with old, old advice. 'This above all: to thine own self be true.' Take care of yourself, and then, if you're lucky, you can help others."

Lani grunted. "Polonius. That tedious old bore."

The Chief grinned at her. "Let's go easy on tedious old bores. I might take offense. Besides, poor Polonius. His advice was trite but mostly pretty good.

I'm not asking you to sacrifice yourself for anything. I would never do that. But if it comes to team versus twp, or team versus Council, I want you with the team. No hesitation."

They sat for a while, thinking. At last, the Chief stirred. "There's a question on the floor. Are you in or not?"

She was still unsure. It bothered her that the Chief really thought that Polonius was saying, "look out for yourself first" and not "be honest with yourself." The second reading was a foundational Union ideal; the first was anything but. She and the Chief would have to have a long talk about that. But some other time, not now. For now, this looked like one of those occasions she had heard about, when the only way forward was right through the messy middle. The folklore here was clear. Jump in, it said. Commit. Get married, or whatever. Fall in love later, if you can.

She nodded with a soft smile. "In, of course, Chief. All I ever wanted."

"Wonderful. You won't be offended if we don't always play exactly by the rules?"

"I can handle that. When do I start?"

"Tomorrow morning. Eight o'clock, fourth-floor conference room. There's something interesting going on; we'll bring you up to date."

# THE CHIEF'S TEAM

The dull and lumpish architecture of the EEE headquarters building was surmounted by the sixth-floor walkway, open to the air and cantilevered over the surrounding streets like the brim of an upended hat. Lani leaned on the railing facing into a stiff breeze and considered the weather, which was turning dirty. Since she was early for the 08:00 meeting and didn't want to appear over-eager, the walkway seemed a good place to kill ten minutes and gather her thoughts. Mostly she thought that, for a desert town, it sure rained a lot in Trenton. She had been told the desert part was all about the balance between rainfall, runoff, and evapotranspiration. Maybe so. But she suspected this explanation was successful at least partly, as Luv Nematode said, because policymakers loved polysyllables. As the first spatters of rain arrived from the incoming storm, she headed downstairs.

The conference room was made for privacy: a windowless internal space with the usual sound and image-display hardware. It had seating for about twenty, but as they filtered in carrying daybooks and coffee cups, the Chief's team came nowhere near filling it. She knew everybody by sight, of course, but EEE was a populous enough twp that she had never had real conversations with half of them. In the front row were Venna and the Chief, then Quan Heinz, Bokun Yardley, and Kero Sandoval, and finally, in the third row, with Lani, Yeg

Coulter. Yeg was the only one with a memorable appearance: squat, shaved head, built like a rock. The Chief must have warned the team that Lani would be joining, since nobody made any suggestion that she didn't belong there.

At 08:00 sharp, the Chief stood up and made it official: "Everybody, you know Lani. She'll be with us from now on. Please make her welcome." And that was that. Then, "Venna, your meeting."

"Listen up, everybody," Venna said. "We have a new one here, on a short fuse." She fiddled with her deck for a moment, and an image appeared on the screen behind her. It was the front door of Lani's favorite leather shop, in the warehouse district. Lani stiffened but kept her expression bland and her mouth shut, wondering what other surprises the day had to offer.

# RIDDLES IN THE DARK

*T*he *Frost's* margaritas were not bad, though sooner or later, the pub was going to run out of ice. The power had failed and the place went dark even before Lani and Evar got their first round of drinks. But Wam, the proprietor, handled the situation with aplomb and with candles in tall glass chimneys, so when he produced the margs, they could tell what they were drinking. The approaching weather that Lani had watched two days earlier had taken its time winding up into a full-on nor'easter, but wind up it did. Now the walls rattled and the gutters hissed with rushing water as the storm got down to business.

"And us a couple of klicks from home," Evar complained. "No way to get back without getting soaked."

"You're soaked already," Lani pointed out. It was true. Eve looked like a water rat at work, and worse, her eyes were dull and her features sagged. In fact, she looked like hell. Lani told her so and asked, "What's the problem?"

"Two days of no sleep is the problem. The Forensic Accounting group brought a fancy new system online on Monday, and it's been 'Eve, we got troubles' every minute since then. Finally starting to calm down, but shit! What a pain."

"Well. I was hoping you'd help me to think some things through, but if you're too fried…"

"No, if I can troubleshoot for F.A., I can do it for you. What's up? Just make it interesting."

"Well, it's interesting. But it sucks. First, like I told you, the Chief came and pulled me off feather-counting and put me to work in his team. So that's great, I guess. But first thing that happens is my great solo nab-a-bad-guy project goes straight down the shithole. I've been scooped. They're all over it. Already."

"Do they know you were working on it?"

"So far as I can tell, no. So that's something, anyway. But about the general layout, they know pretty near everything I do. They know about the cowhide claims, they know about the sales, they know about the dead drop. I don't think they know how the stuff gets delivered to the store, but that's pretty much my only head start."

"So they've been scouting the place since sometime after the last sale?"

"Uh-huh."

"So if it was *just* after, that could explain Venna showing up too late to shop."

"Yeah, I thought of that. But there are some other things. Weird things. Have you been watching the dead drop? Turns out there's another sale on, announced this morning. Starts at 09:00 day after tomorrow and runs only until sixteen hundred the same day. Now we're planning to raid the place that day."

"The team starts up on this investigation on Tuesday, and the dead drop triggers on Wednesday for a sale on Friday? Isn't that mighty convenient? I mean, fits in the work week and everything."

"Yes. Smells bad, doesn't it? I mean, I had to wait weeks for a sale after I knew what was going on."

"Reminds me, I forgot to mention. One thing I did do, before the F.A. shit hit the fan, was search the Daily Drops to see when sales were announced. Turns out there have been five all told, six if you count the new one, going back to July last year, and up 'til now, there's never been less than six weeks between them. Usually seven or eight. This time it's what? Three and a half? Four? This one's different."

"Yep. Yep, I think so. What's new with the *Eapy Fux*?"

"Nothing. Far as I know, she's still piddling around Lake Champlain. I've been busy, not dead. If any of those alarms had gone off, I would've noticed." She waved her empty glass. "Refill?"

"*Ja,* you betcha. My treat. Wam!"

They sat silent while they waited for their drinks, thinking and listening to the storm. It had gotten worse, with thunder and lightning. The thunderclaps sounded like mostly cloud-to-cloud, so walking home wouldn't be too risky. But still. Each year, a lot of Union luvs got killed by lightning.

When Wam brought the drinks, Evar raised her glass. "To private enterprise," she said. "May it wax greedy and sneaky, so EEE has something to do. Cheers."

"Not sure I want to drink to that. Except tonight, I'll drink to anything."

"Good for you. Here's what I think. I think we know one thing for sure. Your busted lock spooked them. They know somebody is watching, but there's been no follow-up. So they're gonna do one more sale, as fast as they can get some inventory here, and then shut down and go someplace else. Make sense?"

"Sure does. I was thinking along those lines myself."

"Okay then, what we don't know. I don't like the way you've been dragged into this at the last minute. It makes me wonder things that I don't like to wonder. I think you can ask the question lots of different ways, but what it comes down to is the Chief's team: are they them, or are they us? Seems to me there just about has to be a connection between your uncle's team and the people running this skin show. But who is giving orders, and who is taking them?"

"I see what you're getting at, I think, but I don't like it at all. I can't believe the Chief would be mixed up in something like that."

"Doesn't have to be him. Could be anybody on the team. How about your girlfriend Venna?"

"May she rot. But not this way."

"Or Bokun the bodacious?"

"Him, too."

"You saw him at the whatsis. The *Clothes Horse.*"

"*Open Horse.* Sure. But that's not a tight link. I went there and got into this.

Who knows what he was getting into? Don't tell me there's only one scam at a time being worked in that place." Lani thought for a moment. "On the other hand…"

"Yes?"

"On the other hand, when I was beating Boke up with that saber, he hung in there and took it. Until I mentioned genetic engineering. Then he lost all his starch. Makes me think he knows something."

"Sounds to me like he's gone bad."

"Hell and damn."

"What's the matter? Besides the obvious, I mean."

"Something the Chief said. About how when somebody starts killing police, it's usually because the cops are corrupt."

"Wait. You mean your little leather business might be tied up with those missing cops? I don't get it. Vanished cops are corrupt. Bokun is corrupt. Therefore Bokun is vanishing them? Not much of a syllogism, kid."

"I know. It's a dumb idea, anyhow. Today's rumor is that most of those missing folks have spotless records. Now people think whoever did them must be psycho—it's a nut case. Nothing like the leather job, which seems to be all about money."

"Yeah. Well. Let's not make things more complicated than they need to be. Leave the MOI out of it. Think about it this way. If Triple-E is clean as can be and the buzzards are looking for one last meal on the train tracks, then they'll be doing just what I said. Then whoever you grab in your raid may be your ticket to the real boss. But if Triple-E is dirty, if somebody on your team's involved, then they'll do more, to throw the honest cops off the track. I don't know what. But you won't be able to trust anything that comes out of the raid; any or all of it could be a plant."

"How would we know?"

"Beats me. I suppose that if the whole thing is some little local entrepreneurial job, then Triple-E is probably clean. But if it links to some wider organization, well, the bigger the outfit, the more likely it is that one of ours is really one of theirs."

"Hmm. Okay. Moving on: weren't you gonna look into whether they're using their pyramid thing in other places?"

"Shit. Yes, I was. I guess I need to get back to work." Evar stared out the window at the dark, flooded street. Exhaustion etched her face. "Fuck," she said. "Look at it come down."

# TEAM SPORT

Following the pattern of most nor'easters, the weather had cleared magically after the peak of the storm. On the morning of the sale, Lani and the rest of the team were out early, enjoying bright sunshine and industriously transferring travel-stained but empty crates among three horse carts and two nearby warehouses that the Chief had rented for the occasion.

At 09:00, on schedule, somebody inside the shop removed the pen-scratched "CLOSED" sign from the front door and replaced it with one reading "WELCOME." Less than two minutes later, the first customer went in, evidently in a hurry. She was gone five minutes later, clutching a paper-wrapped parcel. After that, there was a brief wait, and then a steady stream of people began to cycle through the place.

Cameras placed here and there on both the front and back sides of the building made high-rez video/sound recordings of the whole event. At 09:36 (never do anything on the even quarter-hour), the team moved in. Yeg and Kero walked in the front door while Lani stood guard outside; Venna and Quan broke in the back, with Bokun on guard. The Chief stood on a rooftop across the street, watching the whole scene live and by video link, and giving instructions over their headsets. Another half-dozen plain-clothes investigators blended with the street crowd, ready to join in if there were runners or some kind of melee. Only Venna and Yeg were armed, with official swords they buckled on at the last minute and Walthers with safeties on. There had been some discussion about having Kero take the weapons instead of Yeg, since she was acknowledged to be a better shot. But she was a skinny, small-boned bleached blonde, and the Chief feared that, if it came to trouble, she might actually have to *use* her pistol. This wasn't such a risk with Yeg, who could intimidate with or without weapons.

To Lani, all of this seemed out of proportion. After all, this was supposedly a minor fraud sting, not a late-night attack on a gang of armed hijackers. It was all very well as practice for something more exciting, but nobody expected anything resembling drama. So she too was surprised when they got some, even if it was pointless and banal.

When Yeg and Kero went in the front door, there were three customers in the place. After a couple of minutes, one of them panicked and made a dash for daylight, going out the way he had gone in. He found Lani blocking his way. He was a beefy guy, and if he had just put his head down and blown right over her, he might have made it off the sidewalk and into the street. But his adrenaline was up, and, with unfortunate judgment, he took a swing at her. His left jab, energetic but (she thought) untrained, caught nothing but air. So she showed him a trained one, terminating on his nose. About half power, since she didn't want to break fingers. His head snapped back while his body continued forward until he ran right out from under himself and crashed hard on his back. By the time he sat up, feebly dabbing his face, he was surrounded by street cops who zipped up his hands and feet and propped him against the front wall, looking abashed, with his nose bleeding down the front of his shirt.

"Nice footwork, Lani," the Chief said over her earbuds.

Lani felt pretty good. She had been wanting to knock somebody down for quite a while.

# RAID REFLECTIONS

After the raid proper, there was a surprising amount of follow-up to do: photographing, measuring, mapping, collecting, indexing, packing, and interviewing. First, the lab crew came in to fingerprint and otherwise try to determine how many people and which ones had been using the warehouse spaces, and then the team got their turn with the other chores. All to make sure that when they walked the evidence into a judge's office, they would have answers to any questions that were answerable. These tasks took the rest of the day for everybody. Lani was hoping to sit in on the interviews, but the Chief and Venna kept those for themselves. Despite the general monotony of the jobs, Lani came away with a list of observations that she deemed useful or curious, the details and implications of which kept her awake for hours. None of these items went into her official, newly issued, voice-transcription daybook.

She itemized them in no particular order:

About two-thirds of the junk that had been on the shelves in the outer shop was missing. Some of what she remembered was still there (the horrible bunny slippers, for instance), but most of it was gone, and the rest rearranged to make the shelves look full.

The clerk they arrested for operating the place was not the skinny, vest-wearing, well-spoken luv who had greeted Lani. Rather, he was surly and nondescriptly square, with a beard and a receding hairline. He could not possibly be mistaken for his predecessor.

Between the shop with its counter in front and the warehouse/workshop in back, there was a little living space with two cots, a hotplate, and a walled-off toilet in one corner. The team had spent a while looking at the floorplan that was on file with the city, and it contained no such room. It did show the toilet hookup but placed it in the warehouse area. Lani was glad she had resisted the urge to explore the night she broke in; she would have awakened some opposition, for sure.

Also not shown on the city plans was a door connecting this tiny living space with the main warehouse that took up the largest part of the building. This looked like relatively new construction. The lab techs said there was evidence of recent traffic through that door. This meant that people could, and probably did, come and go from the shop without using either the nominal front or back doors. Lani's photography and in-person surveillance would not have shown any of that. The big warehouse space accessed through the door was empty, but it didn't look or smell as though it had been sitting vacant for very long. Bokun was assigned the job of finding out if it was currently rented, to whom, and for how long.

They found no packing material of any kind in the workspace in back.

A cash box under the counter contained a large but not extraordinary amount of currency. There was not a charge slip, receipt, letter, or other document anywhere in the place.

The pricey goods in the back were neatly shelved and labeled with product numbers, presumably keyed to the inventory on the clerk's deck. There were a little over a dozen items there, mostly boots, belts, and waist packs. They came in a variety of colors and textures, none as finely made nor a close color match to the smooth, light-coffee-hued boots Lani had seen, nor to Muam's handbag.

There would be more to say in the coming days after the experts (maybe including Evar) had made a run at the clerk's deck and after the interviews had been processed and the obvious lies identified. But from what Lani had seen, she had to conclude that the bad guys were way ahead of them. They had fully expected to be raided, had left nothing and nobody incriminating in the shop, and had presumably strewn their path with false leads and traps for the unwary. And from the timeline of events, it still seemed probable that somebody on the team was playing both sides. Worse than that, Lani couldn't shake the suspicion that the real purpose of the raid was to allow the leather-shop gang to go away and play dead, so they could lose the other (imaginary, but they didn't know that) investigation implied by her busted padlock. Maybe even to set her up, the new kid, to take the rap for something.

She recognized the feeling in her stomach. It was how she felt after peeling off during a difficult climbing move, in the fractional second of free fall, waiting for the rope to catch her. Only this time, she might be climbing free. This time there might be no rope.

# MISSED MESSAGES

Sleeping was always a problem for Lani. At the best of times, she slept five hours a night; when her nightmares were acting up, she did with three or less. In truth, she was unsure of the numbers; she felt that she spent a lot of time lying in bed, semiconscious, wondering if she was awake. The adventure in Ohio had added a new subject for her killer dreams. Normally she would have applauded the variety, but in this case, it was clearly a Bad Thing. Each of her life's disasters seemed to require its own ration of terrifyingly disrupted sleep, and if she had to live through many more tragic incidents, she would have to subsist on twenty-minute catnaps forever.

That brought her to the question of why she was, once again, awake at 03:30. The offending dream had not been frightening in the same way as her Hendrikson and Ohio standard nightmares. Rather, it had brought a prickly, creeping dread to mundane events involving people she didn't recognize but whose names she felt she ought to know. By now, she knew anxiety dreams when she had them, and for a time, she lay in the dark, berating her subconscious. "Enough with the terrorism," she complained softly, to avoid waking her neighbors. "Get to the point. Why don't you do me some *good*, for once?" But as usual, her subconscious was not interested in rational discussion and gave no answers. She sighed and turned on the light.

She got up, went down the hall to the loo, and got a cup of hot water for tea. Back in her room, she settled at her desk and flipped her deck open. The first thing she saw was a video post from Evar, marked urgent. It was time-tagged about an hour before, when Lani had been in bed, arguing with herself about whether she was asleep.

Evar's image looked even more haggard than she had been at the *Frost*, if that were possible. She gestured vaguely at the camera. "Answer to your question," she said. "Yes. Lots. Job's running. Take a few hours. Know more when done. Gotta sleep. Come see me tonight. Details." Then her expression firmed up a bit while she added, "Don't you *dare* wake me before twenty hours." And she signed off.

If Lani understood this properly, Evar was trying to say that there were many deep pyramids encoded in the Daily Drop, not just the one they already knew about. But even that could mean anything. And to learn what it really meant, she would have to wait sixteen hours. Well, damn.

One cornerstone of Lani's philosophy was that whatever your ailments— physical, mental, emotional, or moral—their state could be improved by a good stiff morning workout. So she put on her running gear and killed time reading the Trenton news until it was time to start her daily regimen. The *Inquirer's* front page was all politics, with the Chips claque being accused by both the Birds and the Greens of "...advancing policies that will lead us straight back to pre-Collapse chaos!" She dismissed this as hyperbole but also dismissed the whole political enterprise as being of no pressing interest. In a sense, for her, this was true. Twp EEE was special, in that it was effectively an organ of the Union's central government. Therefore, while EEE's twple elected a local rep, as every twp did, whenever reps gathered to vote on anything, the one from EEE could attend and listen and speak, but not vote. Twp EEE was charged with enforcing rules that applied between other twps; it did not have a say in deciding what those rules were. All to say that Lani justified her disinterest in national politics mostly on grounds of practicality. She could see how it might be a fun game to watch, but there was nothing whatever she could do about it. And she had her own pressing problems. Consequently, when she read the

*Inquirer*, it was usually for news of the sports clubs. On this day, she learned that the soccer team she sometimes played for had lost a close one. Big deal.

When Lani got to the starting point of her morning run, she found the Chief's entire team, including even Venna Keithley and the Chief himself, standing there waiting for her. Her brutal workouts sometimes spawned envious gossip within the twp, and her new team had turned out to experience one with her. She was touched by this physical expression of solidarity; it gave her a warm feeling that lasted halfway through the running course she chose that morning. But as she trotted along at well below her normal pace—to avoid embarrassing the less fit—she felt, increasingly, that this intense team spirit came at a cost. That cost wasn't only to do with her physical conditioning and privacy but also with her independence and sense of self. It might even have to do with her recent, subtly poisonous dreams. Venna, surely, hated her guts. Wasn't this public display of her affection really just grudging submission to the Chief's wishes? Could she trust any of these twple?

The rest of the day was routine until the early afternoon when, depending on the day of the week, she would either go to math class at the Uni or retreat to her room to do homework. This was a homework day. On her way into the dorm, she checked her mailbox and found a delivered stamp affixed to a very small package. Mailed packages were unusual. In her room, she quickly found that the attached stamp was null, containing only routing information. In the package was, of all things, a modest sum in Union currency and a handwritten note from Teti Yang. It read:

> *Dear Lani,*
> *Please come see me at the farm any night this week at about 19:00.*
> *Our conversation may take an hour or so.*
> *I enclose cash for stable fees since no one can meet you at that time.*
> *Best wishes, Teti*

"Well, well," Lani said to herself. "Another news break. It never rains, but it pours."

# PYRAMID SCHEMES

Knocking on Evar's door proved challenging since Lani was balancing a flask of brandy and two heavy stoneware tankards of coffee straight from the twp kitchen. But she managed.

Eve answered, wearing sloppy pajamas that Lani had never seen, and wrapped head to knees in a voluminous blanket. Since the temperature outside was all of twenty-two degrees, Lani didn't get the point of all Eve's layers, but she didn't press the matter. She had other things on her mind.

"Son of a bitch," Eve said. "I really am getting old. When I was your age…"

"Back when mammoths roamed the Earth?"

"… four back-to-back all-nighters would have been a piece of cake. Look at me now. A wreck. Well, come on in."

Lani poured a guzzle of brandy into both their mugs, and they sat down in front of Eve's huge screen. Eve sipped her coffee, nodded approvingly, put her mug down, and began to type.

"You wanted to know if there's more in the Daily Drop than meets the eye. Well, once I thought about it for a minute, I saw that it's easy to find out. The thing about old, abandoned file formats is that nobody uses them. Except, of course, for legacy stuff that dates back a hundred years or so, when the OS was young. But there's not much of that in the Drop since the contents are news, more or less by definition. But in that case, all you have to do is go look at the metadata and find files that are typed for pyramid access and—if you're really obsessive—that are less than, let's say, a year old. Then if you find such a thing, the metadata again will tell you where in the image the deep stuff is hidden. So much for zoom-zoom-zooming every picture on the Drop. You with me?"

"I think so. You found some more, didn't you?"

"Yes, kid. I found some more. Lots. Four in the Quebec City paper...."

"Crap. That many?"

"...and a hundred sixty-two in five other periodicals. Mostly weeklies. Since those don't all come out on the same day of the week, if I look through all the last week's Drops, I bet I'll turn up five hundred more."

Lani shook her head. "You wouldn't kid me?"

"Not about this."

"What in the bleeding hell is going on? Tell me they aren't all advertising doll clothes."

"Nope. Very few. There are, I think, three others that are variants on the doll clothes theme. Then there are thirty-two that look more or less like this." She put on the screen a page of gobbledygook, chunked into blocks of varying length.

"Encrypted. No chance of reading any of this stuff unless you can get somebody to spill the keys. But my guess is they are more sensitive versions of ones like this." And she put up another page of text, which seemed to be one paragraph after another of sour, deprecating comments about the world at large. Most made some attempt at humor, but rarely with any success. Lame, sad stuff, each entry signed with an alias. Wubba-Dub, Pathfinder, Sparkles, Acondy, Green-Mountain-Hopper, Tack.

"There are about twenty of these," Eve said. "I think it's pretty clear that these two bunches are all about reproducing what they can of electronic bulletin boards from the early days of social media. And then, by a wide margin, the most common group, a hundred or more, are this sort of thing."

Her next page was a wide, pinpoint-sharp, and highly colorful photo of a huge banquet spread out on a dark wood table. Olives, white bread, little sausages, potatoes done three different ways, carrots, broccoli, green beans, corn, two salads, one with fruit, two gravy boats, butter, jam, and what looked like mustard sauce. And in the center, lord of the table, sat a six-kilo roast of what had to be beef, sliced and glistening. Under the picture was a caption in big red type. It said, "Beef. It's Who We Are."

"Come on," Lani said. "You have to be kidding."

"'Fraid not. Try this." It was a twilight patio scene. In the middle background, a multi-story house made mostly of glass, every room lighted to show tastefully scattered bits of eye-catching furniture, art on the walls, and not a bedroom, loo, or laundry chute in view. On the patio, three gorgeous couples were heavily engaged in making eye contact, displaying soft leather shoes, the women showing soft breasts and thighs. They were thoroughly absorbed, enjoying their white wine, crackers, and cheese while laughing with pure joy at each other's witty repartee. The sure implication was that, ten minutes after dessert, all six would be banging their brains out. The caption was on top this time, in a warm, sunset orange: "Because You Deserve It."

"Haven't we been taught to recognize and despise this sort of thing?"

"Oh, yeah," Eve said. "The worst, sneakiest form of advertising."

"Then how come it works so well?"

"I guess that's the point. What they taught me at school, anyway. Messing with people's primal urges like this, you're playing with dynamite. Anyway, I searched the main archives for a sample of these images. Far as I can tell, these are all, or almost all, shots from consumer magazines from the Crazy Years. In context, all of them were ads for specific products. This one, believe it or not, is selling those shoes."

"Coulda fooled me. But what's the game, then? Why go to all this trouble?"

"Beats me. This is propaganda, and it's subtle stuff. I'm out of my depth; we need an expert."

"And who would that be?"

"Well, I have an idea, but you'll just get mad at me," Eve said. "Think I'm matchmaking."

"Oh, no you don't. Shit, no. Up yours. No way."

"Ah, yeah. Sorry. You need to recruit Patri."

# GENES

The horse was an ill-trained and troublesome stallion, but Lani didn't mind. Managing him gave her something to think about while she rode the six klicks from the Rosedale train station's stable to the experimental farm. She had reviewed Teti Yang's note a hundred times in her mind, reading into it all sorts of things that it didn't say, and she was tired of that. Now if she could only avoid getting tossed off her jumpy mount for twenty minutes, she would learn the truth.

The air was warm and sullen, blending into a darkly invisible overcast sky; there were no stars to inspire her on this trip. The cloud cover and thin fog also made for a very dark night. As long as her nag's hooves kept crunching gravel, she would be all right. She had brought her headlamp but was unsure whether it would help her touchy horse or spook him. So she left it off. Before long, though, she had to resort to humming old songs to push back the crowding memories of that other urgent journey north, alone on a dark night.

At least she was confident that Yang would leave some lights on, so she wouldn't miss the farm cutoff in the dark. This proved to be the case. Before she exhausted her store of tunes, she was able to hitch her mount to Yang's railing and knock on the veranda's screen door. Yang appeared promptly, with a wide smile and a bottle of beer. She gestured with the bottle. "Join me?" she asked.

Again, they sat on the veranda, this time with beers instead of lemonade. For a brief moment, the loudest sound was the mosquitos clustered in their plume of carbon dioxide, trying to get through the screening. But Yang was not inclined to stretch out the social preliminaries.

"Let me tell you what we found," she said. "Or, rather, show you." She opened up her deck, expanded a window that was open and waiting, and turned it to face Lani. It showed a solitary cow, reddish, sullen, and rangy, standing in what might have been a dry-land pasture, regarding the camera.

"That," said Yang, "is your animal. Not a horse, a pig, a dog, a bat, or an anything else. It's a cow. This picture is from the archives. It dates from 1990 or so. This particular breed is called a Brangus; it's a hybrid of 3/8 Brahma and 5/8 Angus stock, which gives a fairly docile critter with high resistance to heat and drought."

Lani took a moment to absorb this. Finally, she asked, "Not a shark or an alligator or something?"

"Nope. A cow."

"So that leather I gave you really is three hundred years old?"

Yang chuckled, perhaps a little grimly. "Not at all," she said. She took her deck back and brought up another picture, this one showing dozens of horizontal stripes, with each stripe composed of tiny vertical hash marks in meaningless patterns. All of one stripe and most of its two neighbors had been highlighted in pink.

"This is a representation of a piece of the DNA we sequenced from your sample. It's on chromosome seven; it codes for some proteins that are important in the cow's immune system. The highlighted part is not found anywhere in the old Brangus DNA sequences in the archives. It is, in fact, identical to a modification that was suggested in a paper written by folks at Bowdoin College eighty years ago. Those guys were looking for a way to immunize bovines against the virus that killed all the cows. They thought this addition to the DNA would work. Whether it does or doesn't, that sequence in your sample's DNA proves that the animal was less than 80 years old. Probably a lot less."

"These people from Bowdoin. They thought their new thing would work, but they didn't know?"

"That's right. They never tested it."

"Why not?"

"Well, it would've been a hard test to do back then. We've learned things in the meantime, so now we can do tricks like breed the blackbucks I showed you. Eight decades ago, it would have been much harder. The main reason, though, is the governing Council wouldn't allow it. Put a stop to all work on bovine DNA, in fact."

"Why on Earth?"

"Fair question. I've looked into the records. It's part of why I took so long with this. At the time, the Council asked, suppose we brought cows back— what happens then? They studied that question to death, up, down, and sideways. In the end, they concluded that if we did that, it would be 'extremely destabilizing.' Part of that was ecological; cows are expensive sources of calories and protein, in terms of water and land use, methane production, and so on. More important, they thought, were the economic and cultural changes that would fall out from a move like that. I could give a long talk on the details, but the short of it is, if cows came back, the twps would wipe their brows and say something like, 'Hey, aren't we champs! We lived through the Bad Days, and now they're over. We can go back to how life was before.' And they would go. And in a hundred years, we'd be right back in the soup."

"Do you think that's true?"

"It's not up to me, Lani. It's a Council edict from when my grandmother was a girl. Besides, this is socio-politics, not biology. I've got no relevant expertise. One day the Council might revisit and change its mind. In the meantime, breeding cattle with DNA like this"—she poked the screen—" is about as forbidden and very likely as dangerous as anything I know." She took a sip of her beer, stared for a bit at her deck, and finally looked up at Lani. "I can tell you this much. That somebody should be playing around with genes like this? With broad commercial promise but without wide reporting and modeling and oversight? It scares the living shit out of me."

Lani sat and drank her beer and tried to think. Her simple little fraud investigation had blown up in her face twice now—in two days. To sell overpriced handbags, somebody was subverting the Daily Drop, reinstating the sins of social media. And the handbags themselves came from what looked like a conspiracy to defy long-set Council policy, to say nothing of possibly leading straight on to a replay of the Bad Days. She couldn't afford to go public with all this because then she would have to confess to her own crimes. And to top it off, if her own EEE twple were involved in these messes, her nosing around could be very risky. The complexity was paralyzing.

Lani raised her eyes and locked her gaze with Teti's. Yang's presence, the calm, certain, unhurried weight of her body and mind, seemed to fill the veranda and filter out into the night. If this was Teti Yang, Lani wondered, what was she? Put that way, only one thing seemed to matter. She was an orphan, torn from her real family, steeped in EEE ways but a late starter, not entirely of them. She was as self-made as anybody in the Union. But if she had a core at all, an identity, she had chosen it, and it was 'cop'. The questions that worried her then became very easy. What would a good cop do?

"Teti...Professor Yang..." she said, "There can't be too many organizations able to pull this thing off. Who do you think is capable? Who might have done it?"

They talked for another hour until Lani was satisfied that she understood all that she needed to know. Yang gave her two copies of a stamp containing the minutia of her DNA work and a dry summary of her conclusions. They hugged at the door, and Lani turned to her horse. She waved as she left the little puddle of light surrounding the farmhouse. Out on the road, the weather had not improved; it was still pitch black.

Once the farm was out of sight, Lani leaned forward and crooned a song into the stallion's ears. Then she kicked him into a full gallop, and for most of a kilometer, Lani let him thunder into the blind dark while she sang out loud, with the night smells around her, her head up, the wind in her hair.

# KAM HIMSELF

When Lani knocked on her door, Evar was dozing at her desk. Lani had guessed that she would be. But it wasn't very late, certainly not by Eve's usual standards, and the matter was urgent. Lani persisted.

Two different people stuck their heads out into the hall to see what the racket was about before Eve finally answered the door. She was wrapped in a shapeless something-or-other and looked awful. Lani brushed her aside and went straight to the refrigerator.

"I need a drink," she said, "and so do you. You'll need it more pretty soon. What have you got?"

"Gin. On the counter. What the fuck, Lani?"

"Not my favorite, but okay. I should make you wait for the news, but I can't. Just spent the evening with Teti Yang. You know my leather thong? From the boot? It's from an honest-to-God cow. Brangus breed. Can't possibly be preserved from the bad old days. Means somebody is recreating cows from old DNA sequences. Gotta be a big operation. Very, very subversive. Here's your drink. Cheers."

Evar sipped. "Recreating? Old DNA sequences? You mean like in *Jurassic* whatsis?"

"Exactly. *Rawhide Park*. With Clint Eastwood, I think, and Laura Dern."

"Well damn me. Maybe you'll be a hero after all. Will you still talk to me when you're famous?"

"Depends. That's what I got. Whadda *you* got?"

Evar frowned and sipped more gin. "Some stuff. Not as good as yours, but charming in its own little way."

"Tell me."

"Sit down and stop vibrating my pictures off the walls, and I will. Sit! I mean it. I can't think when you're like that."

Lani sat and drank her own gin. Made a face, drank some more.

"Good," said Evar. "Nervous system depressant. What you need. So here's my pitch. I ran my search on all the Drops from the last week. Took most of the day, but it's done now. We didn't make quite five hundred hits, but three hundred for sure. More. I need help categorizing where they come from and how often they change and all that, and I've barely had a chance to look at content. But I've turned up some truly oddball stuff. Here's my favorite."

She pointed to an icon, flagged as an audio presentation, fifty-eight minutes long, titled "Kam J's Music Hour." Opened it up. A solo banjo played an intro and then was joined by a tenor male vocalist, singing a simple but catchy tune:

> *Marshall Brunner was a handsome man,*
> *Loved his babies and he loved his land,*
> *Had his beefs and he nursed his grudges,*
> *Didn't love twps and he didn't love judges.*

> *Get out the way for Marshall Brunner!*
> *He's an upper, not a downer.*
> *Worked all his life for a little respect,*
> *Died with a rope around his neck.*

The second verse faded out before it got well started, overlaid with a baritone radio voice welcoming listeners to an hour of liberty-loving music with Kam J. himself. Himself then explained that he was delighted to be there, with this thought for the day: "Liberty meant different things to different folks," he said, "but in the old days, the best liberator of them all was the good old internal combustion engine. Yep, songwriters of the twentieth century loved their women, but they loved their cars more." And to prove it, he queued up The Beach Boys with *My 409*.

"Nice tune," Lani said.

"Sure. Goes on in this vein for longer than I could stand to listen to it. Nostalgia and vague disgruntled talk about liberty. Sounds a lot like your secessionists. What was it? Snarky, adolescent, deniable? Like that. You know this Marshall Brunner?"

"No. Can't say I do."

"Me neither." Evar rattled the ice cube in her empty glass in Lani's direction. "Seriously, kid. We need a historian. We need Patri."

# DEAD LETTERS

A hundred days to go. Talking mere double digits, now.

The Chief had called another eight o'clock meeting for the next morning, so once again, Lani was obliged to skip out on her dance/martial arts segment. This time she was not anxious to make a good impression, but still, she got to the meeting room a good ten minutes early. She spent the time finishing a chore that Venna had asked her to do a couple of days earlier: setting up searches of the EEE mug shot database in hopes of identifying some of the shop customers who had been photographed right before the raid.

She started her searches and was about to close her deck when the first of the other team members arrived. But then she heard Bokun whistling his way up the corridor, and with a shock, she realized she knew the tune. As sometimes happened, her subconscious took control, and before she realized it, she had turned on the deck's video/audio recording. As Bokun entered the conference room, Venna's irritated glance made him stop the racket, and Lani shut down the recorder, typed briefly, and closed her deck. "Marshall Brunner," for sure. Recorded, time-stamped, annotated.

As before, the Chief showed up punctually and turned the meeting over to Venna. The subject, she said, was last week's raid on the shop selling purported cowhide articles. She spent some time on the logistics of the raid, what went right, and what went wrong. Kero and Yeg got flayed with sarcasm for letting that customer escape from the building, and Lani got a grudging commendation for stopping him. The praise was, however, tempered by a politically necessary censure for manhandling a civilian. There were what Lani took to be inevitable and pro forma complaints about the quality of the recorded video. Audio communications were reluctantly conceded to have been okay.

Then Venna turned to the results of the raid, which were disappointing. The desk clerk was a known small-time criminal who had been recruited into the job only days before the raid. He was happy to tell EEE's twple everything he knew, but that was essentially nothing. He did not recognize the man who recruited him and instructed him in his duties. He was paid not very much at the time of recruitment, with the promise of more by mail after the sale was over.

Customers of the shop had been questioned, but they knew nothing beyond how to read the shop's sale times, which they had learned from another unnamed individual, usually in conversations that occurred at the *Open Horse* nightclub. These people were presumably of interest to EEE's tax investigators, but the tax division always had an enormous backlog of likely suspects. Eight or ten more would scarcely make a ripple in their lives.

Finally, the articles for sale at the leather shop had been tested thoroughly and were found to be a promiscuous mix of the processed hides of horses, pigs, and goats. Attempts to ascertain where or when these items had been manufactured or purchased were so far unfruitful.

The Chief took the chore of summarizing. Lani had guessed that he might be feeling embarrassed about investing so many resources but having so little to show for it. But he didn't sound embarrassed. If anything, he was angry. How, he asked, could they have put in that amount of effort and come away with nothing but a few customers whose only overt crime was stupidity? The sale that they raided had been planned, he said flatly, by somebody with a brain. Its only apparent purpose had been to embarrass Triple-E itself, leaving no tracks behind. That meant the damn crooks had organization and resources, too. The one thing that was clear from the raid was that Triple-E was up against some serious opposition. Why, he wanted to know, did the opposition understand Triple-E to the last, least investigator while his team knew *nothing* about them?

Damn shame, the Chief finished, that their hard-won documentation would now just go to sit in the archives. The place where failed investigations went to die.

As the meeting broke up, it finally dawned on Lani that the Chief had gone on as he did because he had come to the same conclusion that she had: one or more of his people were playing for the other team. And, for God knows what reason, he had some hope of embarrassing the rat into the open. This clearly wasn't going to work, and worse, it had warned the traitor that the Chief was wise to the betrayal. It was, she thought with a shudder, as if the Chief was himself a bad guy, and he was *bragging*. She shelved that heretical thought, however. It was impossible to take it seriously. It went against everything she knew about the Chief's character and his history.

Confused and angry, Lani went back to worrying in frustrating circles about Venna and Bokun. Boke, she thought, was purely busted. Though not in connection with the leather shop so much as with the secessionists. Why else would he be whistling the Marshall Brunner song? But the leather shop seemed to be all about money, while Marshall Brunner was about politics. And what about the missing cops, a mystery that she had no stake in, except that it was keeping the whole twp in a tizzy, and it refused to go away. This seemed to be about some nut job and not related to anything. But it was the worst of all— people, apparently good people, were vanished or dead. Suppose that it linked back to her other problems? If it did, that would be a gut-freezing deep-dung situation. She desperately needed to fit all these pieces together.

Lani sighed. Eve was right. They needed Patri.

# MEDIATION

It took Lani most of the afternoon to track Patri down. She finally found him in the History Department's library, sitting by himself at a darkly polished wooden table that must have been five hundred years old, surrounded by books. Actual, physical books lying on the table near him and shelved in battalions around the room's periphery. There was one other person present, a young woman, possibly another student, with a huge afro hairdo, sitting amid her own pile of books at a table across the room.

"Uh, hi, Tree," Lani said. "Got a minute?"

Patri turned to look at her warily. He didn't quite check to see if the exits were clear, but it felt as though he did. "Hi, Lani," he said.

"Is this her?" The Other said clearly, not even looking up from her book.

"Yes," said Patri. "It's her."

There was a little pause. Then The Other said, "Maybe you should ask her what she wants." She still appeared to be reading.

"Good idea," Patri said. "What can I do for you, Lani?"

Lani stood, flummoxed. "Who am I talking to, Tree?" she asked at last. "You or her?"

Patri smiled at her and she could feel her composure melting. "Talk to me," he said. "Just to me."

"She's not too bad," The Other volunteered. "Unless you're put off by those… muscles. Do they bother you, Tree?"

"No, they're okay," he said. "Appealing, really. Okay, Lani, what do you want?"

Lani stood with her mouth open, her eyes jerking back and forth between Patri (who was no longer smiling but whose expression was at least a bit welcoming) and The Other (whose position had not changed by a millimeter; she was still apparently lost in her book). "Uh, um," she stammered. "Uh, I need your help, Patri. I need it a lot."

"Hmm," he said with a slight frown. "Seems to me we have things to talk about before we get to favors. Unfinished business."

"Sorry. What things?"

"'Sorry' doesn't make the grade, does it?" said The Other. Finally, she moved. She turned a page.

"No," Patri said. "I'd call that insufficient."

"What are you talking about?" Lani shouted.

"Can it be," The Other went on, in her same conversational voice, "that she doesn't realize that she owes you something?"

"I think that may be it," Patri agreed.

Lani had lost all orientation. It was like vertigo; she wanted to smash something. "What's going on here?" she demanded. "Did you two plan this charade?"

"Not at all," said Patri. "You have to understand Vaun. She and I are old friends. We've talked about you a bit, but we didn't expect to see you here. Now about Vaun: she doesn't know you. And she's shy. Very shy. She can't address you, or even look at you directly, until she knows you better. Right, Vaun?"

"Good enough for now," Vaun said.

"Vaun thinks, and I agree, that I've got an apology coming from you. Breakups are always hard, but this one was especially unfair, and even mean, and it *hurt*, dammit. I know you can deliver a noble 'please forgive me' when you want to. I've seen you do it with Luv Nematode. I'd like one of those from you. Doesn't have to be long and fancy. Just heartfelt. You have to mean it.

Then we can talk about other things."

"Not before," said Vaun.

Lani found a couch and sank into it. She had no idea what to say or think or feel. She had come seeking Patri on a mission. An important one, for sure, but still basically a police job. And now, without warning, she had dropped into one of those existential whirlwinds where the tiniest move could spawn repercussions that would haunt or serve her for the rest of her life. Herself and Patri, each wandering the world alone, only a hair's breadth from herself and Patri, both dead. Or settled in a nice twp with kids. It was too much. Like O'Brian's Spaniards, she wasn't ready.

"Take your time," Patri said. "I know you've got a lot on your mind."

That stopped her voice. For perhaps half a minute, she sat there with her face working, her hands making jerky, spasmodic motions, and her breath coming in erratic gulps. When she finally tried to speak, what came out was not words but a dry, coughing grunt and a wail. She rolled into a ball and fell over sideways to bury her head in the couch cushions. There she croaked and bawled and couldn't stop crying, no matter how she tried. At last, she felt a warm presence beside her and a hand on her shoulder. She squirmed around so she could hold him, at least a part of him, and gradually got herself together. Finally, she felt able to speak.

"Bloody hell!" she mumbled. "Tree! *Of course* I'm sorry! But you knew it all, I'd just *told* you, remember? Why couldn't you see? I was nine years old. Nine years, and I tried so hard. They say I did everything right. But still, everybody died, Tree. All the same. My whole twp. They left me. They left, and there's nobody behind but me. I think of all that, Tree, and I think of us, and I think of losing you, and I get so *fucking* scared. So scared. I panic. And then I might do anything. Last time, I hurt you. A lot. You! Of all people."

By this time, she was sitting up, talking straight to his face, a bare hand's width away. "So stick around, okay? And let me come back? I know it's asking a lot. But will you please, please forgive me and let me come back? Only do it right now, 'cause I really need you."

Patri held her and squeezed, making it clear that he was taking her back.

They clutched and leaked tears and then separated, but with their eyes still locked. Patri said, "Damn, Lani. You too. Please forgive me. About this scene today. And before. I pushed you way too hard about Hendrikson. Wanted you to tell me how super you are, and never thought about how you would feel about it. Then you threw me out, and I got scared, too. That was weak. I should have trusted you. Trusted you to get things right. Seems like you always do."

"Maybe," she said. "In the end."

"Okay," he said after a while. "We're us again. That's beautiful. But you don't have much time, sounds like. Talk to me. What's up?"

Lani sniffled and closed her eyes, working for control. Presently she said, "It's the fake old cowhide. It isn't old, and it isn't fake. Somebody is breeding cows from recorded DNA against Council edict. There's bad shit in Triple-E; people are going over to the other side. Cops are going missing. Nobody knows if it's only cops or if civilians are, too. Persons unknown are hiding reams of secessionist propaganda in the Daily Drop. We don't know why. It's all connected, but I don't see how. Eve and I, we need you. We need your knowledge and your point of view. Will you help us?"

Patri gifted her with his best smile. "Sure, I will," he said, as his smile turned into an expression of mock surprise. "Why didn't you ask me sooner?"

Vaun had sat, silent and ignored, through this entire drama. Now she spoke up, her big eyes visible for the first time, glinting at Lani from the depths of her afro. "Lani twp Triple-E Maxwell," she said. "I don't know all of what's going on here, but I've heard enough. This is serious trouble. I want in. Whatever it is, I can help."

# COUNCIL OF WAR

It was the *Frost* again, that same night. The thought of corrupted Triple-E twple made them all twitchy, so Lani and Evar arrived ten minutes apart, and Patri and Vaun came in together ten minutes after that. Nobody thought that such lame precautions would make any difference if EEE was actually on their case, but still, it made them feel better. It also gave Lani a chance to explain Vaun to Evar.

"This is serious stuff," Evar complained, just as Vaun had done. "We don't know her. Fucking terrible security." Lani reflected that Eve had been involved in many criminal investigations in her career, but likely all of those had been cyber-crimes. She had always been separated from criminal clutches by at least two keyboards and a data link. Being personally involved, with her body at stake, made her anxious. And why not?

"Patri knows her," Lani assured her. "Has for years."

"Well, I hope that's good enough. What does she bring to the party, anyway?"

"According to Patri, a capital-M Mind. He says she reads everything, forgets zilch, can recall any of it in nothing flat. And she sees connections. Things that seem obvious to duds like you and me, but only after they've been explained by her."

"Sweet. Exactly what I need. Somebody to help me feel stupid."

At Lani's suggestion, they chose a table for six in a back corner of the pub. That way, when the other two came in, they were able to huddle at one end and have muttered conversations with each other without Vaun ever having to speak with Evar and only very rarely with Lani. Vaun may have thought that Patri's and Lani's earlier emotional exchange had given her a window into Lani's soul, but she was still wary. It was clear that in her mind, nothing substituted for long acquaintance.

Evar and Lani spent half an hour reviewing what they knew for the other two. First, the messages buried in the Drop, with samples. Next, the connection with sales at the leather shop leading to the evidence for a compromised interest by members of the Chief's Triple-E team, including Bokun whistling, Venna's unexplained appearance on the scene, and the timing and outcome of the raid. The Missing Officers Investigation, still unexplained and with details, if any, shrouded in twp EEE secrecy. Last, Teti Yang's finding that at least some of the leather was real, recent cowhide.

"I asked Yang who she thought might be behind the cow DNA business," Lani said as she wrapped up. "She gave me a list of half a dozen possibles. But her favorite suspects are from the Genetic Engineering Department at the Montreal Uni. They have the facilities and staff needed to pull something like this off. And I think she's had run-ins with them in the past about ethics stuff. She didn't accuse them of anything, but what she didn't say about them was pretty damning. Anyway, they're located in Chambly, less than a hundred klicks north of Ausable Forks, where the leather smugglers seem to come from.

"All this crap, except for the missing cops, is connected through that silly little leather shop. A lot of it feels like there's some central organization, but if so, we don't know anything about who is involved or their agenda. So my question is, what do we do next? Patri, Vaun? I was hoping you might have some ideas."

Patri and Vaun put their heads together for a quick exchange. Patri nodded, then turned back to Lani and said, "Give us fifteen minutes, okay? We'd like to thrash out some things between us. Then maybe we'll have something sensible to say. Why don't you go have a drink at the bar? We'll call you when we're ready."

Eve raised eyebrows at Lani. "Have we just been dismissed from our own meeting?"

"Only for a little while," said Lani, while Patri nodded. "Besides," she said, "explaining is thirsty work. I could use a drink."

So they went to the bar, sipped margaritas (good ones, with tequila made from Wyoming agave), and let Wam tell them stories of inter-departmental academic warfare. Across the room, P-V (as Patri plus Vaun quickly came to be called) were conversing intently, looking not like friends but like a couple of engineers working a tough problem. That was reassuring.

In less than the stipulated fifteen minutes, Patri signaled, and the four of them reconvened.

"Thanks for indulging us," Patri said. "We have six points and a recommendation. Right, Vaun?" Vaun nodded. "There's direct evidence for most of these; the others are necessary for a consistent picture."

"So...Six points:

"One. You are surely right about there being some central organizing conspiracy. We think the people behind it are very likely few in number and already powerful or rich or both, at least by Union standards. There's not yet enough information to be more specific.

"Two. Most likely, they are trying to build a popular movement with goals that are directly advantageous to them. Hence the propaganda. The secrecy suggests that the goals are, in important ways, contrary to established Union principles.

"Three. So far, the only goal of the conspiracy that we can clearly identify is to re-establish a beef industry, with all that implies. The leather shop is likely an afterthought, or at most a sideline, very likely opportunistic. Say some of their cows died unexpectedly, and they skinned and butchered them and are now using the meat and hide to raise funds for other projects. Or just to undermine the legitimacy of the Union Council.

"Four. The missing cops. We don't know much for sure, but the least hypothesis is that these are tied to everything else. We know the conspiracy is already too big to hide effectively without positive measures to contain security breaches. We think they are silencing people who might expose them. Co-opted, bribed, or killed, in any case, assuring that those people won't talk.

"Five. The conspiracy has already committed very serious crimes. If the main actors could be identified and tied to those crimes, they will surely hang. Even the underlings are in real danger and liable to long sentences. This risk means that everyone in the conspiracy is dangerous. In this connection, the corruption of twp EEE officers is particularly worrying.

"Six. Events are moving fast. It is unreasonable to think that the conspiracy's presumed cattle farm can be kept secret for very much longer. When that secret breaks, they will be head-to-head with the Union government—a fight they can't win unless they control the government first. That means there's got to be a coup attempt of some sort coming, and soon. We don't see how they can hope to do that. But they must have something up their sleeve. They wouldn't be doing what they are doing if they didn't think they could win.

"Are you with us so far? Questions?"

Evar and Lani looked at each other. Evar shook her head. "Not from me. Very clear. Clearly scary. A coup? Really? Lani, can I quit now?"

Lani smiled sadly. "A little late for that, Eve. So, Patri. You said there are likely big shots behind this, people who are rich or powerful. How does that work in our egalitarian, brotherly loving, non-materialist Union?"

Patri smiled sadly. "Just because almost all of us are poor as peasants, it doesn't follow that people who have or want power can't be corrupted. It just means they can be bought cheap."

"Sweet. I fucking *love* people. You mentioned a recommendation? As in, what to do next?"

"Right. The main thing is that we are totally outmatched here. Outnumbered, out-funded, outgunned, still working mainly in the dark. We're holding this heavy hot rock, and we need to drop it on the desk of somebody with the resources and the will to handle it. Established law enforcement is no help. We don't trust Triple-E, and the first thing any other police outfit would do would be to consult them. This isn't the job of the twp representatives or the Council. Or the military. There's nobody left but judges. We've got to go judicial, and we've got to do it soon. That's what we recommend."

"How soon is soon?"

"Dunno. My guess is a week. Vaun thinks tomorrow. Given the practicalities of documenting what we know, maybe we should split the difference and say three or four days."

"Three," said Vaun.

They sat silent for a long time. Finally, Lani said, "Okay. Three days. That's the plan. Who's in?" Around the table, four fingers went up.

"Great. Patri, Vaun—I've never even seen a judge. What do we have to do?"

# PROPAGANDA

At 02:00, thirty sleepless hours after the initial meeting at the *Frost*, Lani sat in her room, collating memos from the group. Evar was adamant about security. She had set up a drop for the group like the one the bad guys used, but better, in case they had to communicate remotely. For the present, she insisted that all group messages should be transmitted as hand-delivered encrypted stamps. Since Lani did not have the specialized skills needed for the others' jobs, she was the hand-carrier. She hoped to finish a draft of the report's chapter on propaganda and communication by 02:50, in time for her next scheduled scooter sweep past Evar's room, to the History Department, and back, starting at 03:00.

She viewed the coalescing picture they were now telling with such alarm, and the schedule pressure they had taken on themselves with such anxiety, that she had given up on sipping whiskey and had switched to black coffee for the duration. In the meantime, she despaired of sorting the various nuggets of information from the last sweep (at 21:00) into neat pigeonholes. The story they were trying to tell was complicated, interconnected, and only sporadically documented; it did not yield easily to neat linear narration. She hoped that Patri could improve on her first draft. More than that, she hoped that he could find ways to minimize the yawning gaps in their knowledge without drawing their judge's wrath by overstating what they knew.

She shuffled through her pile again:

*

*From: Patri*

*Subject: Marshall Brunner*

*Marshall Brunner was a minor historical figure from the 2190s, i.e., the earliest days of the Union. "Marshall" is a title, not a name, corresponding roughly to today's "Bailiff." He belonged to twp Ham, one of the "Next Nine" twps to be recognized by the confederation based in Trenton. Although he got himself elected to a post of some authority in his newly formed twp, he opposed the Union from the beginning and was often in trouble with the local judge. About two years after twp Ham's formation, Brunner was hanged on judge's orders for stealing livestock and spreading disorder to the neighboring twps. In later decades he became a regional, mythical hero, similar to Robin Hood or Jesse James. By the twenty-fourth century, he was largely forgotten.*

*The Marshall Brunner tune was composed in the mid-nineteenth century and has often been pressed into the service of politics. The broadcast lyric appears to have been invented for the present day. Thus, the line "He was an upper, not a downer" invokes Great Lakes' separatist jargon that is less than a decade old. ('Uppers' are those who believe in individual advancement, especially through private enterprise. 'Downers' favor Union-style equality.)*

*

*From: Vaun*

*Subject: Daily Drop hidden propaganda — subjects*

*The pictorial propaganda elements found in the Drop generally promote nostalgia for times before the Crazy Years, when apparently everyone who mattered was free, white, rich, and beautiful. There are, however, three specific foci that together account for more than 90% of the 384 images found in the Drop over the last week. Almost half (190) of these images relate to food and drink, and most often to beef in some form. About 25% relate to automobiles, especially to luxury varieties. Also common are "endless highway" vistas, often highlighting scenery from the old American west. Last, about 15% of items contain promotions for guns of many kinds, or video clips taken from films, virtually all involving citizens using firearms to prevail over armed aggressors.*

*

*From: Vaun*

*Subject: Authors of Drop bulletin board items*

*32 of the items hidden in the Drop are unencrypted bulletin boards. Each contains many entries (about 3500 in all), usually short, virtually all complaining about some constraining aspect of Union life. Each is signed, but the names used are obvious aliases ("Gofer," "Poorboy," "Eapy Fox II," etc.) Across all entries, there are 1942 unique aliases; most of these appear only once, none is attached to more than 8 messages. Textual analysis suggests, to the contrary, that more than 85% of the messages were written by a small number of individuals, almost certainly fewer than ten, and possibly as few as four. Thus, the bulletin boards should not be thought of as public fora but rather as a single marketing platform engaging in theatrics, in which individual citizens may participate to the extent that they also push the product.*

\*

*From: Evar*

*Subject: Drop hidden propaganda—information routing*

*The known hidden Drop items all originate from periodical publications—newspapers or weekly magazines. This is necessary for the kind of communication the conspiracy desires, to obtain frequent updates and allow timely conversations. All of these are, or use, content that passes through "certified aggregators," which are entities that collect material from contributors, and accept responsibility for it following the Daily Drop guidelines. Most newspapers operate as their own aggregators, while the magazines tend to be grouped into sets of publications that have something in common, and each set uses a different aggregator. The hundreds of hidden items we detected last week involve 25 different periodicals, including 6 daily newspapers and 19 weekly magazines. As it turns out, all of the magazines are aggregated through one or another of the newspapers, and moreover, three of the newspapers are operated by the same twp and are aggregated jointly. The upshot is that all of the hidden items pass through one of only four certified aggregators, and all of these are associated with daily newspapers. This strongly suggests that the hidden data operation is managed by only a few people, each of whom has edit permission for the content passing through one of the parent newspapers. The papers involved are:*

*Quebec City Questioner (Quebec City)*

*Allegheny Woodsman (Pittsburgh)*

*Penn Palms Gazette (Swarthmore)*

*Conn River Runner (Middletown)*

\*

*From: Patri*

*Subject: Judges*

*At any time, there are about 200 Union judges. They are geographically scattered, roughly following the distribution of twps. In principle, any twp or individual may file a complaint with any judge at any time. In practice, however, judges usually stick close to their own home locations (except when they form panels), and they deal almost entirely with disputes among twps. Our submission will be from individuals, hence a rarity (though not quite unheard of).*

*Judges have considerable powers and also considerable independence. This means that before one approaches a judge, one wants to know something of her biases and political orientation. We want someone well-connected with the Council, leaning Bird (not Chip), and with a reputation for toughness.*

*Bringing the same case to multiple judges at once is a famously Bad Idea. They will learn of the duplication, assume (correctly) you are trying to game the system, not be happy, and take it out on you.*

*In Trenton, we have several good choices. I recommend Myly twp Jud Chao or Roc twp Jud Partridge.*

*There also appears to be a concentration of conspiracy activity in and near southwestern Quebec. If, for some reason, we cannot put our case in Trenton, we could consider Dortu twp Jud Zeil in Plattsburgh.*

*

*From: Patri and Vaun*

*Subject: Propaganda purposes*

*Propaganda consists of lies broadcast to the public for a purpose. The purposes are universally either commercial or political. Propaganda most commonly seeks to inflame feelings about one or more of five classical subjects: sex, status, religion, tribalism, and fear. Commercial propaganda usually starts at the beginning of this list and works toward the end. Political propaganda does it the other way around. Our case is a peculiar mix of both.*

*The imagery embedded in the Drop seems purely commercial, with strong appeals to sex and status, except that the objects being sold cannot now be bought—so far as we know, nowhere on Earth. The bulletin boards, however, feel like expressions of tribal grievance, except that, at present, there is little inequality to fuel such feelings. We think the underlying notion might be described as temporal tribalism. One tribe is the Union, here and now. The other is the USA, three or four centuries ago. We have nothing; those bastards had everything. So we want what they had, and nothing but the Council prevents us from getting it. Well, at least some of us, the "best" ones. And also the constraints of a ruined planet, conveniently not mentioned.*

*We think that we're looking at a radical plot associated with the Chip claque. In the near term, the aim is to overturn the government using as an excuse a fait accompli, namely an infant cattle industry, complete with a ready-made market clamoring for beef. The symbolic power is outstanding. Note that once the beef industry becomes known to the public, it doesn't matter whether the government opposes it or condones it. If they oppose, the conspiracy can exploit this as a grievance issue. If they permit, then the door is open for other similar abuses. Cars and guns are likely parallel branches of the same sort but not as well developed. If we were to look for links from our conspiracy to black market gun makers, to car hobbyists, and to the fuel ethanol and construction industries, we would probably find some.*

*Longer term, the aim is surely a return to something like pre-Collapse capitalism via incremental changes in Council policies.*

*

Lani smiled and shook her head admiringly. Damn, P-V were good. She was not so sure about herself. Her problem was not a shortage of evidence or ideas. It was too much to do, and too little time.

# WAHRYURASH

After her 03:00 scooter circuit, Lani yielded to biology and snatched a three-hour nap, skipping morning PT. She awoke feeling better than she had in weeks, and she reported to her desk at EEE on time, ready to put in an hour appearing to do twp business while actually composing prose for the summary document in her head. After that, she was due at the twp rehab building for a session with Hap Moran. Missing PT was one thing, but standing Hap up would be something else altogether, would make her feel terrible, and would raise red flags in many places.

The forecast called for thunderstorms, and in fact, the weather looked doubtful when she topped the ramp leading to Hap's second-floor apartment. Still, he liked going outdoors so much that when she took control of his wheelchair, she didn't even ask him before wheeling into the hall and straight back down the ramp. This was just as well, since Hap was having a bad day with his speech, and not even Lani could interpret his mouthings and mumblings. They rolled across the street and into the neighboring park. Lani turned them left toward a part of the park they seldom visited and proceeded at a slow jog to a scraggly stand of palmetto trees. The soil there was sandy and barren, so they could run lengthy non-repeating slaloms around the trunks. These usually amused Hap, but not this time. Something was bothering him. Lani

213

stopped his chair repeatedly, trying to understand what the trouble was, but she couldn't figure it out. The straps that held him in the chair did not seem to bite or chafe him, his pillows were arranged properly, his catheter was not plugged, and in all physical ways, he seemed okay. Finally, she spent two whole minutes watching him closely as his muscles worked and he drooled on his chin, trying to say something. After many similar repetitions, she decided that the common word in all this was something like "Wahryurash."

She turned it over and over in her mind. Wahryurash. Wahryurash. At last, it clicked. Hap was telling her, "Watch your ass."

The wind kicked up as the first fat drops from the approaching storm splatted to the ground. A sudden hard core of ice formed in the pit of her stomach.

As Lani spun the wheelchair to take Hap back to rehab, her small deck buzzed at her. Incoming voice message. Feeling like she was handling a scorpion, she pulled the deck out and answered.

It was Evar, looking frantic. "Lani!" she gasped. "Bad news. Are you sitting down?"

Lani growled. "Get serious. Just tell me."

"It's what's-her-name," Evar gulped. "Yang. Teti Yang. She's dead."

"What? When, how?"

"Last night. The experimental farm. Her body was found this morning. About an hour ago."

"Fuck! Shit, shit, shit! Do you know how?"

"They're talking murder. Torture and murder."

"Torture and…where's this information come from?"

"I've been snooping on internal traffic for about a hundred police departments. Totally illegal. Keyed to the names of everybody who's come up in our stuff. Yang's name was on the list."

"Damn. Anything more about the when and how?"

"No details. One of her co-workers called it in. Don't even know if the police are on the scene yet."

"Okay. Hang on a sec." Lani closed her eyes and thought hard. Several scenarios fit with this news, but the only really likely one was that Teti's grad students were not all as loyal as she had thought they were. One of the Yangsters had sold her out to the other side, and those folks had sent somebody to see how bad the damage was and deal with it. If this was all true, it was dangerous as hell.

The sky was now dropping real rain.

"Okay, Eve, are you there?"

"Yes, Lani."

"I'm blown, Eve. Yang would have told them about me. If they catch me, or even if they don't, you and P-V won't be far behind. You need to run, Eve. Take all your cash and the shirt on your back and get lost. But first, you can connect to the Uni wick; I can't. Call Patri and Vaun and give them the same message. Do that right now. Then I want you gone. Two minutes. I'm serious. Got that?"

Evar looked scared but nodded. "Okay, Lani. I'm on it. Good luck. SeeYaBye." And she clicked off.

Lani grabbed the wheelchair handles and started to run. She couldn't leave Hap out in the worsening storm. "You called it, Hap," she said, over her heavy breathing. "I should listen better, huh?"

She banged through the complex's front door, up the first ramp in record time, around the hairpin turn, and up the second one. Then halfway down the hall to Hap's place, where she elbowed the door open and ran him into the little living room.

"Hey there, Lani," said that familiar voice, and there was Bokun across the room, coming at her with a nightstick in his hand. "Still reliable, I see."

She spun to face him, but it was no good. Someone concealed behind her stung the back of her neck with a taser.

She pitched onto hands and knees with every nerve screaming. Tried to roll onto her back so she could at least kick the bastards, but her muscles spasmed uncontrollably. She couldn't coordinate the simplest motion, not even to yell. As she toppled to one side, she saw gallant old Hap struggling to jump from his wheelchair and defend her. Then they tased her again and carried her away.

# UNDER RESTRAINT

They had a gurney stashed in Hap's bedroom. They loaded her onto it, stripped off her clothes and wiped her down (the tasing had caused her to piss herself), then strapped her to the gurney. When they were done, she could barely wriggle. While they were about this, she got a good look at them. There were only two: Bokun and Yeg, the motherless bastards. Where was Venna? She should be nearby, flaunting her sword and waving the baton for her little band. By the time Yeg and Bokun finished, Lani was beginning to vocalize these sentiments and others, so they punched a wide piece of tape over her mouth to shut her up. Then Bokun grinned at her and slugged her exposed belly. She gagged and fought to breathe.

"You and your foxtrot," he said.

They put her clothes in a bag and a sheet over her and wheeled her out past Hap (who was still mumbling furiously), to the elevator, then down a floor and out the back of the building. There they loaded her, gurney and all, into a horse-drawn vehicle and then out through the rainy streets for a long enough time that she got lost, and Bokun and Yeg got bored. Their desultory conversation was chilling, not so much for what they said as for the implication that they gave fuck all about what she heard. She was theirs, they thought, and would be until she was dead.

"I had plans for this week," Yeg said. "Why do we have to go up there now?"

"Beats me," Bokun replied. "All to do with this bitch, I guess."

"Guess so. But what can we do up there that we can't do here? Doesn't make any sense."

"Fine. You take it up with the boss. Me, I think he's still soft on this little twist. I just hope we aren't stuck up there for two whole weeks. I hate that place."

"It's not so bad. Good food, better'n at the twp. Not hot as here. The work's easy, waiting tables, gofer shit. Next week we get to rub shoulders with Council big fish for a couple of days. It's just I got plans for this week, is all."

"You want to stay away from those big fish," Bokun advised. "They'll sell you out for half a unit. And as for the farm, well, it's a farm. Looks like a farm, smells like a farm. That's enough for me. I came here to get away from all that. Fuck that shit."

"Sure, okay. It's just that..."

"You had plans."

"Yeah."

*

In time they got to where they were going; from the background noise, Lani judged they were close to the main rail station. Yeg and Bokun pulled her gurney out of the horse cart, rolled her up a ramp, and after a ride through interior corridors, closed a door and pulled off the sheet. Lani had been fighting off despair by giving herself a pep talk. She was a cop, goddammit, and a good one, and a good cop would keep calm, notice and remember everything, and look for her chance.

The room was medium-sized, windowless, with walls painted in dull unrelieved institutional beige. The door was wide enough to admit the gurney easily, but it was not a hospital room; it lacked the electrical, gas-flow, and mechanical appurtenances that went with professional medical spaces. On the other hand, there was an additional person in the room, and he was obviously a med tech. There were a couple of blocks of professional offices near the railroad tracks, on the opposite side from the warehouse district. She felt sure that if she were given half a day, or likely only half an hour, she could find this room again. But if so, so what?

The three men removed some of her restraint straps but left her hands and feet secured, with a belt around her waist so she couldn't thrash too much. The tech then started to stick a catheter into a vein inside her left elbow. With a gush of adrenaline, she recognized what he was up to and thrashed as much as she was able. The tech smiled and stepped aside to let Bokun take over.

Bokun slapped her face to get her attention, then took her throat in both hands and pressed the heels of his palms lightly against the sides of her neck.

"Just a little stick, Lani, dear," he said with a wink. "You can go along, or I can choke you out for a while, and we'll do it before you wake up. Your choice."

Lani forced her muscles to relax and mouthed silent curses at Bokun while the tech did his stuff. Bokun stood back, watching her face, and clutched at his heart. "Oh, Lani," he said. "If looks could kill…"

"Where's the boss?" Yeg wondered. "He's late."

"Twenty minutes before boarding time," Bokun said. "He'll be here."

This shocked Lani's limbic system again. "He?" she thought. Surely the boss was Venna?

The tech was fiddling with something that looked to Lani like a timer control on the IV drip. He got it assembled and checked, raised an eyebrow at Bokun.

"Hang on," Bokun said.

They waited for an endless time while the three men, but especially Bokun, pretended they weren't ogling Lani's body. Then the door opened, and the Chief strode in.

For frozen seconds, Lani honestly expected him to pull out his miniature pistol and shoot Yeg and Bokun dead. But no, he nodded a greeting, then gravely stepped over to Lani on her gurney. Her eyes brimmed with tears, and with each step the Chief took, she felt her guts shrivel inside her.

"Sorry about the gag, Lani," the Chief said. "We'll have time to talk later. But I need to tell you that you can cut this nonsense short any time you want to. Just nod for me. If you do, we'll take the gag off, and you can tell me that you believe we are working for the common good, and that you want to help. Then you tell me who else knows about the cows, and everything will be fine. We can move on. We can all help make the Union a better country. Together. What do you say?"

Lani looked around the room and shut her eyes because it was so awful. But with her eyes shut, thoughts came teeming. What was going on here had to be wrong; she had to fight it. But what about the Chief? She knew he had his reasons to despise the government. What if he was right? What if these other rat-rapers were only imperfect tools advancing a good cause? And what chance did she have against them anyway? She thought about dying, and how even in the middle of bad nights, it never seemed a good idea. She thought about Equality, Environment, and Evidence. She thought about Evar and Patri and Vaun. The thought of never holding Patri again was too much to bear. But in the end, she thought about Teti Yang, and how that vast, deep, relentless spirit was gone from the Earth because of these self-satisfied, masticating worms who dared to share this room with her. With a jerk, using both of her strapped-down hands, she shot the bird at the four of them.

The Chief shrugged and signaled to the tech, who started the drip, and Lani's consciousness vanished from the room without complaint, or pain, or memory.

# REVOLUTIONARIES

Lani came groggily awake from a loathsome dream in which she was being fondled by Bokun Yardley. If one could call kneading her breasts like bread dough "fondling." But then she found the dream was real. Boke (the slime) was perched on top of her with both hands on her bare chest and a silly grin on his face.

She jerked and yelped (her gag was gone), and strained her neck to bite one of his arms, but it was no use. He leaned back out of reach, and then, with that lascivious sneer she had quickly learned to hate, he climbed off her and onto the floor.

"Welcome back, Maxwell," he said. "Just warming up, here. We gather for the real event in a few minutes. The whole gang. Turn and turn about, I say. Unless you tell me who you're working for. Fuck knows why, but it would please the Boss if you gave us that much before we get nasty with you."

Lani's head was spinning violently, but even so, she could spot Boke's ham-handed ploy to make her talk while she was still woozy.

"Fuck off," she told him. "There is no gang. It's just you, pencil-dick. Go on. Rape ahead. If you think it'll be fun, you're wrong."

"Grow up, bitch," he advised her. "You know this isn't about fun or sex; it's about power. Which I've got, and you don't. So watch your mouth." And to

220

drive the point home, he leaned over and slapped her face.

Again? she thought. She felt like he had done it before, but she couldn't remember when. She couldn't imagine Bokun slapping her even once and living to tell about it, but somehow she felt that he had. She ignored that unsettling thought, and Bokun, and took stock. She was still bound hand and foot, but now she was on a classy four-poster bed, not a gurney. Her hands and feet were tied to the posts, so she lay spread-eagled and face up on what she thought were probably expensive sheets. A wide towel, now in disarray, covered her from belly to ankles. The room was large for a bedroom, and somebody had paid a fortune to decorate it (wallpaper, hanging art, ceiling fan, ruffles on the drapes). Sunlight streamed through high windows beyond the foot of the bed, and through the windows, she could see blue sky and the tops of some trees.

She felt terrible. Every muscle ached from cramps induced by the taser shots, she had a fierce headache, a raging thirst, and an upset stomach. Her mouth tasted like a squad of marines had marched through it straight out of some tropical swamp. The only part of this that was getting better was her dizziness, which had been pretty severe when she first noticed Bokun playing his sick games but was rapidly fading. She guessed that was from whatever drug they had used to knock her out. The drip in her arm was gone, replaced by a neat little bandage. Well, she thought, whatever else they had planned for her, they weren't going to let her die of an accidental infection.

The last thing she could remember was being loaded on that gurney, trussed like a chicken and hidden under a sheet. More must have happened before they drugged her, but she couldn't bring it back. That kind of memory loss, she knew, was a common side-effect of anesthesia; she wished she could remember more. Not just so she would know what was up with Bokun and the slaps, but because of a remote wordless scream in the back of her mind, flooding her with feelings of terror, loss, and betrayal. She had seen or heard something bad, not long before they knocked her out. Something really bad. She wished to hell she knew what it was.

Lani was still trying to drag back memories that had never been properly made when the door swung open for Venna and Yeg. Venna looked her over with hard eyes that didn't miss much, certainly not the pulled-down towel and Bokun's smug expression. Her mouth twisted, and she speared Bokun with a look that said, as clear as words, *"We'll talk about this later."*

She had nothing to say to Lani. Her only speech was directed to the other two: "Good. She's awake. Get her dressed. No shoes. I'll call for the surrey. Five minutes." She spun on her heel and left.

"Dressed" meant Union standard shirt and pants, no underwear, no belt, and plastic zip restraints on hands and feet. They left about half a meter of slack between her feet, so she could shuffle but not walk or run. To add to its other expensive wonders, the room had a private toilet, which they let her use, albeit with the door open. She gulped water from the faucet until they dragged her away. On the way out, she saw a second bedroom that seemed a twin to the first, and a spacious living area with couches and chairs, a fireplace, and a desk. There was no kitchen. Whoever stayed here (she remembered Yeg and Bokun talking about "big fish"), they ate someplace else.

The sun was dazzling but low in the sky, and it felt like morning. If so, she had been out for almost a day. No wonder she felt rotten. Outside the front door of what she already identified as the guest house was a gravel drive, and across the drive was a full-size house—two stories, heavy stone foundation, two visible chimneys, screened porch all the way around. The guesthouse looked new; the main house was much older, possibly going back a hundred years or so. To her right, the drive passed the main house, curved around behind it, and disappeared. Off in that direction, she could see a high fence and a sliver of an out-building, maybe a barn, a hundred meters away.

From that way came the sound of hooves and a crunch of gravel. The promised surrey appeared promptly, clipping up the drive. As it made the turn, she got a good look at the driver. She stared.

"No," she said flatly. Then, "Unc! Why? NO!"

The scream in her head grew to a deafening screech as her stomach knotted and then revolted. She found herself on hands and knees in the grass, dry-heaving after puking up what little water she had gotten down only a minute earlier. She spat and cursed weakly. Goddam motherfucking son of a bitch!

This was the thing she had feared without knowing it and the thought she had pushed away and denied, seemingly forever. It was the Chief driving. Her uncle. Her favorite uncle was one of them. Probably the fucking boss.

As the surrey pulled up, Yeg and Bokun lifted her to her feet, and Yeg wiped her face with a handkerchief and a scowl of distaste.

"Help her in, guys, will you?" the Chief said, not unkindly.

# TEMPTATION

They bundled her into the surrey, binding her hands to the front rail so she could not slug her uncle, and her feet to the running board so she could not jump out and hop to freedom. The Chief clucked to the horse and made a tight U-turn, heading back the way he had come. He reached under the seat and produced a metal bottle with a straw, and handed it to her.

"Just water," he said. "Thought you might need some." He had, as usual, thought of everything.

She drank thirstily but choked on it as her body shivered with reaction to adrenaline and God knows what else. She slowed down and took little sips, which worked better. After a while, she spoke.

"Why, Chief? What are you trying to do? Why are you doing this to me? We're family!"

He knew better than to take on the family/adoption issue. She was family because his brother had adopted her, and he could ignore that, but he wasn't about to say so. Instead, he took the large view.

"Lani. Don't judge too fast. Look around. Think about how life works these days. When the Union was made, it was a day-to-day fight against the grim reaper. Everyone pulling together, as hard as they could, was barely enough. We needed rules then, and limits, and people who would resist the urge to tinker with anything that worked. But that was a hundred fifty, two hundred years ago. Things are better now. We could loosen up if we wanted. Live a little. But we don't. The Union now is paralyzed, ossified, in every artery, vein, and joint. We, here, this little bunch of revolutionaries and like-minded people elsewhere, we're trying to change that. Just a little bit at a time.

"Nobody wants to go back to the Bad Days, Lani. Really, nobody. But wouldn't it be nice, to…once in a while, on a special occasion…to get together with friends and have a grilled beefsteak? Is that such a terrible thing to want? Or for some of us, especially if we have big families, to live in a house with a yard, instead of being assigned a slot in an apartment complex? To have our own kitchen, eat what we want when we want it? Have you ever seen a flying airplane, Lani? The Marines have a few, you know. They take them out once a year, at night, to be sure the pistons still slide. I've never seen one, but that's what I hear. Couldn't we do things, new things, with a little restricted, regulated, carefully monitored air service? Sure we could. All it would cost us is a little more ethanol production each year. Seriously. We're not slavering red-fanged monsters. We're only trying to jolt the Union out of its funk. Get it going again.

"Why don't you join us? Give up on this holier-than-thou Triple-E fixation, and help change the world? You're a hell of a woman, Lani. In many ways, the best I've ever seen. We need you. Join us. Will you? Won't you? Please, won't you work with us, not against us?"

The surrey had driven about a half kilometer, passing what was indeed an old barn, through a gate, past some irrigated sheep pasture to a long linear hedge, four or five meters high. The Chief drove through a gap in the hedge, revealing a wide fenced plot with large animals grazing in it. Some were reddish and some were blackish, all were long-bodied, with short horns and a fair-sized hump above their shoulders. They sure looked like the cow in Teti Yang's picture. Brangus, no doubt, of varying age, but Lani thought none were very old. About twenty of them. At the far end of the pasture, in a separate fenced enclosure, was a bull, looking lonely.

Lani gazed wearily at the amazing cattle and sighed. "You're quite the spellbinder, Unc," she said. "Always were. I have to admire it. I do. Here you are, promising me the world, sort of. But I don't have to go along, and I won't. What's the best I could look for? Being the hotshot in your crew of domestic killers, running around the country, knocking off people who are better than me? Like Teti goddamn Yang, for instance? Or like my friends, the ones whose names you want? No, thanks. I've been slapped around and groped already this morning, threatened with gang rape. And I bet today will get worse before it's done. But I'm not gonna help you. So much for your loyalty. You take it, but you never give it. To hell with you, then. Screw you and your whole crowd, in fact. With a hot poker. Sideways. I won't help you. I'd rather die."

She finally turned to face the Chief. "Clear enough?" she asked. Then she spat. "How *could* you?"

He returned her stare, stony-faced. "As you wish," he said. "When you change your mind, let me know."

He turned the surrey around and drove back to the barn, where the crew waited.

"You were right," he told them. "It's plan B."

# STORAGE LOCKER

Yeg and Bokun led her into the barn, overseen by Venna and her sword. The barn had a wide sliding door facing the main house and a narrower one at the opposite end. There was a hay loft, storage all over the place, and half a dozen horse stalls along one wall, most of them occupied. With both doors open, it was half-lit and drafty, looked similar in age to the house, and smelled of hay and horses and manure, the way a barn is supposed to smell.

They led her to a short door in the wall opposite the horse stalls. A table sat beside the door, cluttered with tools and containers and an ominous bundle of plastic zip restraints. The door itself looked as ancient as the rest of the structure, except for its handle and lock, which were brand new. The lock was a fancy thumbprint-activated job; the door jamb and lock recess showed freshly cut wood, with chips still on the floor—signs of recent carpentry.

Hanging on a peg in the wall, near the far end of the table, was a holstered, standard-issue Walther. Lani fought a fierce internal battle to avoid staring at it. It was less than three meters away, and she wanted it. Bound and escorted as she was, there was no hope of getting to it. But sometime soon, she swore, she would be loose, and it would be hers, and then Venna would learn how useless her stupid sword could be.

Yeg flipped a light switch beside the door (more new construction) and thumbed the lock plate, which opened with a convincing clunk. He pushed the door open, showing a lighted space beyond, took a pair of diagonal cutters off the table, and cut the restraints off Lani's hands and feet. Then he stood back.

"Strip," said Venna. Her sword was now out of its scabbard, though pointing at the floor.

Lani took off her pants and shirt, and stood still while Yeg redid her hand and foot zip restraints. She doubted that taking her clothes away was about security; it was just a calibrated indignity to prove that they could. She didn't intend to let it bother her. Yeg gave her a little push. "In you go," he said.

She shuffled awkwardly through the door and down a short step onto a dirt floor. The room was perhaps six meters square; up against the back wall, there was a large structure made of solid new wood that might have been a sleeping platform except that it sloped down, not too steeply, from the back wall toward the center of the room. And it had a ring bolt at each corner.

"I don't care for that," she murmured. The door closed behind her, and the light went out.

# IN THE DARK

Lani shuffled forward until her shins bumped into the platform, turned around, and sat down. She needed to let her eyes adapt to the dark, and she needed to think, and both those things felt easier sitting down.

Why were they leaving her alone like this, in the dark? Most likely was that they wanted to soften her up. Let her stew on the fix she was in and get into a panic by imagining all the things they might do to her when they came back. In that case, they wouldn't leave her too long. Half an hour would be plenty for her runaway mind to scare her as much as it could, and they certainly didn't want to come back and find her curled up comfortably asleep on the platform that had to be an adjunct to torture. So they would be back soon. What should she be doing in the meantime?

First came a basic bodily inventory. She still felt rotten, but better than when she woke up. She was thirsty again, but the thirst was manageable, and she was not yet hungry. She was, however, having spells of shivering that came and went, and odd cravings—vivid memories of evenings with Evar, munching cheese and crackers and sipping whiskey.

Aha, she thought. Counting the day and night she had been drugged, it was what? Nearly three days since she'd had a drink. She was in withdrawal. From her alcohol addiction. Brilliant. Just what she needed. Something else to plague her.

Okay, she thought, apart from that, she seemed to be in pretty fair shape physically. Mentally, she still felt a little slow and vague. Leftover symptoms from the IV drip, she supposed. She thought she had done okay head-to-head with the Chief, who was the best talker she knew. So that was good and would probably get better. How about her attitude? Well, she had her check list. She was coldly determined to (a) not tell them a goddamn thing that they could use, (b) get out of this place, and (c) wreak as much damage on these bastards as she could, not excepting her cold-blooded self-satisfied reptile of an uncle. Thinking about him still made her stomach twist, but his betrayal had become a great motivator. She would use that.

All that was internal. Her appearance to her captors was a different thing. For her to escape, they had to make a mistake, or she had to engineer one for them. And both those outcomes would be more likely if they were off their guard. They were trying to terrify her, hurt her, make her know, deep down, that she had no power or resources, and they were calling all the shots. For now, then, her play was to make them think they had her cowed. (She permitted herself a tiny smile at the word, given the circumstances.) She would be pliant, scared shitless, unresisting. They wouldn't believe it, at first. But she would stick with it, they would come to expect her acquiescence, and when they made a slip, only then would she unleash her fire-spitting dragon and burn the assholes down.

So much for mental preparation. She looked around and realized she could see a little bit. The place was not as dark as it might have been. The main light source was the thin crack around the door, but there were also pinholes of various sizes scattered all around the walls. She couldn't see well, but she could see the platform and distinguish it from the floor, and even see dimly into the overhead.

She got up and went to the wall behind the platform and probed with eyes and fingers. The room had a foundation almost a meter high, a stone wall made of rounded river rocks, about the size of cantaloupes, cemented in place. It occurred to her that this might have been the first structure put up on the farm in post-Collapse times and that the barn had probably been grafted onto it later. If so, the mortar would be old, maybe cracked and decaying. With luck, she could dig her way out.

On top of the foundation, the structure was a hybrid of log cabin and frame construction. The walls were made of solid, rough-sawn logs about ten centimeters thick, apparently with no exterior siding. They had caulked the spaces between logs with something, but the caulking had not been maintained lately; flaws in this stuff made the pinholes (some as wide as a finger) that let light in. Studs were spaced against the inner wall; it wasn't clear whether these helped to hold up the walls, or if someone had abandoned a plan for interior siding. There was no proper ceiling, just a half dozen rafters, more of those ten-centimeter squared-off logs connecting the front wall to the back. The artificial lights must have been hung on the trusswork above the rafters and below the roof proper, but she couldn't see them.

She tried moving the platform to see if she could, but it was no go; the legs were anchored in the dirt floor somehow.

The platform, she realized, was large for a bed—almost three meters long and half that wide. It was high enough off the floor that when she stood at its middle, she could easily wrap her hands around the rafter that ran from head to toe above the platform. She had enough slack in her bonds that she could grab the rafter on both sides and do a chin-up, and her feet had even more freedom; she could hold herself horizontal for a few seconds with her hands at one end and her feet at the other. That meant, she thought, that if she let go with her hands and held on for half a second with her feet, she would probably drop on her head and break her neck and skull. So she had a way to kill herself—if it came to that. That was something, anyway.

In one corner of the room, on the barn side, she found five stacked built-in shelves, each about half a meter square. She didn't think she had time for a thorough investigation of these, and she certainly didn't want to be surprised while she rooted through them. There might be something interesting in there, and if so, that was where she wanted it to stay. So she returned to the middle of the platform, facing the door. She summoned some tears to streak her doubtless dirty face and sat, stiffly erect and shivering, until ten minutes later, when the door lock thunked open and the light blinded her with its glare.

# WATER

"That Professor Yang," Yeg said, "she was a tough old bird. Wouldn't think it to look at her, all dumpy and soft like."

Yeg and Bokun had brought in what had to be goat-milking stools, and they sat on them near the lower end of the platform, which put them half a meter from Lani's head. Lani was stretched out on her back, facing the roof, feet at the platform high end and head at the low, with thick, soft ropes securing hands and feet to the corner eye bolts. The guys had brought a third stool, presumably for Venna. It seemed they were waiting for her before starting the party for real. In the meantime, Yeg regaled Lani with tales she didn't want to hear. Doubtless, this was another intimidation tactic. Even though she knew that, it was working.

"She was a surgeon, you know. Long time ago. Anyway, she had that on her bio. So course, I started with her hands." Yeg put a pair of lineman's pliers on the platform where Lani could get a good look at it. "There's nineteen bones in the hand, if you don't count the wrist. Hard to get to the third and fourth metacarpals with those pliers. The jaws aren't big enough. But I busted all seventeen I could reach on her left hand and five on the right before she gave up your name. Crushed 'em, really. Makes a funny little noise, like cracking a pecan. Except you usually can't hear it because of, you know, the screams."

Lani tried hard not to visualize the scene, with Teti tied in a chair and this monster working on her. "Fucking shit, Yeg," she said. "Go practice on yourself, okay? She was worth a hundred of you."

"Oh. Dear me. That's so unfair. Personally, I think of what I do as a public service. The third E, right? All about telling the truth? I just encourage people to tell the truth."

Lani could not think of a single thing to say, but she was spared the trouble because Venna arrived. They had propped open the door to the room. She took off her sword and left it outside in obedience to the first rule of detention: never, ever, bring a weapon into a closed space with a prisoner. She came in, kicked the door shut, and pulled her stool up so she could lean close to Lani's face. "Let's talk," she said.

For the first quarter-hour, it was like any police interrogation, only performed with the subject tied head-down on a slope, shivering, and nude. Lani was invited to tell all she knew about this subject and that, skipping from one to another, sometimes returning or reframing a question so it overlapped with others, always looking for congruences or inconsistencies. It developed that Bokun was not the only one who believed in slapping. Venna would slap her, almost casually, whenever Lani got fresh, or strained her credulity, or she just felt like it. So even though she was expecting it, Lani was taken by surprise when Venna wound up to slug her again, but instead, from nowhere, produced a towel and tossed it over her head.

"Luv, I think you're holding out on us," she said. "Better think that over." Then she dowsed the cloth with water from a jug, cutting off Lani's air.

Lani had read about waterboarding, but that didn't make it easier to take. She could try to minimize her reflexive thrashing, to lower her oxygen demand, and she benefited some from knowing what it felt like to hold her breath for much longer than most people could. But these tricks bought her, at most, a couple of minutes of relative comfort in strangulation sessions that lasted much, much longer. The rest was like drowning, with her vision blacking out and the blood hammering in her ears and every organ screaming in its own way, all for want of air. It went on forever, and it went on long after she was sure she couldn't take any more.

At last, Venna pulled off the towel and let her suck in air for half a minute. "Want to tell us anything?" she asked.

Lani shook her head and said, "No. Fuck..." But she didn't get the "you" out before Venna smacked the wet towel back on, and she was drowning again.

The second round was worse than the first. It probably didn't last as many minutes, but it hurt even more, and it felt a lot longer. This time, when Venna pulled off the towel, she leaned over and, in a relaxed tone, explained that they had more direct methods, but the captain didn't want her permanently damaged. So they were stuck with this waterboarding garbage. And they didn't really know what they were doing with it. It was the first time for all of them, she said, and they might actually kill her by mistake. "Book learning," she said. "You can never trust it." And she started again with the towel.

The third round was, of course, the worst of all. It went on until Lani passed out; they might indeed have been close to killing her. Lani was never sure if she stopped breathing and was brought back only by Venna giving her mouth-to-mouth, or if she imagined that part. Either way, after she had been breathing on her own for a while, gaping like a beached fish, she worked her mouth around the phrase, "Okay. I'll talk."

# JACK AND JILL

They untied Lani from the platform, zipped her into new hand and foot restraints, and sat her up. For a couple of minutes, she coughed hard enough that she feared damaging something—throat or ribs—and then, for a time, she was so dizzy she could barely stay upright. At last, they gave her half a plastic cup of water to help with her hoarse voice.

"What have you got?" Venna asked.

"I...I took photos of the traffic behind the leather shop during the sale three weeks ago," she said. "During and after." Then, spitefully, "Got nice shots of you, Luv Keithley, coming and going. No sword. Going with cash receipts, I guess. You, Lieutenant, a bag lady. How fallen are the..."

Venna slapped her. It was a *pro forma* slap, though. Lani guessed she was surprised and irritated, but not yet alarmed or really angry. She had already decided that by themselves, the pictures Lani described wouldn't prove anything. But she needed to understand how they were taken and whether Lani had been up to something else, something that might actually be a threat. So she spent a long time questioning Lani about her stakeout. When she started, when she stopped, where exactly was her vantage point, did she move around at all, did she try to buy anything? Finally, she got around to the question that Lani had been waiting for but dared not prompt.

"What camera did you use, Lani? The one in your little deck?"

"No. Needed more focal length than that. It was a nice Ralston job, with a zoom lens, up to 150 mm."

"Tripod, too?"

"Yes. Sure."

All this caught Venna's interest. "Where did you get this gear, Lani? It's way out of your price range."

Lani hesitated and stammered. "I…I'd rather not say."

"Tell me, Lani."

"Don't make me. You won't like this part."

"Better tell me, Lani."

Lani bit her lip, gathered her nerve, and launched into it. "I'd only been going there for two days. I was upstairs, taking notes, even though there was nothing going on."

"Get to the point."

"These two cops came up the stairs. I told you I had to leave the back door open. They just walked in and came up to check the place out. Were surprised to see me. They wanted to know what I was doing there, but I didn't want to tell 'em, so I identified myself as twp EEE. When they heard that, they did a saliva check on me, huddled for a minute, and then told me what they were up to. And it was the same stuff as me. Far as I could tell, they knew everything that I did and maybe more. The leather sales, the claims about cowhide. Only they seemed to think the cowhide was real, not a scam. I guess they were right about that."

"Where were these cops from?"

"Twp MetPD2. Big Metro Trenton twp that handles downtown."

"I know where the fuck MetPD2 is." Now Venna was paying attention for real. "These gentlemen have names?"

"It was a man and a woman. They wouldn't tell me."

"They wouldn't tell you? What the hell?"

"They wouldn't tell me. Don't ask me why. I don't know. Security. Maybe they were freelancing, like me. But they wouldn't. Told me to call them Jack and Jill."

"Jack and…pigshit. Boys, get the ropes. Lani is making shit up."

Lani broke and groveled and bawled and managed to get them to listen a little longer without drowning her again. At last, she settled down enough to say more.

"They claimed they were short-handed," she sniffled. "Offered to loan me camera gear and let me in on the final bust, if there was one, if I would get pix for them. So I said yes. I said yes, I would."

"And you got the gear how?"

"Jill and I met at a bar downtown, next day. The *Boatman*. We both brought shopping…"

"Yeah, yeah. And traded bags."

"Yes."

"And you gave them the gear back, and the memory chip?"

"That's right. I met with Jack, that time."

"Did you at least copy the files before that?"

"Sure."

"Encrypted?"

"I'm not a total…sorry. Yes, encrypted. Passphrase, 'I tell you three times."

"Fuck me. Lewis Carroll. You call that secure? How did you live to be as old as you are? Where's the copy?"

Lani told her. Wrapped in plastic, in a dead drop in the back of a certain bench in the park.

"Anything else?"

"Well, when I gave the stuff back to Jack. We got a little, you know…friendly. And he said some things. One thing. He said they had a lead on where the cattle ranch was. Tiny place, he said. Upstate in New York. Caw-sable something. Forks? Are we near a Caw-sable Forks?"

Venna froze, while Yeg and Bokun traded nervous looks. Bingo, thought Lani.

# CHESS GAME

Venna was well-trained, Lani had to give her that. Even after receiving shocking news that her operation was blown, known in at least some detail by twp MetPD2, Venna had not panicked. She calmly asked all the follow-up questions that a good cop would ask, squeezing Lani for more information about Jack and Jill and the circumstances of their meetings, and then going back and asking again and again until she was convinced she had gotten what there was to get. Only then did she and her boys pick up their stools, lock her in, and, presumably, go report to the Chief.

Maybe Bokun and Yeg were distracted, though. When they closed the cell door, they failed to turn out the light. Or maybe that was on purpose, to interfere with Lani's sleep or something. Not that she had any intention of sleeping. But she was grateful for the light; she had not been looking forward to searching the place in the dark. The interrogation had taken longer than she had thought; the chink-holes in the walls showed no daylight. Outside, the sun was down, and without the electric light, she would have been blind as Homer with his head in a sack.

She was reasonably confident that they would leave her alone for a while. She had given them a lot to think about—a paradox, in fact. The Chief would find her Jack and Jill stuff completely incredible. No cops in the world would behave like that, freelancing or not. Therefore, Lani had to be lying. But she *knew* things. Things she shouldn't know. Venna doing her bag job. Even more, Ausable Forks. That had been partly guesswork on Lani's part and all desperation. But Venna's reaction, and the mere fact that Lani wasn't dead now, said that she had played a winning card.

Now the Chief would have to spend the night using special channels, rousting people out of bed to check on her story. Did her blind location exist? Did it show any signs that she had ever been there? How about the camera memory chip? How about Jack and Jill? Did any cop partners at MetPD2 answer to their (specific but non-distinctive) descriptions? Was the Metro twp running an operation on the leather shop? If so, what did they know?

Most of these queries would come back negative, but some would not. This would never satisfy the Chief. Venna and her bully boys would surely be back to try to wring more out of her. But with any luck, not until morning. So now, to work.

She started with the corner shelves. The bottom ones had been cleared out; there was nothing on them but dust. But the top one, above eye level even for a tall man, had a pile of something in its back corner, open to the non-existent ceiling. Climbing up one shelf to get a better look was a problem because of her shackled feet, but she managed. The pile seemed to be a mouse nest. A rodent had transferred most of the stuffing in a pillow to here, one mouthful at a time. It was messy and smelly, but harmless. It might have deterred a lazy would-be cleaner when the place was being cleared for conversion to a torture chamber.

Well, she wondered, what if there was something stuck in that corner before Miss Mouse arrived? Answering that question meant getting her feet up to the second shelf. The move necessary to do that nearly cost her a blind fall backward into the mud puddle at the foot of the platform, but again she managed. By digging with both hands elbow-deep in the pile of shredded insulation and mouse dung, she was rewarded with a small hoard of junk: a sheaf of decayed and water-spoiled topo maps of the Adirondacks; a pair of rodent-chewed work gloves; a dissolving cardboard box containing plastic chess pieces, plaster-filled; a tangle of monofilament fishing line; and two corroded batteries.

It wasn't much. But it might do.

She set aside the fishing line and a couple of pieces from the chess set, and re-buried the remaining stuff in the mouse pile. She hid her booty under the high end of the platform, against the stone foundation, as far from the platform edge as she could reach. Any kind of search would reveal her things, but she was counting on there being no search. Also, she needed to be able to find them easily in the dark.

Last, she put in her best effort to brush residual mouse fuzz off her arms and chest. She was still doing this when she heard voices. She rushed to the center of the platform and curled up as if trying to sleep, seconds before Venna returned, boychiks in tow.

# JUST CHECKING

"Up you go, Lani," Venna chirped as she sidled in, ostentatiously carrying a red plastic water jug. "On your feet." She waved Lani into the middle of the muddy spot from their earlier conversations. She turned away to put down the jug, then turned back very fast, unwinding to deliver an open-handed roundhouse swing that sent Lani toppling over onto the platform.

Lani sat up, probing her jaw with both hands. That was the sort of blow that loosened teeth. Just *wait* till she got her hands on that Walther.

"Just wanted you to know how we feel about you, luv," Venna said. "The boss says you're a smart one, which I doubt. But he also says that you're feeding us scraps, one at a time. He's tired of your little bites. He wants the whole meal. It's time for you to cough it up, dear. All of it, this time. Everything you know. 'Cause if you don't, we'll likely take you out back and cut your throat, and tomorrow we'll feed your corpse to the pigs. Are we clear?"

Lani blubbered and nodded.

"Now didn't I tell you to stand up?"

Lani struggled up and stood meekly, with downcast eyes, letting her nose run, slumping with her whole body.

"Okay. You stand there and speak when you're spoken to. I'm speaking to you now. What else have you got?"

"What makes you think…" Lani said.

"Stop right there. Did you hear what I said? You don't ask questions, I do. What else have you got? Now."

"Well…" she shuddered and gagged, cleared her throat. "Well…Jack did say something about the Drop. The Daily Drop."

"What about it?"

"The, uh, the ad? For the leather shop? Hidden in the Daily Drop? Jack was interested in that. He called in a guy he knows in CompSci at the Uni? Asked him if there could be other stuff in the Drop hidden the same way. So he looked."

"And what did this guy find?"

"Ah, well. Tons of shit."

Venna cocked her arm to smack her again, so Lani rushed to amplify.

"Propaganda, mostly. Secessionist stuff. Lots of stupid ads. With pictures. Ads for food. Ads for beef. Ads for cars. Anti-Union songs. Ads for guns. Treasonous pigshit. I didn't see any of this stuff. Jack just told me about it. But it sounded awful. Breaking every rule, you know? The kind of thing Triple-E should be working against, not for."

Venna slapped her. "You naive little child. You're hopeless. Well, you'll find out soon enough. About this computer guy. There are at least three computer science departments in the Uni. Which one is this guy in?"

"I don't know."

Venna slapped her.

"Honest," Lani moaned. "I don't know! He didn't tell me anything about the guy. No name, no hair color, no favorite music, nothing!"

"Are you *trying* to get hit?" said Venna.

Lani shrunk into herself and stood helpless, miserable and shaking. Venna sat down on her stool. Then for thirty minutes, she cross-examined, going back over everything Lani had ever said since her interrogation started, again and again. Finally, she decided she had all she was going to get. She waved to the boys.

"Your turn," she said. "Make sure she's not scamming us on anything."

Yeg and Bokun swapped her plastic restraints for the soft ropes with slip knots, pushed her onto the platform, and spread-eagled her as before. She screamed a little and begged, but she didn't really resist. They ignored her frantic pleas and dropped the towel over her face with no particular affect or interest. Just a job. Get on with it.

The actual torture was hideous as before but somehow perfunctory. All Venna wanted from her was that she should confess that she was lying about this detail or that. This she was happy to do, but since Lani could never follow up these confessions with real information, Venna correctly assumed that she was only trying to get some air. After that, Venna stopped listening to her answers or even asking questions. It was no longer an interrogation; it was simple, straight-up torture.

When they finally put her restraints back on and left her alone in the dark, Lani had two thin sources of satisfaction. First, they had stopped zipping on her restraints before taking her ropes completely off. There were five whole seconds when she was lying absolutely unrestrained, free as could be. Second was an offhand comment that Venna had made, probably to Bokun, during one of the times when Lani was actively drowning and hence (presumably) not listening. The substance was, "Next time I say to tail some bitch, we fucking tail her. Okay?" From this, Lani inferred that she had not, in fact, been under surveillance any time recently. That meant Venna didn't know about the meetings with Evar and Patri and Vaun, or maybe even just with Evar. With a little luck, her friends were in the clear.

# PERSUASION

They came back a short time later. This time it was only Yeg and the Chief. The Chief looked somber and serious; Yeg wore what looked like the Walther from outside.

The Chief had a milking stool. He set it down a respectful distance from Lani's perch on the torture bench and squatted on it.

"Okay, Yeg," he said, "can you give us some privacy, please? Ten minutes should do it. Don't wander too far. If I yell for help, come in quick and don't worry about me. Just shoot her. That clear?"

"Yes, sir," Yeg said, and his eyes narrowed.

With Yeg out of the room and the door locked, the Chief considered Lani for a moment. Then he shifted around on the stool to face her more squarely.

"Well, kid," he said, "you're a tougher number than I thought. Congratulations. But now you're real close to getting yourself killed, and that would be a shame. I'd still like you on our side. Honestly, I never thought it would come to this. But it has, so let me try one more time to bring you around."

Lani sat mute. She didn't think words would help her at this point.

"You wonder why I'm doing this. The reasons I gave you last time were the party line. They're the reasons we use on the people we want to influence. The average Janes, who are busy doing average stuff and don't think about things much.

"Let me tell you my reasons.

"For me, it started with that fracas at the Hendrikson mine. You remember I came back injured. It wasn't a huge deal—two surgeries, a couple of months in the hospital, eight more in rehab. In a couple of years, I was good as new, almost.

"But in that time, I got to know a whole lot of damaged citizens. Triple-E, sure, but also Marines and Navy and regular street cops. People who got tangled up in farm machinery. Thrown off horses. Struck by lightning.

"Then I took to reading about the old days, before the Collapse, and their prosthetics and their treatments. Turns out they had stuff we don't even dream about. And why not? Because all of it takes materials or processes that we can't make, or won't make, because the stinking Council doesn't approve.

"So I thought, 'change the Council.' But that's easier said than done. I worked for Chip candidates. I ran for EEE rep myself. Got clobbered in that election. Too short-sighted. Too single-issue. Too aggressive. Too argumentative. Too male.

"In the end, I got approached by somebody with more clout than me and with an existing organization that wanted to make some real changes. So I said, 'count me in.' And here I am. Here we are. I won't say it doesn't chafe, sometimes, and never more than now. But I won't quit. There's too much at stake.

"Now, Yeg and Bokun. And even Venna, too. They're monsters. One of these days, pretty soon, I'll make them pay for what they're doing to you. But the showdown is coming up, and until then, I need them.

"So, for the last time. Won't you join us? Won't you? Please don't make me kill you. 'Cause that's what it's coming to."

Tears were streaming down Lani's face, moisture she could ill afford to lose. She had wanted to know why her uncle had become such a bastard. Now she knew. She knew, and she understood, and it didn't change a thing.

She sniffled and took two deep breaths to help control herself. She composed her features and looked her uncle straight in the eyes.

"Unc, listen to yourself," she said. "You've lost it. You've lost yourself. So you've had some bad luck. Maybe with work. Maybe you never got your due. Maybe with a woman."

That made his eyes tighten.

"And now, that failure—whatever it was—has eaten you up. You've started believing your own lies. I mean really. That last bit? About Yeg and Bokun? Expect me to believe that? Sure, you'll sell out your team sooner or later. But in your own time, for your own good.

"Face it. You want what you want. You have reasons. But the Council has to think about everybody, and you and they don't agree. That's life with other people, Unc. Happens all the time. But if...*spoiled brats*...go and start revolutions every time they don't get what they want, then the Union can't work, and we might as well be dead. Will be. Soon enough."

She gazed at him sadly, as she might do with a willful child. "That's logic, Unc. But even if I turn my back on all that, I still can't say yes to you. You're asking me to save myself while everybody I love dies, except for you. I've done that before. I won't do it again."

She clutched herself as best her bound hands allowed while she suffered through a sudden bout of shivering. When that passed, she lifted her eyes to him one last time.

"So that's the deal, Unc. Now you can call in your rabid lap dog and have him finish me off, or go away and leave me in peace. I don't care which."

# PENELOPE

After the Chief turned out the lights and departed, unsatisfied, Lani persuaded her body to relax for a slow count of one thousand to be sure that he wasn't coming back, and to give herself a needed rest. She had enough problems—dehydration, lack of sleep, withdrawal symptoms—without having been the guest of honor at an enhanced interrogation, or in an emotional nuclear exchange with her father figure. She needed a break, if only for fifteen minutes.

After a while, she took stock again. At this point, it was clear that she was not going to change sides, and the shitheads probably guessed that she had told them all she knew. Hers was all bad news, to be sure, but unless she would give them names, her knowledge was no use to them in countering whatever forces they imagined were snapping at their heels. It followed that she was now a liability. They might put her under the towel once more in the morning to see if something good had popped into her head overnight. But if not, then curtains. Unless she could work some magic with two chess pieces and a wad of string.

Well, maybe she could. Patri thought she was super. Now was her chance to find out. It would be chancy and desperate and would need split-second timing. But there was a perfectly good gun hanging right on the other side of that wall. And what else did she have going? And even the little she had would come to nothing unless she could get one of those rocks from the goddamned foundation. So back to work.

She got off the platform at the corner nearest the shelves. She started where the shelves met what she thought was the north wall, which she hoped would be more weather-damaged than the rest. Moving methodically, she went from rock to rock in the top row, twisting and wiggling, feeling for any motion. She worked around the perimeter from right to left and passed the platform. She had almost circled the room and come back to the door, and was beginning to despair, when she found one that had quite a bit of slop. She wiggled, tugged, and pushed. It shifted back and forth by half a centimeter. Maybe less; it was hard to judge distances in the dark. But the mortar had clearly lost its grip on the rock's surface. The only reason the damn thing would not come out was that it was caged by the old, rotten cement. With a crowbar, she would have it out in a minute. She put a shoulder to it and shoved up as hard as she could. No luck.

What she needed was an impact. Put that way, the course of action was clear. Having her hands tied together was a bad problem; she could strike much harder with one fist than two. But there was no help for that. She had thought about cutting the plastic ties with the ragged edges of the flashlight battery casings, but those were all corroded and crumbled at the touch. So a two-hand strike it was. She squatted a forearm length from the wall so she could get some abdominal muscles into the action, identified the target stone by wiggling it, and tried a few practice strikes with no force, to make sure of the placement. Finally, unable to think of any excuse to stall longer, she wound up and hit it as hard as she could with the heel of her right hand, the left one going along for the ride. It hurt, and the rock didn't move. But she didn't break anything in her arm, and she was sure she had heard a little crunch of crumbling mortar. With nothing to lose, she wound up and hit it again. This time there was a lot more noise. When she wiggled the rock, it moved twice as far as before. Once more and the thing popped up out of the foundation as if it weighed nothing, rebounded from the wooden wall with a dull thump, and clopped off the foundation to drop solidly to the dirt, barely missing her right foot. She picked it up and hefted it. Now *that* was a rock.

Just one more thing, and she could commit. She reached far under the platform and retrieved the fishing line and chess pieces. The line was a tangled mess, from which she figured she needed four meters of straight stuff. Finding an end in the dark was infuriatingly difficult, but she couldn't break the line bare-handed, so she kept at it and eventually succeeded. She sat herself down tailor fashion near the top of the platform, resigned to a long spell using hands and teeth to tease the ball of line apart and to extract the loose end, centimeter by centimeter.

# YEG

Lani awoke to the sound of voices outside her door and to a shocked rush of adrenaline that she didn't even try to suppress. Her eyes were barely open, but it was Yeg and Bokun outside for sure. That made it showtime. She would need all the buzz she could muster.

The light went on, the door thunked open, and Yeg marched in, carrying the water jug. Bokun strutted right behind with the towel and the ropes. He shoved the door closed with an elbow, singing cheerfully:

> *"A robin with a yellow bill*
> *Flew down upon my window sill.*
> *'Wake up,' he said, 'the sky is red!'*
> *And so I crushed his fucking head."*

Oh yeah, she thought. They were gonna kill her real soon now. If they could.

"Rise and shine, princess," said Yeg, gesturing with the diagonal cutters. "You have questions to answer. It's a pop quiz."

She whined and struggled to her feet. "No, guys," she begged. "Not that. I'll tell you anything. Please don't…"

Yeg leaned over to cut the tie binding her feet together. As he straightened up, she caught his eye and reached as if to caress his face with her bound hands. "Please!" she wept. "You don't have to do this."

Yeg smiled broadly and, with a teasing gesture, reached out with the cutter and snipped the tie connecting her hands. At the snick of the cutter, Lani shrieked and moved.

The shriek was her best, loudest, glass-shattering high note, the one that drove her parents mad when she was a child. She blasted it unexpectedly into Yeg's face from a half meter away and got a respectable startle reflex from him. He jumped violently and then blazed with anger. Lani's move was to hop up on the platform while flailing her arms about. Her first flail caught Yeg across the bridge of his nose, not hard enough to damage him much but enough to mess up his vision for a few seconds and to make him madder.

She fell backward and continued to screech and windmill as she scrambled upward, all the way to the high end of the platform. There she thrashed her legs and tried to find some purchase for her hands that would let her escape. Yeg shook his head once and swarmed up after her, trying to pin her legs so as not to get kicked. By this time, Bokun was chuckling about Lani's futile panic. As Yeg corralled Lani's knees and scooted upwards to pin her body to the platform, she screamed hysterically at the ceiling, eyes triangulating the rafter over her head. She heaved with both legs to move Yeg ten centimeters to the left, then pulled as smoothly and as hard as she could on the wad of fishing line that, by then, she held securely in her left hand.

The line ran up beside a wall stud, around the header beam, and two meters out her chosen rafter, where it pulled the black knight from its position chocking her rock. After the briefest of delays, the rock rolled sideways off the rafter and fell free for a meter and a half before striking Yeg at the base of his skull, a little off-center. The sound was like a melon dropped on a sidewalk. The rock then bounced harmlessly from Lani's upper thigh, boomed out and down the platform for a bit, and thudded to the floor.

Lani kicked herself out from under Yeg and slithered over him to roll off the platform on the side opposite Bokun. Never very fast on the uptake, Boke was still holding his ropes and staring open-mouthed at what was left of Yeg, who was jerking in the grip of some kind of seizure.

"Hey, Boke," she said with a crooked grin. "Guess it's just you and me, huh?"

# HAND TO HAND

It was more of a fight than Lani expected. She figured that Bokun had the advantage in weight and reach, but he had nothing else going for him. She had speed on her side—and surprise. She had sparred with him many times and had paid attention, so she knew his tricks, quirks, habits, and soft spots. Most of all, she knew that he was fighting because he had to, to get out of the fight, whereas she really and seriously wanted him dead.

Boke tossed away his ropes and circled to meet her in the open space between the platform and the door. Given their sizes and fighting styles, the sensible strategy for Lani was to keep her distance, never giving Bokun a chance to use his strength, pecking at his defenses until she wore him down. Naturally, then, her plan, first chance she got, was to go inside.

Bokun launched a kick with his right foot, which Lani expected; that was how he usually started a fight. But then he pivoted and fired off another with his left, which she didn't expect, and which got him close enough to catch her in retreat with a left jab that grazed her cheekbone. She gave a startled yelp to make him think he'd hurt her more than he had, and backpedaled fast but with an awkward stagger that she didn't intend. It came to her with a rush that she wasn't up to this. Fatigue, sleep deprivation, dehydration, and too much adrenaline were all messing with her reflexes. On a normal day, she would have had him cold. But today, taking him on hand to hand was looking like a terrible strategy. She needed a weapon. She needed her rock.

She was also running out of space to retreat into. She stalled Bokun with a high jab that wasn't meant to connect, then spun a quarter turn, backed quickly, and made a diving sideways escape across the platform and Yeg's body. She skidded over the platform's edge and landed face-down on the floor, with the rock between her and the door, just out of reach. By the time she got her feet under her and scuttled forward to grab it he had run around the end of the platform and was at her again, this time with a hasty kick aimed at the rock. Lani jerked back so the kick missed and hurled the rock at him, but with no arm extension behind her throw and her weight all wrong. The rock floated lazily through the air and tapped him in the chest. It didn't hurt him, but it did upset the timing of his next, best shot—a right-handed overarm blow that was intended to brain her. But she was already bent over, so even before the rock fell back to earth, she had ducked further and moved in under his punch, putting out everything she had to strike with her elbow into his unprotected lower ribs, and not even registering the crack of bones breaking until she was past him, slamming her fist into his kidney with a sweeping backhand blow as she went. He doubled over with a coughing grunt. She turned quickly, did a shuffle-step toward him, and stood poised for a full two seconds while he struggled to lift himself upright and get his guard up. But as he did, when his near knee straightened and began to take weight, she lashed out with her left foot and kicked the knee in from the outside. There was a popping of ruptured cartilage, and he screamed and toppled forward onto his face. She then positioned herself so that when he lifted his shoulders, looking up to locate her, she could step forward with a smooth, coordinated soccer kick and smash her instep squarely into his throat.

Bokun flopped over onto his back, gagging and groping aimlessly. Lani was sure she had crushed his larynx. In minutes, swelling of the damaged tissue would shut off his airway and he would suffocate. Not a nice way to go, but for the moment, he was still strong and dangerous. She felt no sympathy and no urge to move in and try to kill him outright. She had other things to do, and very little time.

Lani danced around Bokun's squirming form and back to Yeg. He had stopped thrashing. She rolled him onto his back and dragged his feet out past the lip of the platform on the other side from Boke so she could pull off his boots. She tossed them aside because, for now, she was fine with bare feet. But she really couldn't ride hours into whatever passed for the local town bare-ass naked. So she undid his belt and yanked his pants off, unbuttoned his shirt, and rolled him over to take that off too. She pulled these on quickly, with no regard for niceties. The fit sucked, but after all, they were Union standard issue; the fit was supposed to suck.

Then came the hardest part, measured in pure muscle power. She jerked Yeg around so he lay on his side, head up parallel to the long edge of the platform. She squatted by the platform and pulled and dragged until she had his arms draped across her shoulders, with his head lolling next to her cheek. Then she rotated and heaved, straightening her legs to end with him in a flaccid piggyback carry. She lugged him this way across the room to the door. There, she shifted her grip on his right arm to his hand, worked around awkwardly until she had his thumb extended, took a deep breath, and pressed the ball of his thumb against the lock plate.

The bolt clunked loudly. She pulled the door open and let Yeg slip off her back and onto the floor. She was out.

# BUCK AND VENNA

Lani was already reaching for the Walther on its peg before her mind registered that the weapon wasn't there. Same peg, right where she remembered. No gun.

"*Shit!*" she spat, suddenly unnerved and trying not to panic. She had been counting on that gun. She scanned the tabletop and had started a visual search of the whole dim, cluttered barn before she jerked her whirling thoughts to a halt. The gun was gone. She would never find it. Nothing else presented itself as a plausible weapon.

What the hell, she thought. *Move.*

Across the barn, then, at a trot, to the horse stalls. She was pleased to find that she could run, after a fashion. Prodded by necessity, her body was making a comeback of sorts. About time, she thought.

There were six stalls, three occupied by curious horses, all giving her the eye. All the full stalls and one of the empty ones had names painted on them. The leftmost belonged to a short, solid pinto named Buck, which she hoped he didn't. Aside from his name, she could not have asked for a more promising animal. He looked like a quarter horse all the way through. If so, he would be quick to accelerate, quick to stop, and sharp in the turns—just what she wanted. If he was smart and well-trained as well, then everything would be fine.

She devoted about twenty seconds to getting acquainted, stroking his neck and cupping her hands around his nose and breathing into his nostrils as he inhaled. Normally she would have spent five minutes in this fashion, but there was no time. Venna and her sword would be along any moment. She opened the stall door and led Buck out. Saddles and other tack hung from the walls, but again she didn't dare take the time to do anything with them. She moved up beside him, talking calmly and winding her fingers into his mane. She had already checked the exits; the back doors were open, and the front ones were closed. There was no time to open the front ones; anyway, she did not want her departure to be visible from the house. Back door, then. She still had no idea how Buck would react to being ridden bareback, but there was only one way to find out. With a two-handed tug on his mane, a big hop and a high kick with her right leg, she was up.

She quickly found out that Buck was a dream: alert and responsive, with no sign of the jitters. He took to a bareback rider as if he had never done anything else. Count on the Chief, she thought, to stock his place with well-trained horses.

She let Buck walk out through the back doors, which were on the low side and, with their center post, narrow as well. He didn't blink. Her intention was to turn right, get onto the gravel road that the Chief had taken her down whenever the crap that was, and then gallop like hell out of there. She promptly found a tall fence in her way and no gate. She made a sharp reversal, urged Buck into an easy trot, and rounded the back corner of the barn onto a wide green yard. The main house was straight ahead. But just to the right of the clear path to freedom came goddamn Venna twp Triple-E Keithley, sword at her side and steaming coffee cup in her hand.

It looked like Venna had come out of the side door of a long low building that Lani had not noticed before. It had a smoking metal chimney sticking from its roof and the general appearance of a bunkhouse and kitchen for the staff. Venna was in the open, fifteen meters from the building's windowless end wall, when Lani and Buck came into view. She sized up the situation with her customary quickness and pitched her coffee cup away, but then she made a bad decision. Faced with conflicting impulses to run for it or to stand and fight, she tried to do both.

She scurried awkwardly back toward the door, also trying to free her blade from its scabbard. Lani meanwhile kicked Buck into a full gallop and charged down on her back like a stooping hawk. Venna struggled with the sword but was prevented from drawing it completely by the wall of the bunkhouse. At the last instant, Lani shifted her weight, hauled back on Buck's mane, and he slammed to a turning, skidding stop. As the horse shied away from the building and his hooves scraped for traction, his hindquarters swung sharply around and smashed Venna into the solid wall, only a couple of meters from the door she was trying to reach. With a struggle, Lani then got Buck to back up. When he felt Venna under his hooves, he spooked and kicked and trampled briefly until he could leap out onto better ground, where he stood quivering.

Lani leaned forward and did her best to calm him. Then she slid off and gave her attention to Venna. She lay in a crumpled heap with blood on her head, not moving. Maybe she was dead and maybe not, but either way, Lani wanted her sword. She couldn't get the belt and scabbard off, though. That paranoid bitch had it locked onto her body in some fashion that Lani couldn't figure out right away. But the sword was already most of the way out of the scabbard. Lani took the blade and left the rest. She quickly realized that wasn't too bad a deal. It was a Union standard smallsword, dull and triangular for most of its length, tapering down to a sharp edge for the last ten centimeters, and a needle point. A dueling weapon, in short, but one that wouldn't cut her leg off just carrying it around, and that she knew how to use if needed.

She remounted, feeling more hopeful than she could remember. She was outdoors under a cloud-flecked sky, with a tolerable blade in hand, on a horse that she had learned to love in about ninety seconds. What could be better?

She had also, however, learned to be cautious. Instead of trotting out into the open again, she eased Buck out from behind the bunkhouse slowly, with her head held pressed down into his mane. And promptly heard a flat crack and the buzz of a bullet past her ear. The Chief was out there, with his little automatic pistol.

# COMANCHE LORE

Lani had to make a fast decision. She could retreat behind the bunkhouse and look for some way to escape without a fight, or she could go out in the open and brave the Chief's gunfire. She had caught a glimpse of his position; he was standing in the middle of the yard, where he commanded all the unfenced routes to the road. Trying to circle the bunkhouse would not buy her anything and might expose her to other dangers if there were people inside. On the other hand, charging him was reckless but not quite crazy. The barrel of that tiny pistol was not even as long as her little finger. The Chief was a very good shot, but no amount of skill would make for accurate shooting with such a gun at more than maybe ten meters' range, especially with a moving target. Besides, she thought she could fool him. The direct assault it was, then, and the sooner the better.

She sat up, straightened her spine, tucked in her chin, and positioned the sword in her right hand pointing straight up in a cavalry salute. Looking every bit the professional, imagining herself as some Kipling character parading before the Queen, she nudged Buck into a slow trot, moved straight out without even looking at the Chief, then turned to face him and halted, as much as daring him to try another shot from forty meters. He stood his ground with his pistol up, pointed straight at her head. It made her eyes itch, thinking about one of those little slugs plowing into her brain.

"Give it up, Lani," he shouted to her. "You can't win."

"Oh, I think I can, Chief. I've killed your goons, and if you don't stop this right now, I'll kill you. Be reasonable. Call it quits."

The Chief thought about this for two or three seconds, then fired again. Another round buzzed by Lani's head, then her heels dug into Buck's sides, and he leaped ahead and galloped hard, a trifle to the right of their enemy. The Chief stood steady, holding her in his sights. Lani felt sure that he would wait until she got close enough that he could not miss and then would shoot her three or four times as fast as he could pull the trigger.

With her free hand, she clutched a handful of mane high up on Buck's neck. Just before she guessed the Chief would fire, she slid to her right and off Buck's back, hooked her left heel in his croup, and hung her whole body down along his right side. From the Chief's point of view, she must have simply vanished. With her right hand, she thrust the sword out under the horse's belly, stretching as far as she could, wishing for longer arms.

Buck held his line for only three strides while Lani kept position, then her sword tip made contact. In an instant, the sword tore from Lani's grip, her heel lost its purchase, the Chief's gun fired, and Buck lurched and slowed abruptly. All of this pitched Lani down and forward. She tried to get her hands out and her feet under her so she could roll, but failed at both and plowed hard into the ground with her face and shoulder before she lost control and tumbled and skidded to a halt.

She lay still for a few seconds before struggling to a sitting posture. The pain wasn't too bad. She was bruised and abraded all over, but those injuries hadn't yet started to hurt. Something was wrong with her right shoulder, but as long as she didn't try to raise that arm, she could manage. When she looked around, she saw Buck, between her and the main house, limping slowly. Then he sat down with a whinny, rolled onto his side, and stayed there. She stood up to go comfort him but then remembered that the Chief was unaccounted for. She turned around, located him, and reluctantly decided that he should come first.

He squatted upright on the grass twenty meters away. She limped over to him and collected weapons. His gun lay on the turf beside him; the sword was a little farther away. She pocketed the gun and, with sword in hand, returned to kneel in front of him. His face was gray, and his breath came in short gasps. He clutched his stomach with both hands, but to little effect. Most of his intestines and a good deal of his blood were already on the grass between his knees.

When she appeared in front of him, he looked up, and his dull expression animated a little.

"Good...trick," he whispered. "Where'd you...learn?"

"My last summer in Colorado," she said. "Me and my brother. We read about Comanches doing that, and we taught ourselves. He broke an arm."

"Sorry, Lani...wish...to hell...you'd...seen things...my way."

"I'm sorry too, Unc. But I just couldn't. You're..."

But his eyes were closed; he wasn't listening. It was too late for explanations.

He reopened his eyes and, for an instant, he looked like the old Chief.

"Lani," he said, barely audible. "This...really hurts. Can you...end it?" He stopped to breathe for a moment. "Please?"

She brushed back tears and nodded. "Sure thing, Unc. Okay."

She got up and studied his face for a short while, memorizing. Then, with a quick, backhanded flick of the blade, she sliced open his left carotid artery and limped away. She didn't wait to see the spurting blood or watch his final slump to the ground. She had seen too much of that kind of thing lately and wanted no more.

# CLEANUP

Buck was an unhappy horse, but it didn't look like his life was in danger. There was a powder burn over the muscle of his left shoulder and a small-caliber hole leaking a little blood, but he would be fine if he got prompt surgery and antibiotics. This eased Lani's mind quite unreasonably. This day she had killed four people she knew well in about that many minutes, and the idea of causing death again—even having to put down a horse—revolted her. In fact, she wondered if all her life had been misspent, every day of it since she was adopted into EEE, at age ten. She had worked and trained to become an invincible killer. To all appearances, she had succeeded. But she had to face facts: when it came down to cases, she just didn't like the work.

There was no sign of activity from the main house, but she remembered smoke rising from the bunkhouse chimney. She had to check it out. She was circling the building to find a different door than the one that Venna had failed to reach, when another man appeared from that direction. He was very tall and thin, and carried a longer and heavier sword than Venna's. Could be a cavalry saber. She studied him carefully, then, a little hysterically, began to laugh.

"Goddamn, Skinny," she hooted. "Is that you? Last seen selling leather goods? I swear, never have I heard about a gang with more jobs for fewer people! What the hell are you doing here?"

"I'm just the cook," he confessed with a shrug. He stood still briefly to take in the Chief's gory remains and the Chief's pistol, now out of Lani's pocket, and pointed at him. He flung his saber away and put up his hands.

"Good thinking," said Lani. "Come over here. Five meters would be about right. A little closer. Good. You can put down your hands. Now strip. While you're at it, tell me how many other people are here."

"I've been serving five. Three more due in a couple of days."

"I know of four, plus you. Where's the other one?"

"He's got the cart. Gone into town for supplies."

"Ah. And where's town? Where the hell are we, Skinny?"

"I think he's gone to Plattsburgh. Ausable Forks is closer, but he wanted special stuff."

"When did he leave?"

"I don't know. Half an hour ago?"

"Okay. You can leave your skivvies on. Bring the boots; I'll need 'em. Come with me. I need some help. You first. To the barn."

Lani hobbled along with Skinny leading the way. She waved him in the back door; if he bolted, she didn't want the front doors open. Once inside, she sat down on a hay bale and said, "Skinny, I need you to saddle me a horse. You know these two horses?"

Skinny nodded.

"Good. I want one with a nice smooth stride. Saddle up the one that's best in that department, okay? And be advised, I know horses and I know guns. So pick me a good one, Skinny, or on my way out, I'll kneecap you with this little popgun. Are we clear?"

Another nod from Skinny. He didn't seem like a subservient sort, really, but swift reversals had him all undone. Lani supposed he must be pretty terrified by now. Killing eighty percent of a chef's clientele between breakfast and lunch might have that effect.

Skinny picked his horse, a bay mare named Goshawk, and went to work on her. While he saddled, bridled, and cinched, Lani slid her feet into his boots and got the sword under her belt so she wouldn't stab Goshawk or herself but was still capable of a left-handed draw.

"Okay, Skinny, two more things and we're done. First, hitch Miss Goshawk to the rail over there by that dude's step. Good. Next..." Lani got up and led Skinny over to the table by the torture chamber door. She shot a quick look at Bokun, lying inside. He wasn't moving, which suited her fine. "...take a handful of those zip restraints and come with me." She led him to the barn's back door.

"Now I want you to zip your hands together and tie yourself to that center post."

For the first time, Skinny objected. "Aww...Miss, don't do that. I won't make trouble for you."

"I know it, Skinny. But do it. Now. Don't worry, I'll send somebody back for you before you get too thirsty."

Skinny moaned, but he did it. Lani's conscience was salved when she saw that he didn't need instruction on how to work the zip restraints. He had tied people up before, just that way.

Lani took a moment to rinse her face and arms in the horse trough. Then she nuzzled with Goshawk for a bit, positioned her nicely by the dude's step, and climbed aboard. Shrugging her bad shoulder made her wish she hadn't. Wincing, she walked Goshawk out past the sullen and barely dressed Skinny. Outside, she stopped and called back.

"Skinny! This guy who left with the cart. What's his horse look like?"

"Big blue roan. Seventeen hands."

"Thanks!" she shouted and rode away.

# TWENTY-FEW KLICKS

Goshawk moved quickly. Once outside the gate, Lani found the going easy. At the end of a private path, she came to a narrow road, which after a kilometer, intersected the main north–south highway. If such a word could be applied to what was really a quiet rural track, only modestly well used. But there were watering stations every so often, and tamarisks and Russian olives for shade, and even occasional directional signs. The first one she saw said twenty-three kilometers ahead to Plattsburgh, eight kilometers behind to Ausable Forks. There were supposed to be judges in both places, but Lani feared that the nearer one might have been corrupted by the Chief and his crowd, so she pressed on.

The air was cooler and drier than she was used to, but not cold. It was a bit too comfortable, in fact. From time to time, Lani would go to sleep in the saddle, waking with a jerk just before she fell off Goshawk completely. This unnerved her. If she took such a tumble, she would likely hurt herself some more; worse, she might not be able to get back on.

About ten klicks on came the first challenge, when she overtook a covered one-horse cart pulled by a big blue roan. As she passed, the driver looked at her, looked again, and shouted, "Hey! That's my horse! What are you..." before subsiding in confusion. Lani pulled up and produced the pistol, but she was herself confused. There was something familiar about this guy. She struggled against the fuzz in her brain for a time, and then she got it.

"Bernardo Chaupi!" she blurted. "Your beard is different. And you've lost your queue. What the hell?"

Chaupi sat back in his seat and ran his hand across the back of his head. "Miss Lani," he said. "With the nanotech blade. You know, I have thought about you often. Especially lately. Luv McRae, he obliged me to make certain… preparations. In case you visited us."

"I bet he did. I guess that was your woodwork? The platform, the thumbprint lock?"

"I am afraid so. No one else at the ranch is, um, handy with tools."

Lani's mind was washed with spatters of memory, filling up gaps, answering previously unasked questions. "I'm beginning to understand things better," she said. "Like the nature of the agreement you two reached, back when. How is that going?"

"It's slavery, more or less," Chaupi said with a frown. "Blackmail and slavery. But perhaps no more." He stared pointedly at her ragged and blood-spattered clothes and at the Chief's gun. "I speculate that Captain McRae is no longer with us?"

"That's so. Nor most of his guests, either."

"Well. Interesting news. And me?" He gestured toward the gun. "Are you going to shoot me with that thing?"

Lani sat and looked and listened. Off to her right, she could see a tiny slice of Lake Champlain. A fresh-smelling breeze blew off it and stroked the spring-green trees along the road. Insects buzzed and chittered, getting on with the business of life. Life.

"No," she said. "I don't think so. I probably should, but I won't. Not today. If I were you, though, I wouldn't go back to that ranch."

"Thank you. I expect your advice is sound. Goodbye, then. Perhaps we meet again, in better times."

"I doubt it. Not unless you learn some manners. But good luck anyway."

She nudged Goshawk and trotted away. Another hour or two, and she could rest.

# KICK IT UPSTAIRS

Lani stumbled while climbing the seven steps from the street to Judge Dortu Zeil's front door. Painfully, she got herself erect again and commanded her body to one more effort. She knew nothing about Judge Zeil except that Patri had recommended her (or him), and she knew little about judges in general except that if you were unlucky enough to spend time with one, the male ones were addressed as "Sir" and the females as "Ma'am." But she was pretty sure she would make a better impression if she did not stagger or otherwise appear to be drunk.

Inside the wide front door was a room with a receptionist. His friendly smile froze in place when he saw the torn clothes, the dried blood, the zip ties, the naked smallsword, the ridiculously oversized boots.

"Uh, can I...help you?" he asked.

"Is Judge Zeil in? I need to see the judge right away."

The poor guy glanced up the stairway behind him, which was enough to get Lani moving in that direction. "You can't see the judge without an..." he began, then switched to a panicky "You can't go up there!"

As she started up the stairs, Lani took a page from the Chief's book. "I can and I will," she said, "And right now, too. Whatever the judge has going is less urgent than this."

At the top of the stairs was a hallway and two doors with frosted glass windows, left and right. The left one had a sign saying "Plattsburgh City Reps Committee"; it showed no lights inside. The right one read "Dortu twp Jud Zeil" and seemed to be filled with streaming sunlight. *How symbolic,* Lani thought, and opened the right-hand door.

Judge Zeil was female. This was statistically likely—the Union leaned unabashedly toward matriarchy—but by no means guaranteed. The judge sat behind an unimpressive desk, surrounded by comms gear. She was tall and matronly, past middle age but not yet old, and wore her white hair cropped short. She had big hands, which lay curled on her desk as she interviewed the two citizens who stood uneasily across from her. She barely glanced at Lani.

"Can't you see we're busy here?" she snapped. "Get out. Wait your turn."

Lani had had quite a while to plan her opening lines. She used them now.

"Beg pardon, Ma'am. I'm Lani twp Triple-E Maxwell. I just killed four members of my twp. I'd like to talk with you about it."

# JUDGMENT

The judge spent some seconds processing. Then her jaw firmed up and she addressed the standing citizens.

"I'll talk with you later," she said. "Now scram. Don't tell anybody what you just heard." She sat then, examining Lani, while the other two made hasty exits.

"Killings, huh?" she said, putting her hands in her lap. "In that case, I've gotta ask you for your weapons."

"Yes, ma'am," said Lani. With thumb and forefinger, she extracted the gun from her pocket and laid it on the desk. Then the sword, grasping it by the forte and presenting it hilt first.

"Thank you," said the judge, sliding into view the heavy Colt automatic that she evidently kept in a holster under the desk. She touched a couple of keys on her keyboard and said, "Faz, can you come up here, please? I need a witness. Bring your sidearm."

She smiled at Lani. "A police substation is across the street. Comes in handy sometimes." Then she snapped on gloves, examined the pistol with curiosity, sniffed the barrel, and looked over the sword, especially the dried blood near the tip.

A cop with a Walther slipped through the door. Judge Zeil nodded her into a corner, where she could see both of them clearly.

"Okay," the judge said. "First things first. Killings. When? Where? How many?"

Lani filled her in. She didn't know what to call the location but was able to identify it on the wall-size map that hung behind the judge's desk.

"Out of my bailiwick," the judge grumbled. "But not too far. Luv Maxwell?"—handing Lani an ID stick— "Lick this, please. And sit down over there before you fall down. Now. That place is two hours away. Judge Ram, in Ausable Forks, was a lot closer. Why'd you come all the way up here?"

Lani thought and worried. But damn. She was going to have to trust somebody, sometime. "My...advisor, Ma'am. He said he trusted you unreservedly. Not so much for other judges, hereabouts."

"Hmm. I wonder what he knows that I don't. Never mind. I need a few minutes, okay?"

Judge Zeil then buzzed the captain of the Plattsburgh police and arranged for a team to be sent to the scene. Cops, lab people, a medic, an ambulance. "Captain," she said at the end, "make it fast, please. Along about 14:30, I'm going to have to inform Judge Ram of these goings-on, and he'll send his own team. I want your people there first. Got me? And don't hand off anything. My investigation, for now." She raised an eyebrow at Lani. "Anything else?"

"A vet," said Lani. "There's a good horse there, got injured in the fight."

"You hear that, Captain? Okay. Don't waste minutes."

The judge slumped in her chair, then turned to Lani. "So how did you kill all those people, luv?" she asked. "Shoot them at breakfast with that puny pistol?"

"No, Ma'am," Lani said. "Far as I know, that gun didn't hurt anybody. Only the horse."

"So you killed four trained Triple-E cops with a standard-issue smallsword?"

"No, Ma'am. Just Captain McRae."

"Pigshit. I mean, well, well. Okay, you don't want to tell me. Let's come back to the other three later. And how did you get so beat up?"

"Fell off a horse, Ma'am."

"The one that got shot?"

"Yes, Ma'am."

"You don't volunteer much, do you?"

"Other people have told me that, Ma'am. I can be loquacious. But it's been a bad day."

"Fine. Anybody who uses words like 'unreservedly' and 'loquacious' on me gets a temporary pass. But I have to know: what makes this mess my business? So far, it sounds like an intra-twp dispute. If so, Triple-E gets to solve its own internal problems its own self. What have you got to say about that?"

"There are reasons, Ma'am. First, Triple-E is not a normal twp. It's more like an arm of the government. If there's malfeasance inside Triple-E, the world gets to know about it. Needs to know about it."

"Noted. I love getting lectured on protocol by rookies. Got any more than that?"

"I'm sure that this group was responsible for the torture and murder of National University faculty member Teti Yang last week. She was twp UniBio. There's been no chance to look for hard evidence of that, but I got an oral confession from the torturer yesterday. Unfortunately, that man is now dead."

"Lani, I feel like you are stalling."

"Yes, Ma'am. But you'll like this last one. When your people get out to that ranch, about half a klick out in the back, they're gonna find a little herd of genetically engineered Brangus beef cattle. They were constructed by direction from whoever was backing my Triple-E fellows. They're immune to the bovine virus. This gene manipulation defies long-standing Council directives. And that's just one part, Ma'am, of a broader seditious conspiracy that involves supporting secessionist groups and hiding Crazy Years propaganda in the Daily Drop. Does that get the judge's attention, Ma'am?"

"Luv Maxwell, you have a smart mouth."

"Yes, Ma'am. I've heard that before, too."

"Okay. For now, I'm sold, pending the report from my team. But I need your full story, and at this moment, you are in no condition to give it to me. So. Sorry to tell you, but I'm gonna put you in jail for a little while."

"Jail? But why? I'm the good guy here."

"It's the way it is, Lani. If half of what you're saying is true, then for now, you aren't safe running around loose. And if it's an extravagant lie, but there are still dead folks out there, then the rest of *us* aren't safe with you running around. So either way, you're going to the lockup for a spell. That'll all be clearer tonight when the team reports. Meantime, I'm having a doctor meet you over there to patch you up and tell me if you should be in the hospital. She'll want to sedate you so you can sleep. If she does, tell her okay, but you've got to be *compos mentis* by midnight tonight. That's when I'll come by the jail, and you can tell me your whole story. Sounds like it's going to take a while. Can you live with that?"

"Yes, Ma'am. One more thing. I borrowed a horse from the ranch to get here. She's hitched outside. Can somebody take care of her?"

"Of course. Faz, will you please escort Luv Maxwell to the lockup and then tend to her horse? And ask reception to cancel all my meetings today. I have to make a lot of calls."

"Yes, Ma'am."

Faz came over, big-eyed, and helped Lani out of her chair. Lani felt she ought to be insulted by the fragile-old-lady act, but only until she stood up. Then she was glad for a strong elbow to lean on.

As they reached the top of the stairs, the judge stuck her head out of the office. "Luv Maxwell? You *are* the Lani Maxwell from the Hendrikson mine business, aren't you?"

Crap, Lani thought. Not again. But it's a bad idea to lie to a judge. "Yes, Ma'am," she said dully. "That was me."

"Good. I thought so," the judge said and went back to her business. Faz's eyes had gotten bigger.

# EXIT INTERVIEW

It had been a long week. For Lani, the strain had mostly come from convalescence and boredom. She had spent the whole time in a fairly comfortable jail cell, mostly with the door unlocked so she could wander and chat with the crew that ran the place and raid the refrigerator. The crew boss was Chut, a stolid old guy who played chess much better than Lani did but would sometimes let her win. Doctor Matu (whose other name she never learned) stopped in to check on her twice a day, changing her dressings and watching her closely for brain bleeds or hell-knows-what. She also provided (at first, insisted on) pills so that Lani could sleep. At first, Lani had accepted these, but after several days she gave them up and returned to her old, bad sleep routine, nightmares and all. Curiously, her recent trials didn't enter into her dreams. When these were bad, these were still mostly about Colorado and twp Moly and the raid. A few times, investigators from the judge's office came by to question her about some detail or other.

After a week of this, she felt ready to do something awful that would put her on a work crew, just to get outside. She missed the sky, she missed her workouts and her solitude, and she missed Patri, Evar, and Vaun, whom she barely knew. When her mood got really bad, she even missed the Chief. It was a relief when she finally got summoned back to Judge Zeil's office.

The place had changed. Two more desks had been moved into the already cramped space. These were occupied by assistants who worked furiously at their decks or held muffled video conversations or (once that Lani saw) passed a note to the judge for her immediate attention. The room across the hall was no longer the realm of absent or somnolent members of the Plattsburgh City Reps. It now was a beehive of investigators doing investigator shit, quiet but very intense.

The judge was different too. She looked like she hadn't changed her clothes in days and hadn't slept for the whole week. Guessing from the general atmosphere, that was probably almost true. She waved Lani into the same chair she had occupied before and slumped in her own with her elbows on the desk and her face in her hands. After a moment, she stirred and looked at Lani with a rueful grimace.

"Well, Junior, you've stirred things up," she said. "You have a good eye for detail, I'll give you that. You'd be amazed how many cockroaches scurry away every time we turn over one of your offhand suspicions. We've got three panels of judges working this thing already, and more to come, I'm sure. Most God-awful stuff I've ever seen. And mostly top-down, too. Not a bunch of little thugs thinking they'd do better if they unionized. Nope. It's people who already have life by the nads, figuring how to twist the little people around their fingers. I didn't think it could happen here. But it could. It did. Would you believe me if I told you…but no, I'd better keep that one to myself, for now."

She broke off and stared out her window for a while, where the sun and clouds seemed to be carrying on business as usual. Finally, she turned back to Lani and fixed her with her no-nonsense gaze.

"Enough about my problems," she said. "I'm letting you loose. Don't think there's any danger to you. We don't have all the vermin rounded up or even identified. But the beans have been spilled; the rest won't see any percentage in revenge. Before you go, though, I need to bring you up to date."

There was something new on the judge's desk: a basketball-sized transparent plastic bubble with a thick aluminum ring on its bottom. It looked like a piece of junk, scarred and abraded on the outside. But as the judge considered Lani, her hands, seemingly of their own volition, reached out and brought the thing to her lap, where she cradled it as if it were a baby.

"First, the bad news. Your pal—mine too, by the way; we went back a long time—Hap Moran? He died the day you got snatched. It's not quite clear if they killed him to eliminate a witness or if his dear old heart finally gave out under the stress."

"Does it matter?" Lani asked.

"Of course not. They were guilty as hell, either way. Anyhow, I'm sorry to be the one to tell you. With him gone, the Union's lost a giant, and the world is a smaller place."

Again acting on their own, her hands put the bubble back where it had been.

"Next. Your friends? Patri and Evar and Vaun? We've gotten in touch with them using Evar's dead drop. Clever, that. Anyway, they know that you are okay and that they can surface. Sounds like they were carrying on without you, as best they could, using public communications. They were maybe a couple of days from having Patri walk into Judge Chao's office when you broke things open. When you get home, they should be back from wherever they were."

"Thank you, Ma'am."

"Last, here's your fanny pack. Recovered from the ranch when we searched the place. Your small deck is in there, and a ticket to Trenton. Also, we took up a collection and added a little roll of cash. Don't be surprised. Go and buy yourself something nice when you get home. Or take Patri out to dinner."

Judge Zeil looked at her with an expression that was almost motherly. "Maxwell and Gibbs," she said. "I like that."

"Yes, Ma'am," said Lani, squeezing back tears. "I expect you would."

# CONSEQUENCES

Lani had been in the mayor's office only once before, when her class had graduated from the twp academy, and went there to be sworn in. Back in what she thought of as the Old Days, before she was shanghaied by members of her own twp, getting invited (if one could call it that) for a one-on-one meeting with the mayor would have been profoundly unsettling. Now, being summoned to the mayor's sanctum didn't impress her; it just wasn't serious. As she walked in, Poirot the bloodhound shambled over to be scratched behind the ears. No, Lani had seen serious, and this wasn't it.

"Good morning, Lani," the mayor said. "It's good to have you back. How's the recovery going?"

"Fine, luv," Lani said. "The collarbone is only a greenstick fracture; it's healing up okay. They'll let me start exercising in a few days." In fact, nearly two weeks after the events, she still looked damaged. Her facial bruises had not quite gone away, and she still carried scabs here and there, but at least she could walk without limping.

"Glad to hear it. Don't push too hard, not to begin with, dear. Listen to the doctors."

"Yes, luv."

"Now, I asked you here to tell you three things. First, I want to thank you

277

for all you've done. I know you started out by breaking some rules, you and your friend Evar. Including, young lady, violating my explicit instructions. I'm not thrilled about the motives that either of you had for getting into this thing. They were short-sighted, selfish, and insubordinate. But all that aside, when things got tough, you two conducted yourselves in ways that were…let me see now…I wrote down some adjectives. Yes, here: 'honorable, ingenious, virtuosic, and brave. Bordering on heroic.'"

"Beg pardon, luv. 'Virtuosic?' Really?"

The mayor sighed. "I know. We're going to give you a medal, Lani. Sort of. I have to write a citation for it, and frankly, dear, I'm not good at that sort of thing."

"How about 'skilled,' or 'tenacious?' And what do you mean, 'sort of?'"

"Ah, good. I can use that…Means we will give you the medal. But then we'll take it away and put it in a box and ask you not to mention it again. The citation will go in the records, but we won't tell the public, and we hope that you won't either."

"Why on Earth not? It's all over the news."

"Yes, but without your name. You've probably noticed."

Lani had.

"You are 'a Triple-E operative,' or some such. Believe it or not, this is for your protection. The public already knows you as the only bright spot in that Hendrikson mine fiasco. Imagine if we added this to your resume. You'd never have another friend who loves you for yourself, or get a quiet night's sleep, or be able to walk down the street unmolested. We're doing our best to make it so you don't have to live like that. Of course, if that kind of celebrity is what you want, then we won't stop you. Feel free to tell anybody you want, anything you want. But my advice is, don't."

Lani digested that.

The mayor held up two fingers. "Second thing. I've canceled your probation review. From now, you are formally off probation and back to normal status. This will cause a little ruckus from the rule-bound corners of the twp, but nothing too serious, I think. And in the circumstances, it would be stupid to risk having panel members impugn your judgment or loyalty. Very bad optics. So you're off the hook on that one."

"Third thing," said the mayor. "Not such good news, dear. You have done a great service for your twp and your country. This isn't the first covert attempt to undermine the Union's principles, but arguably it is the worst so far. Maybe it would have been noticed and rooted out pretty soon, in any case. But in the event, you were the instrument that did the rooting, and people should be grateful, at least here within Triple-E.

"Don't look for that to happen. People inside the twp have lost loved ones. You killed your own father's brother. Never mind you had no choice or that he had it coming; do you think your dad is pleased with you? Or Yeg's brothers? Triple-E is being publicly shamed for its role in the affair; the twp itself may not survive. Confidence in the government is threatened. Two Council members have been hanged for treason already, and three judges, and likely there will be more before the investigations are done. Lots more will be sent to hard labor. Six twps are being dissolved. And all through law enforcement, people like me are being asked, why didn't we do our jobs? In good time, so you didn't have to go recklessly solo to do yours?

"As for me, I've resigned as mayor, effective tomorrow. I had nothing to do with the overt crimes, but many of them were carried out by my twple, on my watch. I should have known, and acted. Folks think I should be ashamed of myself, and I am. I can't run the place under that cloud. That means I've gotta go.

"Point is, Lani, the Triple-E twple are very upset by all this. Your actions are forcing people to deal with changes, big ones, too, and they don't like it. They're angry. They're gonna look for a focal point for their anger. For lack of an alternative, I'm afraid they'll pick you. Maybe you and Evar. They aren't stupid or heartless. They'll know it's not fair. Classic case of shooting the messenger. But until they get over it, which may take years, your life here could be pretty shitty. My advice: keep an eye out for that sort of stuff. Think about how much of it you're willing to take. And have a plan for what you want to do if it gets to be too much.

"I'm sorry to scare you this way, but I think it's my duty. Any questions?"

Lani sat looking at nothing and tried to squeeze out the empty feeling in her middle.

"May I ask something?" she said.

"Yes, of course."

"About Captain McRae? Were you and he ever…connected?"

The mayor stared at her for a long five count. Then she twisted her mouth and looked away.

"Yes. We lived together for a couple of years, a long time ago. About twenty-five years, I think."

"Then what happened?"

"The romance? It worked for a while, and then it didn't. Most of them are that way, you know. I said I wanted to separate, and we did. That was quite hard. I got over it. I'm not sure he ever did."

"Thank you, luv," said Lani. "I needed to hear that."

"I hope you don't hold me responsible for Ryg's…"

"Going off the rails?"

"Yes. Doing the things that he did."

"No, luv. I don't blame you. An old, busted love affair is no excuse for…" She shuddered, sat silent for a moment, and went on.

"I loved him too, you know. Always did. All I wanted was for him to think I was wonderful. Now, what I hope to understand is only, you know…"

"What he was thinking?"

A wee-hours conversation with Patri drifted back to Lani, and she smiled faintly.

"That's asking a lot, luv. Maybe just what he thought he was thinking."

"Well, dear," said the mayor, "I can answer that one. He thought he was thinking about how to make the Union stronger. Many of us do that. Sometimes we get it very wrong."

The mayor stared out the window for a while.

"Listen, Lani," she said. "I can't express how sad these events make me or for how many reasons. Again, I'm terribly sorry about it all. Some of it was my fault. If you need anything that I can give when I'm just a citizen again, I hope you'll ask me. Now, is there anything you'd like me or the new acting mayor to know?"

Lani stirred slightly, picked at the arm of her chair. "I've been sober for sixteen days," she said. "Course, I was in detention for most of that time, but still. And I've got a steady guy. Have had for a while."

"That's wonderful, Lani. Keep it up."

"Yes, luv. I'll try."

# EVAR'S RAVE

Evar was cleaning out her apartment. Lani watched, feeling helpless. With all the comms gear already removed, the place felt empty and cavernous. Even the refrigerator was gone, sent back to twp EEE Mechanical, where it came from. Evar had more personal stuff than most—a couple of memory blocks with her private files, a bound paper copy of her book, her toilet kit, a pair of running shoes she never used, a favorite shirt she had sewn herself. Everything else lay sorted into labeled piles according to destination. Hobbies, Kitchen, whatever. Lani was sad to see The Dress going to Wardrobe, where it would doubtless sit unused forever.

From time to time, Evar sipped from a bottle of vodka. Lani made do with tap water.

"Still smells like solvent," Eve complained. "Housekeeping has been nice and helpful. They come around a couple of times a week to clean the graffiti off my door. Now that I'm leaving, they figure it's safe to repaint."

"Were your scribbles any more original than mine?" Lani asked.

"Naw. Pretty much the same, I think. Adolescent, potty-sexual. Like you said. Threats. I did enjoy the leering toad."

"Probably the same artists."

"Yeah. It's amazing that Internal Affairs can't make them quit."

"First, IA has to want to."

"Right!" Evar stood by her desk with her lip quivering. "Right!" she quavered again, sat down hard in her desk chair with her face in her hands, and froze there for the length of two silent heaving sobs. She looked up at Lani, moist-eyed but fierce.

"You know what they're doing? Those small-souled, shriveled-up crones? They know I'm leaving. They've won. But they won't quit."

"What?" Lani snapped, sharply attentive to anything that threatened Evar.

"They say they've overpaid me. They want me to reimburse them."

"What the hell for?"

"Those twelve days I spent on the run? While you were getting tortured and killing bad guys? You remember those? They want me to reimburse the twp because I wasn't on station for that time. Contrary to Article 2, Paragraph 6 of my contract."

"Pigshit. Didn't you get a twp citation for heroism during those same twelve days? And isn't the amount of money trivial? Let me pay you back, if that's the only problem."

"Yes, yes, and no. It's not the money. It's the fucking principle. They don't get to beat up on me just because they can. Just because I'm, you know…"

"A pariah."

"Yeah. That's the word."

Lani stood and rubbed her face. Shook her head to clear it. "Of all the stupid, vindictive…" she said. "I suppose you're not getting any backing from your boss?"

"Don't be stupid."

"Right. You're leaving tomorrow? So fuck 'em. Go. Don't pay them a cent. If they want to come find you in Freeport…"

"Bangor."

"Will you be with your beau there?"

"Not quite. A lot closer, though."

"Good. Don't worry about payroll coming after you. They won't. If they do, deal with it then. Your new twp will stand up for you, and you can drag those weasels' names through the mud."

Lani made Evar stand up so she could be hugged properly.

"Okay," said Evar, hugging back convulsively, "Consider it done. But what do I do with my principles?"

"The same as always. Do your best to live by them. Every day. And if somebody is giving my granny a hard time and principles aren't working for you, then send me a stamp, and I'll come break their legs."

# LANI

A warm breeze drifted in the window of Tree's upstairs room, carrying the scents of hibiscus, passion fruit, even—was it?—yes, a trace of evening primrose. Lani stood and watched the soft stir of desert trees and the eastern sky that was filling with autumn's stars. Patri, her Tree, lay on the bed, head propped on one elbow, watching her.

"You're leaving, aren't you?" he asked.

She took a long, deep breath, let it out with a shudder. "Yes, my love. I don't want to. I have to."

"I know. I've seen it coming for weeks. Just didn't want to admit it."

"You have? Am I that obvious?"

"Pretty obvious, yeah. But who can blame you? You went through hell. Torture, literally, and you did what you had to, and now your own twple are freezing you out and making jokes behind your back…"

"To my face."

"Really? They're braver than I thought. Or stupider. Still, Vaun and I get drafted to do research and go to meetings and help finish up the work that you started, but whenever you show up, the others treat you like some stinging bug."

"Worse," she grunted. "Empty-headed muscle. Great reflexes but no brains. Or morals. An assassin. A brute."

"Hellfire," he said. "That stinks so bad. Then what's keeping you here? Some feckless grad student guy who can't even finish his thesis."

"Well, it would be better if he would ever wash his sheets. Or his feet."

"Right. There's only so much a gal can take." He got up and came to the window with her, held her gently.

"You know I'd go with you…"

"But you have work to do here. Not your thesis, the other stuff. I know. We all have to sacrifice when we're called. And you've been called."

He squeezed her a little tighter. "Keep in touch, okay? A stamp now and then? I can wait for you. But I can't wait forever. Especially not knowing."

She stared out the window some more. "I'll come back," she said. "Sometime. When I do, I expect to find you and Vaun running the place. For Vaun, it'll be perfect. I don't think she has any idea how to enjoy herself, but if she did, she'd be having the time of her life. You, I'm not so sure. But we need you both. The mess we got into, it was bad. And we won. But it's not like we fixed it and can expect it to stay fixed."

"I know. You're right. This…what do we call it? Crime spree? People ignoring edicts. Killing scientists because of what they know. Abducting and torturing their own twple. Lying to the public. That's all madness, but it's not random. It's a symptom. We won this round, but it will come back. And keep coming until we figure out how to live with change, and stay human. To adapt gracefully. Not to boom and then bust."

Patri paused for a moment, taking deep, slow breaths. Then he smiled.

"This Union of ours. It's wonderful. It's kept us on a good track for a couple of hundred years. Preserved our purpose, our solidarity. Only now, it's getting stuck. More and more often. Times *are* changing. The Union needs to change with them. But that has to be done honestly. Out in the open. Respecting the three E's."

"Aha. Your future, my boy, is in politics. I knew it all along."

"That hurts. But from you, I can take it. Sorry. I *do* talk too much. What about you? Where's your future? What will you do?"

"No idea. Not police work, though. Tree, right now, I can't even say who I am, apart from your best gal. I'll start in Maine, I think; track down Evar. After that, I don't know. West, probably. Something frontier-ish. Maybe north, too. But west, for sure."

"You just need a challenge. And snow in your face."

"You know me so well." She caressed his hands, then pulled herself free. "I gotta go, or I never will."

She dressed quickly, buckled on her little fanny pack, and in three steps, crossed the room to hold him close once more. "Kiss me," she sighed.

So he did, and held his grief until she was out the door.

She left, heading east, toward the train station and toward the blooming Low Earth Orbit swarm and the dawn that would not light the sky for a while yet. She came to the end of the walk that led away from his dorm and turned around. She could make out the window of his second-floor room. It was still dark, and she couldn't see him watching her.

But she knew he was there. And that she would return.

—

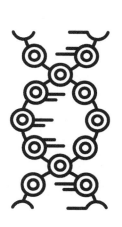

# APPENDICES

- Science Fiction as Predictor: How the Imagined Future Reveals the Past
- Science Fiction as Predictor: Capitalism *vs.* Socialism
- Science Fiction as Predictor: Faith in Reason—E.E. Smith to George Lucas
- Science Fiction as Predictor: Vampires and Zombies
- From the Ground Up: NAU History and Civics for Youngsters
- Where We Came From
- What is a Ttwp?
- NAU Military Weapons: Small Arms and Artillery
- Getting the Point: Swords in the Union
- Stratford Teachers' College: Welcoming Address
- Digital Communications: A First Textbook
- Annual Report of the Union Weather Service
- What the Hell is the Matter with Us?

# SCIENCE FICTION AS PREDICTOR:

## HOW THE IMAGINED FUTURE REVEALS THE PAST
## BY PATRI TWP UNIHIST GIBBS

*Submitted in partial completion of the requirements for the degree of Doctor of Philosophy in the Department of North American History,*
*National University of North America, July 2335.*

**Preface**

Science fiction authors did not usually try to predict the future. This was the case throughout the history of the genre, spanning roughly the mid-nineteenth to the late twenty-first centuries. Rather, most SciFi texts aimed only to be entertaining. What made them "science" fiction usually involved centering the plot on some timely or counter-intuitive scientific concept, or simply setting the action in an invented world, more or less plausible and often tiresomely familiar. In this way, authors could place their characters in extreme situations without the bother of historical research or loyalty to any kind of objective reality.

From a historical perspective, however, even tepidly boring SciFi stories can be useful. This is because, although SciFi works often purported to be about future events or alien beings or astounding new technologies, they were typically rooted in the worldview (and most often, in the anxieties) of the societies from which they came. Science fiction's lasting appeal arose, to a great degree, from its ability to make vivid metaphors for the buried governing obsessions of its own time and place. Thus, we can use even bad SciFi, which exists in abundance, to say something about the psychology of the centuries that were pivotal in shaping our present.

In the following chapters, I will explore several prominent examples of SciFi texts that one can interpret as technically inspired dreams of this sort—dreams that reveal in symbolic terms the deep cravings and fears of their parent cultures.

# SCIENCE FICTION AS PREDICTOR:

## HOW THE IMAGINED FUTURE REVEALS THE PAST
## BY PATRI TWP UNIHIST GIBBS

### Chapter 2. Capitalism vs. Socialism: Summary

As a rule, science fiction authors did not dabble much in economics. Most likely, the reason for this was that the first and most important function of SciFi was to entertain, and Carlyle's "dismal science" did not offer much fuel for that particular fire. In any case, the societies described in SciFi books and movies mostly ignored economics altogether to focus on other things. When this was not possible, the economic systems on offer were sometimes socialist, much more often free-market capitalist, and (with surprising frequency) aristocracies in which all production occurred in an invisible layer of petty bourgeoisie artisans and guilds. Nowhere in SciFi does one see imagined economies that compete in richness or invention with, say, the impossible and absurd genetic creativity of the twenty-first-century *X-Men* franchise.

Socialism was a viable economic model and political program from roughly the early nineteenth century (decades into the industrial revolution) until the middle twentieth century, by which time events in Russia, China, and elsewhere, amplified by capitalist propaganda, had caused "socialism" to be equated with "despotism" in the public mind. A few tales from this era explore socialism as a way to structure the economy, but for the most part (for instance, the Fritz Lang movie *Metropolis*), they illustrate that it is easier to identify the failings of hierarchical capitalism than it is to cure them. Perhaps the best depiction of a fully socialist economy is Ursula K. Le Guin's *The Dispossessed*. Her world of anarchists went a good deal further than mere socialism, however, extending to the absence of laws of any kind. The book was popular among SciFi authors and young, liberal readers, and some fragments of its vocabulary have propagated into current popular usage. But even among enthusiasts, there was general agreement that real anarchy was unlikely ever to work for Terrestrial humans. Prescient, however, was Le Guin's description of Earth's decline while, eleven light-years away, her Cetians were going about their law-free business. The Earth, one of her characters explained, was a ruin. It had been spoiled by humanity, who multiplied and warred and consumed and, in the end, died. All to reaffirm that, as with most historical disasters, our own came with warnings for those who would heed them. Few of our ancestors did.

Plain old capitalism prevails in most of the SciFi that deals with economics at all. The most common trope in such fiction is, however, the heroic businessman—the commercial, industrial, or technical magnate who shows his intellectual and moral superiority by making more money than the other guy. There are too many of these characters to count: E.E. Smith's antagonist Blackie DuQuesne (*The Skylark of Space*), Bob Kane's Bruce Wayne (*Batman*), Robert Heinlein's D.D. Harriman (*The Man Who Sold the Moon*), Poul Andersen's Nicholas van Rijn (the Polesotechnic League stories) and Gunnar Heim (*The Star Fox*), Alfred Bester's antagonist Ben Reich (*The Demolished Man*), etc., etc. The popularity of characters in this mold affirms a libertarian slant among the SciFi audience (rules are for suckers and morons; get out of my way while I get rich) and also a culture-wide obsession with individual celebrity. These attitudes, which Eapy Fox labeled errors of Equality and of Evidence, would serve humanity poorly in the run-up to the Bad Days.

Finally, in the last quarter of the twentieth century and the first half of the twenty-first, authors set quite a lot of mass-market SciFi in universes dominated by entrenched aristocracies, usually hereditary. Isaac Asimov's *Foundation* series plays out in such a universe, as does Frank Herbert's *Dune* series, the *Star Wars* saga, and many more. These works generally do not deal with economic ideas at all. Rather, they exploit the notions of aristocracy and empire to evoke past eras when the staples of traditional romance (noble titles, nifty costumes, horsemanship, sword fights, boundless love) could be played out with a straight face. The readiness with which such fiction was gobbled up speaks more to a public urge toward militarism (with its pageantry and the parallel tragedy of good men dying young), and to sheer escapism, than to any economic ideas.

In all, it seems fair to say that the SciFi genre, which prided itself on looking ahead, provided no preparation for the NAU's system of twps and judges. Nobody in those pre-Collapse centuries could believe how complete a shift in societal priorities would be needed just for humankind to survive. Only when things got bad enough, in desperation, did the Union's makers figure it out for themselves.

# SCIENCE FICTION AS PREDICTOR:

## HOW THE IMAGINED FUTURE REVEALS THE PAST BY PATRI TWP UNIHIST GIBBS

**Chapter 6. Faith in Reason: E.E. Smith to George Lucas—Summary**

The early twentieth century in Europe and America was marked by a swelling wave of scientific knowledge and capabilities, a wave that science, education, and faith in rational thinking rode to new heights. At about mid-century, that wave began to break. Early in the century, SciFi reflected public optimism about scientific progress, as embodied in dozens of broad-shouldered, clear-eyed, super-intelligent scientist heroes, from Hugo Gernsback's Ralph 124c 41+ (1911) to E.E. (Doc) Smith's Gray Lensman (c. 1950). But following WWII, for reasons that we can only guess (perhaps war-weariness, the horrors of nuclear combat, and the rapidly growing material comforts of post-war USA), the previous public support collapsed into skepticism of the scientific viewpoint and, indeed, of rationality itself. In the 1950s, SciFi editors may have been willing to face up to immutable physics in all its grim reality (*e.g.*, Tom Godwin's 1955 story *"The Cold Equations"*), but already the public wanted no part of it.

There followed twenty years of vagueness while SciFi migrated from books to the big screen. During this time, authors who thought of themselves as serious temporarily rejected the label "science fiction," preferring the less constrictive "speculative fiction". A better term might have been "fantasy," but that name had already been appropriated by people writing about broadswords and dragons. Speculative fiction never really took off, possibly because its preoccupations were mainly kinky sex and/or abnormal psychology. From a historical perspective, however, the mindset of readers in those days is clear. Conflict with Mother Nature was pretty much over, they thought; she had decamped to parts unknown after a thorough shellacking by modern doctors, lawyers, and actuaries. So what was worth reading about, except war between power blocs or the strange things that go on in people's heads?

After these decades of near-irrelevance, SciFi reattached to the public consciousness in the form of the *Star Wars* film saga, which generated reliably money-making films of varying quality from 1977 right through the Crazy Years and up to the beginning of serious civil hostilities. The whole corpus of *Star Wars* films purported to be SciFi but had nothing much to do with science. To the extent that even engineering played any role in these narratives, it was only to produce a sequence of increasingly horrific bits of planet-killing weaponry. Thus, science and technical expertise—thought patterns that elevated thinking over feeling—were portrayed as evils to be feared and hated. Opposed to this evil was a curious grab bag of old tropes: WWII aviation tactics, samurai swordplay, and telekinesis derived from obscurely realized eastern mysticism. But audiences had a seemingly insatiable appetite for the stuff. During these times, bookstores often devoted more shelf space to "Angels" than to "Science." No wonder, then, that civilization in this era wandered distractedly to the edge of the abyss and fell right in.

# SCIENCE FICTION AS PREDICTOR:

## HOW THE IMAGINED FUTURE REVEALS THE PAST
## BY PATRI TWP UNIHIST GIBBS

**Chapter 7. Vampires and Zombies**

During the decades between roughly 2000 and 2020, science fiction to many readers meant stories about the so-called undead. This obsession was most dramatically visible in the market for "young adults," whose viewing, gaming, and reading habits were the subject of endless—and often successful—marketing campaigns. Though the ranks of the undead paid at least lip service to many odd morphologies (werewolves, for instance), by far, the majority of such fiction dealt with either vampires (who could live forever if sustained on a diet of human blood) or zombies (once-living people who were brought back to life, perhaps indefinitely but always unpleasantly, by the action of some mysterious pathogen). What was it about this assuredly strange but rather limited subject matter that attracted so many gamers, viewers, and readers for so long? How did vampires and zombies gain such a hammerlock on popular culture?

Given the late-adolescent age range of the target audience, the vampire part is obvious, and its symbolism is easy to penetrate. (Hint: it was about sex.)

Understanding zombies is harder. At the most superficial

level, zombies made great, no-guilt enemies in "first-person shooter" games. Kids of all ages could enjoy blasting down man-shaped targets without, even in the game's narrative, actually hurting anyone who was not already dead. And, of course, this moral head start was inherited by all of the game-spawned videos, movies, and books with similar subjects. But clearly, there was more.

We can infer a deeper reason for zombie allure from Max Brooks's *World War Z*, from 2006. Reading it from our post-Collapse perspective, we become convinced that Brooks's zombies are a stand-in for something else, namely the twentieth-century corporation.

Like zombies, corporations were made from people, but they were not people. They weren't really alive, so they were very hard to kill. In principle, they could go on forever. They had no human sympathy or feelings. Indeed, corporations were monomaniacal sociopaths, interested in only one thing ("human flesh!" or, if you will, "profits!"), and willing to do pretty much anything to get what they wanted. They were everywhere. Worst of all, at any moment, your beloved (wife, sibling, boyfriend, child, fill in the blank)—or even you!—might suffer the fatal bite and turn into one of Them.

Seen this way, preoccupation with the undead was nearly inevitable. The recurring theme of this thesis is that science fiction's important role was to cast abstract menace into material form, which allowed people to deal with it better. If the menace was widely enough feared, authors could sell loads of books, and the public could get in touch with its collective loathings. This recognition was a good thing, in a limited way. It should have been useful to be reminded that Inhuman Beings did really walk the Earth and that just because their peripherals looked like (and perhaps even were) the guy next door, it didn't follow that the Beings would quit hurting people simply to make a buck. They wouldn't, and they didn't.

History now shows us what was needed to persuade humans to abandon the notions of unbridled corporate autonomy and of wealth-based social status. What it took was to kill, within a human lifetime, nineteen out of every twenty people on Earth. Zombies provided a good literary allegory for this disaster. But they were nowhere near enough to prevent it.

# FROM THE GROUND UP:
# NAU HISTORY AND CIVICS FOR YOUNGSTERS
# (ILLUSTRATED)

## BY TWP CHIRON

Appropriate age range: 10–14 years old.
Chapter III. *The Refoundation*. Teacher's Guide

*Summary:*
(1) The worldwide social Collapse in the late twenty-first century inspired the creation of a new political structure in North America. This structure vigorously rejected civic errors seen as leading to the crash. After a time, the structure became the foundation of a new nation, the North American Union.

(2) The Union has two founding documents: *Principia Civium* and *The Book of Judges*. These were created by Eapy Fox, with assistance from what later became twp TrenNJ. They appeared in 2185. They were soon widely read and appreciated as works of genius.

(3) The *Principia* concerns the most significant errors of earlier centuries. It divides these into three families, now known as "the three Es." These are:

    (a) Failures of Equality: policies that encourage the accumulation of wealth and power by individuals or other entities, especially when this is achieved by exploiting the large majority of people.

(b) Failures of the Environment: policies that serve short-term ends by damaging the Earth's resources or ecological balance.

(c) Failures of Evidence-based thinking: activities that exploit flaws in human thought processes to benefit the exploiters. These activities include many kinds of lies, most advertising, and all organized religions.

(4) The *Principia* also suggests how to discourage these errors. This involves the idea of "townships" (not individual citizens) as the most basic unit of society. Typically, a township (abbrev. "twp," pronounced "toop") consists of a few hundred persons. Citizens in a twp direct most of their activities toward a shared goal. Townships are largely autonomous. They are nevertheless subject to limited direction and control from the central government.

(5) The core activity of the central government is to redistribute the proceeds of taxation so that every twp can provide essential goods and services for its citizens.

(6) The *Book of Judges* (not the Biblical one; their only similarity is a conviction that people will make the same mistakes again and again) describes an ingenious system of interlocking courts to resolve disputes among townships. It provides strong safeguards to prevent small groups of judges from obtaining too much power. The judicial system's unique feature is that it does not commit to consistent or even fair treatment of either individual citizens or twps, only to maintaining the welfare of the Union.

*Teacher's Discussion Questions:*

(1) How does the global Collapse in the late 2000s compare with other great humanitarian disasters? You might compare it to the Black Death in Europe, the Thirty Years' War, WWI/Russian Revolution/Russian Civil War, or the Holocaust. What if you consider both human costs and damage to nonhuman species?

(2) Where and when did the structure of the NAU as a confederation of townships first appear? What is meant by "the Original Seven" and "the Next Nine?"

(3) The title *Principia Civium* is Latin. What does it mean? Why did the makers give their book this Latin name?

(4) How is the Union's notion of Equality the same or different from that of the French Revolution? Of twentieth-century communism?

(5) What is meant by "essential goods and services"? Does transportation qualify? Communication? Entertainment? National defense? How does the Union decide?

(6) Discuss some common examples of cognitive errors. How does science attempt to reduce the damage from these? Which of these errors did so-called social media, religions, and pre-Collapse advertising attempt to exploit?

(7) For what reasons did the makers choose several hundred people as the preferred size for a township? Has the importance of any of these reasons changed with time? How do rural twps differ from urban ones? Who deals with disputes between members of the same twp?

# WHERE WE CAME FROM

## EXTRACTS FROM UNDERSTANDING THE PRINCIPIA CIVIUM BY CRUTR TWP UNIHIST HIGHCHIEF

Introduction: Let's dispense, once and for all, with the business of the title. The book gets its Latin title by aping Isaac Newton's more-than-famous *Principia Mathematica,* which made physics a real thing and sent it on its way with a swift kick in the pants. Eapy Fox's thinking was likely similar to that of kids naming a friend "Tiny" because he is very large: the book is called *Principia* because it isn't. In fact, it is unlike Newton's book in pretty much every way. And also because, as Fox herself observed, everything sounds more impressive in Latin.

Mainly, the original *Principia* is orderly, with lemmas following theorems in a stately way. Fox's book is recursive and discursive, returning repeatedly to every major idea and drawing supportive arguments and elucidation from many sources (math and hard science, laboratory psychology, classical fiction, poetry, the pop culture of several centuries, music, art photography, and sculpture), often with only fanciful connections to the main flow of thought. As she pointed out, little of what she had to say was new. Rather, the work's novelty is the way it starts with a handful of diamond-hard ideas and then lays onto these coat after coat of richness and complexity. She was an autodidact, and as many such writers do, she threw everything she knew into her soup. But in the *Principia*, what emerged was not Mulligan stew but that rarest of creations: practical art.

*

Equality: Fox identified failures of Equality as the first and most important of the social factors leading to the near-destruction of civilization in the late twenty-first century. By "Equality," she meant many things, most of them illustrated in what she termed "the first big lie," as follows: In the pre-Collapse world, going back as far as anybody could remember, every large city had in it men (almost always men) wealthy enough that they could buy anything they desired. Boats, women, houses, think tanks, elections, you name it. And in those same cities, often doing work for the Big Men, there were many others who could not afford to house or clothe or feed themselves or their children, or to send their kids to school so that they might live better than their parents. Thus, the first big lie, namely that this state of affairs was morally okay. (The first big lie quickly spawned others, for instance, that this state of affairs was not only okay, it was *necessary*, for the health of the economy. And so on.)

Eapy Fox didn't think this arrangement was okay at all. Encouraging people to work and prosper and better themselves was good, but was that the same as ensuring that a tiny minority could become filthy stinking rich while everyone else starved? This question held most strongly in societies where top-end wealth was so vast that it had no practical purpose save for keeping score. *A fortiori*, it held for corporations, which pretend to be people and have all of people's vices (and more besides), and which are in principle immortal. As Fox put it, "Some people are much more obsessive, aggressive, and predatory than most of us. There is no reason to allow these people to set the terms of the social contract."

*

Eapy Fox's proposed solution to the problem of rich and poor came in two parts. First, she said that society should be organized so that nobody is in desperate poverty. Everybody with a blood pressure, she said, is entitled to the essential goods and services necessary to survive and function in society. Not only food, shelter, and clothing but also medical care, access to transportation, and to a basic level of education. In our own time, the list has expanded to include a personal computing deck, among other things.

Apart from its mathematical bent, the first part of *Principia*'s prescription is traditional (if rather high-voltage) socialism; its aim is to see that nobody is really poor. The second part is not so common because it tries to ensure that nobody is really rich. The means for doing this is simple; it is targeted taxation. But what does "really rich" mean? Characteristically, Fox approaches this question with an example from statistical mechanics, plainly called out as a metaphor, not a formula. (She always insisted on the importance of individual judgment, and never advocated controlling social behaviors with numerical algorithms.)

Fox's protests notwithstanding, the answer comes out as a formula. If $N$ is the number of individuals in your cohort, and $ln(N)$ is the natural logarithm of that number, then you are "really rich" if your wealth exceeds the average for your cohort, multiplied by $ln(N)$.

*

The Union Tax Service does not do anything so drastic or mechanical as slapping punitive taxes on people who exceed the $ln(N)$ expectation when compared to their neighbors. But that is nevertheless the flavor of the thing. Eapy Fox's disdain for material goods reflected that of her culture, and it is a feeling that persists today. More than that, it is manifest in the policies of the Union government. If you want to attract the attention of the Union's tax corps, just collect more material goods, by a factor of ten or so, than the folks around you.

*

For those who find logarithms, exponentials, and other mathematical discussion offensive, Eapy Fox had an inflexible response: "Ignorance of these concepts is dangerous and inexcusable. Go learn them."

*

If you really crave government attention, you can do no better than attempt to (in the pre-Collapse lingo) "go viral." Anything that smacks of exponential growth will bring an immediate reaction. The *Principia* and the Union culture are suspicious of material success but positively allergic to compound interest. In the run-up to the great Collapse, the world saw innumerable exponential bubbles that popped disastrously when they came in contact with the finite world. Even Union children fear positive feedback loops, in part, at least, because they are educated. They know some history, and they know some math: they understand exponentials.

# WHAT IS A TWP?

## CRAD TWP MACHTOOLS OLOWE

**2nd Prize, NAU Grade 10 Essay Contest (Nolpe Masuman, instructor), twp Sch793, Sturbridge**

Eapy Fox invented the notion of twps back before the beginning of the Union, when she was a professor of mathematics at the University in Trenton—the only university in the remaining fragments of the USA at that time. Today we would think it was barely a school, having only about fifty faculty and perhaps five hundred students. But Fox was impressed at how much got done by a group of that size, as long as they respected each other and worked together. During the Bad Days, members of the Uni had struggled and starved, clashed with intruders and looters, and sometimes died in the resulting battles. But they managed to live as a close-knit team that retained its focus on ideas, served a larger community than itself, and moreover kept safe its data archives and the tools to read them and the minimal technology to repair and replace and refurbish parts that failed. She thought that this success story might be replicated in other contexts, avoiding at least some of the obvious pathologies infecting life in the pre-Collapse.

In her thinking about how to structure a new society that would prevail where the previous one had failed, Fox tried to balance a handful of contradictory ideas:

People, she believed, are innately gregarious. They are happiest and most productive in groups, especially groups that strive together for some common purpose.

She thought the size of these groups should not be too large. To circumvent fragmentation into in- and out-groups, the number of members should be reasonably close to Dunbar's number of 150, the number with whom one person can maintain meaningful (if not close) relationships.

On the other hand, even now and more so in Fox's time, most working groups in North America would, of necessity, be small agricultural communities. There is a minimum size for which such units can be reasonably self-sufficient; Fox judged this to be two or three times Dunbar's number.

She knew that to collect such groups into larger units (cities, a nation), all would have to obey some guidelines ruling their interactions and even some of their internal workings. But to protect desirable freedoms, these guidelines should not be more constraining than necessary.

From all of this was born the modern township, the twp. Strictly speaking, there are no invariable rules or laws in the Union; even the most universal customs are no more than guidelines, open to interpretation and variation, if there is a good reason. But subject to the looseness inherent in the Union's style of organization, twps almost always have several common traits:

Twps are groups of citizens of the Union. Each twp keeps a list of its own members, known collectively as its twple. These typically encompass between one hundred and five hundred individuals.

Twps are functional units; the members of a twp work toward a common goal or directly support the twple who do. Twp names usually reflect their goals.

Twps arrange to provide their members with the necessities of life (food, housing, health care, education, and a few others). Funding to achieve standards for these needs comes from the central government, on a per-person basis, with adjustments for local circumstances.

Rural twps typically operate only on a particular plot of land. Urban twps tend to diffuse more into their communities. Near city centers, dozens or hundreds of twps may intermix geographically while retaining their individual identities.

Marriage customs vary widely across twps, but almost all are at least somewhat endogamous.

Twps pay substantial taxes to the central government, which are then redistributed so that every twp can provide to its twple the necessities described above.

The twp is the fundamental unit of Union society; within wide bounds, the central government takes no interest in or responsibility for the welfare of individuals. Twps are required to do this for their own twple. When they fail to do so, judges may intervene. Nearly always, however, judicial intervention is avoided by making it easy to form and dissolve twps, and also for individuals to move between twps.

Each twp makes its own arrangements for internal governance and enforcement of its internal rules. Twple typically choose their governing boards through procedures that are more or less democratic, but details vary widely. Each twp must select a member to represent it to the central government. The central government chooses higher-level officers exclusively from the twp reps via a democratic process in which each twp gets one vote.

Few twps are truly self-sufficient. Thus, twps often join in agreements whereby they provide goods or services to one another. In urban settings, where many twps exist and may overlap geographically, it is common to find specialized twps that run kitchens, or schools, or hospitals, or provide other services for all of the surrounding twps. One of the chief functions of the judiciary is to settle conflicts arising from such inter-twp agreements.

The high degree of autonomy granted to twps has a recognized tendency to create and tolerate local abuses, internal factions, and strife. When these situations become serious, they usually end with the dissolution of the already dysfunctional twp. At present, the Union comprises about one hundred thousand twps. Every year, about two percent of these break up. There is also a slow turnover in most twp's membership, as individual members leave to join other twps, or new members come in from outside. These transitions are considered normal and a validation of the twp system. Judicial interventions are rare, only a handful per year. These actions are usually considered failures, and many of them generate inquiries to determine how they came about and whether blame should fall mostly on the twps or the judges involved.

As Eapy Fox planned, Union twps make up most of the threads in our society's fabric, and they serve many functions. Her original vision took concepts from pre-Collapse structures, including the one-horse town, the extended family, the business corporation, the trade union, the Israeli kibbutz, and the self-organizing social club, to build something that could look like any or all of them but that still maintains a unique Union flavor. Taken together with the judicial structure, they form a strong but flexible system whose elements evolve with time, but that has a connecting structure that has held the Union together for more than a century through many challenges.

# NAU MILITARY WEAPONS SMALL ARMS AND ARTILLERY

## FREEPORT ENCYCLOPEDIA 2334

Within a decade of its formation, the NAU recognized the need for a national military to defend its borders and to combat the piracy that threatened its merchant fleet. After several false starts, the military structure solidified into two branches: the Navy and the Marines. The choice of weapons to be used by these services was then made quickly. Although nearly every weapon developed during the previous four centuries was, in principle, available, the original leaders of the military were acutely aware of the new country's sharply constrained resources, its minimal manufacturing base, and the impracticality of obtaining help from beyond its borders. For these reasons, they put great emphasis on ease of manufacture, reliability in harsh conditions, long service life, and commonality of ammunition. These constraints, particularly the need to avoid exotic materials and fabrication methods, led to a limited arsenal that drew entirely from early to mid-twentieth-century multipurpose designs.

The most familiar and recognizable of these arms is the Kalashnikov AKM; all Navy and Marine personnel are trained in its maintenance and use. The Walther PPK is the standard sidearm of Union police forces, as well as for some military applications. Its small size is valuable when concealment is important.

In the modern era, the Union's antagonists (and indeed the Union itself) have lacked the infrastructure to support either civil or military aviation. For this reason, specific anti-aircraft artillery is absent from the NAU list of weapons.

The list of supported weapons has changed little in more than a century, largely because, in that time, new technical challenges from outside the Union have been rare and minor. Production facilities for NAU weapons generally are kept in mothballs for decades at a time and are restored and operated sporadically and for minimal production runs when needs are identified.

**Small Arms**

*Pistol:* M1911A, cartridge .45ACP = 11.43mm, short-recoil automatic feed.
Walther PPK, 1936, cartridge .32ACP = 7.65mm, blowback automatic feed.
*Machine Pistol:* Uzi, 1954, cartridge .45ACP = 11.43mm, blowback automatic feed.
*Infantry Rifle:* Kalashnikov AKM 1947, cartridge 7.62x39mm.
*Machine Gun:* MG3 1960, cartridge 7.62x51mm, recoil-operated, 1000 rpm, belt feed.

**Artillery**

*Light:* Oerliken 20mm autocannon, API blowback operation, 450 rpm.
*Heavy:* Japanese 12 cm/45 Type 10 Naval Gun, fixed 120mm semi-automatic 10 rpm (modified).

# GETTING THE POINT: SWORDS IN THE UNION

## BY ISHOD TWP HOBBY SOLINGEN
## THE EDGE MAGAZINE, OCTOBER 2335

We have many swords in the Union, of many different types. There are blunt epees, foils, and sabers, meant only for sport. There are razor-edged katanas that would have looked at home in seventeenth-century Japan. There are rapiers and claymores and scimitars, cavalry sabers and naval cutlasses, two-handed broadswords two meters long, and Roman gladii you can hide in a briefcase. And there are the ones you see all the time: the standard-issue Union smallswords. For those of us who are obsessed with edged steel, there is an endless variety of the things, to say nothing of the fascinating details of how they were made, what they were used for, how experts wielded them, who originally owned the genuine antiques and what *their* stories were, and how present-day swordsmiths learn their skills and obtain the materials for their blades. In fact, delving into such details is the primary purpose of *The Edge Magazine*, and this kind of writing fills our pages every month.

But that's not what I want to do here.

This month, the question I wish to discuss is this: *Who are the people who, in today's Union, a moderately civilized nation-state, walk around in public wearing swords, and why in the name of sense and logic do they do so?*

It turns out there is a straightforward answer to this question. Two answers, in fact.

The first answer need not concern us very much, as it hardly has anything to do with edged weapons. This answer, briefly, is *fashion*. Swords worn for fashion are generally not swords at all but rather elaborate sword scabbards with fancy hilts affixed to their tops. Such a scabbard may not contain a blade at all. If it does, often it is not made of metal, and if it is, it is probably metal that will not take or hold an edge. Why people think they look good wearing such things is another story, and one that I will not go into here.

The second answer is more interesting. It is not, as many imagine, a historical relic from the time when the Union was a so-called "dueling society." One similar to, say, that populated by the French gentry in the time of Cardinal Richelieu. The reason that this answer fails in the case of the early Union is simply that it was never a dueling society. It is true that some duels occurred in the late twenty-second and early twenty-third century Union, but these were slipshod affairs, more like the old-west "gunfight at the OK Corral" than real dueling set-pieces. Of course, in most of those fights, guns were used instead of swords, and this in spite of guns being very rare and expensive, just as they are today. In fact, the only reason for dueling opponents to agree to swords was that, in a well-run fight between novices, a sword duel might be impressively bloody, but hardly ever kills anybody. The early Unionists were, after all, practical people.

But for the last hundred years and more, police and some others have carried swords. Now if dueling history is not the reason, what is? The answer lies in the great rooster bubble of 2199. Union Equality policies have usually prevented people from acquiring vast windfall fortunes from economic bubbles, in which some privately held commodity suddenly becomes immensely valuable. Nevertheless, there are always some people who are relatively well off, and when an opportunity arises to speculate on a very profitable sure thing, they will do that and hope to hide the proceeds from the tax man. Such an opportunity arose in the summer of 2199 when samples of a breed of genetically modified chickens were made available for testing only to a restricted group of Pennsylvania farmers. The chickens in question are quite standard today, but then they were seen as vastly superior to existing breeds with respect to size, disease resistance, size, egg-laying ability, flavor, and size. They were super-chickens. But just as word of these birds got out, there was a hiccup in the genetic processing line, and it became clear that, at least for the near future, the only supply of augmented fowl was the dozen farms of the original hen testers.

This turn of events gave rise to a very un-Union-like surge in the population of aspiring chicken thieves, drawn from other professions by the outrageous selling price of fertilized eggs, hens, or (especially) roosters of the new breed. The original farmers all belonged to a single township, twp ChikNegg. They at once appealed to their marshall (what we would call a bailiff today) for protection, who quickly concluded that, with a staff of two, the twp ChikNegg police force was not up to this challenge. He therefore appealed to the local judge, who pushed through an overnight labor draft to provide a modest army of deputy marshalls. The head marshall himself happened to have a relative who operated a warehouse stocked with obsolete weaponry, including quite a number of inferior swords. He was able to negotiate a contract on favorable terms, and soon the twp ChickNegg constabulary was not only numerous but also armed with highly visible weapons. This action quashed the Rooster Rebellion in its early stages. The chicken rustlers didn't want a fight; all they wanted was raw material for *coq au vin*.

This ludicrous episode did, however, serve a serious purpose. It caused several observers in the still tiny government to rethink plans to ramp up firearm production for the use of police and security forces. They reasoned that making more guns would simply spawn a black-market arms race, with probable horrendous results. But if the police carried not guns but swords, and actually learned how to use them, the entire crime-and-punishment environment would remain fairly non-violent. These thoughts eventually became policy, and police forces across the still-growing Union came to be armed with cheap but adequate dueling swords. Hardly ever with guns.

As for the swords themselves, they were (and are) nothing special. The Union smallsword is a lightweight stabbing weapon with a blade 70 cm long and a utilitarian bell and crossbar hilt. The blade is ground to be dull and triangular for most of its length, with a short single-edged cutting section near the tip, tapering to a sharp point. The steel is typically a chrome-moly alloy made for mass production, not superior quality.

That brings us to the present, in which the sword is explicitly a badge of authority. Today, if you see a person walking down the street wearing a nondescript dueling sword, you can be sure that a judge, or a mayor, or some other person with considerable clout is standing in the background. The sword doesn't need to be drawn. Its mere presence tells you that when this person commands, you had better obey, or at least listen.

# STRATFORD TEACHERS' COLLEGE: WELCOMING ADDRESS

## WAYT TWP STRATTC VAN VLECK
## SEP 5, 2334

Women and men, men and women of the class of 2337. As the mayor of our twp, it is my pleasure and honor to welcome you to STC. Also to be the first to make you aware of, and (if I may presume) to inspire you to prevail over, the challenges that you will soon encounter here.

STC (or "The Strat," as it has come to be known) is by all accounts among the best of the teachers' colleges in our Union. That is saying something. Just to get here, to be standing where you stand, each of you has proved your ability and your motivation time and time again. When you graduate, you will be among the best molders of youth on Earth, fit in every way to propagate our Union values, our knowledge, culture, and devotion to the planet, on into the years ahead. To you, this may sound absurd, boastful, puffed up, and fatuous. It is not.

Remember that when the Union was formed of the Original Seven twps, one encompassed the University; four were agricultural; one was a consortium of bakers, cooks, and food transporters, and one consisted of school teachers. Among the Next Nine, there was a second teachers' twp. This means that at the Union's beginning, among its population of six or seven thousand, almost a thousand taught school or directly supported someone who did. Through all its years, the Union has been willing—nay, eager—to spend lavishly so that our children may have the best education possible. We in the Union have nothing much in the way of luxury goods, but we have citizens who, by the time they reach adulthood, know about as much as books can teach them, and much more besides. As they grow older, lived experience adds to their understanding of the world and, in the end, multiplies it many fold so that, as citizens, they make better decisions and behave as responsible humans should. The cultures of the Crazy Years taught their children to be good consumers and lousy citizens. We are doing the opposite. That, I am convinced, is the chief reason why we are here, while other cultures have been drifted over like Ozymandias. It will be your challenge, each of you, to continue in this fashion.

Don't think this will be easy. At the Strat, we will work you as hard as you have ever been worked. Some of you have been in the military already. This will be harder than that. The hours will be long, the competition fierce. Sometimes you will feel that you are getting nowhere; you will be tempted to quit. You will wonder what the reason is, why we are mistreating you so. Rest assured that there are reasons behind the seemingly unreasonable demands that we will make on you.

First, know that things will not get better after you graduate. You will have long hours, heavy class loads, children who need special help merely to get along. Children who can fly, but only if you are there when you are needed, and not a minute later. After three years at the Strat, you will know, and know for sure, that you have the resources to meet the urgent needs of your students. Resources of intellect, of stamina, of wisdom, of humility. You are going to need those qualities and that confidence.

Second, society is going to put enormous trust in you. Not only to teach its children but also to lead, to act as examples to your community. When difficult issues arise, people in your twp will look to you. In the years before the Collapse, almost all legislators and public leaders were trained as lawyers. That crazy system got its just deserts during the Civil Wars. Nowadays, there are no lawyers, in the old sense, and instead, people look to us, the teachers. Well over half of the twp mayors in today's Union were first trained as teachers. Just as you will be trained. Responsibilities will come your way. Our most salient purpose in running this college is to make you, our students, able to handle these responsibilities when they appear.

I am sure that you have all heard the old adage, "Those who can't teach, do." This is a silly sentiment, and you should pay it no mind. Believing it will only lead to trouble between you and the families of your young charges. But perhaps you are not aware that in the pre-Collapse days, our forebears said it the other way: "Those who can't do, teach." This sentiment was not merely silly, it was horribly dangerous. Historians agree that disrespect for learning was one of the key pathologies that brought civilization low, a couple of centuries ago. In other words, you fine men and women will have the most important jobs imaginable. How well you do them may well determine the survival not only of the Union, but of all human life. Those of you who are paying attention will notice that I am repeating myself. I do this not because I am old and doddering, though I am, but because this part is very, very important. All people everywhere are counting on you. Don't let them down.

And finally, please don't forget this: Training of your mind and your will are good things, but they will not take you far unless your body can keep up. Besides, this is the damn Union. Physical capacity is the foundation for everything else. So at

05:00 tomorrow, I expect those of you who are able to come to the practice field for a brisk run. This old man will be very disappointed in any of you who can't outrun him over a measured two kilometers.

I'll see you there.

# DIGITAL COMMUNICATIONS:

## A FIRST TEXTBOOK
## EVAR TWP DIGLAB NGUYEN

**Introduction**

Moving binary data from one place to another represents a significant portion of digital activity in today's Union. This has not always been true; in the first hundred years or so after the advent of computers in the mid-twentieth century, merely moving data around constituted *almost all* digital activity. Of course, even then, people wrote software, built numerical models, designed bridges, created visual images, and so on. But in terms of sheer investment of human effort and commitment of digital infrastructure, the largest share by far was devoted simply to acquiring, maintaining, and using digital bandwidth.

Although this preoccupation with instantaneous communication no longer prevails, there is still much to know about the purposes and methods of digital communication. This book attempts to illuminate both the social issues that have driven communications technology over the last three centuries and the technical solutions that have evolved to allow necessary communication while avoiding societal destruction.

This book's first and shorter part deals with digital communications hardware. During the first century following the introduction of computers, development was driven by the apparently limitless opportunities for increasing the density and hence the speed of digital circuitry, and by runaway market-driven experimentation with functionality and user interaction. With the arrival of the Bad Days, both these sources of innovation reached their natural limits, and stalled. From then on, personal computers (now called "decks") were considered fully developed tools, like shovels: available in a few variations but not susceptible to fundamental improvement. Thus, today's mid-size "laptop" deck would be immediately recognized and usable to a time traveler from two hundred years ago. The last major peripheral change was to add gene-sequencing hardware one hundred thirty years ago; major OS updates are now released about every thirty years. A benefit of this technical stasis is that malicious deck security violations are now very rare. Not only have the financial motivations for hacking largely disappeared, but also centuries of experience with virtually unchanging platforms have squeezed out nearly all points of attack. The defects of our current stability are similarly obvious: users get little or no choice about what tools they use for given tasks, or about how these work. For example, at one time there were hundreds of typefaces available to whimsical creators of digital text. Now, if the couple of dozen standard fonts do not suit your needs or aesthetic judgments, you are out of luck.

The second part of this book deals with the social constructs within which the digital communicator lives and works. By far the most influential of these is the nominal ban (actually a closely held government monopoly) on long-distance high-bandwidth communication channels. This restriction originates early in the Union's history, when "cowboy coms" (unconstrained long-distance individual communication) became identified with a wide spectrum of social and political dysfunction, and indeed with mental disease in individuals. The oldest form of this restriction, still in force today, involves partitioning the Union into many (at this writing roughly 35,000) disjoint geographical communication zones, known as "wicks," each containing only a few twps. Communication within a wick is high-bandwidth and easily accessible. Between wicks, it generally is not. To move large quantities of data farther than one's current wick, one must rely on the Post, which uses the railways to ship large-capacity information storage units across the country in days or less. The main exception to these rules is the government-operated Daily Drop. This service transmits updates of every kind (weather forecasts, entertainment, newspapers, catalogs) to each twp every 24 hours, using government-controlled high-bandwidth channels. In addition to the Drop, there exist many exceptions, cut-outs, and workarounds that, when deemed necessary by the Council, help to solve communication problems that would otherwise be intractable. Much of the discussion in the book's second part deals with these exceptions and how to find and use them if normal methods fail in your application. Understanding how to exploit this large set of side-channels, with rules of access that are often *ad hoc* and sometimes contradictory, is the chief requirement for a successful career in modern communications management.

# ANNUAL REPORT OF
# THE UNION WEATHER SERVICE

## SUBMITTED APRIL 3, 2335
## SUMMARY FOR MANAGERS

This annual report was prepared pursuant to the charge laid on twp Meteo by the Union Governing Council to provide a yearly description of the evolution of the Earth's climate, the weather prediction activities of the twp, and the desired future extension of the twp's activities.

**1. Climate Evolution.** There are no major surprises in the standard climate indices for the last year. Carbon dioxide atmospheric loading remained at about 920 ppm, while proxies for global surface temperature and land temperature were stable at +6°C and +10°C, relative to 1950–1980 baselines. Precipitation patterns were largely normal, with most of the annual rainfall in most locations concentrated in a few large events. Atlantic hurricane activity was slightly below the recent normal, with only 34 major storms last season. Mean sea level is now 5.7 m above the 1990 baseline, rising at a steady 1.7 cm per year.

Although climate evolution appears modest at this time, we cannot be confident that this situation will persist. $CO_2$ levels are stable for now, but the likely behavior of other atmospheric gases, notably methane, may not be so simple. Great quantities of CH4 are now being released from seabeds and far-northern permafrost. Ice processes in Antarctica and Greenland may be surprising, as may variations in the global oceanic circulation. Thus, although disruption of the base climate two centuries ago was not wholly unforeseen, the climate system may still have other, possibly larger, shocks in store.

**2. UWS Prediction Capabilities.** Short-term (three to five days) weather forecasts in populated areas of the Union remain significantly worse than those that were commonly available three centuries ago. This loss of capability results from sparse (in many regions, non-existent) weather observations, which are needed as input data. By modeling scenarios involving improved observation facilities, the UWS has developed three proposed programs that would make significant improvements in our forecasting ability. The programs are:

**A.** We should drastically increase the number and quality of weather reports obtained by part-time observers, especially in sparsely populated areas. The Council should thus require each free-standing twp to train and equip one or more of its twple as apprentice meteorologists. Together with this labor draft, the Service should design and equip tens of thousands of simple weather stations to be used by the new apprentices.

**B.** The Council should mandate improved weather stations and transmitters for our Navy and merchant ships at sea. Reports from the mid-Atlantic and eastern Caribbean would help to predict the tracks and strengths of tropical storms. The UWS is already researching means to reduce the degradation of shipboard propulsion and navigation under prolonged exposure to high winds and heavy seas. Work is also in progress on "spoofing" the radio direction finders now commonly used by pirates to locate our vessels. Such technologies will improve shipboard morale and hence the motivation for crews to obtain and transmit the required data.

**C.** We have almost no weather stations in the Western Waste. The only exceptions are along the current Western Rail Line, which connects Columbus, OH with Walden, CO, an unsupported run of some 2300 kilometers. Attrition of unmanned weather stations along this route is high, largely due to vandalism and thievery by the region's highly mobile vagabonds. For adequate forecasts of violent supercell storms, we require that more stations be manned and defended.

# WHAT THE HELL IS THE MATTER WITH US?

## TRENTON INQUIRER
## FRIDAY, NOVEMBER 14, 2335

### LETTERS TO THE EDITOR

*From Wam twp UniLit Marquez*

In this space, I keep reading about how wonderful we Unionists are. About how if not for one little thing, broken pavement on Rutledge Street, or lack of apples in June, or poor maintenance on city scooters, or some other damn thing, if not for that, life here in the Union would be splendid. Perfect, in fact. Idyllic, susceptible to no improvement whatever. Other societies have sought Shangri-la, they say, but we have found it.

Horse piss, I say. It's true that we are mostly not starving anymore, and nearly all of us have roofs to keep the rain off. In terms of basic material needs, we are doing fairly well. And look! Anybody who wants one gets a free deck (or two or three). Fine. Great. But what about culture?

Who is the best novelist now writing? Can you *name* a novelist now writing? I can't, and literature was once my business. Where's the poetry that speaks to life in the Union? When did you last hear an original piece of music? We have one middling-grade chamber orchestra nationwide. Have you ever been to hear them? When was the last time you listened to a new popular music band? You know, a singer, a couple of guitars, a drum? Last year? Ten years ago? Never?

Our entire cultural life is replayed from the archives, served up by our decks from catalogs we find on the Daily Drop. I know of a few theatrical clubs, but even they are mostly reviving plays that our seven-times-great-grandparents knew by heart. They now make the occasional movie up north, but those are still clumsy knockoffs of films from before the Collapse. Why don't we have our own art? Something that binds us to a common purpose (beyond mere survival)? Something that comes from ourselves?

It's laziness, I think. And cowardice. We who pride ourselves on our industry and courage are lazy and fearful when it comes to examining our own lives.

I think each of us has an artist inside. Some can make good art, most not so good. But all of us should be proud of our culture's art and our own, and care about it and make it whenever we can. But almost none of us do. This dry place in our lives is shriveling the community's soul and blighting our way forward. Killing our search for a life that transcends mere rejection of past errors and achieves instead something new and better.

Luvs: this is our life, and nobody can change it but us. Start now. Go and do good work.

# WOULD YOU LIKE TO KNOW MORE?

In *The Brangus Rebellion*, Judge Zeil says that she and Triple-E veteran Hap Moran "went back a long time." What was that about?

To find out, and to read something of their relationship and adventures in the younger North American Union, sign up here for a free copy of my novella *Space Museum*.

**www.rrcorvi.com/sign-up**

# WITH THANKS AND A SMALL REQUEST

Dear Reader

My thanks for reading *The Brangus Rebellion.* I hope you enjoyed reading it as much as I did writing it!

If you did, please take a moment to leave a review on the book's Amazon page.

Reviews can have a great impact on potential readers. You can do me no greater favor than to tell other readers what you thought.

*R. R. Corvi*

# ACKNOWLEDGMENTS

Thanks to those who read early versions of the book, and who responded with kind and on-target criticism. First to Chris, from whom I learned the most important thing: what and whom to be interested in. Also to daughter Andrea, Dr. Mommy Kozai, a wise and perceptive reader as well as the best person I know. Then friends and colleagues who read the book and told me what they thought: Richard Kautz, Andy Howell, Alan Nelson, Christy Stebbins, and Travis Metcalfe. Thanks also to the developers of the AI *Marlowe*; its statistical insights proved helpful.

Finally, thanks to my production team. Editors Nick Hodgson and Mairead Beeson sharpened the text immeasurably. Designer Mark Thomas gave the book a wonderful look, outside and in. And Production/Marketing expert Denis Caron and his team pulled these pieces into a coherent whole, showed me how to navigate the maze of publishing, and did the heavy lifting to give *Brangus* a chance to find its audience.

# ABOUT THE AUTHOR

Timothy M. Brown, retired astronomer, writes fiction under the name R.R. Corvi. The "R.R." does not stand for anything. Rather, *RR Corvi* is the name of a variable star in the astronomical constellation Corvus, the Crow. In Greek mythology, Corvus was the sacred bird of Apollo—a not especially devoted servant of the Sun god. Feel free to make what you will of these allusions; Tim chose the name because he liked the sound of it.

Tim grew up in a literary family and read extensively from their collection of Sci-Fi and adventure paperbacks. Authors Robert Heinlein, Arthur C. Clarke, and Isaac Asimov were early favorites. As a child of Sputnik, Tim grew fascinated with all things technical, earned degrees in physics and astrophysics, and pursued a long career in astronomy. In 2016, the National Academy of Sciences awarded him their James Craig Watson Medal for contributions to astronomy.

Tim and his wife, Rosie, ski and hike in the Colorado mountains and indulge their grandchildren whenever the opportunity arises. Tim also makes telescopes and related gizmos in his shop and uses them to fortify his long-term love of the night sky. *The Brangus Rebellion* is his first published novel.

Made in the USA
Middletown, DE
25 September 2023

39365579R00197